# Chuck Life's a Trip

Hans Joseph Fellmann

A Russian Hill Press Book
United States • United Kingdom • Australia

R
H
P  Russian Hill Press

ISBN: 978-0-9995162-9-4 (softcover)
ISBN: 978-1-7341220-1-5 (ebook)
Library of Congrress Control Number: 2019911305

Cover Design by Ivan Potter-Smith

To my gahts:
The most baumish friends a Chuck could ever wish for.

She extends her hand and you take it,
The world splitting open at her back,
A thousand colors come gliding forth
Like tentacles of blood moving through ocean water,
They slither in your ears and around your eyes,
Down your throat and up your spine,
Soon every ounce of your being is infected,
Its chemistry glowing with the promise of her

~ H. J. Fellmann

# CONTENTS

WORD TO THE READER i

CHUCK ROOTS iii

L-TOWN 1

BANGKOK 7

ANGKOR WAT 26

DELHI 40

JAIPUR 58

AGRA 66

DELHI TO MANALI 72

MANALI 77

BACK IN DELHI 132

LONDON 136

BERLIN 143

PRAGUE 156

ČESKÝ KRUMLOV 179

BLED 199

LJUBLJANA 215

PLITVICE 221

SPLIT 225

HVAR 229

DUBROVNIK 250

MOSTAR 268

KOTOR 275

THE ROAD TO SHQIPERIA 279

TIRANA 283

KRUJA 289

BACK IN TIRANA 293

SARANDA 295

CORFU 298

ROAST (Result of a Small Town) 343

ABOUT THE GLOSSARY 347

GLOSSARY 349

# WORD TO THE READER

The following is based on an actual trip my best friends and I took during the spring and summer of 2006. Although certain names, places, and events have been altered to suit the flow of the story and to protect identities, most of what you are going to read is true, if not in fact, then in spirit.

It is important to note that what transpired on this journey changed all our lives irreversibly. Before embarking, most of us at least entertained the idea of leading a 'normal' life somewhere on down the line. As with any addiction, though, we reached a point of no return. A point where more of us was defined by the drug pumping through our system than by the blood that originally nurtured us into being. This is an account of our crossing that point, laid out before your eyes in all its embarrassing glory. If the words that impart it offend you, frighten you, or piss you off, then so be it. No one ever grows up smiling the whole way.

.

# CHUCK ROOTS

Before you dip into the pages of this trip, there are a few things you need to know about me and my friends. The first and most important is, we don't talk like other people. By this, I don't mean that we have speech impediments or mumble. I mean that we speak a dialect of English that we created called ROAST—Result of a Small Town. There's a comprehensive glossary in the back. The small town in reference is Livermore, California. It's the town we all grew up in.

As kids there, we got into a lot of shit. By twelve, most of us were smoking, drinking, fighting, doing drugs, and stealing; anything to ease the staggering boredom of a nut-freckle town that had little more to offer than a string of fast food joints and a rusty flagpole. An average day for us consisted of ditching class, jacking booze and cigarettes from a general store staffed by geriatrics, then getting drunk and high under a creek bridge. Afterward, we'd pick someone's house to crash at. We'd wait for their parent(s) to fall asleep, then when the night was good and thick, we'd run out there and spit in its face. To keep our folks from understanding our conversations about these unsavory activities, we invented code. For example, getting drunk was "gettin' D" and smoking weed was "lollin'" (after *pakalolo*, the Hawaiian word for pot).

Over time, our little dialect grew in size and complexity. Within a few years, we had words and phrases for everything from mastication to masturbation. We also developed sounds, gestures, and a unique form of sarcasm to accompany our speech. This meant we could talk about whatever the fuck we wanted in front of our parents—or anyone else for that matter—and nobody would be the wiser.

Around about the time ROAST was developing, my father's career in the pharmaceutical industry took off. His company sent him all over the world to crazy places like Novosibirsk, Belgrade, Osaka, and Bruges. He didn't see my mother, sister, or me much on account of all his business travels. To make up for it, he brought us bags of presents and stories from abroad. When he was due home from a trip, I'd be ecstatic. The instant I heard his wheels crunch into the driveway, I'd run to the front door and wait for him. My father's a huge, German motherfucker, so I could feel his footsteps under my feet as he walked up. I'd get to the point of nearly crapping my He-Man shorts, then he'd burst through the door and shout, "Hey-hey." He'd always be carrying a bundle of shiny packages checkered with foreign stamps. After he dumped his bags and got in his sweats, we'd all pile around him on the sofa. The man had a knack for building tension. Instead of just handing out gifts, he'd start with a long and wild story of how he found each one. Sometimes it was in the Caribbean on a scuba dive through eel-infested waters, other times it was in the Orient on a hike up a misty mountain, atop which sat a little old man with yellow nails and a wispy beard. Whatever the case, by the time that gift was in my hand, it coulda been a fuckin' rat turd; I wanted to be out there with the killer eels and the guru with the bad hygiene.

Unfortunately, I was stuck in Livermore, which would have spelled total boredom if it weren't for my shitkicker buddies and weird cultural background. As mentioned previously, my father is a humungous, tank-footed man of German descent, whereas my mother is a tiny, mouse-footed woman of Mexican descent. Next to my silo of a father, my mother looks like a little brown bean; a reality that belies the size of their respective families. This disproportionality is made most apparent whenever we throw a party at our house and invite both sides. To a stranger, we probably look like an Amazonian tribe preparing for a meal of shipwrecked Europeans, post-mutiny. Despite this, my father made sure I'd never forget that the staunch blood of Deutschland courses through my veins. I'm reminded of how he did it every time I have to pull out my joke of a driver's license.

Having a purely German name like Johann Klaus Felmanstien didn't stop my mother's side of the family from trying to Hispanicize me entirely. I was the first male grandchild; a huge deal in Latino culture. My Mexican grandfather, Papito, naturally sought to adopt me as his own. Since my real father was always out working his ass off so we could survive, my gramps got his wish. For most of my youth, I spent every waking second with Papito. During the day, we'd take trips to the mall or the park, and at night he'd sing me Mexican lullabies under the moon while I fell asleep in his arms. Anything we said to each other was entirely in Spanish. For all intents and purposes, I was a full-blooded Mexican who just happened to have a ginormous bearded father with pasty skin and a strange accent.

It didn't occur to me that I was different till I showed up at school with an accent like a Salinas berry-picker and a name straight off the pages of *Mein Kampf.* There was really no cultural glove for a beanerschnitzel like me to fit into. For the few Mexicans around, I was too light-skinned with a name they could barely pronounce. For the hordes of whites, I was too Hispanic . . . with a name they could barely pronounce. Fortunately, I found a band of genetic miscreants who shared my predicament. Their names were Mason McKinney (the Scottish Frenchman), Tim Frazelli (the Nicaraguan Italian), Bert Thompson (the Irish Polack), and Kip Zakynthos (the Greek Jew). Together we twisted our dicks into the bellybutton of Livermore. Together we created ROAST.

The thought of traveling with these guys on a massive scale didn't enter my mind until I was seventeen. The day I started my senior year in high school, I got a call from my rich Aunt Chloe.

"Yer pops tells me yer gunna be graduatin' from high school in June," she hiccupped. I heard a wine glass clink in the background. I choked down a chuckle.

"Uh, yeah?" I said.

"Well, I wanna give you a lil' present, Johaaaannzy. Anywhere in the world yer lil' heart desires to go, you just tell yer Aunt Chloe an' she'll fix yer ass up with a ticket there."

"Really?"

"Yep. But don't go thinkin' this is a fuckin' freebie. You gotta put in some slave work. Wax ma Beemer. Fuck, wax ma legs. I don't give a damn. And get yerself a job out there in Liverlips too. I ain't gonna bankroll yer whole fuckin' trip."

The minute I hung up the phone, I began designing a nine-week odyssey that stretched from Casablanca to Bratislava. It barely took me a day to finish the thing. Once it was done, I got on the horn and tried to get all the guys to come. Unfortunately, they already had senior trips to shit spots like Cabo and Cancun in mind. My friend Devon Molenberg, a guy I met freshman year who was loosely associated with our group, was the only one willing to come. I was bummed the rest couldn't but stoked to at least have one partner.

For the next nine months, Devon and I did anything we could to stack cash. Monday through Friday, we slung pizzas at some crummy parlor in town, and during the weekends we did odd jobs for various family members. Various in my case simply meant Aunt Chloe. I can't count how many of my Saturdays and Sundays I spent at her ritzy hilltop mansion scraping pigeon shit off her deck or smashing black widows in her shed. While I worked, she stood out on her lawn in her kimono swilling chardonnay and barking orders. It made my job a bear of a son of a bitch, but when it was finally over, and I had that golden ticket in my hand, all the crap just melted away.

On June 17, 2000, the day after our graduation, Devon and I split for Europe. We had nothing but the packs on our backs and wads of sweaty foreign cash in our pockets. Our trip was epic. We sipped Chianti at the apex of the Eiffel Tower, dove from limestone cliffs in Sorrento, and schlepped through the forests of Transylvania in search of haunted castles. I wept when it all ended. Devon was bummed as well, but he wasn't a natural travel addict like me. While he went on to pursue a career in psychology, I remained hooked on the idea of traveling.

My addiction lasted all through my college years at the University of California, San Diego. When I wasn't in class jotting notes, I was researching a score of exotic locales, trying to piece together another giant trip. To motivate myself further, I set up a world map on my wall and stuck pushpins in all the places I had been. At night I would stare at it, reveling in the places I had already explored and lamenting over the gaping blank spots I had yet to visit.

With money I earned from more pizza deliveries and the odd Aunt Chloe job, I did Asia with my father in 2001, then Scandinavia by myself in 2002. The trips covered some of the blank spots and had their share of poignant moments, but they lacked one key ingredient: my buds.

In the summer of 2003, I finally convinced Mason to come with me to Brazil. We raised Hades together on the streets of Rio for two solid weeks, then crossed the entire South American continent by bus. We came out the other side with enough bruises and stories to fill three lifetimes. When Bert and Tim got wind of what they were missing, they ditched the loveseat and hit the road with us. In the summer of 2004, we all went overland from Cancun to Costa Rica. Although Kip and others weren't present, the spirit of our group still thrived, and our dialect grew richer and more colorful. After Central America, traveling was a part of who we were. It elevated us from being a group of jive-talkin' mugs to a nascent culture with a slick argot and a specific practice. That said, there were still elements missing from the equation. None of us was entirely conscious of what those elements were, but one thing was certain: we needed another trip.

On a hot night in April 2005, Mason, Tim, and I were chilling on the couch of our San Diego apartment. The hookah was out, and we were puffing it lazily and sipping Fat Tires. Suddenly, Bert came charging through the front door. He had a big grin on his face and a dusty old box in his clutches.

"'S all that bitchiness?" Mason asked.

Bert plopped the box down on the coffee table. "Euro-trip videos from '85," he said. "My grandparents grunged over last weekend and blew me up with them." Having nothing better to do, we stuck the videos in. I don't know what it was about a bunch of old fucks puttering around the Bavarian countryside in a Fiat that got our trip juices flowing again, but the prospect of a big one swelled in our collective mind like an engorged whale cunt, and we just had to take a bite. The timing was right for it too. Bert and Tim were getting ready to graduate from San Diego State, as was I from UCSD. And Mason, who was also enrolled at UCSD, didn't give a fuck about finishing the last of his two years there. We agreed that in April '06, exactly one year later, we'd set off on the biggest trip any of us had ever done.

Over the next five months, I mapped out an eighty-five-day juggernaut that took us to fifteen countries across Asia and Europe. I know some of you more seasoned travelers may be thinking this is peanuts, but for a group of hoodlums from a small town in the States, eighty-five days, fifteen countries, and two continents is a big deal. By the time we'd bought our tickets, Livermore was buzzing with talk of our adventure. That's when we got word from Chuck Sunday, a high school friend we hadn't heard from in years.

Judging by his name, I know the guy doesn't sound like much. Maybe just some potbellied prick in a ball cap who bides his time between watering his lawn and scratching his nuts. While these things are fully true of him, there's more to Chuck than just that. Not only can he blow through a Double Whopper meal in under five minutes, he's sporadically grouchy and famous for snapping your head off when you least respect him. Though these talents are impressive, they pale by comparison with his most salient—an uncanny natural ability to veg the fuck out. Unlike us, he doesn't need pot or booze to put himself in a drooling stupor. No, Chuck simply needs to park his ass anywhere he sees fit and commence lounging. This proclivity for relaxation has always had a calming effect on the boisterous dynamic of our group. Shit, just having him around, loafing like a big fat panda, helps us deal with stress and hardship better. Because of this, we'd decided long before to honor him by creating a word in ROAST using his name. To "chuck out" roughly translates into standard English as to relax, but it's more than just that. It means to chill with gusto, to unwind completely and let the stress of the day dribble from your joints. Chucking out is a joyous affair for all of us. We do it whether we're on the road or in L-town.

When Chuck told us he was going to meet us in Europe, we were ecstatic. So much so that it gave us an idea for a group name. One drunken night we made it official. We were now "the Chucks," living out through our trips what we humorously referred to as "Chuck life."

# L-TOWN

T he night of April 9, 2006, was our last in the States. Our flight to Bangkok via Hong Kong was at six the next morning. We still wanted to go out and have a few drinks to celebrate. We planned to head out at eight. To be ready in time, I started my trip-shopping extra early. I'd have spread it out over the previous week, but every odd family member had crept out of the woodwork wanting to take me to a goodbye lunch or dinner.

I came back home at six with a dozen shopping bags. They were filled with toiletries, water bottles, guidebooks, etcetera. I laid everything out on my bed and started in. I tried to cram my pack with all of it, but it wouldn't zip up. "Fuck it," I said, tossing shit everywhere. "I'll do this later."

To get my mind off packing, I reviewed the itinerary. As my eyes ran from spot to spot, I saw the travel scenes in *Indiana Jones* where his route is mapped by a crooked red line. The theme song filled my ears as I read our destinations off: Hong Kong, Bangkok, Angkor Wat, Delhi, Agra, Jaipur, Manali, London, Berlin, Prague, Český Krumlov, Linz, Bled, Ljubljana, Zagreb, Plitvice, Split, Hvar, Mostar, Kotor, Tirana, Siranda, Corfu, Bari, Frankfurt.

Images of each place flashed through my head. When my reverie peaked, I could reach out with my fingertips and tap the pools of water surrounding the Taj Mahal. The ripples I made doing this turned into a trill. The trill turned into a loud ring. I came crashing down from the ceiling and back into reality. With my head still spinning, I answered the phone.

"Dude, it's eight," Mason said. "I'm groogin' over now to pick up you and the other Chucks."

"Ait," I said.

I didn't have much time. I ran a wet towel through the cracks, threw on a collared shirt, and blasted myself with Axe. My mom, dad, and sis warned me not to stay out too late. "You'll miss your flight, sweetie," Mom said, planting a giant smooch on my face. I wiped it off with my sleeve and cut. Mason squealed up to the curb in his beat-up red truck. I opened the door and a cloud of pot smoke came billowing out. Mason waved it away with his hairy arms. When it cleared, I got a load of him. He was wearing stained camo shorts and a Brazilian Bikini Team T-shirt. His ginger beard was thick and gnarled. It looked like a Venusian sea creature clinging to his face.

"I see you're ready for the nahs," I said.

He glared at me with the two pools of bloody emeralds in his skull.

"Get me," he said.

Since it was right up the road, our first stop was Tim's. As usual, his goofy father, Emilio, answered the door. He was in a holey wife-beater and boxers. A dumb smile was growing on his lips.

"Sorry, we don't want any Girl Scout cookies," he said.

Mason and I picked our fingernails and waited for the air to clear. Emilio stood there chortling.

"Haha. Okay, you guys can come in," he finally said.

We left him at the door and ran upstairs. From outside Tim's room, we could hear a strange buzzing. We pushed his door open and looked in. Tim was crouched over a misshapen chunk of wood, drilling holes into it. Next to him was a hollow, lopsided tower. It was fashioned from a gutted TV, a mangled snake cage, and a banker's box stripped and inlaid with Plexiglas. A naked light bulb hung from the top. A knotted tree branch twisted its way up the middle.

I wrinkled my brow and drew my head back. "What the hell is this garnk shit?" I asked.

Tim ignored me and continued drilling. I looked him over with a dimpled-pity grin. His hair was a sweaty mess of spikes. His triangular chin was peppered with ants, and his eyes were two brown dimes. A cigarette-ash turd hung from his lips. Mason lifted a fist to his beard and snickered. The drill buzzed and buzzed and buzzed.

"Tim," I yelled. "What the fuck are you making?"

He shot his eyes at me, and the drill whined to a stop. He stared at me for a moment, then thrust his skinny elbow into the side of the tower. A crack-eyed squirrel went shooting up the tree branch. Mason dropped to the floor, laughing.

"It's our last night to pop off in L," I said, "and you're in here making a palace for a bitchin' squirrel?"

"I'm ready to bunt," Tim said. "I just wanted Nutty here to have a lil' place to chuck while we blew up."

"Nutty?"

"Chea hea. He's a baumish lil' guy. I found him outside playing with Mofo today."

Mofo was Tim's anal-retentive black cat. I secretly hoped he'd make a quick meal of Nutty the Squirrel the minute we left.

Our next stop was Bert's. I was riding shotgun, so it was my duty to go and get him. When I got to his door, I took a deep breath. I looked back and saw Tim and Mason laughing at me.

"*Dios mio*," I muttered.

I raised my fist and rapped against the wood softly. Nothing happened, no one came. I knocked again a bit harder. Like an idiot, I hit the wrong spot and set off the Thompson's wiry doorbell. To the crackling tune of "Yankee Doodle Dandy," a flurry of squeaks and barks exploded from within the house. Bert came pounding down the hall.

"Shut the fuck up you little pricks," he screamed.

I opened the door myself just in time to see him kick one of his Dachshunds in the butt. The furry little sausage went sailing across the kitchen floor, yipping in agony. Bert's mom Shelly came in from the backyard with crinkled eyebrows. When she saw what was going on, she freaked.

"Oh, Berty, don't kick my Lambo."

"Fuck Lambo," he shouted. "And fuck Ferarri."

With three big lunges, he cornered the dogs till they were spilling all over one another in fright. He raised a fist at them and sneered. The dogs' eyes widened brightly. He brought his knuckles right up to their snouts. At the last second, he flattened his hand. He patted both their heads and chuckled.

"Let's cut," he said to me.

I looked him over and raised an eyebrow.

"You really going out like that?"

He was wearing a wrinkled Hawaiian collared with two missing buttons. His pasty gut was hanging out the bottom, and his fro was blasting out the top. His cheeks were the color of deciduous trees in fall, and his eyes were raisins coated with blow. He looked like a disco bum who terrorized the beaches of Honolulu. I snickered at him. He ignored me and slipped his thongs on.

"Ait, Mom. I'm bouncin'," he said. "Tell Dad I said late."

On our way to the truck, Shelly poked her head out the window. She waved to get our attention then lifted a greasy paper bag in the air.

"You forgot your pickle sandwich, Berty."

Bert cut into a swagger and threw up his hand in disgust.

"Toss it."

Shelly frowned and disappeared behind the blinds. Bert looked over at me.

"I mean really? Fuck am I gonna do with a pickle sandwich at a bar?"

We piled into Mason's truck and took off. Our final stop was the Blue Moon Saloon downtown. My watch read 8:40.

"What time's Sebastian meetin' us?" asked Bert.

Tim was sparking a joint. "Roun' nine."

I rolled my eyes. "I really hope your lil' brother doesn't act like a faggot on this trip."

"He wob if you wob."

4

"Yeah, we'll see. He might just flat out gettem, this bein' his first time blowin' up. Good thing he's only groogin' for half."

We pulled up at the Blue Moon—or the "Blue Balls" as we called it on account of us never getting laid there. Despite it being a Sunday night, the place was packed. There was a line of half-drunken wannabe cowboys and gangsters trailing out the door. We were able to push past them and get in first because we knew the doorman, Skinny.

"You guys out celebratin' 'fore the big trip?" he asked.

"Fuckin' chea hea," we said, pushing through.

Inside we could barely move. It took us ten minutes just to get up to the bar. When we finally did, we ordered Fat Tires all around. We chilled with our backs against the counter and sipped. Some friends rolled by and gave us daps on the trip. As we cheers'd them, we heard a noise. It was the sound of skin being thwapped under cloth. We looked out and saw the crowd rumbling. One by one, drinkers popped from sight. A whirl moved through them, cackling with electricity. It slowed at the wall of people in front of us. Two big hands reached out, pushed the wall in halves. Out stepped Sebastian, still laughing. He was wearing a black leather trench coat and a Cuban top hat. His jet goatee was shaved to a perfect spade. He had plugs in his earlobes the size of wine corks. He stopped laughing and looked at all of us.

"Let's fuckin' explode!"

Everyone busted up but me. Sebastian ordered three shots of booze. He downed them one after another and let off a huge belch. Then he turned around and grinned at us with tequila-stained teeth and whiskey tornado eyes.

"Wanna see some baumishness?" he said. Before we could answer, he ripped off his coat, shirt, and hat. His enormous gut came spilling out over his pants and his hair flew up in disarray. He whipped around and pointed over his shoulders with both thumbs. On his back was a sloppy tattoo of Lord Krishna, puffing smoke from a hookah.

"It looks like a three-year-old did that shit with a crayon," I muttered.

He turned around with the face of an infant chimp who'd stubbed

5

his toe. Mason cut in.

"So where'd you get that ink?"

Sebastian scratched his belly and ran his fingers through his locks. "L-Town Tats," he said. "And it's hella weird cuz I didn't even tell the artist I was explodin' India. Hoo hoo, just kinda looked at me n' *knew*."


The next seven hours were a blur. All I remember is swilling Scotch and spinning circles on the dance floor. When I came to, I was in bed naked. A snoring mammoth was lying next to me and gripping the head of my cock. I carefully unpeeled her fingers and slipped out of bed. Once I was dressed and outside, I called Mason. Thankfully, he was willing to come across town and get me. He picked me up and had me home within twenty minutes. When I stepped through the door, my towering father shat himself.

"It's four-fifteen," he screamed. "Pack your crap and let's go."

I apologized profusely and ran upstairs. I crammed my pack to the splitting-limit and zipped it up. I grabbed my money belt, iPod, and shades. I leaped in our van and we cut. At 5:20 a.m., we arrived at the SFO parking garage. The McKinneys, Thompsons, and the Frazellis all arrived shortly thereafter. We checked in and raced to the security checkpoint. We heard the final boarding call for our flight over the PA. My tiny mother ran up and squeezed me tight.

"Please be safe out there," she said.

The crack of her voice made my eyes tear. We hugged for a good long minute. When we let go, she reached into her purse. "You bring this back to me, you hear?" she said. She pulled out the little amethyst egg she always gives me before I travel. I nodded and took it from her hand. My father and sister then walked up. We all came together and formed a bundle of warmth. Halfway through the hug, I poked my head above the sniffles. I saw my buds doing the same thing with their families. When the hugging ended, our folks told us to get in a line. We stood shoulder-to-shoulder with giant grins. The cameras flashed, and the waving hands went up. We slung our packs over our shoulders and winked.

# BANGKOK

We arrived at Bangkok International in the late afternoon. We'd been traveling for almost thirty hours straight and looked like a gang of zombies after an acid bath. We schlepped off the plane and grabbed our packs and stacks of baht, went outside, and jumped in the first van to the center. As we weaved through the concrete arteries of the city, I stuck my head out the window. The air was thick with humidity and reeked of pineapples and rotting trash. I mused at the jungle of corporate towers. Every so often, its vast gray web was pierced by the golden spire of a Buddhist temple.

Our van dropped us off in the middle of Khao San Road. The thoroughfare was clogged with hippies in tank tops, sandals, and dreads. *Tuk-tuks* beeped and forced their way through the river of backpacker grime like white blood cells. Snack stalls sizzled and smoked, and little tan people hung flowery decorations on Buddha statues for the start of Songkran (Thai New Year) the next day.

We waded through the tumult till we came to a side street called Soi Rambutri. Despite being lined by hostels and bars, its backpacker presence was significantly less than Khao San's. We checked out a few joints there. All were roach-infested dumps with used condoms between the sheets. A lanky Nepalese man in an oversized shirt recommended we check out the Tandu House. It turned out to be a veritable refuge from the miasma of Khao San. There was a fountain courtyard and whitewashed walls, an internet café, and a spotless restaurant. Mason and I got a double with a shower. The others took a triple across the hall.

After a nap, we walked to a dive bar down a littered alley. The place was mostly for backpackers, but there were a few toothless locals puttering around. We chose a table outside and ordered a round of Big Changs. After five of the suckers, my head was swimming. I felt that gnawing burn inside my shorts. I darted my eyes around. Bert raised his eyebrows suggestively. I looked over my shoulder. Two Thai chicks in pumps and short dresses brushed against my back. One turned around and winked. Then they both split in a swish of shiny black hair.

"Go blow her up," Bert said, waving me on. I took a pull from my beer and sprinted off down the alley. I heard Sebastian yell out, "Oh, I gotta see this."

With the others at my heels, I ran after the two girls. The alley ended at a dumpster and fed off to the left. I slowed down at the corner. When I turned it, I found the two girls standing there, checking their makeup. The one who had winked at me looked the nicest. She had long, tan legs, firm breasts, and a chiseled face. I cracked my neck, straightened my shirt, and approached her. I could hear the others chuckling behind me.

"Hi," I said, offering her a hand. "I'm Johann. What's your name?"

The girl stepped forward. She slipped her bony hand into mine and grinned.

"Ong," she said. Her voice was metallic and grating. It sounded like she was talking through a broken intercom.

"What was that?" I asked.

"Ong," she said louder. I noticed a lump the size of a crabapple dandle against the skin of her neck. I wrinkled my eyebrows. Then I froze.

"Um, okay Ong, it was great meeting you," I said. I tried to pull away. She simpered and squeezed my hand tighter.

"Ih wuh nice tu mee you, tu," she said. Her eyes held mine with their scary gaze. Little needles of blood had collected around her pupils. My heart raced and blackness filled my veins.

"I gotta go," I said, ripping my hand away.

Ong stepped back with a surprised look. Her friend said something to her in Thai, then they both walked off.

"Phuuck," I puffed.

When I turned around, I saw the others roaring with laughter. I marched up to them with my arms out and barked, "You fucks knew?"

Mason put his hand on his chest and tipped backward. He was laughing so hard he almost collapsed to the ground.

"We didn't wanna stomp on yer good time there, gaht."

I shrugged it off and wandered around with the Chucks for a few more hours. When it became apparent we'd be getting no pussy, we cut for the Tandu House. We found a group of mostly girls chilling and drinking outside the entrance. We grabbed a spot in the middle of them and went to it. Tim picked a beat-up teenybopper and Sebastian and I took a triad of Swedes. Mason and Bert went for the same Thai streetwalker. Her name was Oh, and she was thin as a chicken bone with caramel skin and lazy eyes. Mason and Bert showered her with compliments. At first, she took to Bert, presumably because he was the prettier of the two. She nudged in close and pursed her big lips up at him. He threw his head back and laughed.

"Hey Mason, why don't ya' grab a shot of me with this nah?" he said.

Mason thinned his mouth and aimed his camera at the pair. Bert fanned his collar and wrapped his arm around Oh's neck. Oh completed the shot by slipping her hand into Bert's crotch. When Mason saw this, his eyes widened. Then his beard swelled up like an angry porcupine and turned the color of lava. Bert and Oh smiled, and the camera went "click." I winced for Bert.

Before we move on, a dab about Mason's personality needs illuminating. I call it a dab, and it is most times. When provoked though, that smudge on his profile consumes his being entirely, rendering him the most shameless bastard on the planet, especially when it comes to the ladies. To complement this, or as a direct result of it, the single most distinguishing feature on his body, his red beard, seems to intensify in pigmentation and increase in size till it's nothing short of a hirsute rash of hellfire. And once Mason's beard reaches critical mass, you're fucked.

After the picture was taken, Mason plopped the camera in Bert's hand and eased in next to Oh.

Bert tried to break the two apart by fluffing his curls and talking loud, but it was no use. Oh had her skinny arms laced tight around Mason's chest. She was staring up at his volcano of a beard with her jaw swinging and her pupils bugged. Mason looked down at her and smiled with his creepy hazel eyes. He slithered his arm around her shoulder and pinched her nipple. She giggled and buried her face in the forest of hair on his chest. Mason looked up at me and nodded.

"Toss me the key, Johann," he said. "This lil' ney needs a good snittin'."

I scowled and tossed him the key. Tim stood up with his teenybopper and asked Bert for the key to their room. I looked up at him and sneered.

"You really gonna fuck that bitch?"

Tim's girl tugged at her skirt nervously and stared at the ground. Tim glowered at me and took her by the hand.

"C'mon," he said.

After they left, Sebastian and I tried to coax the three Swedes into coming up to the room. They smiled politely but refused our advances. Bert noticed our flailing efforts and came over to try and help. He worked up his best Irish accent, something he does to seem exotic when we travel.

"Ya loik fockin' Oirishmon?" he said, jabbing his beer at the girls.

I rolled my eyes. The girls just laughed.

"Yeah, we like dem." one said.

Sebastian went crazy-eyed when he heard this. He must have forgotten that not two minutes prior he'd been speaking to them with an American accent.

10

"Ay so ya lika de Irish, do yer lassies?" he growled.

The girls crinkled their noses. Then one of them shouted, "You sound like a big gay pirate."

Sebastian grinned and rose to his feet. With both hands, he grabbed the fat of his belly and started doing a circular jig. The girls howled at him, then got up to leave. As they walked off, Sebastian stood there, baffled.

"Nice goin', playboy," I said to him. "You really add to the crew."

He looked over at me with a sad dumb look on his face. Then he hung his head and lumbered off toward a beer stand.


I woke up at seven the next morning on the triple room floor. A horrendous wail was needling itself into my ears. I looked up and saw Sebastian. He was shirtless and perched on the bed with a bamboo flute pressed to his lips. Each time he blew, it sounded like the high-note pipes on a rusty church organ being punched full blast. He got up, still blowing, and kicked the balcony door open. The grating whistle of his instrument waltzed with the roar of the streets below. I dragged my ass up and over to where he stood. I looked out and saw thousands of daylight tweakers spraying one another to shreds with high-pressure streams of water. Songkran had officially begun, and Sebastian was its gigantic chirping herald.

All of us were ill-prepared when we left the Tandu House. There wasn't a single water gun or soy paste packet between us. The minute we hit the streets, we were pounded by jets of stinging liquid. Hundreds of smiling Thais charged us and smeared our faces with gunk. We elbowed our way onto Khao San and spilled into a river of warring Songkraners. A swarm of wet *kathoeys* surrounded us, giggling effeminately and grabbing at our cocks.

"One of those bitches just practically M'd me," Bert yelled.

We ripped through the circle of ladyboys and threaded down the storm of squeaking super-soakers. My face was in ribbons from the cut of the sprays. We saw a side street with a curry shack in the distance.

A barrage of soy bombs came raining down on our heads. We sidestepped them and blew through a wall of bodies and exploding liquid. The door to the curry shack came tumbling around us.

"Dude, we fuckin' gottem out there," I said, collapsing into a plastic chair.

The six of us—Oh had tagged along—were covered in beige paste and soaked to the bone. We looked like waterlogged mummies. All we could think about for the next hour was recharging. We ordered a pair of Big Changs each, curried everything, with sticky piles of coconut rice.

When the soy paste had dried, and our food comas subsided, a restless feeling began to surface. It seemed the people outside were laughing and partying at our expense. We lifted ourselves from the table and gave each other knowing glances.

"Let's pass these faggots treats," Sebastian said.

As luck would have it, the restaurant was connected to a larger shopping mall. Two doors down from us was a water gun store. We walked inside it and found rack after rack of brightly colored supersoakers. They looked like extraterrestrial firearms confiscated from a crash-landed saucer. We each bought the biggest gun we could carry. To complete our arsenal, we grabbed some soy paste bombs and black sunglasses. The man behind the counter chuckled and filled our weapons. We pumped them to the breaking point, slipped on our shades, and kicked open the door.

Sebastian was the first one out. He was shirtless and had the two neon giants he'd purchased raised level with his head. To his right was a giggling mass of Thai schoolgirls dousing each other in buckets of water. He whipped around and locked onto one of the girls' faces. She was laughing hard and completely oblivious to him. He flexed his tatted back, cocked his guns, and grinned.

"Blow me, bitch," he said.

Two streams as thick as ape dicks jetted from his nozzles. They zipped over the asphalt and slammed point blank in the middle of the unsuspecting girl's face. In slow motion, her mouth expanded and her eyes shut. She thrashed her head from side to side and screamed. Sebastian held the streams till the skin of her cheeks sagged. When he finally relented, she was sobbing.

The girl's friends hissed at us. They refilled their buckets at a gushing fire hydrant and splashed our bodies with gallons of freezing water. We unloaded against their faces till they recoiled like a nest of frightened snakes. When the vapors cleared, they had vanished.

"C'mon, Chucks," Sebastian said. "We still got fools to treat."

Just ahead of us was the warring river of Songkraners. We ran and jumped into it like crazed mercenaries, blasting everything in sight. The liquid flow of the crowd engulfed us, processing our bodies down its tracts like a loose string of turds through the intestines of a giant sea serpent. When we came out the anus, we were caked in tan feces.

After the insanity had drained us, we retired our super-soakers and crashed. I had to sleep on the triple room floor again because Mason was in our room screwing Oh. An hour later, there was a knock at the door. I got up and opened it. There were Mason and Oh.

"Chucks wanna sauce?" Mason asked.

We nodded and slipped our thongs on. We walked down to the courtyard and chatted about where to have dinner. As I was suggesting a place, I heard a series of squeaks. Suddenly a load of cold water blasted me in the face.

"What the fuck?"

I looked over and saw Oh cackling, with a super-soaker in her hands. I went to grab it from her, but she sprayed me in the face a second time.

"Haha, you li' dat," she said, flicking her tongue at me. I grimaced and picked up a nearby hose. I turned it on full power and sprayed her in the mouth. She dropped her gun and lapped sensually at the stream of water. I clenched my teeth, tossed the hose, and walked off.

Despite having crashed on the triple room floor again, I woke up the next morning happy. The reason for this was I'd be seeing my friend Takka later that day. I had met her back in '01 when I was on vacation in Thailand with my father. She was our private tour guide for the Bangkok area. She had a voluptuous body, soft voice, and dark skin. She was ten years my senior, but that didn't bother me. She still had the energy of a hyperactive teenager in bed. This is what earned her the nickname Takka, short for *takkataen*, which means "grasshopper" in Thai.

Takka arrived at our hostel at eleven. She was wearing tight jeans, a cotton blouse, and polarized sunglasses. A begonia was perched delicately above her ear. She carried a white umbrella to keep the sun off her skin. When we saw each other, we hugged. I immediately felt that bubble of warmth form between our chests. I moved in for a kiss. Takka pressed a finger to my lips.

"Layta," she said, smiling. "Now I will show you my city."

We split up into threes and got tuk-tuks to the Grand Palace. The road there was clogged with monks in orange robes and drunken Songkraners firing water guns and hurling soy bombs. The decorations and fanfare seemed to have doubled since the day before. Piles and piles of crushed flowers, smoking shrines, and exploded water balloons littered the surrounding streets. We cut through a huge procession where elephant-back temples sparkled amidst a sea of joyous brown faces. We were almost trampled to bloody pancakes in our little tuk-tuks.

An hour later, we arrived at the Grand Palace. Its grounds were more beautiful than I had remembered. Their most pronounced structure, the Phra Sri Ratana Chedi, looked like a delicately carved mountain of gold-leaf toffee stretched and hardened to a needle point. The temples surrounding it were inlaid with complex mosaics of semiprecious stones and mirrors. Blue-skinned sentinels with tusks and bejeweled swords were posted at the entrances. I must have taken a thousand photos.

When we entered the compound, its walls were ringing with the haunting chants of monks in prayer. To this eerily spiritual background music, Takka taught us of the kings who had inhabited this place. All nine were of the Chakri Dynasty, which has run from 1782 to the present day. The most revered of them was King Rama V, or Chulalongkorn.

"He modernize our country and protect us from being control by the British and the French," she explained to us. "It because of him that Siam never been colonize."

While she spoke of this man, she had tears in her eyes. I chuckled silently and opened my guidebook. I saw a photo of the current Thai king, Rama IX (a.k.a. Bhumibol). He was smiling like he'd just finished having a tremendous orgasm.

"Check this fuckin' guy out," I said.

Takka looked me directly in the eyes and scowled.

"This not funny."

"Why not?" I said, raising my hands. "He's just a figurehead."

"He is not just figurehead. Our Bhumibol, he stay up many nights to try and solve problems of our country. He go to villages to try and see what he can do to fix Thailand and he do this every day. He could live with riches in this palace we build for him, but he prefer to stay in smaller palace and live more normal like us to show how much he love and respect common people. Please do not be angry when I say, Johann, but I do not see your leaders doing this."

I tried to imagine Bush and Cheney out there doing the things Takka had mentioned, but it was a stretch. Far more ridiculous than Bhumibol's expression.

Takka then took us to Prasat Phra Debidorn, a temple within the Grand Palace. Its roof was a four-pointed shell of red and green tiles that ascended in tiers like robotic snakeskin. At its center sat a stone bastion ornately carved in Angkor Wat style. Propping everything up was a tight row of blue and gold colonnades. They glistened with jewels. As we removed our shoes at the entrance, Takka explained how lucky we were.

"We Thai only open this tempo to public once a year."

Inside, everything was silent and still. Dozens of locals were laid prostrate, whispering thanks to the icons in front of them. Each icon was a life-sized version of a Thai king, made entirely of gold. Seeing that much solid gold in one place nearly made me choke. Where were the guards? I thought. When I saw Takka get down on the floor and weep, I understood why none were needed. No Thai in their right mind would ever think of touching those statues, let alone stealing them. A strange electricity encircled my heart. I got down on my knees next to Takka and started to pray. I looked up at the other Chucks and raised my eyebrows. They bit their lips and walked away.

After the ceremony, we went back to the Tandu House. We rested a little, then hit the streets. Songkran was in full swing. It didn't take long for the other Chucks to get swallowed by its crazy, colorful maw. Before I knew it, Takka and I were alone for the first time in many years. We slid into each other's arms and kissed. The silence of our little bubble reduced the carnival around us to a distant roar. Takka looked up at me and smiled. "Les go to your room," she said.

Mason was still out there partying when we arrived. We celebrated by stripping down to our birthday suits and making love in the shower. Our wet embrace spiraled out of the bathroom and onto my bed. The friction from our rhythmic clapping split my elbows open against the white sheets. Blood oozed out everywhere and mixed with the scattering of condom wrappers. We left for her place an hour later, laughing at the mess we'd made.

Takka lived on the other side of Bangkok. It took a good forty minutes to get there in her little Toyota. I expected her to be living in a small apartment. I was shocked when we pulled up to a decent-sized home. It had an outdoor garden and a bamboo fence. The inside was decorated with Buddhist relics and boasted three bedrooms and a full-size bath. She led me to her bedroom and threw me on her bed. We made love till our bodies gave out and fell asleep damp and naked in each other's arms.

Takka got an alarming call shortly after we woke up. Her friend's father had just passed away, and she was calling Takka to inform her about the funeral date. This put Takka in a stupor. For the entire ride back to the Tandu House, she spoke very little. When we arrived, we found the others in the courtyard nursing their hangovers. Mason looked up at me from his Sprite and pinched his eyebrows.

"What the fuck happened in our room?" he asked. "Looks like you hooked some fool up in there."

"We blew up," I whispered. "Anyway, now's not the time to talk about it. Takka's friend's dad just gottem so she's feelin' *good*. We gotta do sumthin' to get her mind off it."

We decided to take her to an Indian place on our street. We ordered tons of food and drinks and insisted on paying for everything. This seemed to bring her out of her funk. That is, till we went back to the hostel and found Oh waiting for us there with her daughter.

Poh was the spitting image of her mother only with pigtails and more clothing. She was bouncing around the courtyard like a spun-out jellybean singing Thai nursery rhymes. Oh was smoking a cigarette and chatting on her cell phone. Mason went up and gave her a big, wet kiss.

"You mi me?" she asked, with the phone still to her ear.

"Ch," he said.

We all went up to Bert's room. Oh immediately gave Takka daggers. While we were blabbing amongst each other, I saw Oh lean in and mutter something to Takka in Thai. Takka's face tightened to a point. She slung her purse over her shoulder and walked over to me.

"I must go now," she said. "I have tour to give."

I walked outside with her and asked her what Oh had said.

She hesitated with a scowl. "She ask me very rudely if I fuck you. She is bad woman. Tell Mason be careful with her."

Before I had a chance to say anything to Mason, he emerged from Bert's room with Oh and Poh.

"We're gonna drop Poh off at her granny's then come back n' blow up," he said. "I got an extra key from the front desk so if you bunt, it fuckin' matters."

"Go huge," I said. I turned back to Takka.

She was frowning deeply. "I come back at eight o'clock," she said, walking off. "Please be here."

At around seven, Mason and Oh came back up to the room. Oh was being her usual annoying self. Mason looked a bit ghost-faced. I pulled him aside and asked him what was up.

"Dude, I kinda gottem," he said.

"Whaddaya mean?"

"With Oh. Don't tell the other Chucks, but when we got back, we took a bower, and I snit her in the ass without a fronny. When I pulled out, I had blood on my dick."

"What? Are you fucking crazy? She's a Thai prosty!"

Mason looked like he was about to panic. His eyes bulged to the point of bursting, then a sleazy coolness suffused his demeanor. He lit up a cigarette and shrugged.

"Well . . . if I gottem, I gottem," he said.

I laughed. "Maybe ney ney ain't that bad," I said.

He puffed out a chuckle of smoke and pointed across the room with his cigarette tip. Oh was stretched across the bed with Sebastian's nipple in her mouth and Tim's crotch in her hand.

"Gimme yo iPod," she shouted, squeezing Tim's dick harder. He handed the thing over with a whimper. She plugged the headphones into her ears, kicked to a standing position, and started bouncing up and down, screaming out the lyrics to "It's My Life" by Bon Jovi.

When she shouted "Ih mah liiii" for the umpteenth time, I lost my cool. I leaned into Mason's ear and said, "Tell her to fuckin' bunt."

He looked around and saw that everyone was grimacing. Tim walked over.

"She's getting' fuckin' garnk," he whispered. "Plus, I'm worried that if we leave her alone, she'll pilf our shit."

Mason raised his eyebrows. He walked over to her and politely told her to beat it.

"Why?" she shouted. "You thing I wan steal fran you? If I wan steal fran you, I neba fuck you. I jus have my fren come and kill aw of you. Then I steal fran you."

Her eyes were swirling with madness. She cackled hysterically and

18

threw her arms in the air. Mason grabbed her by the elbow and jerked her out of the room. I heard her cussing at him in the hallway.

"At least I got my nipple sucked," said Sebastian.


"I have a surprise for you today," Takka said, nudging me awake. It was nine in the morning. I could barely open my eyes.

I groaned. "Can't the surprise wait for later?"

"No. We must wake up your friends and leave now so you don't end up party all day."

"Well, could you at least tell me where we're going?"

"Floating Market."

"The Floating Market? You took me and my dad there last time. That's no surprise."

"Be patient, Johann, and go wake friends up. You have to trus me."

We arrived at the Floating Market during rush hour. Its maze of chocolate rivers was flooded with long-tailed boats carrying cheap toys, buckets of fish, pyramids of fruits, vegetables, etcetera. We boarded our own long tail and slid into the splintering chaos. A dozen old ladies in rice paddy hats sidled up to our boat and shoved their goods in our faces.

"One dolla. One dolla," they screamed.

Everything they offered had the interest factor of a scrotum-pinch. We begged Takka to take us out of the main thoroughfare.

"Not till you all try something," she said. She whistled one of the old ladies over. The woman floated up to us, brandishing a toothless smile. With her wrinkly hands, she showcased her main product. It looked like a prickly green football.

"This is durian," Takka said.

Before we could blink, the old woman whipped out a machete. She brought it down on the fruit with a resounding crack, then handed Takka a freshly cut half. The meat inside looked like calf brains glazed with butter. It reeked of rotting onions.

"That smells like ass," Tim said.

Takka smiled. "Yes, it stink. In Thai, though, we say about this fruit, 'Smell like'a hell, taste like'a hebin.'"

She passed the stinky durian half around, and we each scooped out a hunk.

"You ever sauce this shit before, Felm?" Mason asked.

"Ch. It's like she says, dude. Smells like hell, tastes like heaven."

He gave me an incredulous look and stuffed the durian hunk in his mouth. The rest of us followed. I was prepared for the taste. My friends weren't. In synchronized motion, their faces soured, and the durian shot from their lips. Tim even puked a little.

"More like smells like hell, tastes like shit," Bert said, gagging.

Takka and I almost keeled over the side of the boat laughing.

"You like?" she said through the tears.

"Yeah, I like," Bert said. He was still spitting little bits over the side. "I just hope that's not our fuckin' surprise."

Takka chuckled and took the oars. She rowed us from the main thoroughfare and into the channels surrounding it. All the boat vendors and riverside stalls instantly disappeared. Fishing villages, stilted homes, and vine-covered Buddha statues took their place. Except for the occasional birdcall, there was little to interrupt the sound of the water swishing past our boat. It lulled me into a place of crystal meditation.

In the midst of my thoughts, our boat bumped to a stop.

"We are here," Takka said.

I looked up and saw a gigantic, seven-headed cobra glaring at me with all fourteen of its eyes. Its heads fanned out from a six-foot tower of green coils upon which rested a sign that read "Cobra Show Thailand." My heart skipped. Before we'd left on the trip, I had begged Takka to take us to a cobra farm. She'd refused, claiming she's terrified of snakes.

"I had a horrible dream once that one ate my ho body," she'd told me. "I will not go even near a cobra farm."

Thinking it was a lost cause, I decided not to pester her about it, so I was stunned that between then and now she'd gotten up the gumption to take us.

She waited outside for our van while the five of us milled around the farm. There were a few walls of ill-kept cages housing specimens of various sizes and temperaments. Once we got our fill of browsing, we sought out the owners of the place. All of them were dark, sinewy country boys with vein-streaked arms, tank tops, and black shades. Only one of them—the main handler—spoke any English.

"Sawasdee krab," I said to him.

The man pursed a tiny smile. "What you need?" he asked.

"We want to know if we can try cobra blood."

He laughed. "You wan dring?"

"Yes."

He conferred with his associates. They all snickered.

"Tweny dolla ea'," he said.

None of us knew the price for this sort of thing. We handed him the cash, and he stuffed it in his pocket.

The second he walked off, I got queasy. At first, I had been excited about us all drinking cobra blood. But the knowledge that an innocent creature had to lose its life so we could do this was starting to eat at me. I voiced my concern to the group. Tim cocked his head at me and squinted.

"Think about it, Felm," he said, cracking his knuckles. "You think that cobra gives mad shits about you? He'd pass you treats in a second if he could. Plus, you care millions about saucin' pigs n' cows off. What's a bitchin' cobra? This'll be a baumish experience, gaht. You should just say damn and care."

The handler came back five minutes later with a hissing burlap sack. He held it in front of our circle of shocked faces and opened it. Inside was a gray serpent coiled up to the size of a basketball. Its eyes were furious yellow dots.

"You're gonna get 'em lil' guy," Mason said.

We followed the handler to a dirt lot in back. There beside a wooden shack stood a tall metal post with a laundry line tied to it. The handler wrested the snake up by the face and pulled it hissing and coiling from the burlap sack. He grabbed the end of the line and tied it around the snake's neck. The constriction from the rope made it writhe with panic. A slug of bright yellow feces came squirting out its anus.

"That cobra just took its last shit," Sebastian said. The handler left and came back with a tray full of items. Among them were five wine glasses, a tin mug, a bottle of rice whiskey, a razor, and some toilet paper. He popped the top off the rice whiskey and dribbled some of it in his cupped hand. He ran his whiskey filled palm down the entire length of the cobra's body, scrubbing it of feces, scales, and dirt. He repeated this a half dozen times, then went over to the tray again. This time he grabbed the razor.

"Fuck, gahts I'm coo on this," I said. "I don't wanna gettem and get sick."

"Dude, *way* Felm. You'll be ait," Sebastian assured me. "They're cleaning that shit hella good."

I looked over at him like "What the fuck's it to you?" Before I could verbally bitch smack him, Mason cut in.

"I *care* what you guys do, I'm blowin' up," he said. "I already paid for this shit."

Bert and Tim both nodded in agreement. I was swamped.

"Ait, fuck it," I said. "Let's explode."

After cleaning his razor and pouring some rice whiskey into his mug, the handler walked back over to the snake. One of his buddies crouched down and gripped its tail while the handler positioned himself in front of its body. He handed his buddy the mug and gripped the snake at the neck. In one slow, deliberate motion he squished its blood down toward where his buddy was holding. When the two men's hands met, he stuck the razor to the snake's belly and zipped a three-inch incision into it. Its flesh tensed, then relaxed. With two fingers, the man dug into the pink of the incision and wrestled out a fluffy curtain of guts. A long, thick artery rich with blood ran the length of the curtain. He poised the tip of the razor against the beating artery and cut. A fountain of maroon blood came spurting from the intestinal curtain and down into the mug. He intensified the flow by running his clenched fist along the length of the snake's body again. When the mug was full, the cobra's body looked like a long, deflated balloon.

My feelings of guilt were exacerbated when the handler let go of the snake. Its tail coiled and thrashed against the metal post, smearing blood and bits of black organ meat all across it.

"Now we *gotta* sauce its blood," I said. "It'd be fuckin' fair to that lil' gaht if we didn't."

The handler filled each of the wine glasses with the dark cocktail and handed them to us. I could feel the warmth of the cobra's blood under my fingertips. I looked down at my glass. I could see my sad red reflection in it. Mason elbowed me from my stupor. Then he raised his glass.

"A toast," he said. "To this cobra, whose blood will now make us brothers."

We all looked into each other's eyes. I could feel that strange electricity again, buzzing between us. We pulled our drinks in close, tipping the glasses. Our mouths opened, and the blood poured in.


I woke up the next morning with screaming black eyes. It felt like there was a badger trying to slash its way out of my skull. Takka was lying next to me in a similar state. The previous night had been a blast with her two friends, Buki and Pae, till the lot of us got thrown out of the club.

I nudged Mason awake, then went up to the triple room. Bert was lying naked in bed with Buki, and Pae was in the bed opposite them, squeezed in between Tim and Sebastian. Everyone was out cold. I stuck two fingers in my mouth and whistled.

"Time to bunt," I screamed. People only groaned and rolled over. It was an hour before any of them actually made it out the door.

Outside, Bert said his goodbyes to Buki.

"I'll call ya in two days," he said.

"You betta."

She bounced up and planted a tiny kiss on the tip of his nose. He straightened the palm trees on his shirt and winked at Mason across the courtyard. When the bus pulled up, all of us got on, including Pae. Unbeknownst to me, Takka had invited her to come with us to Angkor Wat.

The trip to the Cambodian border was surprisingly decent. Our bus had air conditioning, comfy seats, and ample leg space. It even dropped us off at a little Thai restaurant for lunch. I felt less like I was traveling through Southeast Asia and more like I was traveling through Northwest Europe. This stood in stark contrast to the horror stories I had read about travel by bus to Angkor Wat. Many bloggers had written that it was the single most hellish trip in all of Asia.

Musta been a buncha pussies, I thought.

My cockiness lasted till we reached the Cambodian border. For five solid hours, we sat on the floor of the stuffy control room, sweating our clothes soggy and filling out useless forms. When the guards finally let us through, we had lost a dozen gallons of water between us. My face looked like a big prune.

The instant we stepped foot outside, we were swarmed by street urchins. They were dark-skinned and greasy with fast eyes and few teeth. Some begged for money with cupped hands. Others threw their cheap goods in our faces and pleaded with us to buy them. One boy caught my attention. He had a dusty crop of brown hair and a biscuit of dried snot glistening beneath his nose. An infant was hanging naked and lifeless from a sash he had slung over his shoulder. I felt terrible for the little pair, so I handed the boy a few Cambodian riel. His cronies must have spotted me doing this because they left my friends' ankles and crowded around mine. With a phalanx of screaming children in front of me, I shot my eyes back at our luxury Thai bus. The fast-increasing distance between me and it made the harshness of this new reality set in. I scowled and drew my eyes downward. They followed the road to where its pavement crumbled into a river of red earth. When they were level with the horizon, our Cambodian bus pulled up. It looked like a row of filthy aluminum shacks haphazardly welded together. My heart sunk.

"Wew'cum to Cambodia," the little boy said and giggled.

# ANGKOR WAT

I watched out the bus window as the countryside crawled by. It was greener and more open than Thailand's. Wooden villages dotted its belly. Surrounding it was a loose-knit jungle. On occasion, we'd curve around a range of limestone cliffs. They rose from the plains like the backs of dragons. It soon began to rain. It started as a trickle then quickly developed into a torrent of grape-sized water drops. Our driver braved the forming mud slicks till the engine coughed itself to death. We had to get out so repairs could be made. While we stood in the rain, children from a roadside village came creeping out of their hovels. They wore smiles but exhibited little of the fanfare the Thais usually bring when greeting foreigners. We thanked them for posing in a few photos with us. They only grinned and stood silent.

Back on the bus, I willed myself into a light sleep. The rain had turned the dirt road underneath us into a river of mud and rock. Every time I closed my eyes, they were jolted back open. I resigned myself to looking out the window again. It was nightfall now. The only illumination came from the few decorations people had put up for Songkran. Villages in the distance looked like handfuls of fireflies scattered across an endless black canvas. It was like seeing Christmas in deep space.

Ten hours later we rolled into Siem Reap. Its streets were sparsely paved and cluttered with trash. Tall skeletons of buildings hung in the darkness. Beggars and three-legged dogs scurried back and forth. Our bus let us off at a dirt alley next to an abandoned gas station. We were forced to find accommodations with no directions other than what was in our guidebook. We looped through the city's dingy causeways searching for anything that resembled a hostel. Most of what we came across were gaudy, French-style hotels, gated off from their surroundings. On a side street off the main drag, we finally found a budget hotel with vacancies. It was an oasis of teakwood and palms amongst the concrete ghosts. Takka and I took a room together, as did Tim and Sebastian. Pae opted to share a triple with Mason and Bert. Despite having ridden for fifteen hours, we were all in the mood to kick a few back. After we unloaded our crap and freshened up, we headed off toward a dive bar the hotel owner had recommended.

The bar looked like a rundown colonial outpost. It had creaky ceiling fans, a few old pool tables, and a mahogany counter with high stools. The owner was a shifty-eyed Dutchman with a potbelly and curly hair. I ordered a Jack and coke from him and sat down at the bar. I struck up a conversation with the guy next to me. He was a British soldier named Vaughan who had been living in Cambodia for the past few years. Everything about him screamed English football goon; the glistening bald head, crooked teeth, giant gut, penchant for beer-guzzling. It wasn't until he began expatiating on modern Cambodian history that I took him seriously.

"The thing about this country," he said, "is that it's never been given a proper chance. I mean, the first thing Pol Pot did after he changed the name to 'Democratic Kampuchea' and instituted his bloody 'Year Zero,' was round up anyone with five measly brain cells using his Khmer Rouge army and blow 'em all to smithereens."

"Why the fuck did he do that?"

"Well, think about it, mate. He didn't want anyone trying to steal his show. His objective was to create an agrarian communist country composed entirely of ethnic Khmer workers he called 'old people' or people who weren't tainted by westernization and capitalism. The 'new people,' a.k.a. intellectuals, urban businessmen, ethnic minorities, etcetera, were believed to be threats to the Khmer regime and thus thrown into labor camps or killed. Pol Pot murdered one point six million of these poor bastards, and he did it with the belief that of the eight million Cambodians in existence, he only needed a couple of million to create his utopia. Everyone else was expendable, or as the Khmer proverb goes, 'To keep you is no benefit; to destroy you is no less.'"

"Jesus," I said.

After that, the conversation with Vaughan tapered off. I sat and sipped my beer in silence. I thought about the villagers I'd taken photos with earlier. Suddenly their reluctance to speak didn't seem so odd.


Our main objective for the next day was to see as much of Angkor as possible. We were out of the hotel by seven-thirty. The van we'd arranged for the night before was already waiting for us in the courtyard. Our driver, Supal—a tubby little ghoul with a cheerful disposition and a mouthful of baby gold teeth—greeted us with a handshake.

"Where you need go first?" he asked.

"We need money, tickets, and breakfast, in that order," I said.

Supal nodded. He ushered us into his giant tin can, and we clunked off.

Downtown Siem Reap looked less daunting in the daylight. I noticed more greenery and whitewashed balconies. There even seemed to be something of a café culture; remnants, no doubt, of French rule. When we finished changing money and buying our tickets for the park, Supal let us off to eat at one of the cafés. It was aptly named "The Khmer Experience." We sat out on the terrace and ordered our food— omelets, toast, yogurt, and cereal. It was almost a given that we'd have to wait a bit longer for our meals since most of Southeast Asia has a looser concept of time than the West, but I've seen slugs on opposite ends of my yard meet up and fuck faster than these idiot Cambodian cooks could crack an egg. In the end, only three of us, Sebastian, Bert, and I, got our food. Mason and Tim just scowled at their empty plates. Takka and Pae got so impatient they went to the kitchen at the back and cooked their own meals. Needless to say, we didn't tip.

Supal arrived a few minutes after we finished eating.

"You like Khmer Experience?"

"Oh, it was *coo*," Bert said.

Supal furrowed his brow. "What coo?"

"It means we're looking for something a little more authentically Khmer."

"Angkor City authentic Khmer," he said, smiling.

Supal parked our van in a dirt lot a half mile from the city entrance. The main temple, Angkor Wat, was blocked by a high wall of trees. We got out of the van and had to side-skirt a gang of street urchins selling postcards. When we refused to buy any, they snubbed their noses at us; one little girl even started to cry. Another, whom Mason had ignored completely, told him to fuck himself. We were howling as we started on our walk.

The path curved around fallen trees and boulders consumed by moss. A few times we thought we were lost. The sunlight that splayed from the canopy marked our way. I felt like I was on the set of *Raiders of the Lost Ark* in search of a golden monkey head.

"There's the exit up there," I said, pointing to the horizon. Like clockwork, the botanical hands of the jungle parted their chest plate. Revealed was the temple complex of Angkor Wat. Its main building towered in the distance like a giant's throne. At its center stood six stone hives, organized in a diamond shape, with the largest at the front. The towers were atop a rock altar that stepped downwards and outwards into a massive stone footing. The only way in was through an ornately hewn door below the main tower. Leading up to this door was a path lined by palm trees. The grandeur of everything sucked our lungs flat.

"Where did they get the inspiration to build this thing?" I asked Takka as we walked.

"The Hindu King Suryavarman II reign from 1113 to 1150 A.D. He get his inspiration from Mount Meru, where Hindus believe all their gods live. This place is like Mount Olympus for ancient Greeks. The King build it for Vishnu, a very powerful Hindu god. But inside you will see many Buddhist statues and monks. This because Cambodia was convert to Buddhism in thirteenth century."

For the next three hours, we explored the entire complex. Our journey took us through a labyrinth of stone passageways that shrunk and expanded till they led us to a grand courtyard. Carved into its walls were scenes from the Hindu epics *Mahabharata* and *Ramayana*. Most depicted alien-faced gods massacring or blessing men in one of the thirty-two hells or thirty-seven heavens of Hindu mythology. One scene caught my eye. It was of a man in royal Hindu regalia kneeling before a beautiful floating woman. I inched closer to get a better look. As I did, the hairs on my forearms stood on end. This reaction spread throughout my body like rapidly growing ivy. An electric hand curled around my heart. My eyes slipped closed in bliss. I smiled.

"You okay, Johann?" Takka asked.

I flinched. My hands were shaking. "Uh, yeah," I said.

"What you looking at?"

"I'm not sure. This place is weird."

Takka slanted her eyes at me fondly. "I know," she said. "It have special magic. Come, les see the rest."

Takka led us through a high stone archway. On the other side, we found a plain of grass backed by walling. Bald monks swathed in bright orange robes were milling around with bundles of burning incense in their hands. We sidestepped them and rounded a corner where a crumbling stairway led up to the entrance to a tower. It must have been over a hundred feet high. Its steep incline was such that you could stand on one step, and with a slight lean, use the steps above as back support.

We trudged up the hot steps, burning our hands and feet as we climbed. When we reached the top, we were rewarded with a panoramic view of the temple-dotted jungle. A little Cambodian man with skin as black as licorice greeted us at the doorway.

"You wan buy?" he asked, proffering us his wares. Everything he had was in two reed baskets hanging from opposite ends of a bamboo stick he had balanced on his shoulder. Nothing looked all that interesting.

"We're fine," Sebastian said.

The man gazed at him with an odd glint in his eye. "I know wha you wan," he said, grinning. He reached into his trousers and produced a long, black staff. It was wrapped in a scaly tail that ended at the top in a cobra's head.

Sebastian's eyes lit up. "Baumish."

The man only asked for a few bucks. He then vanished with a giggle into the darkness of the temple.

"What the fuck?" I said. "Did you tell that old fart about the cobra farm or something?"

"Noooo," Sebastian said. "It was like with my Krishna tattoo. The fucker just *knew*."

I leered at him, on the lean. "Haha. Yeah, he *knew*," I said. "Knew you were a faggot."

Before Sebastian and I could go at it, Takka cut in. "I take you guys now to anatha tempo," she said. "This one even more beutifo."

She took us to the Temple of Bayon. Its outer layer was just a crumbling mound of rock covered in vines. We entered it nonchalantly, snapping photos of the orange- and white-robed monks threading across the stone tiers in front.

"What do the different colored robes mean?" I asked.

"The orange is for men and white is for women."

"There are female monks?"

"Not exactly. They are *mae chee*, laywomen who dedicate life to Buddhism. Only men can be ordained. In Thailand, I wore robes for two years. We all must do this as Buddhists."

"My, aren't I an idiot?" I said.

We crawled up through a dark passage that opened into a terrace of stone towers. Each tower was taller than the last and emblazoned on four sides with the same serene face. The sea of faces followed my every move with smiling eyes. I felt like I was in a medieval Hindu fun house.

"Who's the dude?" Bert asked, pointing to one of the carvings.

"Most people think this is King Jayavarman VII's face. He is the one who build this tempo."

After a minute, we came upon a small shrine encased in ribbons of smoke. Inside was a golden statue of the Buddha with pots of incense and flowers at its feet. An old mae chee with a shaved head and buck teeth sat in front of it. She curled her finger at us.

"What's she want?" I asked.

"You are her guests here," Takka said. "She wan bless you."

"Okay."

We entered the shrine one by one and got down on our knees. We pressed our hands together and bowed to the statue of Buddha. The mae chee crept over and batted us each on the head with a bundle of smoking herbs. She snickered as she did it to Sebastian, presumably because his gut prevented him from kneeling down all the way.

"You're kina gettin' 'em there, Sebastian," I said, pointing.

He looked at me with a blank expression on his face.

"Blow Ned," he said.

The woman paused her blessing when she heard this. She looked up at me and smiled.

"Blow Ned," she repeated.

Bert dropped to his side and started convulsing with laughter. It took him a full minute to come to.

"Fuckin' A, Felm," he said, panting. "You came all the way to Cambodia just to have a bald female monk tell you to blow Ned? God, you gottem."

"Who is Ned?" Takka asked.

Ned, God rest his conniving little soul, was (and still is, to a certain degree), the supreme pariah of our group. Since the day we met him till the day he died, he used his boyish grin and pathetic whining to con us out of money, love, and favors. At one point or another, he lived with all but a few of us; crashing on our apartment couches and eating all our food. He always promised to compensate us for his incessant scheming and mooching, but never delivered. In retaliation, the lot of us dubbed him anathema to the Chucks. He was one of us, but only insofar as we teased him. Our favorite way of doing this was to tell one another to blow him. This became so commonplace that we began saying, "Blow Ned" to express disdain for pretty much anyone or anything. That is, until he died of congestive heart failure in 2007. On occasion, we still slip up and tell one another to blow the guy. And despite the disrespect of it, our continued use of this phrase keeps old Ned alive in some form. During the trip, Ned was still around so we used the expression freely. Even so, we never heard it from anyone outside our group. You can imagine my surprise when a female monk in Cambodia told me to suck the guy off. I nearly died myself.

That night, we took Takka out to dinner. She refused to accept any money from us, so this was our way of thanking her for being our guide. During the meal, she and Pae indulged in the alcohol. By the end, both girls were exceedingly drunk. Bert and I weren't feeling much pain either. When the bill was paid, the four of us decided to see what we could dig up from Siem Reap's night scene.

We took to the streets laughing and stumbling over our feet like inebriated clowns. Pae, who was normally reserved and only slightly flirtatious, began hanging off Bert's neck like a knotted sweater. She lapped at his ear and whispered filthy things to him. Since he'd consumed enough booze to fill a small aquarium, her mild size issues and chipmunk face conveniently escaped his attention. He even laughed when she bit his earlobe.

"Does she always act like this when she goes out?" I asked Takka.

"No." Takka chuckled. "Only when she drung. When we drung, we both go crazy."

We charged into the first club we found. It seemed cold and angular from the outside. Inside we found hundreds of smiling

Cambodian twenty-somethings tossing back Angkor beers and slithering around to trance music. We pushed and swerved our way up to the bar. The bartender didn't even take our order. He simply lifted a bucket of lukewarm beers. I took one and looked out at the crowd. People were dancing and twisting their fingers through spinning webs of green lasers. It was a semblance of a good time.

"I'm gonna go blow up out there and see what's what," I said.

I went out on the dance floor. At either end, I noticed two raised platforms topped by steely-faced guards in Armani suits. When they spotted a beer in my hand, they climbed down from their towers and escorted me off the dance floor. "No drinks," they spat in unison. As they climbed back up on their perches, I watched the faces of the clubbers around me. They were pinched with silent fear. It was like being in a dance library. I decided it was time to cut.

The next place we went to was still quiet but had a lighter ambiance. Some people were sitting in dark corners with drinks to their lips. Others were heel to heel, gliding around noiselessly on the dance floor. We took our place among the forest of bar stools in the back and ordered. Pae and Bert were all over one another like chicken pox. I tried to coax Takka into dancing with me, but she opted to finish her beer.

"You go dance," she said, smiling. "I wan watch."

I shrugged and staggered out there with my head between my shoulders. When I got to the center of the floor, I stopped. A small ring of space was afforded me. I closed my eyes and absorbed the atmosphere. Everywhere around me people were moving. The strobe lights above were beating like rabbit hearts. Each time they flickered, my eyelids turned bright red. The song did its build-up, and I began to gyrate. That eerie electric sensation pulsed through my body again. I ripped the rubber band from my ponytail and let my hair enshroud my face. The music intensified, and I thrashed my head back and forth. The circle of people around me widened. A ceiling light clicked on and blasted down on me. When the song hit its apogee, I threw my head back and opened my mouth. A vein-thickening wail came sailing out.

It ripped a wide hole in that bastard Cambodian silence. My reality peeled away in curls. I saw a vision of a frosty mountain range with a blue moon glowing high above it. A woman's voice spoke to me from the sky. Her words were strange but beautiful, like fire being swallowed by bubbles. I strained to decipher the tongue. I could only memorize the sounds.

When the message clipped off, I tumbled down the steps of insanity. My eyes flapped open, and I was left gazing at the crowd around me. Everyone was wearing contorted faces and wide eyes. I was a sweaty, scraggly-haired spectacle of a man. I walked slowly back to my stool. My friends were staring at me in astonishment. I took a sip of my beer and smiled at them.

"What?" I said. "I was having a moment."


The next morning, Takka and I didn't wake up until noon. When we finally made it out the door, we found Mason in the hallway, laughing. I asked him what the deal was, and he pointed back into his room.

"Ask Bert," he said.

I walked up to the threshold. I saw Bert sitting knees-to-elbows on the bed with his face pointing at the floor. A lit cigarette was dangling between his fingers.

"What's up, gaht?" I asked him.

He stuck the butt to his lips and took a long pull. As the smoke slithered up his cheeks, he thumbed over his back. Behind him was a plump brown body swathed in a red towel. It was Pae.

Bert flicked his cigarette out the window and walked up to me. His face was drained of color.

"I gottem last night," he whispered. "The fronny busted while I was snittin' it."

"Pae fuckin' has anything," I said.

"No dude, you don't understand. It was just after I jizzed. She might be preggers now."

Mason started laughing again and clapping his hands. Takka scowled at him.

"Don werry," she said to Bert. "I know she don wan baby now. We make sure it is okay."

Pae opted not to join us to the bus stop. It was just as well; six people fit better in two tuk-tuks. Our shitty bus was already at the station when we arrived. While the others got on, Takka and I took a few moments to say goodbye. She had dolled herself up and put a flower in her hair.

"I wan you to remember me looking happy," she said, smiling. As she finished her sentence, a sad expression melted down her face. I curled her hair behind her ear and kissed her on the lips. She smiled again.

"See?" I said.

I got on the bus and waved to her till she was a little brown dot. When she popped below the horizon, I turned around and grimaced. The road was more hideous and bumpier than I had remembered. I was having trouble just putting my earphones in. Everyone else seemed miserable as well. The only one who was dealing was Sebastian. He was shirtless and slouched over his backpack, snoring like a tranquilized bear. I snapped a photo of his sagging man-tits then drifted back into my head. The vision I'd had in the club was the first thing I thought of. I replayed it over and over again in my mind, trying to squeeze any drip of meaning I could from it. Nothing made any sense. I contemplated saying something to the Chucks, but a gut feeling told me to wait.

Six hours and six hundred nerve-rattling bumps later, we arrived at the Cambodian/Thai border post. Since the bureaucrats there were extra sluggish, and the building was full of locals, we had to wait outside for our passports in the blazing heat. The five of us set up shop around a storefront gutter and clicked into self-mode. Tim scribbled odd shapes and designs in his visual journal, and Mason tinkered with his oversized camera. Bert inhaled fruit waffles with a tiny fork, and I sat and observed. At the epicenter of our activity was Sebastian. He was lounging on the asphalt like a Komodo dragon with a belly full of goat. Everything about him reeked of Chuck life. He had the gold-rimmed aviators, the ratty clothes, the sweaty pits, the wedge of gut poking out from under his shirt. His neatly shaven goatee had grown into a black forest that was crawling up the sides of his face. When he smiled, it looked like a string of chicklets in a licorice whip field. To complete his look, he had hung his cobra staff across his body. He was a living, breathing microcosm of the world we had created.

Bert was next to truly recognize the importance of this spontaneous moment. He got up from his chair, fixed his collar, and cracked a smile.

"Fuck. Look at Blow-up Guy over here." he said. All our attention was on Sebastian now. His grin sunk into a joyous cavern.

I woke up the next morning in a rare state. From the moment we'd hit Bangkok, Sebastian had been a shark on fire, demanding we all pound shots, one after another. I staggered into the courtyard of the Tandu House. Bert and Tim were chatting with Buki, and Mason was enjoying a meal with Oh and Poh. Sebastian was sprawled out over a tabletop with his arms dangling off either end. I snickered at him.

Our flight to Delhi was in a few hours. We said our goodbyes to the girls and took a shuttle to the airport. Inside, the line from the Air India desk stretched out like a crooked snake. We stood behind it and tried to be as inconspicuous as possible. All the Indians kept looking back at us with big white eyes.

"You think we're gonna gettem over there?" Bert asked me. "I mean, look at how these fools are lookin' at us. It's like they think we're fuckin' Albert just for trying to go to their country. Maybe we should just say sick and bunt to Europe."

"No fuckin' way," I shouted louder than I'd expected to. "India's a must."

An Indian guy in front of us wearing a flowered shirt looked back and laughed.

"You gentlemen are in for a rreal treat," he said.

The five of us gulped.

As we boarded our plane to Delhi, the man's sarcastic warning reeled through our minds. We took our seats at the front and wiped our brows. In all our fretting, we didn't even realize we'd boxed someone in.

"Hi," she squeaked. "I'm Jess."

We turned around and saw a woman sitting there smiling. She had greasy black hair, olive skin, and hazel eyes. Her tiny frame was draped in a red chemise. Silver jewelry dripped from every one of her bodily extensions.

"You guys nervous?" she asked.

"A little," I said.

The plane engines kicked to life, and we started moving down the runway. I could feel my stomach tying itself up in knots. When we lifted off, I pinched my eyes shut and swallowed my heart. Spidery black fingers started crawling across my face. I smelled the stench of a thousand dead infants. I was ready to claw my way through the roof when we kipped up and leveled off.

To distract myself, I turned around and struck up a conversation with Jess. She was still smiling.

"I . . . I'm Johann," I said. "And, uh, these are my buds from . . . back home."

"You guys are all traveling together?"

"Yeah, we do something like this every year. It's kind of a tradition."

"Wow! You guys are from Cali right?"

"How did you know?"

"I went to Chico State."

"Jesus, small world. You doin' India also?"

Her eyes bulged. She quickly softened her expression with another smile. "No, no, not this time. I'm en route to Switzerland. India is a wonderful place, but you have to be extremely prepared for it. I take it this is your first time?"

"How did ya guess?" Bert said.

"Haha. I was the same way, too, when I went five years ago. It was tough, but I stayed for over a year."

"Did you get sick at all?"

"Oh, horribly."

My anus tightened. "How sick?"

"Let's just say my eyes turned yellow."

"My God. Any advice?"

"Yeah, don't drink the water."

I swallowed hard and looked out the window. At first, I saw only night. Its cloak swelled and softened till we were surrounded by gray clouds. As we dipped through them, our plane began to rattle. My palms got slippery and my chest heated up. I gripped my armrests and tightened my gaze. The belly of the cloud field lit up with red light. When we pierced it, an endless patchwork of glowing streams unfolded. Each of the tiny worm-ways was teeming with blood cells.

"Damn," I said, leaning in closer. Just as a mobile signal causes radio feed to blip and beep, my view of the city became obstructed. What started as a few streaks quickly erupted into a flurry of white leaves. I thought we had slammed into a flock of seagulls.

"What the hell is all that?" I asked.

Jess looked out her window and puffed. "Oh, it's just the pollution."

"Jesus."

A second later, our landing gear descended. We came barreling into Delhi International with our wheels squealing and our cabin shaking. When our plane choked to a halt, I let out a sigh that almost took the contents of my bladder with it. We Chucks were officially in India. God save us.

# DELHI

The interior of the airport was humid and yellow. The smell of rancid diapers permeated the air. We cupped our faces and went to customs. It took us a full hour to get through. The baggage claim was on the other side. Our bags were circling the conveyer belt like frozen turds. We grabbed them and slung them over our shoulders. We got some money, then went outside to look for a cab. I was expecting to be gagged by smog and rushed by taxis. Delhi surprised me with a cool breeze and a trickle of interested drivers. I chose one, and we walked down to his car. A few porters in pastel shirts materialized from the darkness and slipped our packs from our backs. Mason paid them each fifteen cents and got in the cab.

"You guys can all pitch in and help pay for my room later," he said.

As we neared central Delhi, the filth and intensity of our surroundings increased in waves. Paved roads dissolved into rivers of gravel. Trees and shrubs melted into mounds of trash. Every thoroughfare became cluttered with skinny beggars and cows and women in bright saris. There wasn't a single patch of space not overwhelmed by activity. We careened through this madness in our creaking taxi, gripping at what was left of the roof handles. Our driver was a smiley, toothless man with tamarind skin and a lit cigarette hanging from his big lips. He cackled wildly and honked his horn.

"Where'rr you going?" he asked, snapping his fingers.

"Main Bazaar," I yelled.

He blipped his head in acknowledgment and laid on the gas. We were heading straight toward a wall of cars. "Look out," I screamed. At the last second, we zipped through a fissure in the gnarled steel and popped out the other end. I looked over at Bert. His face was dead white.

"I miss Thailand," he said.

Our cabbie dropped us off on a dirt road that zigzagged through a thicket of apocalyptic building shells. Everywhere we stepped were cow pies and bums in fetal bundles. We wandered up the street in search of anywhere inhabitable. It was the middle of the night so most hotels were closed.

"Let's just do this place," Mason said, pointing to shabby joint with a bright interior. We schlepped our crap inside and got a triple and a double for eight dollars a person. The Frazellis shared the double.

Inside our room, it was dank and smelly. The walls were stained orange and the bed was hard as Plexiglas. We stripped down to our boxers and turned the wall fan on. It sputtered to a stop within seconds.

"I'm gonna take a fuckin' bower," Bert said, whipping his boxers down. When the door to the bathroom closed, I clicked on the TV. An Indian couple in bejeweled regalia were dancing across the screen and singing. It sounded like they had helium in their lungs and marbles in their throats. Bert heard the horrible noise and yelled from the shower. "What the fuck's goin' on here, gahts? We're in goddamned India."

The sound of hard knocking woke me up in the morning. I pried my sweaty body from the sheets and went to the door. It was Sebastian.

"Dude, me n' Tim found a baumish lil' hostel up the road called The Rama," he said.

"You guys'r coo on this place?" I asked.

"Yeah, I'm not payin' eight bones a night for cockroaches to crawl on my balls in the mo'nin'. The Rama's only two. Plus, it's got hella backpackers."

We checked out of the Roach Motel and went to The Rama. It was cheaper, but by no means an upgrade. Most of its wiring and plumbing was lumped together in one big snake that coiled up inside the walls of its six-story stairwell. I know this because every third tile was either cracked or broken. What's worse, the place was home to thousands of mosquitoes that nested indiscriminately around the nooks in its waterlogged ceilings. My arms were flecked with red dots not thirty seconds after we entered the reception area.

"Do you guys have air conditioning?" I asked.

A coffee-skinned man with a flat nose and gold bangles dripping from his wrists looked up at me from his Hindi newspaper.

"Yes sirr, we do."

"Thank God," I said.

Bert got a double with Mason. Tim, Sebastian and I shared a triple. Our room was nothing short of hideous. It had three beds the size of slave cots whose mattresses sunk inwards like taco shells. Its walls were skuzzy, and its bathroom reeked. Its floor was a patchwork of muddy footprints. The air conditioner on the windowsill looked more like a busted engine.

"Does this thing even work?" I said, clicking it on. It rumbled to life just long enough to cough out a single puff of cold air. Then it sputtered flat. I ran downstairs fuming and explained this to the man with the newspaper. He threw his hands up in defeat.

"I'm terribly sorry, sirr," he said. "But I told you it verrked ten minutes ago. I didn't say it vood verrk forever."

I bit my tongue and sagged my head. It was a two-dollar room in Delhi. What the fuck did I expect?

To escape the heat of our rooms, we went upstairs to the rooftop restaurant. It was a breezy little oasis protected from the sun by an aluminum canopy. We decided to stay and have some food. While I munched on my veggie curry, I noticed that everyone around us was speaking Hebrew. It seemed very out of place. But it enlightened me as to why I had spotted a prayer room full of Hasidic Jews two floors below.

After settling the five-dollar bill, we shuffled downstairs and stepped into the sun. A frenetic river of cattle, motorbikes, and glistening Indians gripped our feet and sucked us into its flow. We went sailing down a canyon of filthy signs and telephone lines, gawking at things as we passed. There were bloody meat shops with hanging lamb cadavers, men in ragged clothes, *sadhus,* and rickshaws and slicks of shit and mud. There were cow pies and dirty feet, fruit stands with buzzing flies, glass pipes and plastic jewelry, vendors with no teeth. At every corner, a smelly confluence of each knotted to a lump and bumped us farther down the line like a group pinball. When we came to the end of it, we were spent.

With creaky bones, I stepped into a nearby clothes store and grabbed a couple T-shirts depicting Hindu deities. When I came out, I found the others snapping photos of a cow in traffic. Cars and even buses went completely out of their way to avoid hitting it as it lumbered across the street. People who knew better stood on either side of it to avoid getting creamed. Those who weren't hip were all but targeted by oncoming cars. I mused at this for a long, hard moment.

Back at the hostel, I napped for a bit. The sounds of laughter woke me. I opened my eyes and saw Bert sitting ghost-faced on the edge of my bed with a bottle of whiskey in his hand. Sebastian was cackling at him hysterically.

"What the hell happened?" I asked.

Bert looked at me with his mouth open. I thought he was going to shit himself.

"I went out to get some snalk, and I almost gottem," he muttered.

"Whaddaya mean you almost gottem?"

"Well, I was walking down the street all hella Albert n' not payin' attention, and I got hit."

"By a car?"

"Fuck yeah, dawg," he said. "I got hit by a cow."

The room collapsed into tears.

The five of us went upstairs to drink away our bovine woes. As we sipped whiskey and chatted, Tim asked me what I liked most about traveling. I tapped my lips with my index finger and thought. It came to me like a slow fart.

"The way it makes me grow," I said.

My response provoked an "aww" from our environs. I cricked my head to the right and spotted the source. He was a slender chap with greasy skin and hairy arms. His bald head was shaped like an upturned egg, and his eyes were cool and focused. He sat with his legs crossed, sipping tea on a lean.

"I like that," he said.

"Thanks."

"Mind if I join you guys?"

"Not at all."

The man unfolded from his chair like an oiled pocketknife and glided over to our table. The second he sat down, I could feel his aura seeping into my skin.

"My name is Mace," he said.

"Hey man, I'm Johann."

While the others introduced themselves, I stared at a soggy flower floating in Mace's teacup.

"What the hell is that?" I asked him.

"It's bang. Sort of like pot flower tea. You can't get it in New Zealand. That's why I keep comin' back here." Mace's accent was so subtle and his voice so smooth I could barely discern the twang in it.

"How many times have you been here?"

"Six, well, seven times now."

"Jesus. Seven times?"

He smiled. "I'm nothing. I know people who came here intending on staying a week and never left. India has a strange way about it. Things here can change you so profoundly that you can never take them anywhere else. The only solution is to stay forever."

"Well, we've only got a month."

Mace grinned. "That's enough to squeeze your soul," he said.

Our conversation lingered on spirituality. Mace had a ton of experience in the field.

"I once lived on an American Indian reservation," he explained. "I became very good friends with the shaman there, and he eventually sought to initiate me into his tribe. As a rite of passage, I was to run fifty miles nonstop through the desert with a mouthful of water. If I swallowed it, I'd fail."

"Damn. Did you finish?"

"Yes, but it was extremely difficult. Halfway through, the heat, coupled with my desire to swallow, brought me to the brink of madness. I started seeing creatures from the spirit world manifest in front of me. Some encouraged me, but some tried to prevent me from finishing. When I got to the end, I felt like dying. The shaman nursed me back to health. It was a crippling experience, but in the end, I was bonded to that man and his tribe forever."

"Wow," I said, staring off.

"Yeah, it was pretty intense. Anyway, that initiation rite wasn't the deepest spiritual experience I've had in my life."

I snapped out of my head and looked back at him.

"No?"

"No. That was getting sick here in India."

That rush of horrible blackness suffused my chest. It coated my throat and chattered my teeth.

"R-really?" I said.

"Yeah. I was bedridden for two weeks and lost sixty pounds. It's my own fault though. I refused to take any medicine in an attempt to beat the disease naturally. While I tried to wait it out, I had all sorts of weird dreams and visions. At one point I even thought I saw God."

"Oh yeah? What did he say to you?"

Mace took a sip of his tea and flashed his eyes.

"Go to the doctor."

Tim and I got up early the next morning to go sightseeing on our own. As the two Chucks who'd known each other the longest, we wanted a little time just us. We went upstairs to get a quick bite. In mid-chew, the other Chucks came shuffling up the steps. Mason had fluffed his beard and had on his black shades and leather cowboy hat. Bert had shined his curls and donned his best Miami Vice shirt. Sebastian was wearing a beige body suit, a Muslim prayer cap, and a beaded necklace. The gold-rimmed aviators on his nose were squeaky clean as were the ruby eyes on his cobra staff. Tim and I looked at each other and chuckled. "I guess we'll get some Felm n' Tim time later," I said.

Delhi must have known we were coming to see it that day because it had dolled itself up too. Its streets were teeming with dung and beggars, and its sky was three fireballs shy of Armageddon. We stepped into its dizzying wake and got scooped up by a rickshaw.

"Where you go?" the driver snapped.

"Jami Masjid," I said.

After chugging through an endless river of smog and horns, we arrived at the foregrounds to the mosque.

"What's so baumish about this bitchin' place?" Bert asked.

"Ooff," I replied. "Alls I know is that it was built by Shah Jahan, same dude who built the Taj. And it's the biggest most bargaretty mosque in India."

We got out of the rickshaw. From where we stood, we could see little more than a ghostly silhouette of Jami Masjid. We threaded a path through a mess of dogs, cows, and prayer-capped devotees. As we neared the mosque, its swaying image gained clarity. Soon we were standing face-to-face with the marble juggernaut. It had onion-shaped domes, pinstriped colonnades, and a shiny black gate. It looked like a candy palace from a children's storybook. The steps up to its entryway were covered with lounging Muslims. "They're waiting for call to prayer," a man told us.

"Aw real?" Bert said. "Then let's cut."

"Nah, man. I wanna see this," I said.

I ran over to a small market and bought a prayer cap and a body wrap. The speakers on the minarets were crackling when I returned.

"I think it's about to start," Tim said.

I popped my cap on and wrapped my bare legs. Just as I did, the air around me tensed. Like a swarm of buzzing hornets, the *muezzin*'s voice spewed from the speakers. Black-bearded Muslims of all shapes and sizes came swishing up in their white gowns. They barreled past us, waving their hands in the air and chanting. When they hit the steps, all of them fell silent. I heard Bert snicker behind me. I distanced myself from the group. I stood alone on the opposite side of the gates. I watched as hundreds of believers dropped to their knees. They waited with cupped hands for the *muezzin* to cry "Allaaaaaaah *ho akbar*!" The instant he did, they prostrated themselves in unison. I could hear them under the veil of silence, weeping quietly. That strange electricity started tingling in my stomach. It crawled its way up through my organs till it reached my eyes. I hung my head and cried.

"Well, that was fuckin' tight." Bert said when the prayer ended.

An immense anger swelled up inside me. It burned behind my face like a bonfire.

"Let's grooge around the mosque and see if we can get inside," I said, gritting my teeth.

Bert gave me an evil little glare and nodded. We followed a path around to a crowded back alley. A mustachioed vendor sat at a table peeling a severed goat head with a knife.

"Is this the visitors' entrance to the mosque?" I asked him, pointing to an opening in the side gate.

He wobbled his head. Then he sliced off the goat's face.

"Okay . . ." I said.

Taking the guy for a slow wit, we walked up to the opening in the gate and asked the guard standing there. He was a portly Sikh man with a feline grin curling up between his beard and blue turban.

"Is this the entrance to the mosque?" I asked him.

His eyes twinkled, and his head began to wobble. It looked like an underwater worm trying to wriggle itself into the mud and away from the mouths of hungry fish. Mason furrowed his brow and thinned his lips. "Is this the damn entrance or not?" he barked.

The guard wobbled his head again. Mason bolted forward. "Fuck it," he said. "I'm rollin' in."

The rest of us followed him. Bert stood still and lit a cigarette.

"I'm gonna wait here n' beef 'em," he said. "I fuckin' care mad about seeing the inside."

"Suit yourself," I said.

We pushed past the guard and up the steps to the mosque. Its interior was a sooty expanse of tiles divided into sections by dog-eared prayer rugs. At the center was a square-shaped well filled with green slime. Crowds of Muslims were kneeling at its edges, bathing their faces and praying. We walked past them and into the dark corridors of the main structure. In every corner, a believer sat Indian style, bowing his head prophetically and reading from the Koran. Together, the voices of these men sounded like the wispy beginnings of a schizoid delusion. It was creepy and sublime.

We toured the length of the prayer area. Then we walked back into the courtyard. As we were getting ready to leave, an Indian man with a camera crew approached us.

"Would you kindly do an interview for Indian National Television?" he asked.

"Sure." I said. "But what for?"

The man scratched his head and pointed to a crumbled area of the mosque's interior.

"You see this?" he asked. "A week ago, one bomb went off here. Eight people die."

"Jesus. Well, what information do you need from us?"

"Just some small information about the American experience here." He snapped his fingers and the cameraman zoomed in us on. Sebastian's eyes lit up. "I got this baumishness," he said, pushing to the front. "Here. Interview me."

The crew laughed and put the mic to his lips. He tweaked his aviators and grinned. "So whaddaya wanna know?" he asked.

"Well, first did you hear about this bomb going off?"

"Nah, not this one," he said.

"Well, how does this frightening knowledge affect you as an American tourist?"

"Ooff. I'm not really that scared, I guess."

"You mean after 9/11, you don't feel that you could be a target for terrorists when you travel?"

"If I'm a target for terrorists, I'm a target for terrorists anywhere I go, doesn't matter if it's India or Indiana. Shit, 9/11 happened in my own country. I guess what I'm trying to say is, there's threats everywhere, terrorists or no, but that doesn't mean I'm gonna sit on my ass and not see the world just cuz a bunch of guys in Kandahar have bombs and don't like me. Shit man, I'm here to blow it up too."

The interviewer looked slightly confused but seemed to understand some of what Sebastian was trying to convey. He thanked us all and walked off. Sebastian hung his cobra staff over his shoulder and laughed. "Told you gahts I had that shit," he said.

I sniffed at him and walked off. The others followed behind me. We picked Bert up at the entrance. Our next stop was the Red Fort across the way. Getting there was nearly impossible because of all the cars. Not one driver knew the meaning of the word "lane." As we crossed the street, we were almost flattened to road wax half a dozen times. I remember thinking it'd be less of a gamble to leap into a pit of starving crocs with a severed dingus than brave the streets of Delhi.

By some miracle, we made it across unscathed. We looked ahead and saw the Red Fort. From the outside, it hardly seemed like much. Its environs were so filthy it looked like Lord Shiva had swallowed a dump truck full of garbage then shat it out every which way his butt would spray. Crawling through this soiled refuse were a hundred Indian families and their naked babies. As we approached one of the mothers, she lifted her infant by the legs and pointed its ass toward us. With a resounding gurgle, the infant tightened its cheeks. A stream of stinky nacho cheese came squirting out its asshole.

"Fuckin' iul," we yelled, jumping back.

With shit-speckled feet, we ran to the entrance of the fort. It was tall and imposing with umbrella-top towers and tit-shaped domes. We passed through the archway, heads skyward, musing at the mottled designs that bathed its skin. When we reached the end, our faces dropped. Two long-bearded guards were pointing assault rifles directly at our throats.

"Let's just bunt around 'em," Bert said.

Inside the fort bazaar, I asked a woman at a jewelry shop what was up with the guards.

"They are here to protect us if someone attack fort like they attack mosque," she said.

"Why would they attack the fort?"

"Vee don't know. Terrorists, if these are terrorists, usually attack symbols of power ven they hate someone. The Red Fort has been a symbol of Indian sovereignty since Shah Jahan built it in fifteenth century. It is one of the most recognized monuments in Old Delhi."

I thanked the woman for her information and went outside to tell the others. As I explained the reasons for the guards' presence and gave a small history lesson on the fort, Sebastian took off. He went swaggering around the grounds, tapping his staff and yodeling like he owned the place. His display caught the attention of a group of local teens. They came running up to him with starry eyes and cameras cocked.

"May we take some photos with you?" they asked.

"Chea hea," he said, waving us over. The teens dumped their cameras into our hands and implored us to capture the moment. With shouts and pointing fingers, they crowded around Sebastian's gut and lit off a big group smile. Sebastian stood at their center, grinning like a baked Buddha with his arms outstretched. A dozen cameras clicked off at once. I stood in the background with my arms folded and my eyebrows spiked. A sneer crawled across my lips like a spider leg.

There was a call for me at the front desk at nine the next morning. I answered it with a grunt.

"Hello? Johann?" an Indian man said.

"Yeah, who is this?"

"It's Andupa. Are you rready for me?"

"Shit. Um, yeah, give us half an hour."

Andupa was the nephew of Kunti, one of my father's coworkers. She had contacted him before we left, asking him if he could take us around Delhi on his day off. He'd said he would and emailed me shortly after we'd arrived. I'd given him our information and such, but after that, I hadn't spoken to him. In all the commotion of the previous few days, I had forgotten he might be coming. I rushed to get ready.

Though I had told Andupa half an hour, he didn't arrive until after twelve.

"Bad traffic," he said, stepping out of the cab.

He was wearing blue jeans, a polo shirt, and white sneakers. His hair was neatly cut, and his moon-shaped face was clean shaven. The only distinguishing marker on him was the thin silver bangle he wore around his right wrist. He shook each of our hands and smiled warmly.

"Ver vood you like to go today?" he asked.

Since the day before had been such a rat race, we decided on one place that was simple but unique.

"The Baha'i Lotus Temple," I said.

"Ah, the Lotus Temple. Very nice."

"You've been there?"

"Yes, a few times with my Baha'i friend. It is very beautiful. Many Baha'i people from all over the verld come to this place."

"What the hell is a Baja or whatever?" Bert asked.

Andupa laughed. "A Baha'i is a follower of Baha'u'llah, the founder of the religion. He create this religion in Persia over one hundred fifty years ago to spread verld peace and unity. His followers believe he is a messenger of God just like Abraham or Jesus."

"Sounds bitchin'," Bert said, looking at me from the corner of his eye. I ignored him and got in the cab.

Minutes later, we rolled up at a big field. From where we parked, the Lotus Temple looked more like a white alien nipple than any religious structure.

"It's kinda small," I said to Andupa.

"It grows quickly," he said. No sooner had we stepped foot on the brick path leading to the entrance than the temple shot up from the horizon like the head of a giant sea creature. In the sun, its marble exterior looked like glimmering folds of marshmallow all neatly bent into a huge lotus. A stream of people were entering under its shiny eaves. Not one of them spoke.

"Everyone's hella chuck," Sebastian remarked.

At the steps, the terraces surrounding the lotus tumbled away revealing nine pools of water. Clusters of multicolored people were gathered at their margins blinking and smiling at one another.

"Fuck's up with the nine pools?" Bert asked.

"There are nine because this is the highest number in the Baha'i faith," Andupa explained. "It symbolizes power and visdom. But the pools also keep peaceful atmosphere. Everything must be peaceful in Baha'i place of vorship. You vill see vat I mean inside."

We followed Andupa through the entrance. Inside, there were no pulpits, no altars, no mosaics, no gods, saints, sacraments, or psalms. In fact, the only thing inside besides a circle of marble columns was a hexagonal collection of pews dotted with people in silent prayer. Each of them was of a different race, gender, and creed. We sat next to an old man wearing a Muslim prayer cap. Across from him was a Hindu woman with a black braid and sparkling purple sari.

"Are these people all Baha'i?" Tim whispered to Andupa.

"Only some of them. Baha'is allow every rreligion to come and pray at their temples. It is a bit like rreligion for people of all rreligions."

When the silence of the temple became more nagging than blissful, we decided to cut. Since we didn't have anything else planned for the day, Andupa suggested we get lunch.

"C'mon," he said. "I know a crrazy place."

His crazy place turned out to be a tourist dive called Sikh Made. Everyone inside was bloated, white, and sweaty. The walls were decorated with Indian kitsch.

"What's so *Sihk* about this place?" Mason asked.

"Nothing, rreally." Andupa chuckled. "But the food is good, and the couches here are very comfortable."

We flopped our asses down on a pile of sparkling down cushions. We listened with one ear as Andupa rattled off our lunch order: *dhal makhani* (black lentils with butter and cream), *sag paneer* (cooked spinach with cubes of fried cheese), garlic *naan* (tear-shaped flatbread), *shish kabob* (grilled meat and vegetables on skewers), spicy mutton curry . . . The list went on and on. Each delicious but potentially disastrous item he named made our stomachs widen with hunger and then cringe with fear. It was like anticipating the first bite of a turd coated in the most decadent Belgian chocolate.

An hour later the food came. Everything looked so sumptuous and saucy that we just had to dig in. We indulged to the fullest, having seconds and thirds. All the haunting flavors of each dish made the risk of later shitting ourselves to skeletons seem worth it. Even so, we were eager to know if there wasn't something on the menu that might ward off a gastric catastrophe.

"I'll order some *lassis* and spiced water for you guys," Andupa said.

Moments later, the waiter came back with three drinks. Two were white and one was green.

"So what are all these?" I asked.

"The two vite ones are sweet and salty lassis. The green is the spiced water. You should save this one for last."

His mischievous smile made me feel uneasy. I went for the safest of the bunch first—the sweet lassi.

"Tastes like blended cheesecake," I said, passing it to Tim. "Not bad."

Confident now, I reached for the salty lassi and took a healthy swig. It was like having a goat ejaculate into my mouth.

"Jesus," I said and belched.

"Vash it down vith the spiced vater."

I grabbed the glass of creamy green slop and dribbled it down my throat.

"God, that tastes like peppered gorilla snot."

Andupa slapped his thigh and cackled.

"You tricked me, man," I yelled.

"Oh, come now," he said, grinning.

Andupa redeemed himself by paying our $200 bill. We thanked him through pinched faces.

"Not at all," he said, leading us out the door. The sun was still blazing. It made the sweet and sickening things in our stomachs churn harder. We gripped our guts and milled around for a while. We turned a corner and found a huge white cow munching on a hunk of greasy trash. As it chewed, I noticed that passersby were oblivious to its presence. It was as if it was just another person, wandering amongst the kiosks and eating their lunch. I shook my head and smirked.

"I hafta ask," I said to Andupa. "What's the deal with the cows? I mean, I know they're sacred, but do you guys worship them or what?"

Andupa puffed through his nose and chuckled.

"First of all," he said, "no, vee do not vorship cows. They are animals. It is better to say vee appreciate and protect them. This is because throughout our history they have given us many things including milk, butter, and curds for food, dung for fires, urine for elixirs, and backs for transportation. Our society vas built largely by their verk. In the past, Hindu Brahmins used to sacrifice and eat only bulls.[1] But some say this practice stopped from the vegetarian influences of Buddhism and Jainism.[2] Now both male and female are protected in our country and free to do as they choose out of respect for their gifts to us."

We all thought for a moment about what Andupa had just said. Bert was the first to chime in.

"Well, fuck," he said. "We Americans love dogs so fuckin' much we have *shows* for them. So I guess that shit with the cows ain't *that* weird."

---

[1] A Brahmin is a member of the highest caste or *varna* in Hinduism.
[2] Jainism is a sixth-century Indian religion whose followers practice noninjury of animals and believe perfection can be attained through reincarnation.

Everyone cracked up, even me.

Andupa got us a cab back to The Rama. He promised to return a few hours later to take us out on the town. All of us were chuck as fuck. We passed out till nightfall, then had a little dinner. When it was time to get ready to go out, only Bert and I were up for it.

"I haven't had a decent explosion since Thailand," Bert said.

"Me neither."

Andupa arrived at nine-thirty and took us via taxi to the outskirts of Delhi. There was a shopping center there that looked like any in the States. Its crowning feature was a three-story KFC.

"Where are we going?" I asked.

"The girls vill be at a hookah lounge inside the center."

"Girls?"

"Yes, I've invited some friends to meet us there."

The rendezvous spot was tucked under the KFC. Despite its clandestineness and crummy location, its interior was rather nice. There was a neon wet bar lined with crystal martini glasses, mosaic wood flooring, and alcoves of black leather sofas. The girls were waiting for us in the alcove just past the spiral staircase.

"Johann and Bert, I'd like you to meet Amita and Anita," Andupa said.

For having such similar names, the two girls couldn't have been more different in appearance. Amita was thin and tan with straight brown hair and sapphire eyes. Anita was curvaceous and dark with wavy black hair and onyx eyes. I went for the seat next to Anita but Andupa snatched it from me. Thankfully, I was able to recover and grab the seat next to Amita before Bert got it. After ordering cocktails and mint hookah, we all got to chatting. Anita said she was from Tamil Nadu, and that she had a husband and a son.[3] She spoke some French which kept me from solely dedicating my attention to the smoke rings I was blowing against the lights. When the conversation began to drag, I shifted my sights to Amita.

"Where are you from?" I asked.

---

[3] Tamil Nadu is the southernmost state of India.

"Uttaranchal, up in the north."

"Yeah, I know where it is. We're heading up to Himachal Pradesh in a week or so."

"Oh, you know a bit about India then?"

"Some," I said.

"So tell me, what do you like best about it?"

I fanned my collar and grinned. "It's the oneness of the diversity that impresses me most," I said. "Each state, each region, is populated by a multitude of groups with vastly different cultures and languages. Comparing one to the next in some cases would be like comparing apples to asses, and yet the vast majority of them consider themselves Indian. Take you and your friend Anita. You're from opposite ends of the country, speak different languages from different language families, you look completely different, and yet you both consider yourselves Indian. I believe this is because despite your differences you've shared a deeply intertwined history on the same slice of land. And isn't it ironic that two so very different people from so very different regions have almost the same name? A cheesy example I know, but it kinda proves my point."

Amita grinned. "You must have been from India in your past life," she said.

"Thanks," I replied. "You might be right."

Bert and I woke up the next morning feeling like dog balls. After the hookah, we'd partied at some club till 4 a.m. with Andupa and the girls and swilled God knows how many drinks. The other Chucks were feeling like general crap as well. We didn't make it out the door until after noon. The rickshaw ride to Grand Central made things infinitely worse. Not only were we packed five deep on a scooter-propelled buggy the size of a scarab beetle, but all our gear was piled on top of our laps, crushing our legs. As we jostled through the thickets of pollution and traffic, my stomach was about to explode. I gripped it with my free hand and leaned out the window. Just as I did another rickshaw whizzed by, almost tearing my head from my neck.

"This city won't even let me puke," I mumbled.

I pulled my head back into the cabin. Our driver then enhanced my misery by cranking up his music. It sounded like the wailings of a helium-lit banshee. I wanted to douse my head in gasoline and light it on fire. Strangely, as the track skipped along, it lolled me to a state of bliss. I looked at the driver to see if the music was having a similar effect on him. Underneath his twisted mustache, I saw a toothless wedge of pure sunshine.

"So that's how they do it," I said.

"Do what?" Mason asked.

"Cope with this fucking place. Indian music drives you happily insane."

When we arrived at the station, my nausea resurfaced. The lines at the ticket windows were more like angry clumps of bees shifting this way and that. They buzzed over dozens of bums who flapped their arms and groaned like impaled seals. We kicked our way through this mess and up to a service window. The fingerprint smears on it were so thick and oily we could barely make out the woman's face behind them.

"Ver you go?" she barked.

"Jaipur."

"So sorry, 3:00 and 5:40 buses all sold out. Next please."

"We're fucked," I said, turning back to the Chucks.

"Well, I'm fuckin' kickin' it here another day," Bert yelled.

"Excuse me, dear sirs," a voice said from behind us. "May I be of some assistance?"

We turned around and saw a pudgy Indian in a black leather jacket.

"How?" I asked him.

"I have an airr-conditioned jeep. For 25 US each, I can take you dirrectly to Jaipur."

My stomach eased.

# JAIPUR

We pulled into Jaipur just after nine o'clock. Our driver dropped us off at a little hostel called The Green Forest. It was a haven for hippies, but that was no matter. It had a nice terrace and the rooms had fans. We dropped our crap off and looked for food. We were sick of curry, so we opted for McDonald's. The burgers we got were all beefless and stinky. We choked them down with sodas and split. We walked back to our rooms and collapsed into our beds. We were out within seconds.

We met at the breakfast table the next morning. All of us felt sick from the previous night's food, but none as sick as Sebastian. He came last to the table, schlepping his ass across the sunny terrace like a partied-out gorilla. There was no cobra staff in his hand, no top hat on his head. He was a bloated, dead-eyed version of his blow-up self.

"Donald's fuckin' gave it to me," he groaned. With a resounding plunk, he plopped into his chair and stared straight ahead. I considered taunting him about his weak bowels, but I refrained.

"You gonna pop off the Pink City with us today?" I asked him.

"Fuck *yeaaaaah*," he grumbled. "I'm saucin' then I'm chuckin'."

"Ait," I said. "Well, we're bunt'n."

Before we could sightsee, we had to buy our 6 a.m. train tickets to

Agra. The station we got them at was a dump but not nearly as chaotic as Delhi's. We stood in line and folded our arms. Just in front of us were two soft-bodied blondes with Birkenstocks and tattered backpacks. I leaned into them and raised my eyebrows.

"So what state are you guys from?" I asked.

"Oh, we're from Virginia," the slightly thicker one said. "I'm Eliza and this is my sis, Mary."

"Why are you guys here?"

They gripped the silver Ohm symbols around their necks and glanced at one another.

"Spiritual reasons, I suppose," Mary said. "Virginia's not exactly the most open-minded state when it comes to that sort of stuff. We came here to get away from all that and gain some new perspective. You can imagine our parents' reaction when we told 'em we were gonna live on an *ashram* in Goa."[4]

"Jesus, how'd that work out for ya?"

"Great, until the one time I strayed from my diet." Eliza looked at her sister and laughed.

"Haha. What happened?"

"Well, Goa isn't like the rest of southern India. It serves a lot of meat cuz of all the Portuguese influence, so the cuisine is the most wonderful blend of both types of food. Well, one day Eliza and I decided to cheat on our vegetarian diets and have some chicken curry. We ate from the same fucking plate and I was the only one who got sick."

I felt a rush of panic. "How sick?" I asked.

"I contracted amoebic dysentery and lost thirty pounds."

My face went flush.

"What?" Mary said. "Haven't you gotten sick yet?"

"No. Well, kinda. I've had a stomachache and felt like puking but nothing serious."

"Ha. Well, it'll happen. Everyone gets sick in India."

Right then, a tiny black spider materialized on my brain. It crawled

---

[4] An *ashram* is a religious retreat most commonly found in South Asia.

to a remote flesh-nub, then extended a sharp leg. With a click, it picked it open like a raspberry drupelet. Poisonous red juice leaked into the meaty grooves. I disappeared screaming into my mind. When I came to, I was in Bangkok with my father. He had his hand on my shoulder as I sat on the toilet pissing blood out my ass.

"You shouldn't have eaten that damn street food," he kept saying. His words were like a horrible mill cycling over and over. They pulled fear from one spot, lifted it high, then sent it crashing and spilling down all over another. I saw my perception of India flailing in it like a speared fish. The only thing I could do to save it was blink hard and change the subject.

"So Jaipur, huh?" I said.

"Yeah," Eliza replied. "We're on a little vacation. Been here a few days."

"Yeah? What's there to do around here at night?"

"There's a hookah lounge called Mr. Beans. It ain't bad."

I saw Bert smile from the corner of my eye.

"You guys wanna meet up with us there tonight?" I asked.

"Sure," Eliza said. "We'll meet you guys around nine-thirty."

"Cool."

We bought early morning tickets to Agra and took a rickshaw to the Pink City. I was expecting to be impressed, given its history. Back in 1727, Maharaja Sawai Jai Singh II dubbed Jaipur the capital of the Kuchwahas (a clan of ruling Rajputs). Over time, it gained fame because of its orderly design and grandiose royal architecture. Its nickname, which mainly refers to its older quarter, came about in 1853 when residents painted the area pink in honor of a visit by the Prince of Wales. The ubiquitous pink hue of its buildings is still maintained by the city's residents to this day.

We were dropped off at the city gates. A congested flow of donkey carts, trucks, buses, and rickshaws was lurching itself in spirals around us. At our backs, the rickety shops and checkered walls of the city rose to cradle this mess. Everything was pink alright, even the asses of the monkeys picking scraps from the gutters. Besides the sheer madness of the downtown area, I failed to see anything outstanding about the Pink City.

"Let's bunt to the Amber Fort," I said. "I heard that's kinda baumish."

We grabbed a cab. The Amber Fort was twenty minutes outside of town, through a wasteland of crusty hills. When we were almost there, we made an impromptu halt as a parade of elephants went lumbering into the green waters in front of the battlements.

"Let's get some shots," I said.

Stepping out of the cab, I was stymied by the view. With its rusty pinks and yellows, the buildings of the Rajput fortress looked carved from the desert itself. As our cameras clicked, a man approached us on elephant back.

"Twenty-five dollarrs forr elephant rride?" he said.

"Fuckin *baaaaad*," Bert said.

The trail took us through a square of violet flowers. There was a fountain at the center bubbling softly.

"God, I'm bot," Bert yelled. He ripped his shirt off and dumped his head in.

An old lady tending the gardens hissed at him.

"What?" he said.

"This is a national treasure, man," I said. "Plus, didn't you read the sign?"

It was directly above the fountain. The English read, "Please be fully clothed upon entering fort." Bert ignored it and walked off. When he reached the fortress walls, he stopped.

"I gotta take a phat-ass friss," he said.

"There's a bathroom back at the entrance," I said.

He looked over his shoulder and said, "That's dayz back."

He whipped out his pecker and began urinating against the colored bricks. The tiny snaps of his splattering piss ran cracks up my patience. I looked over at Tim, who was equally disgusted. We walked off and left the others behind.

As we entered the labyrinth of the fort, Tim stopped and turned.

"Know what that made me think of though?"

"I dread to think."

"Remember that time when you jumped up during naptime and started playing air guitar with your little penis in front of the nuns?"

Tim and I had gone to the same Christian preschool.

"Ha-ha. Yeah. Sister Maria got so furious she yanked me into the bathroom and washed my mouth out with a dirty bar of soap. I fuckin' *cared* though. I just laughed and did it again."

Tim pitched forward and cackled hoarsely. "Or h-how 'bout that time when we hung out for the first time at my house, and you begged to play with my special He-Man doll, and when I finally gave in, you stripped all his armor off and made Skeletor buttfuck him in front of our moms?"

"Hahaha. Yeah." I wept. "That was the shit. And hey, remember on Sebastian's first birthday, when he was about to blow out his one bitchin' candle, and I stuck my head in there and blew it out before he could?"

Tim pinched away a smile. "Yeah, I remember that. You were being kinda nice."

"Oh, whatever. You were laughing."

"Haha, maybe a little. Oh yeah, and what about that time . . .?"

We went back and forth like this till we reached a sunlit stairway. We walked to the top of the fort. From there, we saw a conglomeration of pink rooftops slithering between two breast-shaped hills. It looked like rosé spilled between the tits of a supine woman. I absorbed the panorama with deep breaths. My mouth dropped when I faced the courtyard below. I saw Bert there milling around with his shirt still off. He was completely oblivious to the grimacing locals around him.

"He's got mad respect," Tim said.

"Yeah. For other cultures." We looked at each other and smiled. "I'm thinkin' Bert just earned himself a nickname. 'Culture Guy.'"

"Tmph. I was thinkin' more 'Respect Guy.'"

After a crummy elephant ride in town, we went back to the hostel. The others were exhausted as usual. Bert and I, despite our tiff earlier, were eager to meet the Virginian hippies at Mr. Beans. The two of us took off just before nine. We arrived right on time. The place was clearly a locals' haunt as there wasn't a whitey in sight. We picked a table near the entrance and waited for the girls to show. Half an hour passed, and it quickly became apparent they weren't coming.

"Let's just order a faggot," Bert said.[5]

When our hookah came, Bert started puffing it nervously. Both his knees were jittering, as were his curls.

"What's up, gaht?" I asked.

He took a long pull from the hose then passed it to me. As the smoke dribbled from his lips, he explained.

"I'm hella homesick man," he said. "That's part of the reason why I've been acting so tight lately."

"You have been kinda garnk," I said.

"I know. I just hella feel like my relationship with my other friends in L is gettin' 'em. Fools respond mad to my emails."

The "fools" he was referring to were his friends Buddy, Beau, and Dan; a raucous gang of FAS-afflicted rednecks who exclusively wore grape-smugglers and steel-toes. The three of them, especially Buddy, always ripped on me back in high school. I never associated with them because of this. Bert, however, had a longstanding friendship with the pricks. That is, until he started traveling with us. Our influence was slowly opening his mind. As a result, these "friends" were starting to identify with him less and less.

"At least you still have us, gaht," I said, patting him on the shoulder. "I mean shit, we're blood brothers."

He looked down at the ground and buried his thumbs in his cheeks. A frown bent his face.

"Yeah, about that," he said.

"Woo?" I asked.

"Well, I kinda said sick to skinkin' that cobra blood."

"Dude, I saw you."

"Ooff." He shrugged. "When you guys weren't looking, I spit it out."

---

[5] For 'faggot' in this context, see the ROAST dictionary.

"Why man?"

"Eeff. I was scared I'd get sick. Plus, I knew deep down what it meant, and it made me feel weird. Now, I regret it though."

I felt like someone had chopped off my finger. I thought hard for a moment. "Mark my words, Culture Guy," I said. "We'll find some way to reinitiate you on this trip."

He smiled weakly.


I awoke to the sounds of Sebastian yelling through the walls. It made me wanna scoop my eyes out with a spoon. I got up and marched over to the Frazellis' room.

"What the hell's goin' on in here?" I asked, opening the door.

I saw Tim lying face down on the bed with a finger in each ear. His baby bro was in the bathroom naked, plucking his teeth with dental floss and humming at the mirror. "Taj's gonna be so baumish," he yelled, tossing the floss over his shoulder.

"Is that what all the bitchin' yelling was about?" I said.

"Chea hea." Sebastian beamed.

"Blow up Dude's feeling better now," Tim mumbled into the sheets. "He even woke up early just so he could bower and bunt on time."

I looked at my watch. It was 4 a.m.

"Whatever," I said. "It's almost time to skunta anyway."

We got to the station at five-thirty. Because transportation in India costs less than gumballs, we had unknowingly bought first class tickets. We boarded Cabin #1 of the train. Its squeaky seats and stained floors made it a dump by Western standards. That it had leg room and a rattling air conditioner made it rather snazzy by Indian standards. Everywhere was empty, so we spread out like vultures and crashed.

Five hours later, I woke up to Sebastian yelling again.

"What the fuck is it this time?"

"Ooff, dude," he said. "The sign outside says 'Agra,' but we're not slowing down. I think we're gonna grooge right past it."

I poked my head out the window. We were coming to a desolate station with a few workers shoveling gravel out front. I saw the sign for Agra.

"The train'll stop," I said.

Thirty seconds passed, and we were still moving. BUG's eyes widened. "I'm goin' for it, gahts," he said.

"Goin' for what?" I asked.

Without answering, he grabbed his cobra staff and top hat. With a "Zalt!" he kicked open the cabin door and swan-dived toward the platform.

"Jesus."

From the window, we saw him crash to the concrete like a sack of grapes. He went tumbling forward with his staff clicking the whole way.

"I gotta make sure my bro didn't gettem," Tim said. He closed his eyes and jumped out the cabin door. Fortunately for him, the train had already stopped.

# AGRA

Sebastian was sprawled out on the concrete like a murder victim. We ran toward him as fast as we could. We arrived to find him smiling and unscathed. The sun was glinting against his black beard and aviators.

"You scared the shit out of us," I yelled. He raised his eyebrows and laughed. All we could do was join him.

Back at the station, one of the workers told us we had gotten off at the wrong stop. "Anotherr trrain vill be coming in forrty-five minutes," he said. We parked our asses and tried to wait it out. A half hour later, we were drenched in sweat and out of water.

"Let's just get rickshaws," I said. We grabbed two in a parking lot nearby. They took us to the correct train station where we bought 5 p.m. tickets to Delhi. On our way out the door, two new drivers practically forced us into their rickshaws.

"Vee take you to Taj Mahal," they yelled.

On the way there, I was stunned by Agra's state of decay. Its roads were cracked to pieces, and there were hills of trash everywhere. Picking amongst them were dozens of emaciated cows. Their ribs shone against their skin like the bellows of so many accordions.

I distracted myself from this grim sight by burying my nose in my guidebook. A blurb that had little to do with the Taj Mahal itself caught my attention. It talked about how the restaurants outside the main gates were infamous for serving tourists poisoned food. The alleged intent was to get the tourists sick enough to seek medical attention, at which time corrupt doctors in collusion with the restaurants' owners would show up and provide treatments for exorbitant fees. According to the guidebook, a tourist couple had died a few years back from their food being poisoned. Since then, business had plummeted.

When we arrived, I told the others about what I had read. Everyone seemed worried except Mason.

"Oh I'm *sure* we're just gonna fuckin' die if we sauce at one of these places," he said.

"You're really gonna chance it?" I asked.

"Watch me." With us behind him, he walked into a little dump across from the ticket booth. The inside was swarming with flies and there was garbage all over the floor. Tim looked at Mason and scoffed.

"I bet you'd gettem here even if they didn't poison the food," he said.

Unfazed, Mason sat down and ordered a cucumber sandwich. The waiter served it to him without a plate.

"Sauce it up," I said. He raised the sandwich to his lips and snickered. In three bites, he consumed the entire thing. He then lit a cigarette and smoked it casually. Part of me wanted him to start choking just so I could have my fears justified. When it looked like he wouldn't, I got up to go to the bathroom. That's when his eyes rolled back in his head.

"Jesus man, you gottem," I screamed.

Mason gripped his neck and hacked violently. I thought he'd swallowed his tongue.

"Somebody do something," I yelled.

Tim sprung up and ran over there. As he outstretched his arms to perform the Heimlich, Mason stopped convulsing and grinned.

"You fuckin' asshole," I said.

To avoid choking the prick ourselves, Tim and I let Mason go in with the others to see the Taj first. We waited with the packs outside and listened to music.

An hour later, Chucks came walking up.

"Was it as coo as yer gay ass thought it would be?" I asked Sebastian.

"Chea hea," he said. "Don't look at it until you get past the Great Gate. That'll make it *extra* baumish."

Tim and I bought our tickets and went in. We passed between a pair of small towers shaped like conquistadors' caps, and onto a path flanked by red sandstone archways. At the end was the Great Gate. It was mountainous, with four faces that each contained a large domed hollowing. Everything was neatly painted in coral and flecked with white.

"It looks like a giant wedding cake," I said.

We kept our heads down as we entered. We stared at the ground till our tiptoes met the edge of a stair, then we looked up. The scene unfolded in stages. First, I saw a rectangular fountain, boxed in by juniper hedges. The hedges ran like dominos till they hit ivory steps. These steps gave birth to an onion-domed jewel cradled neatly by four minarets. The entire structure gleamed like the inside of a seashell. I staggered up to it and away from Tim, adjusting my camera. I wasn't watching my feet. I went stumbling over something and crashed to the ground. My camera pitched forward and hit the pavement with a loud crack. I picked it up and found that the memory card was jammed.

"Goddammit," I screamed. "Of all the fucking places to break a camera."

A little boy nearby laughed. I looked at him and scowled.

"Vood you like a guide, sirr?" he asked. "Please, I must repay you for your accident."

"You tripped me?"

"Yes, but it was my accident too."

"Bullcrap."

I started to walk away. The little boy jumped in front of me.

"Please, sirr," he begged. "Let me guide you."

I looked him up and down. He was dressed in a dirty red vest with baggy pants and a rhinestone hat. His entire outfit was faded from years of use. I assumed he was a street urchin who was somehow able to get his little hands on a costume so he could act as his own tour guide. His plight seemed one of equal determination and hopelessness. My heart melted.

"Fine, go," I said.

The little boy smiled. "First, what you must know," he began, "is that the Taj is not a mosque. It is a tomb."

"For whom?" I asked.

"You ever love a girl?"

"Let's not get into that."

"Haha. Okay. Well, this man who built it, Shah Jahan, he love his third vife, Mumtaz Mahal, more than even you love your camera. But, she die while she give birth to their son number fourteen. So in 1632, he start to build the Taj Mahal; her tomb. It take him twelve years, and he use 1,000 elephants to bring all materials from all over the vorld. Sadly, when the Shah finish his masterpiece, his evil son Aurangzeb take power and put him in prison at Agra fort. He could only see his Mumtaz from vindow. It vasn't until his death that they bury him next to her in the Taj. He is vith her again now."

When the little boy finished his story, he smiled and held out his hand.

"You'll get yer money bud," I said. "First tell me about the inside of the tomb."

"Of course," he said. We went inside the tomb. The marble walls were covered in black Arabic calligraphy. It looked like a powerful spell encrypted in some mythical language.

"What's all this?" I asked the boy.

"These are verses of the Koran," he said. "The Mughals vere Muslims, so they put this vriting in their tombs to protect and bless the dead."[6]

The dead in question were in the center of the room. They were

---

[6] The Mughals were a ruling class of Muslims descended from invading Mongols, Turks, and Persians; they ruled most of India from the sixteenth to the nineteenth centuries.

cased in long and ornately carved marble sarcophagi. Seeing the two of them lying there together called up memories of the tapestry I'd seen in Angkor Wat. That strange electricity crackled around the nodes of my heart again.

Outside the Taj, I paid my friend handsomely for his service.

"What's your name, little man?" I asked.

He gripped the ten spot and shoved it into his pocket.

"I'm Pasha," he said.

"Well, I'm Johann. Nice to meet you."

Just as I went in to shake his hand, he shot his foot out and tripped an unsuspecting tourist. The old fart went tumbling to the ground.

"Gotta verk," he said.

I walked away chuckling.

After leaving the Taj, we cut to grab a bite in a neighborhood known as Taj Ganji. It was a seedy little area with crumbling buildings stacked on top of one another. We threaded our way through in search of a restaurant. The guidebook recommended a joint called the Maya Café. We found it down a trash-littered ally. We climbed its steps to a balcony overlooking the street. There was an open kitchen filled with smoke. The stench called up memories of county fair latrines. To avoid it, we sat at the back.

"This place might give it to us," Bert said.

As we sneered at our environs, we were approached by our waiter. He was a monster of a man with oversized hands, black skin, and a bowl cut. He looked like a giant Indian Beatle with acromegaly.

"Yourr orrderrs?" he asked.

We squinted at our menus and frowned. The only thing that looked even remotely appetizing was the Tropical Pizza. We all ordered one except Mason. He lit up a smoke instead.

"You're not saucin'?" I asked him.

"Fuck yeah," he said. "I already sauced at the Taj. And by the looks of this place, you guys are gonna be the ones who gettem."

I choked down a knot in my throat. "The sauce here'll be baumish," I said. "I ain't trippin'."

Baumish turned out to be what looked like a deflated basketball slathered in snot and pineapples. I had trouble just lifting a slice of it to my lips.

"Is it saucy?" I asked Bert, who was already a nibble in.

"It ait," he said. I looked back at my slice. A shoelace of nasty cheese was dangling from the tip of it.

"Hey gaht, you sure that shit's baumish?" I asked Bert again.

He dropped his food and locked his face. "Yeah man, it aiiiit," he barked. "Sauce yer shit arredy."

I cringed and bit into the slice. It tasted vaguely of asshole, but I was starving. I scarfed the whole pizza without incident. Just as I was swallowing my last bite, I looked up at our waiter. He sat across from us in the Thinking-Man position. But instead of resting fist-under-chin, he had one of his carrot-sized fingers jammed up his nose. He froze when he saw me staring at him.

"*Hijo de puta*," I muttered. Any normal person would have elected this moment to remove their finger from their nose. But Frankenbooger kept his fully lodged; he even wriggled it around to cast my eyes off him. Horrified, I looked over at Mason. He was stretched coolly across his chair smoking another cigarette. An arrogant grin curled up on his lips. He winked.

"Have fun tonight."

# DELHI TO MANALI

W aking up was miserable. I'd only slept for three hours the night before on account of our horrendous train ride to Delhi and my fucked-up stomach. Now, I had to pull myself together and go to the bus station with Tim to get our tickets to Manali. The two of us showed up there half asleep. The line was atrocious as usual. The only thing different about it was this time it had a hefty Israeli component. It seemed all the Israelis were on a mass exodus somewhere. I asked the dreadlocked Israeli in front of me where they were all going.

"Dharamshala," he said. "We go there first, and then maybe to Manali. After that, Kasol."

"You guys all travel to the same places at the same time?"

"Most of us. You never heard of 'Israeli trail'?"

I laughed. "No. I mean I know a lot of you guys come here after the army."

"Yes, and we usually start in Goa, then to Mumbai, up to Rajasthan, to Delhi and Agra, and then to the north. If you are going north now, you will be on the Israeli trail as well."

Homeboy wasn't bullshitting. When we got back to The Rama, half its residents—who were largely Israeli—were packed and getting ready to catch buses up north. There was a congregation of them upstairs eating, smoking, and chatting in Hebrew. They dwarfed our little group.

"Fuck, there's small amounts of 'em out n' about," I remarked.

Mason sneered at the comment. "I know," he said. "*Israaaaaaeli* cool, isn't it?"

I couldn't help but chuckle.

At noon, we—and the hoard of Israelis—grabbed our shit and made for the buses, a mile away. For some ungodly reason, we decided to walk it. Halfway there, I felt my insides twisting and my shoulders sizzling from the heat. I didn't know whether to scream or shit myself. My only consolation was that I knew I'd have a "double-sleeper cabin" with Tim on the bus. In my mind, this at least ensured that I would be able to stretch out and relax for the twenty-two-hour ride.

My hopes for a decent trip shrunk when I saw our bus. It was dented to shit and barely bigger than a large minivan.

"How the fuck did they fit double sleeper cabins on this bitch?" I spat.

Tim pursed his lips hopefully. "Maybe it's bigger and more chuck on the inside."

We boarded with high hearts. They dropped when we saw the interior. Not only were the seats filled with animals and screaming babies, but there was nothing that looked like a sleeper cabin let alone a *double* sleeper cabin anywhere in sight.

"Where the hell are we?" I asked the driver, showing him our ticket. He snickered and pointed to what I had thought were the curtained-off compartments for people's hand luggage.

"You've got to be fucking kidding me," I said. We stumbled to the back of the bus where our cabin number was listed and whipped back the curtain. There was a cramped space behind it scarcely big enough for a child's coffin.

"Looks like we got double buttfucked," I said.

We took our shoes off and squeezed into the tiny compartment, head to foot. Tim's feet have a nasty tendency to get hairier in the heat; India had turned them into werewolf paws. As soon as the stinky beasts were planted directly in front of my nose, our bus engine jittered to life. We pulled away from the parking lot in a cloud of black smoke. Then I passed out.

I awoke hours later when our bus came to a grinding halt. It was eight-thirty at night, and we were stopping to get something to eat. As this was the middle of Satan's nowhere, our options were slim. It was either the roadside stand selling what looked like barbequed possum's tail or the dimly lit restaurant with floors dirty enough to make a swamp hog faint. We opted for the latter because everyone else on the twenty northbound buses outside had. It was as good a choice as any.

We sat at a big table with a dozen Israelis. The one next to me recommended I order something vegetarian.

"Your first time in India?" he asked me.

I nodded and looked his way. He was a grimy little shrimp with hairy arms and a bony face. He looked like he had been on the road for half a decade.

"You probably khate this place now, no?" he asked.

"It takes some getting used to," I said.

"Hahaha. Yeeeeessss." He brought his lips back into a smile that revealed a curtain of yellow teeth. I winced.

"Do you like it here?" I asked.

"I love it. But India is a khard place to love. You see right now you are sick, you khav kheadache. It stinks. You khate it. This is because you khav only been khir one week."

"How did you know?"

"I know. There is very simple formula for India. At one week you khate it, at two weeks you can tolerate it, at three weeks you kind of like it, and at four weeks you never want to leave."

"Oh yeah, why is that?"

"Because this is when you will realize that khir you are truly free."

I pondered the Israeli's statement through dinner. I got on the bus, gripping my gut. The engine groaned to life and the wheels pulled away from the curb. We got as far as the Punjabi border when a cadre of cops brandishing Kalashnikovs stopped us and boarded. They seemed to be searching for someone. With the noses of their firearms sniffing at people like hungry dogs, they swept down the aisle and shouted in Punjabi. They found their man crouching behind a plump

Indian woman in the back. They stuck their guns to his face, lifted him from his seat, and escorted him out the door. A one-sided screaming match ensued just outside my window. At the end of it, the man forked over a few crumpled rupees. The chief, a portly gentleman with a wattle of fat jiggling under his chin, snatched the money from his hand, glanced at it, and started barking.

"I guess those bones were fuckin' enough to pass," I whispered to Tim.

Seconds later, the border guards stuck their weapons to the man's back and walked him into the darkness. We drove off, leaving him behind.

I shivered back into my cubby and tried to get some shuteye. I was able to at least shut my eyes, but they were quickly bounced back open by the tossing and turning of our bus. We were coming to the more mountainous, and thus more precarious, region of northern India. It didn't help matters that our driver was now nursing a bottle of whiskey and taking rips off a boner-sized hash blunt. As we sloshed back and forth, I glanced out my window. Just inches from our tires was a mile-wide crevice deep enough to swallow the clicks of the rocks our bus kicked over its edge. I cringed at the idea of spilling into it like so many other buses I had read about. According to our guidebook, the road from Delhi to Himachal Pradesh was one of the most dangerous in India and claimed dozens, if not hundreds, of lives by bus-related accidents each year.

Three hours and 300 hairpin turns later, we arrived at a string of latrines nestled under a rocky overhang. My guts were now in an absolute uproar. I made a beeline for one of the shitters. On my way out the door, Bert came tumbling down from his cabin, bent and groaning. His face was pale, and his arms were wrapped around his stomach.

"Fuck. This blows on so many levels," he croaked.

We ducked into what looked like two adobe prison cells. Each was affixed with one naked light bulb hanging from the ceiling. Underneath was a rectangular slot carved out of the concrete. The mounds of feces below were illuminated by the light from above. I pulled down my pants and inched my ass over the hole. When I was in a comfortable position, I pushed. Nothing came at first, so I pushed harder. It felt like I was going to force my intestines out. While I sat there trying to squeeze dimes from a quarter, I watched a weird-looking spider crawl up the wall. Every few seconds, he paused and jotted back and forth in situ. When he finally got halfway, I crushed him with the heel of my sandal. If I wasn't going to make it, neither was he.

# MANALI

S omething foreign slithered into my nose. It lifted the walls of my lungs and softened them to a cool blue. I pried my eyes open and looked out the window. We were rolling into a parking lot surrounded by pine trees.

"Where are we?" I asked Tim.

He was twisted face down with a shoelace of drool slithering out from his mouth. The bus driver answered my question.

"Manali," he barked.

Then I realized what I was breathing. It wasn't smog or feculent odor. It wasn't the cheesy stench of Tim's beast feet. It was fresh air.

We crept our way off the bus like partially reanimated corpses. The sunshine and the scenery kicked a little more life into us. There were green mountains sprinkled with wooden shacks, flowerbeds, and wedges of forest moving in from every angle. A slender man with bright fingernails and black skin sauntered up to us and smiled.

"I am Gumtha," he said. "I vork forr Tourist Inn. You need rroom?"

Bert grimaced and waved him on. "Whatever, Kunta," he said. "Anywhere we can chuck."

We followed Gumtha to a rickety van, and he took us to his place. It was a cedar lodge with hot water, spacious rooms, and balconies with views. There was even a meadow out front where fat white cows munched their cud.

"Vee have rroom service as well," Gumtha said.

We got a double and a triple for three bucks a head. I took the double with Bert because the others wanted to blaze, and I hated the smell of hash. Bert and I walked to our room and opened the door. There was a single queen-sized bed against the back wall. My face hung from my skull like hot putty. Bert kipped into gear and threw himself across the bed. "I'm fuckin' chuuuuckin'," he yelled. He wrapped himself tightly in the sheets. Then he started spouting shit off like, "Get me the remote. Get me my meds. Order me some sauce. Bring me some nahs."

I tossed the remote at his fro. Before he could bark any more orders, I got in bed, snapped my eyes shut, and passed out.

Six hours later, something forced my eyes open. It started as a purring in my stomach but rapidly devolved into rib-knotting pain. I jumped up from the bed and raced to the bathroom. I could barely get my shorts off fast enough. I sat down, and my ass plug went flying into the toilet. It was followed by a dozen gallons of scalding diarrhea.

"Good God," Bert screamed.

Once my asshole jittered to a slow, I cleaned up and hobbled back in the room. I felt like I had just shat my skeleton out.

"India officially gave it to me," I said, collapsing on the bed.

Bert took the cue and raced into the bathroom. His ass went off like a cannon in the toilet.

"Soup's on," he yelled.

I laughed weakly and held my gut. I could feel the eels of poisonous shit still swimming around in there. When Bert came out of the bathroom, I went back in. We played musical toilets till 3 a.m., then fell back to death.


The next morning, I crawled out of bed and unloaded my guts in the toilet. I was sat there for a good twenty. When I came out, Bert was still dead where he lay. He looked like a giant slug in a crepe, wrapped in all those blankets.

"Let's sauce," I said.

"Mmmmm."

I knew he'd be bedridden for at least another five hours. I left him be.

Our food spot that day was a place I had found in the guidebook called Riverside Café. It was perched on the banks of the Manalsu Nala just across the bridge to Old Manali. The grounds were a dump, but the environs were stunning. The mountains around us looked like the shoulders of gray gods dusted with clouds, and the river below us like a torrent of shredded ghosts marching diagonally. The café's owner, Kung—a wavy-haired Tamang from the hills of Nepal—came to take our orders.

I was hoping the items on his menu might reflect his heritage. Unfortunately, all that was listed were standard dishes for weak-stomached tourists.

"Why don't you serve any Tamang dishes?" I asked.

"No one would buy," he said, smiling.

I scowled back at my menu. While the others ordered cheese sandwiches, I tried to decide between the Himalaya Burger and the Himalaya Sandwich.

"What's the damn difference?" I asked, pointing.

"One have lettuce," Kung said.

With bellies full, we made our way back across the bridge and toward what Mason swore was "Old Manali." His sense of direction is usually keen, so we didn't argue with him. We followed him up a hillside path. When we got to the top of it, we were standing smack dab in the middle of the forest. The only sign of civilization was a saddled donkey defecating on a clump of mushrooms.

"Is this our cab driver?" I asked.

Mason yanked his beanie past his ears and shot ahead of us. We continued behind, laughing at his back.

For the next two hours, we followed him on his proud odyssey. The journey took us through acres and acres of deep, green trees and lush vegetation. We found nothing that even remotely resembled Old Manali. When our feet tired, we squatted across a cluster of boulders and rested. From atop the highest boulder, I noticed a wooden cone poking up through the forest canopy.

"What's that?"

Mason fumbled with the map for a bit, then crumpled it shut.

"Ooff," he said. "Let's just bunt up there and see."

We lugged our asses up the trail to a clearing in the trees. At its center was what looked like a giant upturned beehive. It had three pine tiers, each of which cradled a ray of sunlight. A monk in a red robe passed in front of one and it lit him up like a butterfly.

"What is this place?" I said.

"The Hidimbi Devi Temple," Mason read from the guidebook.

According to the Hindu epoch, *Mahabharata*,[7] the goddess Hidimbi used to roam the forests around Manali. There are many tales of her adventures. The most famous of them involves her horrible twin brother Hidimba and his lust for human flesh. Our guidebook gave us a summary of what happened.

*One night Hidimba sent his sister out in search of fresh meat. She combed the woods for hours but found no one. Just as she was about to give up, she stumbled across a Prince called Bhīma. He was passing through the woods on a war campaign with his mother and four brothers; Yudhishthira, Arjuna, Nakula, and Sahadeva. At first, Hidimbi planned to slay Bhīma. But his stature and confidence wooed her from afar. She decided then to make him hers. To seduce him, she approached him as a dark and voluptuous woman dripping with silver. She courted him long into the night. As time passed, her waiting brother Hidimba became increasingly suspicious. He set off into the woods only to find his sister embracing what should have been his meal. He lunged for her, but the prince intervened. He killed the cannibal god after a long battle. Hidimbi then fell on her knees and begged the prince to marry her. He agreed on two conditions: 1) That she allow him to spend the time between sundown and sunup with his family, and 2) That she accept his will to leave after the birth of their first son. She agreed. And after their son Ghatotkacha was born, Prince Bhīma left with his family. For a time, Hidimbi was with her son. But he soon began to display his father's prowess for battle and*

---

[7] The *Mahabharata* is a ninth-century Sanskrit epic which primarily focuses on the struggle for power between the Pandava and the Kaurava dynasties in the kingdom of Kurukshetra located in the modern Indian state of Haryana.

*eventually took off on his own war campaigns. Hidimbi was left to roam the Manali forest alone. Locals claim she still does to this day.*

We walked up to the maw of the temple. A wave of tension crept through me as I entered. The air smelled of dust and rat feces. I looked down and saw a ring of boulders on the floor. I peered in closer and noticed that one of the boulders was covered in dark splotches. I asked the praying man next to me what they were. He cocked his specs and smacked his lips.

"They do animal sacrrifice here," he said. "The blood go dirrectly into hole underneath. This is Hidimbi's mouth."

When I heard this, my bones started rattling in their joints. I tried to keep myself from shaking by hugging my chest and locking my knees. I could only hold it for a moment. Then, Boom! That bizarre electricity bolted up through my system and shot jaggedly out my eyeballs. I sprinted out of the temple and to the outhouse across the way. I popped a squat over the fetid hole and groaned. An aquarium's worth of painful water came screaming out my ass. When it finally stopped, I wiped up, limped home, and crashed.

The next morning, I felt a bit better. I was still punchy from the previous day's events, but the twelve hours of sleep I'd gotten sanded down the edges on my nerves. I had a scenic but boring meal at the Riverside with the Chucks. After that, I wandered up the hill toward Old Manali and into a little internet café. Up until this point, I'd had very little contact with my family; it always seems to take from the purity of my experiences abroad if every two days my parents update me on the shape and size of our dog Buffster's latest carpet accident. Nevertheless, I sat down and fired them off a couple emails.

About halfway through, I was distracted by the smell of goat's cheese. I stopped typing and looked to my right. Sitting next to me was a tow-headed girl with thick arms and a cleft chin. She looked like a Nordic lumberjack.

"I'm Gertrude," she said, cracking her neck to one side.

"I'm Johann."

"German, too, eh?"

"Distantly. My father just gave me this name as a joke."

"No, zis is good name. Especially since only *old* men in Germany still have it. It is my grandfaza's name, too, haha."

"Your grandfather? I was under the impression that Johann was a young and sexy name in Germany."

Gertrude wailed like a shitting sow. "Who told you dis? Your faza?"

"Well . . ."

Gertrude kept laughing. I folded my arms and scowled.

"At least he didn't name me Adolf," I muttered.

"Hey, it's okay," Gertrude said. "I von't tell other German girls your name if you tell me ver is a good und cheap hotel."

I smirked and recommended the Tourist Inn. She said she'd check it out.

"Wanna meet at nine o'clock der to have a party?" she asked.

Normally, I would have denied Paul Bunion. But I wasn't in the mood to be choosy, especially after learning I was the laughingstock of young Germany. I politely accepted her offer and finished my emails.

Next on the list of things to do that day was set up a trek to Hanuman Tiba, a Himalayan mountain some two days' walk from Manali. I went back to the hotel and grabbed the others. The first place we tried was in town. It was a shady joint with dirty floors and beady-eyed agents. The assholes greeted us with fake smiles then tried to rape us for a hundred bucks a pop, before food and gear. We told them to suck wind and went to ask Kung's advice. He told us about his friend Rajesh at Alpine Trekkers. We thanked him and went up there. It was a clean and friendly place with walls covered in pictures of grinning mountaineers. A long-haired man with high cheekbones and a shoe-brush mustache greeted us from behind the front desk.

"How may I help you?" he said.

"Are you Rajesh?" I asked.

"Yes. Please, come sit."

We told him Kung had sent us. Within ten minutes, we had worked out a deal for a fully guided, all-inclusive, three-day, two-night trek to Hanuman Tiba for seventy-five dollars each. We even got to choose our own menu.

"Give us three days to prepare," Rajesh said, smiling. "Vee vill leave from here Tuesday at 10 a.m."

We celebrated the trek by taking down multiple plates of spicy Kullu food. We were glued to our toilet seats the entire evening.

A dozen dumps and episodes of *No Reservations* later, Bert and I heard a rapping at the door. I opened it and there was Gertrude. She was wearing timber boots, all-weather pants, and a flannel shirt. The only thing missing was a Babe belt buckle.

"Paul," I blurted. She jumped back and pruned her face.

"Paul?"

"Yes, um, paul-ese come in, Gertrude," I said.

"You Americans are strange," she said, ducking past me.

Bert caught his first look at Gertrude mid-drag. Cigarette smoke stuttered up from his nose.

"You run a bait-n-tackle shop?" he asked.

"Excuse me?"

"Uh, so whaddaya guys wanna do tonight?" I asked.

"Does anyone smoke?" she asked. She reached into her pocket and produced a rolled-up bag of weed. It looked like matted tree moss.

"We're cool," we said.

The three of us hit the streets in search of a place called Club Vroom! We found it on top of a ski lodge, shaking the pines around it with blasts of cheesy trance music. Its interior had no real decorative theme. Elk horns juxtaposed Japanese rice curtains, black lights, and big-screen TVs. I squinted at all of it.

"Let me buy you guys a round," Gertrude said.

She came back with three mugs of yellowed bath water. We found a table near the door and sat down. In front of us was a troupe of wasted foreigners dancing and crawling up onto the bar. An Indian DJ encouraged them from a corner by incorrectly repeating rap lyrics. At one point, I think I heard him say, "Ain't nuthin' but a ghee thang, *baaaby*. Club Vroom! is tha best one, *baaaby*."

Bert and I were unmoved by the mayhem. Gertrude had a sparkle in her eye.

"Would you guys like to have E wiz me?" she asked.

The thought of rolling balls at Club Vroom! with Gertrude and the goofballs was almost laughable. We politely declined. "Drugs don't sit well with me," I said.

Gertrude shrugged and popped a tablet in her mouth. My prick inexplicably inched forward.

When Club Vroom! finally lost its antique charm, we went back out on the road in search of somewhere new. Our wanderings took us way out in the sticks where the asphalt was eaten over by shrubbery. The only thing ahead was a flickering street lamp.

"This is gettin' bitchin'," Bert said.

Just as we were preparing to turn back, the distant beat of music reanimated our senses.

"Where is zis coming from?" Gertrude asked, grinding her teeth.

We spotted a junkyard with a noisy club at the back. It was surrounded by two rings of barbed wire fence. Gertrude and I promptly jumped the first. Bert's clumsier attempts at climbing prompted three guard dogs to come firing out of the gloom. They chased us, nipping at our heels till we jumped the second fence. This put us at the club's foreground. It was a wasteland of oversized children's toys floating in pools of murky water. The strangest of the exhibits was a gathering of beat-up rubber duckies wearing sunglasses and smiling at one another.

We climbed the steps to the club and pushed open the door. The whole place couldn't have been bigger than a pawn shop and was filled with strobe lights. The geek at the front stopped us and demanded we pay 250 rupees (about 8 bucks) a piece. We looked around at the almost exclusively male clientele and laughed.

"Why would we pay eight bucks a pop to toss our sausages on the pile?" I asked.

He looked puzzled. Bert snickered. "There's no bitches, bro," he shouted.

I looked over at Gertrude, hoping she wasn't offended. She was scratching her arm and smiling at the wall.

"Let's fuckin' bunt," I said.

The only place left to go was the hotel. We got back within half an hour, exhausted, and weirded out. Bert didn't even stick around for a closing chat.

"I'm too chuck," was his excuse.

While I knew this was partly true, his real reason for leaving was to give me a chance to make my move. I did it just as Gertrude was walking into her cabin.

"You need some company?" I asked.

She pursed her lips and let her eyes dangle from their sockets. I was almost certain she'd give in and say yes.

"Nope," she said and shut the door.


Morning came at noon. I rubbed my eyes open and looked around the room. There were piles of dirty clothes strewn everywhere. Cigarette butts were poking up from various ashtrays like strange fungal growths. Our TV antennae were hung with Bert's stained underwear. Our bathroom was a bubbling brown swamp. Our trash can was overflowing with soiled toilet paper we'd been unable to flush. It looked like a heap of slimy frog's eggs. I wandered over to the other Chucks' room to see how it was looking. From corner to corner, it was spliced by sagging clotheslines. Mason, Tim, and Sebastian were each tending to their own, fitting it gingerly with soggy socks and boxers. Between pin-ups, they paused to scratch themselves and puff smokes. I felt like I was at a decommissioned project block run by the Camorra.

We went to the Riverside to eat and escape our nasty rooms. We ran into a couple there named John and Annie who were also staying at the Tourist Inn.

"Our place is a dump, too, because of our laundry," Annie said.

"I feel like I'm back in the Peace Corps washing all that stuff by hand."

"You were in the Peace Corps?" I asked.

"Yeah, why?"

"Because you just reminded me. I applied for that shit like six months ago, but haven't heard back yet."

"Yeah, it takes a while. I waited almost fourteen months for my placement."

"Damn. Where did they end up placing you?"

"Tanzania. They put me in a little Masaai village in the middle of nowhere. There was no electricity or running water, so I had to do everything by hand."

"Was it worth it?"

"Yes, but it was frustrating. They sent me there to do 'community development,' but I spent more time smacking mosquitoes off my arms and boiling in my hut. The little things are what really got me through; making friends with the elders in my village, bathing my baby host sister, watching my host brother aggravate our cow by poking it in the udder with a stick."

I chuckled.

"What's your focus?" she asked.

"Teaching English," I said. "But I may switch to something else."

"Okay. Well, a word of advice. Don't do community development unless you really enjoy sitting on your ass."

"I'll keep that in mind."

As my service was still months away, I was able to put it back out of my head. I shifted my sights toward souvenir shopping. I headed up the road with the others to Old Manali. Our first stop was a jewelry shop called Sylus. The place was filled with glittering hunks of semiprecious stones set in silver. I crouched down at one of the display cases and began browsing.

"Hello. I am Sylus," a man behind the counter said. "How may I help you?"

His clipped voice matched his specs and bowl cut.

"I'm looking for a pinky ring," I said.

Sylus reached under the glass and pulled out a tray of fat-stoned rings. I drooled.

"Lemme see that one," I said, pointing to a two-ouncer inlaid with garnet. He handed it to me, and I slipped it on my pinky. It fit perfectly.

"You like rrings?" he asked.

"Yeah, I collect them from every place I go. It's like wearing each destination on my fingers."

"Vell, this rring you like is not from Manali."

"Oh?"

"It is from Rajasthan."

I looked down, turning the ring in slight disappointment. A thread of light hit one of the garnet's dark corners and flashed red at my eyes.

"I'll take it anyway," I said.

"Yes." Sylus grinned. "It seems to like you."

After dropping a hunno on the beast, I was proud to call it my own. That is, of course, until Mason came out of the shop five minutes later wearing the exact same ring.

"Dude, you don't even fucking wear jewelry," I yelled.

He choked up a satisfied smile and dismissed me with a jerk of his beard.

"Garnet's my birthstone," he said. "I have more of a right to wear this than you do."

Before I could respond, he charged ahead to the next string of shops. He had clicked into ultra-buying mode—a defense mechanism he sometimes employs to take attention off his mimicry of others. By the end of his day-long shopping spree, he had bought two rugs, three flutes, a sitar, a garnet ring, five bags of incense, and a Buddhist prayer bowl. He walked back to our hotel with all this crap on his back, staggering like an over-burdened donkey.

"Why the fuck does he always blow hella bones on such bitchin' shit?" I muttered to Tim.

"That's Mayt'n," he said. "His beard won't pinch a nickel to save his mother, but he'll blow all his scrill on nahs and cool fuckin' lil' trinkets. I'll tell ya one thing though, he's gonna have mad bones for

Europe, and I for one am *fuckin'* payin' for him."

"Oh, me too."

The next morning, Sebastian and I were the only ones who made it out of the hotel. Our intention was to go shopping for the trek, but we ended up wandering around New Manali in search of more souvenirs. Our journey took us through a dozen Tibetan novelty shops selling all the same tourist crap—rugs, pots, candles, incense holders, monk's robes. There were even photos of the Dali Lama grinning from ear to ear and flashing the thumbs up. Now that I had my ring, the only other thing I was looking for was a mask. My room back home is filled with them.

In one of the musty underground shops, I found a cache of old masks that looked cool. Most of them were bug-eyed depictions of Hindu deities coated with layers of dust. A portly monk wearing glasses and a red robe was wiping each clean with a rag. He looked up at us and smiled when we walked in.

"How may I help you?" he asked.

"I'm looking for a mask."

He puffed air through his nose. "Well, you've come to the right place. Which type you were looking for?"

"I dunno. Something local?"

He scratched his bald head, rustling up thoughts with his fingertips. When he noticed my ring, he raised his eyebrows.

"I think I know."

He drew a creaky ladder from the corner and posted it up against a wall of shelves. He climbed till he reached the top and pulled down a mask so caked with dust I could barely make out its face.

He climbed back down and held the mask in front of me. With a swirl of his rag, he wiped off ten years of collected grime. The face revealed was that of a full-lipped Indian man with a black mustache. He wore a crown of sparkling garnets.

"This is Prince Bhīma," he said. "He was the lover of the goddess

Hidimbi whose temple is built here."

The words escaped my mouth before I could process their meaning. "I'll take it," I said.

Now thirty bucks poorer, I went back outside with Sebastian to finally start buying supplies. As we searched for a trek shop, I felt strangely compelled to look over my shoulder. Amidst the crowd of shoppers and bums, I saw a woman. She was draped in silk and silver with bunches of black curls spiraling down her shoulders. Her eyes were a shade of blue found only in gemstones. She smiled at me with red lips.

"Mother of God," I choked. She stared at me for a moment. Then she whispered something inaudible. I walked toward her to find out what she'd said. She lifted her heels and flitted away.

"After that nah," Sebastian yelled.

I grinned at him and we both took off. We followed the woman through dozens of crowded lanes and switchbacks. A few times I thought we'd catch her. In the end, we were left staring at a brick wall.

"Fuck," I said, kicking the dirt. It clouded up around me. When it dissipated, I saw a sign that read, Himalaya Clothes Shop."

"I guess I'll just bunt in here," I said to Sebastian. "You can beef 'em out here or whatever."

The owner of the shop was a pencil-thin Tibetan girl with puffy cheeks and sharp eyes. Her hair ran down her back in a long, thick braid.

"What you wish?" she asked me.

I wanted to tell her that I wished for my woman with the gemstone eyes. I cracked my teeth and exhaled.

"Uh, a jacket," I said. She brought down a green jacket with big pockets. It looked decent.

"What's your name?" I asked.

"Lhamu."

"Okay. I tell you what . . . I'll buy that jacket if you come have lunch with me."

A cloud of rouge suffused her face. I thought she might faint.

"No thanks," she said.

"Please, my treat."

"No, no. My mother will kill to me."

"Well, you should at least think about it. I'm going on a trek to Hanuman Tiba tomorrow, and I'll be back in a few days. Give me your answer then."

Before she had a chance to respond, I slipped her a bill and split with the jacket. She smiled at me under her red cheeks.

It was the morning of the trek. Our laundry was still damp, our bags were still unpacked, not to mention we all felt like crap. We were to meet Rajesh and his crew at ten sharp outside Alpine Trekkers. It was already half past when we got out the door. With packs full of soggy clothes, we hiked across the bridge and over to the Riverside. Kung took mercy on us and served us up cheese omelets and hash browns.

"You wan me tell Rajesh you will be late?" he asked.

We nodded weakly.

We arrived at Rajesh's over an hour late. He was waiting patiently for us out front with bags of supplies and two other guys.

"These are my aids, Dinesh and Chittesh," he said. Dinesh was a tall, bucktoothed teen with shaggy hair and a long face. He looked a bit like Jar Jar Binks. Chittesh was significantly shorter with a potbelly, crabapple cheeks, and a mouth like a Cheerio. I kept thinking he'd break out in songs of yuletide mirth.

"Shall we?" Rajesh said, ushering us all up the crooked path with a slender hand.

We plodded along like cattle up a sand dune. Indian jewelry shops, Israeli restaurants, and Tibetan haberdasheries gently gave way to a strange wooden suburbia. The houses that comprised it were four-story ebony beasts that stretched up from the tiny path like malevolent sequoias. The blue sky hung above them like a floating ocean of glass. I whipped out my camera and started snapping photos. People inside must have heard my clicks because their heads came popping out their windows like cartoon mushrooms.

As the road brushed suburban life from its shoulders, an almost eerie greenness flooded our vision. We heaved up into it, straining our lungs till they squeaked and burned. We were soon surrounded by nature. To our left was a hill of pines folding over the horizon. To our right, a snowy ridge whose jaggedness reminded me of a Stegosaurus's armor. When the sun started crisping our faces, we sought refuge in a nearby temple. Its womb stunk of feet and sage, and its ceiling sagged low. We had trouble just entering.

"What's this place for?" I asked Rajesh.

"This is temple to Hanuman and Krishna," he said.

Sebastian's perpetual grin widened. He was about to remove his shirt, but I scowled the effort dead.

"Don't act tight in here," I snapped.

He blew me off and went ogling at the statues lining the walls. I did the same. All the statues were bronze renditions of the gods dusted with saffron and dressed in *leis*. I searched for one of Hidimbi on the off-chance Rajesh had been mistaken. I came up nil.

Back outside the temple, we hit a trail that wove its way up through a network of Kullu villages. Each was different, Rajesh explained to me, in dialect, dress, and custom. Some of the villagers wore red paisley scarves and spoke vulgar dialects of Kullu. Others donned green sashes and hats and conversed in Tibetan vernacular. Every time we came to a new place, I noticed a difference in preferred livestock. Some had sheep, some had goats, some had chickens, and some had stoats. Despite these glaring differences, three things remained consistent throughout. There was always a mammoth stack of hay in the middle of the road. There was always that roadside old bag frowning at us with one tooth poking over her upper lip. There was always a lone cow, chained to a post, shitting on its hindquarters and chewing its cud lackadaisically. My favorite of the dozen or so villages we passed through was undoubtedly the one that specialized in growing pot. Half its entire crop area was devoted to the cultivation of man-sized weed stocks bursting with purple buds. I looked out across them and smiled. The scratching of black nails across my back made me shiver and keep walking.

As we reached higher ground, the sourness in my stomach began to resurface. I tried squashing it with a cheese sandwich, but that made it worse. My only recourse was to walk steadily without pause; for some reason, continual movement kept my guts from exploding. I maintained an even pace. Eventually, I reached an internal equilibrium that was bearable, even pleasant.

Then Mason spoke. "Let's grab some baumish shots here in front of these mountains," he said.

We had come to a spot in the road where the brush was low and the mountains behind it boomed. It was an excellent photo op, but I knew if I stopped, the fate of my boxers would be very much similar to that of Keanu Reeves if the bus had dropped below fifty.

"I gotta keep movin' Mayt'n or my guts'r gonna fuckin' hook 'em," I said.

"Oh clean the sand outta yer vag and get up here for one lil' pussy pic."

I bit my lip and fell in line with the others. When my footsteps stopped, my rectum clicked.

"I'm gonna shit my fucking pants," I screamed.

"Just a couple more shots here, Felm," he said.

While the man fired off photo after photo of us from every conceivable angle, I stood there in agony with my butt cheeks clenched. After ten minutes, I could stand it no longer.

"Can we bunt now?" I asked.

"Ooff, hold up. I wanna have Rajesh grab a couple with me in it."

He handed the camera over and knelt in front of us. I contemplated dropping my pants and showering his head with ass rain. Someone up there must've read my mind. No sooner did I draw the string on my pants than a curtain of raindrops came ripping down across us.

"We must keep moving," Rajesh said. "This rrain vill get vors."

Within five minutes, the sky was a flickering mass of black clouds. Our once dirt path was quickly turned to a river of sludge. It was impossible to walk steadily. My stomach grew more and more angry. I was determined to make it to camp before I let it all out. On three occasions, we crossed rapids via creaky wooden bridges. When I saw them, I was reminded of the driftwood ladders the Chucks and I used to hammer together when we'd build tree houses. Memories of those times were what I concentrated on while crossing. This prevented me from poking my eyes downriver and slipping in panic. It also prevented me from shitting myself.

Two hours later, we arrived at our camp in Solang. The valley we were in was filled with boulders and surrounded by crooked peaks. The recent pockets of springtime heat had reduced these peaks' snow levels to such a point that only their deepest cracks and grooves remained full. This gave them the look of hooded giants run through with big white veins. Our tents were placed at the base of these mountains, precisely where the largest artery of snow was. It stretched down toward the ground like a lightning bolt frozen in time. I wanted to stay and help the crew set everything up. But nature was cussing at me to make do. With a packet of Wet Ones in one hand and my guts in the other, I ran for a patch of forest. The second I dropped my drawers, a liter of warm peanut butter exploded from my ass. I quickly ran out of moist towelettes and was forced to use bush leaves.

"Please don't be poison ivy," I said. When the humiliating ordeal was finally over, I schlepped back up the hill and collapsed in my tent. Sleep consumed me before the sting in my anus dissipated.

I rolled out of bed that evening soaked and starving. Everyone was gathered in the communal tent, so I joined them. While I had been sleeping, Chittesh, Dinesh, and Rajesh had been preparing dinner for us. We ate it together with heat lamps at our backs.

"This is so saucy," someone said. Our meal was a feast of fried *paneer* (cheese), pickled cabbage, potato vindaloo, and dahl makhani. It was all homemade and steaming hot.

When dinner ended, Sebastian poked me in the gut.

"Felm's prolly gonna hook 'em again and frit his pants from all this sauciness," he blurted.

The others cracked up. I just sat there and fumed.

"You think that's funny, huh?" I said.

His comment, however lighthearted, sparked that sour feeling of animosity I had for him. Being that he was younger, less experienced, and considerably less traveled, I felt it an act of insubordination for him to crack jokes at my expense. I reacted as you might expect an egomaniacal prick with a god complex and a sore stomach to react.

"Fuck off you fat-ass tagalong bitch," I spat.

The good-natured cheer on Sebastian's face melted away. It left behind a serious gaze, the likes of which I had never seen before.

"What?" he snorted. "Did you drop more bones than me, so you think this is *your* trip now? Go fuck yourself, Felm."

The Chucks all cracked up. Sebastian grew a long, self-satisfied smile. I wanted to neuter it from his face. I curled my fist into a ball of granite. I knew if I used it, the whole trip might implode. I scowled and retired to my tent.

I woke up to the sounds of sizzling food. I was still furious at Sebastian for his comment, but my hunger outweighed my anger. I opened my tent and went outside. Rajesh and his crew had again prepared a feast for us. This time it was cheese omelets, toast, OJ, and fresh fruit. Everything went down easy enough thanks to my now-empty bowels.

After breakfast, we took to the road in earnest. We charged up dozens of mushy hills, almost slipping and falling with every step. The only concession this harsh area offered was an occasional peek through the mist-folds that cloaked the surrounding view. More than once, I caught a glimpse of streams pouring like clear blood from stab wounds in the snowy mountains and dribbling down into the forests below. The apex of our ascent was hardly climactic, however. What was supposed to be a panoramic-view op turned out to be a swift retreat into a hilltop cave to avoid a sudden onslaught of rain. It would have been bearable had some animal not recently taken a huge steaming crap there. Due to the smallness of the rock eaves above us, we were forced to huddle around the monster turd pile as if it were a campfire, while we waited out the storm.

After five hours of shit piles and near-death slips, we arrived at the base of Hanuman Tiba. Sunlight was peeling through the fingers of the storm, lighting up the mountain like a volcano spewing gold. Our crew took advantage of the favorable conditions and set up shop. We'd have helped them, but we were just too goddamned chuck.

We awoke from our naps to find a crackling campfire. Rajesh and his crew had prepared spicy chow mein, grilled cheese, and cucumber salad. Our plates were set atop our own individual stumps around the fire.

"God, this looks so baumish," Sebastian said.

We took our seats with the others and began eating. A conversation started to ripple between the eight of us.

"May I please know . . . vat are this strange vords you use when you talk with each other?" Rajesh asked.

Dinesh and Chittesh both wobbled their heads to note that they wanted to know too.

I laughed. "Well, we kinda invented a way of speaking from being together so much," I replied. "It's like our own little dialect."

"It's called ROAST and it's bauuumish." Sebastian said.

"You mean like the dish?" Rajesh asked.

"No," Mason said. "Like the Result of a Small Town. ROAST."

"We invented it to keep our parents from knowing what we were talking about," I said. "Now it's what separates us the most from other people. It's what makes us special."

"You mean there aren't other Americans who use this vords?"

"Nope, we're the only ones you're gonna meet who do."

"Can you please teach us some?" Dinesh asked.

I smiled. "Which do you want to know?"

The three of them grinned at one another. "Bad vords," they said in unison.

I ran them through a crash course in ROAST cuss words. Dinesh, who seemed the most eager, was the first to give it a shot. He pursed his lips crookedly and mouthed out a phrase.

"I vant to bav some snuss. Please grunge over and let me snit it, you baumish nah."

The five of us pitched over our stumps and fell to the ground cackling. Rajesh and Chittesh giggled uncomfortably.

"Did I say this correctly?" Dinesh asked.

"Sure did." Bert wept.


We rolled out of our tents at 7:30 a.m. We sat down for a breakfast of cinnamon pastries, fruit salad, and milk coffee. We were told to finish our meals quickly as the sun was intensifying. This could mean snow burn and/or blindness if we weren't careful.

"Where exactly are we walking to?" I asked Rajesh. He pointed to the base of Hanuman Tiba.

"There," he said.

"The way up is covered with three feet of snow," I said. "How the hell are we gonna get through?"

Chittesh went into his tent and brought out a giant bag. He dropped it in front of our feet.

"This how," he said. What spilled out was five pairs of spiked snowshoes the size and weight of cinderblocks. Just looking at them hurt my feet.

"These are boomish," Mason said, slipping his on effortlessly. I struggled to get mine on. When I finally did, my flat feet were pinched with pain.

"You got anything more comfortable?" I asked.

Mason scoffed. "Don't be such a pussy, Felm."

"Get me, faggot," I yelled. "You know my feet are fucked up from all the broken bones I've had."

"Yeah, yeah."

With no other footwear options, I rose from my stump and made toward the mountain. The others, Mason in front, bolted ahead while

Bert and I lagged behind. Right away, the insides of my boots started grazing the skin off my soles. To take my mind off the pain, I soaked in the beauty of my surroundings. In front of us, a demi-coliseum of peaks towered above a stretch of icy earth. The sun's heat had punched holes in it giving it the look of Dalmatian fur. When the pain in my feet finally became unbearable, I paused in the middle of the ice sheet. Not two seconds after I'd sat down, Dinesh came running up with a frantic look on his face.

"You not to sit here," he cried.

I looked at him cockeyed. "Why not?" I asked.

"You will fall trrooo."

Just past my ass was a snake of water gushing from under a snow fold. A step farther and I'd have broken through the canopy and been swept away.

"Fuck," I said.

Shaken, I followed Dinesh and Bert until we reached the top of a snow hill. Hanuman Tiba stood directly in front of it, flexing its big white muscles in the sun. Equally flexing was Mason in his black shades. He greeted us with a smirk.

"Took you fags long enough," he said.

"Fuck off," I muttered.

I could tell by the look on his face that Dinesh didn't want a fight to erupt. He intervened politely.

"Let's to slide down the snow on our stomach," he suggested.

The five of us shrugged in agreement.

For the next hour, we took turns doing tricks down the embankment on our bellies. My feet and body were still hurting, so I had to take it easy. This pushed Mason to be as showy as he could. A half dozen times, he went sailing down the snow on his belly with his ankles in his grip and his big red beard pointing the way. After the sixth time, he gave me a little jab.

"Catch all that?" he asked.

"Nah dawg," I said. "I guess I'm not as fuckin' *awesome* as you."

The comment only encouraged him further. He even started

picking on Bert who was too tired to snow-slide.

"Blow it up a lil' ya Jew fro puss," Mason said.

Bert looked up at him from where he was sitting. He took a deep breath and let out a long, hard " Brrrrrrrrrrrrrrrrrr."

When the winter sports ended, Rajesh and the crew told us we should head back. Mason immediately slithered up front and led us as naturally as he could. Bert and I lagged behind again. After a moment, Bert turned to me and snickered.

"Think I can tag that dirty bearded Scot from here?" he asked, packing up a snowball. Bert had been a minor league pitcher for five years. He was good, but Mason was damn near the size of a pea in our field of vision. I narrowed my eyes and sized up the distance between us and him. It was easily a hundred yards.

"Fuck yeaaah," I said.

Bert gave me a smirk and cocked his arm back. It zipped off like a hummingbird's wing.

"Get me," he spat.

I watched in awe as the snowball arched through the sky and plummeted toward Mason's head. Had the man known what was coming he'd never have removed his hat to wipe the sweat off his brow.

Smack! The sound of the snowball hitting his crown sent crows flying. Mason lost his balance and went tumbling forward.

"Bingo," Bert yelled. Mason spun around with his beard glowing like a demon's eyes. The first person in his line of sight was Tim.

"D'ju throw that shit?" he growled.

Tim was still catching his breath from his corky little laugh. Mason burst into copper flames.

"Fuckin' get it," he yelled.

He heaved an ice ball directly at Tim's grill. It exploded against his teeth like confetti.

"Oomph, oohh," he said. He packed up a snowball of his own and threw it at Mason. It sailed right past his head.

"Wait a sec," Mason said.

Tim couldn't throw for shit or beans and Mason knew it. There was only one person who could have nailed him that dead on.

"That's right, bitch," Bert shouted.

"Oh, you're gonna gettem, Brutal Uzbek pussy."

Mason packed up another snowball and ran up the hill toward Bert. I met him halfway and nailed him in the beard with one of my own. Just as he was about to divert his attention to me, a snowball flung by Sebastian cracked him across the jaw. Now it was all-out war. I saw the opportunity to belt Sebastian in the face with my balls and I took it. It was revenge for his insubordination two nights prior. Tim cracked me for trying to fuck up his game in Bangkok. Bert cracked Mason again for the same. The whole thing devolved into an ugly mess. When it finally ended, we trekked back to Manali without saying a single word.

The next morning, I rolled out of bed and went up to Rajesh's alone. I wanted to get away from Manali and needed some advice on where to go next. He advised me that the coolest place nearby was a town called Rishikesh in Uttaranchal, the next state over.

"The Ganges is still somevat clean there and they have many ashrams for meditation," he said. "You vill be able to do plenty of thinking on your problems vit your friends."

This sounded decent to me. At the very least I could chill there. I bought a bus ticket and went back to the hotel. Bert was in the room packing and watching Anthony Bourdain reruns. He and I hadn't pelted each other too bad so we were on speaking terms.

"You see the other Chucks?" I asked him.

"Everyone but Man Bear Pig," he said.

"Where'd he bunt off to?"

"Eeff."

I decided to go over and at least wish the other two happy trails. Sebastian was heading back to the States, and Tim was leaving for Europe with Bert the next day.

Tim and Sebastian were in their room folding clothes and sharing a spliff. They looked up at me lazily when I walked in.

"Ai' la' gahts," I said, throwing them a fist.

Tim gave me a half-hearted dap, as did Sebastian. I considered leaving it at that. Just then Mason came lumbering in. His beard looked redder than average.

"Well, there goes Pakistan," he grumbled. "I was thinking of going there tomorrow, but I just checked my fuckin' bank statement and I have mad bones. Guess I'm stuck here for the next two weeks."

Tim and I glanced at one another. Neither of us said anything.

Mason lit up a spliff and tossed his money belt on the bed. I smiled and eased my way out of the room. He let me get as far as the threshold then looked up at me. I could tell by the soft redness in his eyes that the hash was beginning to loosen his anger.

"My yoga instructors, Kim and Theo, invited me to sauce at their pad tonight," he said. "Grooge with me if you want."

"You have yoga instructors?"

"Yeah. What do you think I was doing while you and Bert were crapping your guts out or sleeping off your hangovers?"

"I don't know, cropping your beard?"

"Oh, that's a great one. Anyway, come if you want. They make good food."

"Ait," I said.

We met up at 7 p.m. and headed out. His yoga instructors rented a small shack near the bridge toward Old Manali. Kim greeted us at the door in a pair of saggy red pajamas. She was a mousy little Thai girl with mischievous eyes and a bright smile.

"Please come in," she said. The floor of their house was covered in OHM-embossed yoga mats. The only piece of furniture was a mattress in the back that was shrouded down from the ceiling by pink curtains. Theo sat in front of it spooning up bowlfuls of *tom yum*.[8] When he saw us, he smiled.

"Welcome to our little spot," he said, with a raspy English accent.

---

[8] *Tom yum* is a hot and sour soup of Thai origin. It is usually cooked with shrimp, mushrooms, lemongrass, and other ingredients.

We sat in front of him where our bowls were placed. Kim padded up and sat by his side. She looked like a tiny brown child next to Theo, who was tall, gaunt, and pasty with raised cheekbones and bulging blue eyes.

Mason and I busted out a couple bottles of Old Monk rum we had bought on the way. Once the drinks were flowing, the topic of partying came up.

"Is there anywhere around here besides lame-ass Club Vroom! Where you can grab a beer?" Mason asked.

Theo thought for a moment. "I take it you've been to the club with the rubber duckies out front?"

"I have," I said.

"Well, besides that, Manali really only offers you one thing."

"What's that?"

"Full moon raves."

Our eyes widened. "Jesus. When's the next one?" I asked.

"It's not for sure. They try to do them when the moon's at its biggest, but that's difficult because raves are illegal in India. To trick the cops, organizers will spread fake rumors about raves in hopes that they'll eventually give up their pursuit. So far, I've heard of two fakers. I know the DJs around here who throw them, so I can keep you posted. A real one should be happening within a fortnight."

The prospect of a full moon rave was enticing, but my tickets to Rishikesh were already bought and paid for. Not to mention attending it would mean spending the next two weeks with Mason. We were now on speaking terms, but dinner with Kim and Theo had only pushed the beef between us below the surface. I figured it would just be better if I split.


"Fuck me," I yelled, looking at my watch. I hopped out of bed and bolted into the shower. It was already 10 a.m. and my bus to Rishikesh was leaving in an hour. I scrubbed down and toweled off. I threw some clothes on and started packing. Bert was in a similar frenzy. His, Tim's, and Sebastian's bus to Delhi would be leaving shortly after mine. We checked out fifteen minutes later. We decided to stop for an extremely quick bite at a place called Nunchucks as it was right next to the bus station. On the rickshaw ride there, I felt a grumble in my stomach. I took it for a simple case of gas.

When we arrived at the restaurant, I jumped out of the rickshaw. I set my pack on the ground, so I could pay the cabbie. As I was reaching for a bill, something nudged up against my asshole. Prolly just a tom yum fart come a' knockin', I thought. I took a gamble and let it fly. A second later my face froze.

"What's wrong?" Tim asked.

I was wearing breezy shorts, so I had very little time before the diarrhea streaming down my thighs became visible.

"Watch my fuckin' shit," I said.

I bolted across the restaurant to the bathroom in the back. It was empty, so I shuffled inside. I looked down and my face dropped. Not only was the fucking toilet busted, but there was no toilet paper to speak of. I stripped my shorts and boxers off in disgust and searched them over for shit streaks. The loose leggings had saved my shorts, but my boxers hadn't been so fortunate. Had Nunchucks provided toilet paper and a working john for its clientele, this ugly mess wouldn't have been so ugly. As it was, I was forced to make an example.

"Here's to you sweetheart," I yelled.

After positioning one leg over the sink, I cranked the faucet on and began scooping handfuls of water up against my soiled ass cheeks. The sink soon looked like a coal miner had just washed his dirty hands there. As I was finishing up, the doorknob creaked and bumped up against my naked culo. I saw the mirrored reflection of an Indian busboy recoiling in terror.

"So soddy," he said, bowing profusely. He shut the door quickly behind him. Others in the restaurant had still no doubt seen me in my birthday suit with a leg on the sink and a hand to my crack. The ensuing snickering confirmed it.

"Fuck this place," I said. I chucked my sullied boxers in the trash bin. At that moment, two acts of revenge seemed appropriate.

Now that my stomach was completely empty, I was forced to actually sit down and order something at the restaurant whose bathroom I had just defiled. I grabbed a quick plate of mutton *momos* (dumplings) and wolfed them down, saying little to the Chucks. They were all giggling at my misfortune from across the table. When I finished eating, I bid them a curt adieu and ran to the bus station. It was exactly two minutes past eleven when I arrived. I was confident I hadn't missed my bus.

"I'm soddy, sir, but your bus has arredy left," the woman at the ticket counter told me. I clenched my teeth and kicked the ground.

"You're fucking kidding me," I screamed. "Nothing ever leaves on time in this goddamned country." I slung my pack over my shoulder and ripped my ticket up.

"Manali it is," I said.

As I passed Nunchucks, I saw Mason inside smoking a cigarette and staring out the window. He looked as down in the shits as I did. I went in and gave him a civil little nod. He looked up at me and snickered.

"Miss your bus?" he asked.

"You know me. The other Chucks ardy bunta?"

"Yep."

"Well, whaddaya wanna do?"

He smoked and thought for a moment. I could see the steady unsureness in his eyes.

"Ooofff." He shrugged. Just as we were getting ready to say sick, an accented voice from outside squeaked up between us.

"Jo'khaaaan," a girl yelled. We ran outside to see who had shouted. It was Kefira.

In the confusion of the past two weeks, I had completely forgotten about Kefira. She had rejected a pass I'd made at her our second night in Delhi; something I really didn't care to remember anyway. If there was any anger lingering in my bones about the incident, it vanished when I got a load of her. She had on a slinky tank top that barely covered her mango-shaped tits and her orange fro was done up so I could see the nape of her tiny neck. I imagined grabbing it from behind and forcing her head downwards.

"Kefira," I yelled, running up and hugging her. She threw her skinny arms around me and belted out a laugh.

"What are you doing here?" I asked.

"Ah, I am khir with my friends," she said. I looked behind her and saw a trail of rickshaws packed with Israelis. Amidst the dirty feet and dreadlocks, I noticed a few cute chicks.

"Where are you guys headed?" I asked.

"The King's Palace," she said. "It is good place."

I looked over at Mason who was ogling at some of the chicks. His nostrils were flaring over his beard.

"Wannaaa . . .?" I asked. He hesitated for a moment. I saw his beard darken and then fade to light.

"Ait," he said.

On the way to the King's Palace, I mused at the sky with my lips pursed to a playful dot. When we arrived at the spot, my mouth fell open like an old man's asshole. Our hotel was so gaunt and rickety, I almost shat myself again.

Mason snorted. "Some fuckin' palace."

A little Indian man with a Snickers bar mustache and a seedy grin came out and showed us to our room. We were on the top floor at the very back.

"This is it?" I asked as he pushed open the door.

Our room was a twelve-by-twelve flea-bitten shithole with concrete floors, one old mattress, and stained walls. The bathroom was littered with trash, and the back door opened to a wedge of concrete lingering some thirty feet aboveground.

"Well, this is a royal butt fuck if I've ever known one," Mason barked. "How much you gonna charge us?"

"Therein lies the deal, my good sirrs." The hotel clerk bowed ceremoniously and let the price squeak from between his cheeks. "One American dollar each."

"Sold," I said.

The Palace didn't turn out to be all bad. There was a great view of the mountains from our balcony, and there were curly-haired, big-titted Israeli chicks everywhere. Before I snapped one off in the john, I spotted Kefira going into the room next to ours. She told me she and her buds would be having a little soirée later that evening.

"Just to come when you are done doing whatever you do," she said.

I laughed. "Alright, you lil' monster."

After a crap and a shower, I mentioned Kefira's party to Mason.

"I'm saucin' at Kim and Theo's tonight," he said, glancing up from his Clive Barker novel. "After though."

"Oooh, I'm actually kinna saucy, too," I said. "Can I—?"

"You're just gonna invite yourself?"

I was about to bite back.

"Nei nornin," he said. "I'm sure they'll fuckin' care if you grooge with me."

Mason and I showed up at Kim and Theo's at around eight with a couple bottles of Old Monk. A freshly made meal of coconut catfish and pineapple rice was just being served. Kim put down placemats and plates.

"Please have seat," she said.

We dropped down and lunged for our food. Theo cracked off the meal with some wild news.

"Mates, there was another fake tonight," he said. "Fuckin' cops went for it like candy."

"Shit. What happened?" I asked.

"Indian mate a' mine passed the word that there'd be a rave tonight in the back forest. When the fuzz got wind of it, they rushed out there to see if anyone was setting up. They just ran by not too long ago. Watched 'em come back with shifty eyes but no perps. Bastards are out for it tonight. Lucky nothing's really going down."

"When do you think the real rave'll be?" Mason asked.

"Can't say yet. Chances are, I won't know until the day of. This bollock's gonna go on till the cops give up."

When we finished eating, we spun the cap off the Old Monk and continued our chat. I was curious to know about Theo's past as his long, weathered face told me stories.

"How big did you used to blow up back in the day?" I asked.

He gave me a puzzled look. Then his eyes brightened. "Quite a bit more than I do now at thirty-three," he said.

"What changed?"

"I did. Or rather an incident changed me."

"Ooohh, what?"

He inhaled deeply and grabbed the bottle. He took a big swig of rum and began.

"It was five years back. I was out with me mates one night in London, and we were getting good n' pissed. One of me mates pulled out a baggie of microdots and started passin' 'em around. I was feeling brave from all the booze, so I popped four."

"That's fuckin' burly," Mason said.

"Burly's an understatement. I got so fucking smashed, I thought I was losin' me fuckin' head. I started panicking and what not, seeing shit like leprechauns and elephants and what all fuck that wasn't there. Soon voices were telling me I was gonna die. In the middle of the club, I started screaming and ran to the loo. For a second, it was alright there, then I looked in the mirror, and me face started melting off me skull. I closed me eyes to erase it, and when I opened 'em, everything went white. For the next hour, I laid there on the floor crying cuz I was so piss scared. I remember thinking, this is what a madman feels. After that, I couldn't do the hardcore scene anymore."

Theo's story scraped open my nerves. Black thoughts started bubbling up and strangling my brain. I quickly changed the subject. We dithered on topics such as yoga and ashrams for the next couple hours. At eleven, Mason and I scooped up our remaining booze and bid our hosts farewell. We promised to return.

"Please, welcome," Kim said, smiling.

Back at the Palace, Kefira's little party was in full swing. There were at least two dozen Israelis on our floor swilling drinks, puffing hash, and popping pills. Mason and I stumbled into her room and greeted her. She coughed out a cloud of smoke and threw her arms around me.

"Jo'khaaaan," she yelled. "You come."

"Wouldn't miss it," I said. I introduced her to Mason.

"Nice to meet you," she said. "Now let me introduce my friends."

The chattering died down. She spun in circles around the room introducing each person with the point of a wobbly finger. "This is Caleb and his girlfriend Malka. And this is Nava, Tamara, Eliora, Gil, his girlfriend Adi, Yoel, Adi again, Yoel again, Dani . . ." on and on and on. I felt like my head was going to explode when she finally finished.

I was stuck in the maw for a good bit. All the Israelis were asking me inane questions like, "What is American doing in India?" and "Khow you like our food?" It took some finesse, but I was eventually able to break away and get Kefira to come with me to my room.

"Why to your room?" she asked me, as I shut the door behind her.

I leaned in close and puckered my lips. Just as they reached hers, she broke out laughing.

"Don't try this funny shit," she said.

I ignored her and leaned in again. She stopped me at the mouth with her tiny palm.

"Let's go see what your friend doing," she said.

"He's whatever."

"Not whatever. Maybe if we find, you can kiss khim instead." She opened the door and jumped back in surprise. There was Mason, leaning over the balcony rail and barfing out his coconut catfish all over the lower patio.

"Opa," she yelled.

I tried to get her to close the door and stay a while. She just nipped at my nose and ran back to the party. Mason was now my date for the evening. I spent the next hour sipping warm rum to the sounds of his puke splattering against the concrete.

Mason was still violently ill when I woke up. I could hear him vomiting in the bathroom with the door shut.

"How much did you skink last night?" I asked him.

"Small amounts," he groaned. "I tried to blow up with that chick Tamara. Uuhhhhh."

"You mean the one with the giant boobs and the buck teeth?"

"Chea hea. She said tight to me, so I went and just got hella D. Then you faggots opened the door right when I was yakking off the balcony."

A sly grin crept across my lips. "You wanna sauce some breakfast?" I asked. "Lil' hummus? Lil' *bureka*?"

There was a pause. I heard a new shower of vomit erupt from Mason's mouth and explode into the toilet. I left the room chuckling.

I spent the rest of my day lounging and writing outside. By nightfall, I found myself in the presence of Israelis again. I shared a bottle of Old Monk with a guy named Caleb, whom I'd met the night before. After his first sip of juice, he looked over at me. "You try *charas*?" he asked.

I shook my head. "What is it?"

His scruffy jowls bowed like a pumpkin slice. From underneath his Rasta beanie, I could see his brown eyes sparking.

"It is solid hash oil, stronger than strongest weed. You will try it."

"I'm okay," I said.

"What? Why not?"

"Bad experience."

"What bad experience? This shit is good and easy to smoke." He reached into his pocket and pulled out what looked like a marble dildo. It was hollowed out in the middle and engraved with flowery mosaics.

"This is a *chillum*," he said. "You mix charas with tobacco and put it in top." He reached into his pocket again and pulled out a baggie with a black cube of gunk stuck to the corner. "Now you take a small piece of this shit, and you roll it into little balls and mix it with tobacco."

When the concoction was ready, he stuffed it in the front end of the chillum and held the flame of his lighter to it. As the wad cherried, he puffed at it from the bottom. Thick ribbons of smoke came slithering up from between his lips. His eyes went red.

"Now you try," he said, passing it to me.

"Really man, I'm cool," I said.

Before he had a chance to push me again, an ambient Israeli grabbed the chillum and started puffing away. Others around him followed. Within two minutes the room was so filled with smoke, I felt a contact high creeping up on me. The walls started to darken.

"I'm gonna go to bed," I said.


Caleb left with his girlfriend two days later; something about someone having stolen a hundred bucks from his room. He'd made a big show of it. Though understandable, it still kinda soured my taste toward the Israeli crew. On my way out to breakfast, I locked our front door from the outside just in case. I'd have invited Mason to come with me, but homeboy was still sick in bed.

I took a stroll into town and searched for a place to eat. Every restaurant was packed with Israelis. Atop a small hill, I spotted a joint called Dragon Bite Café. It had a great view and a sunny terrace without a soul. Upon climbing its stairs, I found that the 45° angle from which I'd perceived said emptiness had only created an optical illusion. Sitting not five feet from the edge of the terrace were a dozen clans of noisy, hash-smoking Israelis. Since there was one free table in the corner, I sat down there and sulked. The waiter came by and took my order.

As I picked at my *ziva* (puff pastry stuffed with cheese) and hummus, I was able to block out most of the ambient chatter with a bit of Chili Peppers. I sank deep into their nostalgic mist of guitar twangs and cool voices and forgot about my predicament. Just as I reached the zenith of low-eyed chuckness, a presence arrived. The man came struttin' up outta nowhere like gangbusters with eyebrows bouncin' and pearly whites flashin'. Everyone on the terrace exploded with cheers. You'd think their messiah had finally arrived, but nope, it was just Mr. Big Cheese, Mr. Fuckin' Saturday Night, comin' up, shakin' hands n' takin' names. He had all the characteristics of a Vegas pimpin' Jew mobster; the shiny curls, the billion-dollar smile, the thin gold chain with Star of David danglin', and the crooked-heel, tooth-pickin' daddy swag. The only thing missing was the silver suit; our man wore camo shorts and a sweater. As he stood there smoking and laughing hoarsely, I began feeling sick to my stomach. I signaled for the check, paid it, and rose. As I did, MBC looked over at me. Our eyes met for a split second—an opportunity I used to convey my disgust.

"*Pinche cabrón*," I muttered.

I left the restaurant in a foul mood. Drinking might have taken the edge off, but it was too early for that. I decided instead to do something that always puts me in a good mood … jewelry shopping. Sylus's was just up the road. I sauntered in whistling and asked the man to show me a ring tray. He side-skirted the twelve Israelis pining for his help and brought me out a bed of fatties. A silver behemoth inlayed with blue chalcedony caught my eye.

"How much for this one?" I asked.

"Ten dollars," he said, blinking thoughtfully from behind his giant specs.

"Jesus, that's cheap."

"Yes, it is, and sexy too. Maybe if you slip it on you vill have some cheap sex."

The two of us busted up laughing.

The instant I slipped the ring on, its coolness fused with my bones.

"That's very beautiful," a voice next to me said. I looked to my left and saw a girl. She had wavy black hair pouring down her shoulders and bright hazel eyes. I could smell rose perfume blossoming from her wide cleavage.

"Thanks," I said, blushing.

"You're welcome. What is your name?"

"Johann. You?"

"I'm Shiran. You're from California, aren't you?"

"How did you guess?"

"I noticed your accent."

A sharp ear for accents *and* hot? My pecker went goofy-eyed.

"Well, I must go now, but I like your taste in jewelry," she said. "Maybe we'll meet up sometime at Club Vroom! I really like that place."

"Oh, me too," I cooed. "Best club in Manali."

The fact that I had just sacrificed taste and resolve for a possible piece of ass weighed little on my conscience. I had a new ring, a new mood, and a new future rendezvous to look forward to. When I got to the room, Mason seemed chipper enough to dance with. His news put me in even better spirits.

"Kim n' Theo invited me to sauce tonight," he said, combing his beard. "You can grooge, too, if you want, pussy."

"Thank you, pussy. I shall."

That night Kim had whipped up a wicked meal of ginger pork and pineapple rice. Everything was set out for us when we arrived. As soon as we sat down to eat, I turned to Theo and raised my eyebrows.

"Any chance of a rave tonight?"

He shook his head. "Sorry mate, another fake got sent through the rumor mill, but that's about all. It may be a couple days still."

I frowned and continued eating. Kim slapped my knee. "Don't be sad," she said.

"Oh, I'm not. Just a little impatient, haha."

She smiled slyly. "Want to know what I do when I feel sad?" she said.

"What's that?"

"I kiss my Booboo."

Theo stopped chewing and widened his eyes. "Kim let's not do this," he said.

"Yes," she retorted. "This will help him."

She got up and ran to the "bedroom." She came out a moment later carrying an oversized doll.

"This is Booboo," she said, holding him out to me with both

hands. Booboo was the size of a chubby toddler with wide-set frog eyes and thin lips. His shaggy acrylic hair was fading in patches, and his face was half-abraded from years of nuzzling. He was wearing a Little Devil T-shirt and flashing the rocker horns with his left hand. He looked like a satanic cabbage patch kid.

"You wanna give him a lil' kiss?" Kim asked. "You will so much feel better."

I winced endearingly and scotched away. Mason laughed into his fist.

"Have at it, mate," Theo said. "Lord knows she makes me kiss the damn thing when I'm pissed n' defenseless. Then I have to sleep next to it like it's our child. I can't tell you how many times I've woken up in cold sweats swearing the lil' bastard took a shot at me bollocks."

"Oh stop," Kim snapped. "Now, just kiss him, Johann."

"Ahhh, I better not," I said. "Just ate n' all. Wouldn't wanna puke n' ruin his snazzy doo."

Theo and Mason pitched forward and banged the ground with their fists. Kim just sat there with Booboo looking puzzled.

"Okay, then." She pouted. "I'll put him in his bed."

"Great," Theo said. "Now let's grab some charas and Old Monk and blast that bloody thing outta our heads."


The next morning was a bust. Not only were Mason and I two gags from death, we'd stumbled home dead alone from an all-night pussy-hunt at Club Vroom! with Kefira & Co. While Mason opted for lounging—besides just having a hangover he was developing some sort of throat infection from all the charas—I was still determined to redeem myself. I decided to pay a visit to the only other chick in town I knew—Lhamu.

The timing couldn't have been more choice; the pockets on my jacket were just starting to come undone. When I came and showed Lhamu, she took this, and *only* this as my reason for returning.

"I'll have my auntie sew them up," she said, taking the jacket from me. She handed it to her auntie, a white-braided hobbit wrapped in a parka, and went back to inspecting her merchandise. I contemplated taking off for lunch until the job was done. My wiener wouldn't let me.

"So uh, what are you doing this week?" I asked.

"Work," she said.

"Oh." An awkward moment started to swell. I quickly squashed it. "Well, I understand. But if you're not too busy, you wanna go somewhere with me? I've only been in Manali for a few days, and I don't know my way around. If you were my tour guide for a day, I'd take you out to lunch."

She paused for a moment then turned around. Her eyes were pinched with suspicion.

"Just as friends," I said with both hands up.

"I guess maybe I can show you some places later this week," she said. "But you be good boy."

"Scout's honor."

Lhamu gave me her digits, and I left with a smile. I putz'd around the city for a while then made for the Palace. When I got back it was only eight, but I was pooped. I was just about to click off the lights and jump in bed when I heard people laughing above us.

"I'm gonna go see what's up," I told Mason as he laid there gripping his gut. I walked upstairs and found one of the rooms with its door ajar. I pushed it open hoping to find Kefira having a naked pillow fight with her friends. The little monster was nowhere to be seen. On the bed, where I'd imagined she'd be, was Mr. Big Cheese.

"From the restaurant, yeh?" he asked me.

"Yeah," I said. I was expecting the guy to tell me to get lost. He flashed a grin and waved me in.

"Come party with us, man."

Mr. Big Cheese had two other buddies with him. One was a smiley, black-bearded fellow with book specs and a flavor saver. The other was a dark-skinned gangly fellow with reptilian eyes and a cold demeanor.

"This is Ezra," Big Cheese said, referring to the former. "And this is Yoel."

"Hey," I muttered. "I'm Johann."

"Well, Jokhann, is nice to meet you. I am Dov. Wanna smoke with us?"

"Nah, I'm cool."

"Okay, well, don't mind us. We are preparing."

The trio had a little smoke station going. Ezra was rolling balls of charas, Yoel was busting apart cigarettes, and Dov was fiddling with a plastic Sprite bottle.

"What's that for?" I asked Dov.

"Bong," he said. "But you khav to first burn the edges." He sparked a lighter and held it to the neck of the bottle. Its plastic warped and wrinkled till it was the color of phlegm.

"See khow this area is now smaller?" he said, pointing.

"Yeah."

"Now, you just go all the way around." He let the flame dance around the exterior of the bottle till it pruned and shrunk. When it was half its former diameter, he pulled away. "And there it is. Perfect smoking tool."

What he held in his hands looked more like a deflated douche bag than the perfect smoking tool. But I could see where he was going with it.

"Now what?" I asked. "You gonna add some water, poke a hole, stick the bowl in, and pack it up?"

"You got it, man,"

Dov and his crew proceeded to do just what I had said in precisely the order I had said it. Their finished product bore a suitable resemblance to a bong.

"And now we light it," Ezra said, holding the contraption to his lips. He cherried up the bowl with his lighter and sucked till the neck of the bottle was curling with smoke. When he pulled away, his eyes melted from his skull.

"Gooooood shiiiiiiiit," he said.

For the next half hour, the crew smoked themselves starry. Yoel and Ezra shrunk into their own little worlds, but Dov smiled at me.

"Wanna sit outside and drink?" he asked me.

"Sure," I said.

We sat on the balcony under the big blue night and chatted. It wasn't long before the conversation cut beneath the skin of pleasantries.

"Being in India really give me time to think about all crazy shit that khappen to me," he said.

"Yeah? Like what?"

"Fuck man. *Craaazy* shit. I just got out of army, you know? And so much stuff khappen to me, like I remember one night in my first week I couldn't sleep. I just lay in bed with my eyes open thinking. Then I khear this one boy start to scream. I recognize this is the voice of boy nobody like in my platoon because khee is a lazy one, and khis laziness get us to do extra work. Well, I look over and I see this boy get tied to khis bed by some other assholes and they are tearing khis clothes off. I want to khelp khim, but I can't believe what I see. They just started to rape khim like animal and beat khim on back. When they finish, khee is crying a lot but nobody does anything because they khated him for being lazy bitch. I khated him too. This is when I knew this army was bad for my spirit, so the next night I tried to escape. The police shot at me, but they miss. In the end, they captured me and took me to army jail. I got to go back to army and eventually finish."

"That's fuckin' nuts," I said. "How did you deal?"

"I still deal," he said, staring into his glass. "This is why I smoke. I get very bad anxiety from the things I khav seen."

"Yeah, I can relate."

"But don't think my life is the khard one," he piped. "Yoel khas seen the *real* bad shit."

"What kinda *real* bad shit?"

"Like worse than me. Khe's Iraqi Jew, you know? And they are khard motherfuckers because they khav to be. When Yoel was just boy, he worked streets in Baghdad as drug dealer. You know khow fucking dangerous is this? You khav not only police chase you but other drug dealers. And Iraq is not very safe for Jews. I will tell you this because you are my friend now. To protect khis life and make money, Yoel khad to kill people."

"Jesus, how many people?"

"More than you want to know."

Not wanting to push things further into dark waters, I changed the subject to something lighter.

"So what's with Israeli chicks, man?" I asked. "They're fucking impossible."

Dov took a sip of rum and chuckled. It almost seemed like he was laughing at some private joke.

"You can't get them khir," he said. "Don't worry what other guys will tell you."

"Why not?"

"Because there are just too many other Israelis around. One girl fucks American boy and the khol world will know. If you want to get with Israeli girl, you must come to visit me in Tel Aviv. It is big party city, so people are more anonymous. Also, I will be able to introduce to you many girls."

"Fuckin' A man," I said. "And if you ever roll out to Cali, I'll do the same for you."


I thought of calling Lhamu the next morning but decided to wait. After a shower, shit, and a shave, I bounced out with Big Cheese and his crew to Old Manali. We did a bit of shopping then hit up a place called El Sombrero for brunch. The others wanted to do Israeli, but I insisted we eat at this place. I have a thing for trying Mexican food in different countries. And not because the food is good either; it's usually shit. But as a person of both sardonic humor and Mexican heritage, I like to see how bad different cultures fuck up "our" food.

I ordered the enchiladas hoping for a disaster. However, the plate I got looked pretty decent. Everything was covered in fresh sour cream and red sauce. The cheese and chicken filling smelled well-spiced, and the beans on the side were miraculously refried. I shoveled a big dripping bite into my mouth.

"Khow you like?" Dov asked.

"Goob," I said. The first few chews were nice. Then my tongue shriveled. "This tastes like fried foreskins," I yelled.

Dov nearly hacked up his goat meat quesadilla. "I guess you will add this to list of shitty Mexican places, eh?" he said.

"Big time."

The smegmaladas irritated my stomach. But instead of backing off, I got smashed with Dov and the others, then hit Club Vroom! As usual, it was splitting at the seams with drunken Israelis. I pushed my way through a gyrating mess of them and sidled up to the bar. My only objective was to get a drink and keep my drunk going. That changed when I looked to my left.

"Shiran," I yelled. "What's up?"

"Nothing," she said. "Just chatting with my friend here. Hope you have a good night." She turned away and continued her conversation.

I slouched and tongued at my straw.

An hour later, I went outside for some fresh air. I saw Shiran and her friend crouched behind a bush. Shiran had her hand on her friend's back and was reassuring her in Hebrew. The girl took two deep breaths, pitched forward and puked.

"Jesus. Is she gonna be okay?" I asked.

Shiran looked up at me and smiled. "She will be fine," she said.

Once her friend had passed out, Shiran and I got to chatting. She was more engaged this time.

"What can you tell me about California?" she asked. "As you know it is my big dream to go there."

My eyes lit up. I knew the weight being from Cali carried with broads abroad from my cousin Dom. He always told me the same story about it in the same cosmopolitan voice every Christmas day at my *Tío's* place.

"So this guy Rolf and I are in Dubrovnik," he'd always start off. "We're at a café in the old town having our Perriers when these two fine-lookin' women come swaggering by. They're both Italians with curly hair and big boobs. We make eye contact with them and they walk up to our table."

At this point, Dom would usually stop to cross his legs and take a hit of Merlot.

Cue my line. "So what happened?"

"Well, they ask us both where we were from, and Rolf gets all smiley and arrogant. He sits up in his chair, puffs his chest out like Popeye and goes, 'I'm from Belgium.' The ladies are just like *whatever* and then turn to me and ask me where I'm from. Naturally, I sit back all cool and hit 'em with the news: *California*. You should have seen their pretty faces, Johann. They wanted to fuck me right there at the table. Mind you I had a ménage with 'em later on at the hostel. Rolf wasn't too happy about that at three o'clock in the morning, haha."

Images of greasing Shiran on a silver throne backstroked through my mind. But before I had a chance to open my mouth and seal it, a crew of drunken Israelis came roaring up on their bikes. They grabbed Shiran and her snoring friend and threw them on their rear seats.

"You need ride too?" they asked me, laughing.

"Yeah. Where are you guys going?"

"Riverside Café to eat. Don't worry, we'll come back for you."

"Okay." I waited at a table outside the club. After an hour, I stumbled home, feeling like a swamp toad with a scabby asshole.


All my efforts to cajole an Israeli girl into sleeping with me had failed utterly. I was in need of a female companion, even if it meant settling for one with whom my relationship was strictly platonic. When I called Lhamu the next morning, she seemed willing, almost mildly excited to meet up with me.

"I know right where to take you," she said.

We met up in downtown Manali at noon. She was wearing tight jeans and a black tank top. Her gold-flecked hair was pulled back into a delicate ponytail.

"You look nice," I said. She smiled thinly and said the same of me.

"So where are we going?" I asked.

"Have you seen Hidimbi Devi Temple?"

"Yeah, it was the first thing I saw."

"Well, you have not seen it like I will show you." That odd electric pulse spidered up the walls of my chest. I clipped its legs and asked Lhamu about herself.

"Well, as you know I'm Tibetan," she said. "So much of my life concerns my people."

"How so?" I asked.

"Everything pretty much. Since almost fifty years our government is being run from Dharamsala because of the Dali Lama was kicked out of Tibet. Now, they take care of all Tibetan people around India. Our living quarters, school placement, healthcare, culture events, everything is provided from them. Even our shop here in Manali, they help us with building that."

"Are most Tibetan exiles in Himachal Pradesh?"

"Many, but in the winter, we go to Rajasthan to work. There are many Tibetan shops in Jodhpur where my family had a shop."

"Had?" I asked.

She looked down at the ground. "Yes, last year a horrible fire burn many Tibetan shops in Jodhpur, including ours. Nobody know what cause it."

I assumed it was a hate crime but didn't want to push the issue.

"And what about you?" she asked. "Will you tell me about yourself?"

"Sure," I said.

What I assumed was going to be a casual chat about my likes and dislikes quickly devolved into an all-out interrogation where I was the fettered spook, and she was the fat-faced Russian crime boss with a hot poker to my naked genitals. She grilled me about practically everything: marital status, drug and alcohol use, past girlfriends, living habits, work ethic, morals, family values—the works. Whenever she got a response she didn't approve of, she wasn't shy about flashing a hairy eye. When the grueling interview finally ended, I felt like a house of cards Rosanne Barr had just plopped her fat ass on.

Luckily, we were just arriving at the temple. There were scores of Kullu villagers and Tibetans all gathered outside the entrance.

"It's way more crowded than it was before," I remarked.

"This because of the festival soon," she said. "People are coming to pray to the one who protects our mountains."

As each person entered the inverted beehive, a bearded Hindu priest or Brahmin dressed in a flowing white robe dotted the center of their foreheads with a finger full of red paste he picked from a golden bowl. It was like nothing I had ever seen.

"What's with the red stuff?" I asked.

"He is giving them a *tilaka*," she said.[9] "He puts it on their mind's eye so it may open when they pray to Hidimbi Devi."

I stepped up to the threshold of the temple and faced the Brahmin. He looked directly into my eyes and smiled. I smiled back awkwardly. I figured his change in character was motivated by my being the only foreigner come to pray.

"You have it," he said.

"Have what?" I asked.

He fired his finger delicately against my forehead then stood back. Like a tulip after a rainstorm, the wrinkles in my frontal lobes began to bloom. I was dizzy and disoriented. When my lobes locked into place, my mind buzzed. Everything around me—the candles, the smoke, the darkness, the rocks, the moss—took on a lucid hue. I could sense strange energies pouring off my environs and fusing with my inner core.

With jittering eyeballs, I thanked the Brahmin and moved deeper into the temple. Those prostrated in front of Hidimbi's maw made a space for me to pray. Lhamu, freshly dotted, knelt next to me.

"What do I pray to her for?" I whispered.

"Something close to your heart," she said.

I closed my eyes and reflected. My sense of self immediately

---

[9] A *tilaka* is a mark, usually worn on the forehead by Hindus during rites of passage or religious ceremonies.

dribbled downwards. There was chaos in blue rings, faces, and names I couldn't pronounce. I clawed deeper and deeper, ripping away at years of flesh, repression, and anger. When I reached the horizon, the glow of it nearly burnt my eyes from their sockets. I had to shield my face till it lessened and could be read. The words were enigmatic but very real. They told me what I told my cupped hands.

I called Lhamu the very next day. To my delight, she was willing to come out with me again.

"We will take the bus to Solang Valley," she said.

On the ride there, she didn't talk much. She just kept brushing her black hair and staring out the window. I hoped she was working up the guts to kiss me. When we arrived at Solang Valley I saw that at least the setting for a kiss was appropriate. The icy mountains and the forested hillsides were bathed in silky light. We picked a spot on a hilltop with a panoramic view. Two adjacent stumps provided the perfect seating arrangement.

"Do you know what that is?" Lhamu asked, pointing. Her finger directed my eyes to a river spilling through a space between two boulders. The answer seemed obvious.

"It's a waterfall," I said.

"Wrong. It's not just a waterfall. According to legend, it is Hidimbi's tears that she started to cry when Prince Bhīma left her. She's still crying for him."

My heart clicked. I leaned in and tried to kiss her. I got just up to her lips. Her face melted sadly, and she turned away. I recoiled back into myself and stood up. I snapped photos and rambled on about nothing. She joined me eagerly. We spent our day together without mention of the incident.

In the evening, we parted on cordial terms. I promised I'd call her again and went back to my room. Mason had left a note there telling me he was at the doctor's getting his throat checked. I finally had a bit of time to myself to think. As I sat there on the balcony staring at the mountains, I fell into the deepest hole. It felt like my soul had stepped into an elevator that was plummeting faster and faster toward the center of the earth. My eyes went green and my mouth hung open. My fingers unfurled like dying petals.

I perked up a shred when Mason returned. The doctor had given him some medicine for his throat, and he was already feeling better. He even had ideas about going to Kim and Theo's.

"They invited us to sauce if you wanna roll," he said.

"Sounds ait," I said.

We cut at ten with a couple bottles of Old Monk. The air outside was smooth and the moon was bulging in the sky like a ripened peach. Theo was already getting his fix when we arrived. He was sprawled out on the floor with rum to his lips and spirals in his eyes.

"You're not gonna believe this, mates," he exclaimed.

"What is it?" I asked.

He sat us down hurriedly and poured us drinks. Once we'd sipped them, he broke the news.

"It's tonight," he said, fanning his hands.

"That it is," Mason seconded.

"No mates, I mean it's bloody tonight. The rave, the fucking full moon rave!"

My throat tightened and my eyes swole. I could feel my testicles crackling in their sack.

"It's tonight?"

"Yes, mate. Tonight." Mason got a look like, What are you kiddies blabbin' about? He took to chopping down fantasy in classic fashion.

"How do you know this isn't just another one of those bullshit mock raves the DJs talk about just to throw off the cops?"

"Oh mate, you gotta trust me," Theo said. "I told you I know these guys."

"Yeah, but how do you know it's for sure?"

"I do because I have faith . . . and because they paid off the cops."

"See, now that I can believe," Mason said, chuckling.

The promise of a full moon rave now ballooned in our hearts like the full moon itself.

"So where exactly are they gonna have it?" I asked Theo.

He flashed me a bag of crooked teeth.

"That's the beauty of it," he said. "It's not gonna be in some abandoned warehouse or shitty trance club. Oh no. These DJs got something extra special picked out this time. See, this time they're gonna have it . . ." He retracted as our ears grew. When they were wide as houses, he laughed. "Naaaaah," he said. "I'm gonna keep it a surprise for you gentlemen. Let's just get thoroughly pissed instead."

When the witching hour crawled up our backs and whispered in our ears, we poured up boozy concoctions and kicked the door open. A haze umphed up from the ground and expanded like a phantom's hand against the dirt path. There were three fingers to its palm. One pointed into town, one pointed to the hotel, and one shot left into a thicket of screaming blackness.

"Which way do we go?" I asked.

"Which way ya think, mate?" Theo said.

We cut to the left where the path grew rocky and twisted. Shadows flitted back and forth, giggling at their fingertips and looking up at us with wild eyes. We took swigs of our potent mixture and let the wind around us peel off our inhibitions. Once our skin was good and tender, the face of the moon came peeking out from behind the black pagoda tops of the forest and soaked our bodies in ghostly oils. There was a plusssshhhh and then a sting. I could feel the moonlight creeping into my pores, fusing with my cells and restructuring my makeup. When the process was complete, I was manic—a lunar beast feverishly sniffing out trance beats from the dark hills. At first, what I detected was faint, like the bump of a pulse through leather. I let it hook me with its promise and went crashing down the path in a rage, the others behind me, swirling and drinking and ejecting shouts into the bosom of the night. We came to a corner in a flurry where two dead-faced cops were stationed. We greased their palms with 200 rupes a pop and pushed on. The ground beneath our feet immediately warped and broke out into a slope of ashen rocks. Its dance led us downward to where the cliff faces crumbled and the earth was a tree-lined stage.

"This is it," Theo shouted.

The candlelit womb of boulders was teaming with night-crazed freaks, pumping their fists in the air and screaming for release. Surrounding them were half a dozen trucks with open backs. Some were equipped with fridge-sized speakers blasting techno beats into the maw; others had lit countertops with skinny smiling Indians offering shrums, pot, poppers n' booze.

The four of us tossed our arms skyward and went ululating Indian-brave-styly into the frenetic eye. We were engulfed by sweaty limbs spinning and satanic faces grinning. I was charged, even enraged. My hands took on spirits of their own and tore off my shirt and ripped out my hair-tie. With skin gleaming blue and teeth clenched, I cut into a tornado that stretched out across the eons. When my whirling finally came to a still, I was separate from the crowd and facing the mountain.

At first, I only saw darkness. Then a hazy figure entered my view. I felt a rash of goosebumps swell up against my naked back. The figure moved toward me, gaining clarity with every step. It stopped right in front of me and materialized. It was a pale-skinned woman with black curls and periwinkle eyes. Her dress was a jagged slice of night and her fingers were dipped in red. She blinked softly, and my bones unhinged.

"What's your name?" I asked.

She leaned in and took my hand. The second her skin touched mine, a rush of warmth suffused my body. My feet tingled and my limbs lightened. When my last toe kissed off, she said, "I'll tell you for a dance."

In a delicate corkscrew, the two of us floated upwards. We went past the treetops and mist, past the wispy clouds streaking the sky. The fact that I was hundreds of feet from the earth made little difference. All I could concentrate on was this woman's eyes. They were full and slanted like a tiger's. Hunks of tear-blue jewels dotted each of their centers. The more I looked into them, the more I was pulled from the shackles of my own flesh. I danced with her till my skin went gray.

A century of waltzing passed. She pulled me in closer as our silhouettes cut up into the moon's glowing ring. I looked down and she looked up. My arms were around her waist, and hers around my shoulders.

"Will you tell me your name now?" I asked. She dotted her mouth and shrugged to one side.

"You already know it," she whispered.

When our lips touched there was a blinding flash. I was ripped from the cradle of time and sent tumbling through a wormhole in the sea. Leagues of watery images swam past my stricken face. I saw everything that had shaped me up to that point.

When I came to, I was the size of a skittle with a bowl cut and a flannel. My Mexican grandfather Papito was looking down at me with tender eyes. A smile stretched across his weathered face. I smiled back then turned to the night. It was a churning black ocean with Stardust for froth. Bobbing in its midst was a full, crystalline moon, twinkling at the edges. My eyes grew wide and my smile grew wider. I shot a tiny finger toward it and cried, *"Mira la luna."* Upon uttering this, my two halves fused. My woman had told me her name.

With it still ringing in my ears, I was ripped back into the sky and flown into her embrace. I was brimming with happiness.

"Your name is Mona," I said.

She smiled and let go of me. Her home was pulling her away, and I was losing my ability to float. When she was just a speck in the distance, I heard her cry out in a foreign tongue. Her words were the same I'd heard in Angkor: *Liker ade peste o bengypen.*

I drifted down, back into the sea of ravers spilled out across rocks. No longer were they twisting or tumbling; the effects of the pills and booze had long since worn off. The only thing that kept them from crashing was the promise of the sunrise. The sky was already a heady shade of cornflower blue. I got on my knees and upturned my palms. Just as I closed my eyes, I saw a wedge of gold poke up from behind a chip in the ridge. I envisioned the sun's brilliant arms stretching out across the valley. When their warm fingers struck my face, the cheer of a thousand maniacs filled my ears.

"That shit was *un*-baumish," Mason said, as we stumbled back to the hotel.

We were both grinning and feeling good. The words flowed freely between us.

"You blow up with any nahs?" I asked.

"You didn't see me?"

"Uh, no."

"I was poppin' off with lil' ney ney half the night. She was fuckin' *un*-nah. Hella long golden hair, crown of flowers, baumish fritties, white summer dress. She had these crazy deep blue eyes."

My heart skipped. "What kinda blue?" I asked.

"Like suck your fuckin' soul blue."

"Did you get her name?"

"Ooofff. She told it to me, but I forgot it right off cuz I was too D. I was gonna chuck with her on the rocks after n' loll n' ask her again, but she skunted before I had the chance."

I'd have chatted with Mason further, but I was far too fucked. My lips were cracked, my eyes were red, and my hair was a scraggly mess. I had a kink in my left knee and was hobbling up the hostel steps like a cartoon crook with a ball and chain clamped to his heel. As I pushed our door open, my knees buckled. The second I hit the sheets, I clicked off.

Mason and I were bedridden for a full 48 hours. When we finally pried ourselves from the room, we found the Israelis cutting *en masse* to Kasol. We bid them adieu and thanked them for a baumish time. Then the question was what to do next. Both Mason and I had the same flight leaving out of Delhi for London in three days. We decided that since Indian buses are extremely unreliable, it would be best if we left two days in advance instead of one. This meant we had to split by the morrow. Mason was still feeling "fuckin' chuck" and wanted to chill, but I wanted to use my last day to say late to my Manali peeps.

During my little tour, I said goodbye to all the people that had defined my stay. I visited Kung from the Riverside, Dinesh, Chittesh, and Rajesh, our guides, Sylus the jeweler, and even Gumtha from the Tourist Inn. All of them greeted me with smiles and sent me off with a handshake or a hug. When I'd finished all my rounds, I paid a final visit to Lhamu. She was closing up shop as business was slow. I startled her with a hand on the shoulder.

"Johann, you scare me," she said.

"Nah, I'm not falling for that crap," I said.

She smiled slyly and asked me why I'd come. I told her I was leaving the next day and she looked genuinely upset.

"Will you ever come back to Manali to visit me?" she asked.

"Sure. I'm always bouncing around the globe."

She gave me an incredulous look and pulled out a pen and pad. She wrote me her address and email and handed it to me.

"You are welcome to stay with me at my home any time," she said.

I didn't know what else to do but thank her and write down my info. As I handed it to her, she looked me in the eyes and said, "Go with God." I told her I would.

On my way back to the hostel, I stopped at an internet café. It had been weeks since I'd last checked my email, and my connection to home was slowly fading. There was an overload of messages from my mother warning me not to do such-and-such and scolding me for not having written or called. I filtered through the kaka and sent her back a brief email telling her I was okay.

From my father, I had only one message. It read like a fortune cookie: "Hope all is well out there. Best, Dad."

Besides messages from back home, I had received a message marked URGENT from the Peace Corps. I opened it expecting, even hoping, that I'd been dropped from their placement list. It was a short message. It read: "We've started the selection process for your country of service. You'll depart by late September." The reality of this hit me like a mallet to the groin. I'd be out before fall for almost two and a half years.

I walked back to the hotel hoping Mason was there and available for a chat. I found him on the terrace puffing charas from a long, marble cock. His droopy red eyes read "Too stoned to talk." He mumbled something about Kim and Theo's for dinner, then slipped off into nothingness. I decided just to chuck and say fuck it. I crawled into bed and passed out.

A couple hours later, I awoke to the squeaking of mattress springs. I opened my eyes and saw Mason sitting at the edge of the bed. He was staring at the wall, grinning oddly. It looked like someone had taken a melon-baller to his brain.

"You aright, gaht?" I asked him. He didn't respond. I sat up and crinkled my brow. "Mason, are you alright?"

He arched his back like a walrus and poofed out an "Ark." Then he tumbled headfirst over the bed-line. I heard a violent smack. Then came cooing and gurgling.

"Jesus Christ," I screamed. I ran over to where he had fallen. He was on the concrete, twisted at the neck with a pool of puke and blood fanning out from his cheek. I lifted him from the stringy grip of his fluids and sat him back up on the bed. His eyes were black dots, and his face was bedsheet white.

"Mason, Mason," I shouted. "Can you hear me, gaht?"

He blinked a few times then recoiled in shock.

"Wha happah?" he asked, lifting a hand to his bloody lips and nose.

"You fuckin' gottem again, dude," I said.

Mason had a history blacking out from drug abuse. Two years prior, at the top of a waterfall in the Costa Rican jungle, he had smoked an assload of pot with Tim and had had a violent seizure right there on the rocks. He was out for ten minutes and even stopped breathing. Tim was only able to resuscitate him with handful after handful of cold water.

Thankfully, I was able to bring him back with only a few shouts.

"We're gonna chill here tonight," I told him after his eyes had stopped wobbling. "Fuck Kim n' Theo's."

He nodded and hobbled to the bathroom. After he finished washing up, he came over and chilled next to me on the bed.

"Ya know you really passed my nerves treats," I told him. "You need to choo oot on all the loll."

He looked down at his thumbs and frowned.

"I know man. I sometimes gettem with that," he said. "I've just been feelin' garnk lately cuz my stomach n' throat've been hookin' 'em."

"And that's why you've been lollin' n' skinkin' so much? Fuckin' *baaad.*"

He puffed through his nose. "Well there's other reasons too," he said.

"Which are?"

"Well, that nahs have been payin' *maaad* attention to me lately. Ever since Oh, I've been havin' tight luck with that."

"Least ya had her," I said.

"Yeah, but even with her, shit was coo cuz you guys, especially *you* Felm, were *coooo* about her blowin' up with us. I know lil' cheatie acted sick sometimes but eeff, you guys fuckin' had to be bitchin' like that n' hella dis her n' distrust her n' shit."

I thought for a moment. I decided a belated apology was in order.

"Sorry, gaht," I said. "I'd say it to Oh, too, but I'm prolly gonna fuckin' see her again."

"'Anks, ga'. Still means somethin'."

Mason proceeded to tell me the story of Oh's life; a saga of hardships that included rape, drug use, domestic abuse, and teen pregnancy. I was very moved. And what with Takka being in the same distant country, I could relate to my buddy's plight more than ever.

"I miss my lil' Thai nah too," I said.

Mason nodded with closed lips. His eyes were vibrating with tears.

"This is always the story with us Chucks," he said. "Even if we do nah out, we always skunt off n' leave 'em broken n' bleeding. Not to say that's not baumish in some respects, but let's face it Felm, we might just gettem in life when it comes to ever having what our parents have."

"Yeah," I said. Just then the thought of Mona popped into my head. I was gonna kick her back down but figured, Fuck it, why not try n' tell the guy?

"This shit's gonna sound *un*-weird," I said. "But ooff dude, I gotta let it out."

Mason raised his bushy orange eyebrows and looked over at me. His mug was a mix of sarcasm and wonder.

"What is it, gaht?" he asked.

"Nah," I said, retracting. "You're just gonna think I'm a *sane* fuckin' man."

"Felm, I arredy think you're a *sane* fuckin' man. Anything ya tell me's gonna make a damn bit'a difference."

His beard had a point. I took a deep breath and let it fly.

"I think I may have seen something at the rave," I said.

"Huh?"

"I mean I did. I did see something at the rave."

"So did I," Mason said, chuckling. "Hella fools gettin' sobe and actin' phat."

"No man, I mean I saw someone. Some *chick*."

"O . . . kay? And?"

"Well ooff, she kinda gave me the impression that she was a goddess."

"Felm?" he said, trying to pinch a smile off his lips. "Did you, I dunno, sauce any shrums before this chick came rollin' up? You know how cool you can get when that shit's in ya."

"Duly noted," I said. "But there were no shrums involved. I'm seezly, Mayt'n. I really fuckin' saw this chick. She was this pale queen with curly black hair n' blue eyes. I was bein' all Felmania-ish and goin' nuts and dancin', n' when I got separated from the crowd that's when she came up. I was fuckin' stunned. I thought I was seein' things but when she spoke, I knew I fuckin' *was*. I had even seen this chick before. You can even ask Sebastian cuz he saw her too at the market here dayz back."

Mason laughed. "Ait, Felm. I believe ya, choo oot. Just tell me what happened."

I told Mason the story of Mona, how we danced, how we kissed, how I realized her name. I thought he was gonna laugh at me, but he just sat there dumbfounded.

"What is it?" I asked.

I waited a full minute. Mason rubbed his eyes and turned to me.

"You know that nah I told you I was dancing with at the rave with the flowers in her hair?" he said.

"Yeah?"

"Well guess what I just remembered her fuckin' name was?"

# BACK IN DELHI

Delhi hit us like a jackhammer to the face. All at once, its torrent of cows, horns, smog, rickshaws, rot, filth, fumes, shacks, beggars, bombs, temples, tombs, and fuck-all-crazy, came jutting into our grills and hacking apart our eyeballs, ears, and noses with the feverish pulse of a cleaver-wielding lunatic on a full moon night. Our only defense was to cough and choke till our lungs sputtered into obeisance and our eyes took on perma-squints. We slid into the nasty streets and hailed a rickshaw to Main Bazaar. Our destination was where our maddening trip had pretty much started: The good ol' Rama.

By the time we got there, we were exhausted. We crapped out in our room for a few good hours, then planned our evening. Mason had his heart set on a final stroll. I decided to hit the roof and see who I might run into. There were a few chicks hanging around up there, but nothing worth gawking at. I sat down and ordered a Sprite to kill time.

"You've grown a bit," a voice said.

Startled, I turned toward the edge of the terrace where the voice had floated from. Sitting at the only table there was our guru, basking in all his shiny bald glory.

"Mace," I cried. "Didn't think I'd run into you again, man."

He grew a thin smile and stirred his cup of tea. It seemed he hadn't moved from his little perch since we'd left.

"I told you I'd see you later," he said.

"Well fuck. Mind if I join you?" I asked.

"I can move over there," he said.

He lifted himself from his seat and glided over. The steam curling up from his tea made his eyes widen.

"So how have you been?" he asked, sitting down.

"Cool. You were right, this place fuckin' carved me up. I've never seen so much insane and beautiful shit."

"Yeah? How did your other buddies take it all?"

"Mixed bag really. Tim, that skinny-ass dude, I know he loved it cuz the fucker practically looked Indian by the time he left. Fool got tanned as hell. And Sebastian, well, he fuckin' loved it here, too, cuz people treated him like a damn celebrity. He's prolly back at home right now telling all his dickhead friends how he was a god over here, haha. And Mason, man, I know he loved it cuz he just bought up a bunch of shit and was able to rough it in the hills like he always does. Plus, he was able to get down and super spiritual and do a ton of yoga and charas and all that crap. He got sick, but whatever, we all got fuckin' sick. That's just part of the nature of this place. It takes a lot, but it gives a lot in return.

"So yeah, I'm not worried about any of those guys. They loved India, you know? Really, the only one I'm worried about is Bert. I mean the guy's a fuckin' homebody. He acts tough and all cocky, and I know he loves traveling or he wouldn't do it, but underneath I get the feeling he's scared shitless. Especially of these kinda places."

"I got that impression too," Mace said.

"Really?"

"Yeah, he just seemed out of his element here. Where did you say he's gone to now?"

"He's in Europe with Tim. We're meeting up with them in a couple days and doing the East and the Mediterranean, like Bosnia, Croatia, Greece, all that."

"Those places will be good for him. The people are passionate and inviting, the weather is nice, and the culture is different but not so different that he'll be put on the defense. I have a strong feeling that you'll see him come into his own on this trip while he's in Europe. And that, in turn, will make all of you come together as a group."

"You really think so, man?"

Mace smiled. "I know so."

After Mace melted into the walls, I played pool till midnight with some sweet-lipped Italian, then went back to her apartment. I spent four solid hours there pounding shots with her Irish and Israeli roommates, watching *The Others,* and explaining the intricacies of Hinduism and Indian history as I had learned them. At around four-thirty, I walked back to The Rama through the shadows and the cows, all drag, without so much as a stink on my fingers. It was a bummer, but the call of the spirits brightened me up.

When our crap was packed and our nuts were jacked, we stepped outside for a rickshaw and tipped a final two at The Rama. We'd miss the place, but bigger things were screaming our names. On the ride to the airport, I was juiced as our smiley-eyed driver had it in him to sing his lungs out to a few high-pitched Indian ditties. He cranked the volume to the roof, and we locked shoulders and went wailing down the disheveled streets of Delhi with Mason laughing at our backs. We were all high battery charged when we got to the airport. I stepped off the rickie with a glow in my fingertips and slipped my pal a bill. He flashed me a single brown tooth and sped off with visible music coiling from his open windows. Mason and I chuckled and slung our packs over our shoulders.

Now, in the airport, we could almost taste the pull of far-off places. It was strange to be overcome by such excitement for foreign lands when we were already in the weirdest of the weird. I tried to keep this in mind here, but nothing seemed *Indian* anymore. All the people looked mixed and blurred. All the screens bore spots unheard: Istanbul, Abu Dhabi, Bangkok, London, Berlin, Moscow, Beijing, Tokyo, Masqat.

Masqat? Fuck, going to that palm-studded outpost in the middle of the big desert made Tirana stink of Toronto. Plus, the gate for departure there was right next to ours. What would a little excursion to Oman hurt anyway? Mason and I had a moment where we seriously considered doing something drastic. Our motto *du jour* was, "We'd make 'em pop if we grooged to Masqat." Nothing but a heightened sense of earthly love came from it though. We were free to take off anywhere, but poor little Kip would be left holding the big red bag in Britain if we did.

"Let's just bunt to London," I said. "The Chucks are waiting."

# LONDON

Mason and I stepped off the plane all coke-jittered and shifty-eyed. We had three things on our minds: get through customs, find Kip, and sauce. The first was easy enough as we were Westerners and had nothing to declare. I felt bad for the Indians, especially the Muslim ones, who were "randomly" selected to have their bags checked.

Once through, we went to the outer terminal where we knew Kip would be waiting. The poor bastard had come in nine hours before us. We found him sitting on a steel bench next to his perfectly proportioned pack. His specs were tweaked, and he was staring at the fluorescent bulbs like an idiot savant with a troubling thought glued to his brainstem.

"What's up, Kip?" I yelled, shocking him out of reflection.

"Y-you guys blow up in India?"

"Fuck yeah, gaht."

He flashed us a smile that made us shield our eyes. His teeth had been bright before the trip, but now they were glittering like a Tiffany's bracelet in the sun.

"Damn Kip, you get those babies whitened *again?*" I said.

"Shoo," he said. "Nice n' baumish for the nahs here."

We stepped outside after a pull on the Underground. The number of bitches struttin' up n' down the sidewalks of Leicester Square made our heads bobble. I thought my noggin might go sailing off my neck and spin circles across the street with bug eyes just to catch a peek up one of their dresses. This is when I realized we weren't in Kullu anymore. And it wasn't just the ass that did it. London had clean streets, orderly traffic, gray skies, dead trees, crisp air, and dogs instead of cows. The only whisper of India was the few curry joints run by blue-turbaned Sikhs peppering the boulevards. You'd think we might have gotten nostalgic and gone for a plate of vindaloo, but nope. We headed straight for the most egregiously Western spot on the whole damn planet: Mickey D's.

Once the greasy meat in our stomachs was awash in a sea of sparkling sugar water, we focused on hostels. We hit a place in Soho called Piccadilly Backpackers, but it was all booked up. On word from the clerk, we headed to Bayswater. After an hour of stomping around, we found a joint called The Hyde Park. They had three dorm spots for twenty quid a pop. We checked them out, but the beds were dinky as fuck and stacked on top of one another like sardine cans in a crate. We shrugged our shoulders and put down the cash. The second we did, the cheap Scot in Mason's soul chomped on his wooden pipe and went kickin' up a smoky ol' storm.

"Our plane for Berlin boards at 7 a.m.," he said. "It's 10 p.m. now, so we're only gonna be here for like five fuckin' hours. We might as well say house n' chuck down at the bar."

Kip and I couldn't argue with the man's logic. We agreed to ask for our money back. Luckily, the guy at the front desk was a pal and gave it to us on the condition that we ordered drinks from the bar. We assured him that wouldn't be an issue.


"Felm, getcher ass up," Mason barked.

I came to with a stiff neck and crossed eyes. Everything was blurred with slug trails.

"What the fuck?" I said.

"We gotta skunt now. Our bus leaves for the airport hella soon, and there isn't another one for dayz."

My watch read 2:50 a.m. We had ten minutes to make it to the bus station.

We hit the black streets and shuffled as fast as our withered legs would carry us. We made it to the station with minutes to spare. Our bus rolled us out to London Stanstead. We schlepped inside and found our flight. The Brianair counter was just opening. The lady who took our tickets was a pudgy, chicken-skinned bitch squeezed into a blue airline suit.

"Tickets and passports," she said.

We handed them over. She perused everything with a scrutinizing eyeball. "We're weighing your bags as well," she said.

We threw our bags on the scale. Amazingly, none of them was over the two-ounce weight limit. We breathed a sigh of relief.

Chicken-skin lady snapped her fingers. "Open all your bags and show me their contents," she said.

I wanted to club her over the head and boil her up in a stew. She made us take out every single item, including our sweaty boxers, so she could inspect them personally. I thought Mason was going to throw a clot when she started fiddling with his prayer bowls. Lucky for her, she put them back before his beard changed color.

When the nightmare was over, we stood in a horrendously long line at the security check. It was 6:30 a.m. when we finally got to our gate. We had half an hour to chill before we boarded. Like we usually do in otherwise boring situations, Kip and I sat together in a corner, people-watching and making smartass remarks. For the first bit, we didn't really see anyone worth ripping on; just a few old fucks with walkers and Gilligan hats mumbling to one another and drooling. Then through the front hall came a dude that was all swag. He was wrapped in a gold jumpsuit with the image of an Uzi emblazoned on the front. His fluttering fingers were dripping with gumball machine rings. He had a do-rag, a goatee, and a toothpick shooting out the corner of his mouth.

"Look at fuckin' Ali G up there," I said.

Kip burst into a childish cackle. I hushed him before he blew our cover.

Ali licked his lips and ran his palms across his do-rag as if it were his hair. Then he spotted a chick nearby. She was all ass with wavy black hair and a button nose. She held a tiny cellphone to her ear.

"Watch ol' Ali fuckin' gettem with this nah," I whispered to Kip.

Ali cracked his neck and jutted his chin. He swished up to her and shot off a mouthful of gold-rimmed teeth. Little Miss Cellphone faced him with butterfly eyes and gave him the fuck-me smile. The blood rocketed up into my cheeks.

"This is horseshit." I said.

Kip started weeping and clapping his hands awkwardly. "I . . . I guess *you* hooked 'em," he cried.

"Oh, fuck that. If that faggot can pull that nah, I can pull one too."

"Haha. Well, it looks like ya might get yer chance."

Kip pointed to a girl who was walking through the front hall. She was a six-foot blonde with long legs and a pair of eyes so blue they could have skinned the paint off a Lambo. She tick-tocked passed us in her designer boots and took a seat across the way. It took me a good minute, but I huffed up the courage to go after her.

"Wish me luck," I said, pulling my beanie over my head.

I strode up to my lady with a knot in my throat. She was sitting on the floor with her knees up and her claves X'd. I squatted down in front of her and leaned in. She looked up at me and smiled.

"Those for me?" I asked, pointing to her roses.

She blushed. "Haha. No. They are for my mother. She is very sick."

"I'm sorry to hear that. My name is Johann. What yours?"

"Zefiryn, but you may just call me Zefir."

Judging by her hair color and her vaguely Slavic accent, I assumed Zefir was from Poland. I chanced the city.

"You from Poznan?" I asked.

"No, I am from Szczecin. But very good you guess I am from Poland. How you know this?"

"Your accent. I'm good with languages."

"Really? Well, then tell me, can you spell Szczecin?"

My anus tightened. "Um, sure. It's S H. I mean, S Z."

"Haha, I'm just to joke with you," she said.

My anus loosened. I heard giggling from nearby, but I shrugged it off.

"So what were you doing in London?" I asked.

"Oh, just shopping. How about you?"

"I'm on vacation. I was just in India and Thailand with my buddies, and now I'm on my way to Eastern Europe with them."

"Wow."

I traced Zefir out an imaginary map of our travels. She seemed more intent on staring at my fingers.

"Where do you buy all these rings?"

"Oh, all over," I said, fanning my fingers. As I named off each ring's country of origin, I heard that infernal giggling again. When I shot my eyes over to catch the culprit, it abruptly stopped.

"Wow. You are such an adventure man," Zefir cooed.

"Haha. Thanks. And speaking of, if you ever come to America, I can *bravely* show you around."

"Oh, are you from New York?"

"Well, no, but—"

"Then L.A. Oh, Johann, I *love* L.A. So much shopping and nice clothes. Will you take me around your great city?"

Anyone who knows me knows that I think Los Angeles is a concrete abomination that should be stricken from the map in a furious blaze of hellfire. But, since I'm a spineless worm and have no real morals or ethics I adhere to, I just went ahead and let this chick think I was from that sun-beaten megalopolis of fake trees, fake tits, and even faker people.

"Yeah, sure," I said. "I'll take ya around. Only if you do me one favor."

"And what is this?"

"Let me sit next to ya on the plane."

Since the plane was half-empty, I didn't have any problems

grabbing a seat next to her. Once we were settled in, we continued our conversation.

"So you're going to see your mom, huh?" I asked.

"Yes, she is waiting for me now."

"How sick is she?"

"Very. She will die soon." Zefir said this so matter-of-factly it stunned me blank.

"Aren't you . . . upset?"

"No."

"Jesus, why?"

"Oh," she said, yawning. "Because I can communicate with the dead."

I didn't know whether to piss myself laughing or just piss myself. I think I did a bit of both.

"You can communicate with the dead?" I repeated slowly.

"Yes. This is how I know mother will never be far from me. When my sister died five years ago, I started my communications with her too. We talk all of time, but sometimes is hard for me to know what she is saying or understand, you know? Johann? You okay?"

My prick was still reeling from having been bonked on the head by my jaw. As it finally came to, so did I.

"Yeah, I'm fine," I said. "In fact, can I tell you a story?"

"Sure."

For the next half hour, I recounted the whole string of events that transpired at the full moon rave in Manali. I even asked Zefir if she knew the meaning of the cryptic phrase Mona had called out to me just before she'd disappeared. Zefir repeated the phrase, *Liker ade peste o bengypen,* out loud a few times just to get a feel for it. On her fifth repetition, her eyes grew wide.

"Yes, I do know this language," she said.

"Well, what is it?"

"It is Romany, the language of Gypsies."

My cock winced.

As our plane was landing, Zefir gave me her info and some words of advice.

"There are many Gypsies all over East Europe," she said. "Find one of them and have them translate this sentence for you."

"Okay," I said. "Can I see you again?"

"Yes, maybe. Give me a call tomorrow."

# BERLIN

"So you gonna nah out with this chick?" Kip asked.

"Ooff. I don't know if I'll ever see her again," I said. "Bitch blew me up though."

"In what way?"

I looked down at him and scratched my head. Kip was a first-time traveler and relative newbie to the group; relaying something as odd as a theophanic hallucination and subsequent conversation on the experience with a self-proclaimed medium might've blown his little brains out the back of his skullcap. I put my hands up and shrugged.

"Eeff. She just cockteased me a bunch," I said. "Anyway, we figure out where we're goin' yet?"

Mason came lumbering up with his bags all hangin' off him and a map of Berlin stretched out in front of his face. His brow was furrowed and his eyes were focused.

"See, we're at Schonefeld Airport, near Brandenburg," he said, stroking his beard. "But pussy-ass Bert n' Tim sent us directions to The Factory Hostel where they're at from Tegel Airport in Reinickendorf cuz that's where they flew into, so their directions fuckin' mean shit. The way I figure it, we basically walk five minutes up to the train station, take it six stops and then transfer to the M6 line; then we go up to the Lansberger Allee station in Prenzlauer Berg district, and we can walk to the hostel from there."

Weeeeew. My head was spinning dreidel circles back and forth across my shoulders. I have the directional sense of a deaf and drunk bat, so it never ceases to amaze me how Mason can sniff out precise directions to even the most obscure locations without breaking a sweat.

With Mason at our front, we stepped into the cool Berlin air and walked to the train station. Everything along the way, from the slate bricks to the tram tracks, to the rows of trees encircling the airport, was clipped and cut and organized in such a fashion that one could almost hear the whirr of precision instruments making it just so. Despite its austerity, I could feel a measured warmth emanating from my environment. It was almost as if all the care that had gone into creating everything had rubbed off and was now filling the air. I pondered this uniquely German paradox as I rode the neural network of trains and lines that Mason had mapped out. I'd have reached a conclusion as to why things were the way they were in Berlin and greater Germany, but a *doner kebap* shop just off our stop snagged my attention. The place was run by a chatty little Turkish man with a Friar Tuck cut and tawny skin. For two euros fifty, he served us up lamb kabobs the size of newborns and ice-cold beers aptly named Berliners. By the end of our meal, we were all ready to chuck. Thankfully, our ginormous, cube-shaped hostel was just outside. We went in, asked the front desk for beds in Bert and Tim's room, took our electric key cards, zipped up the steel elevator, buzzed into our room, tossed our crap to one side, and fell face first on our gleaming white bunks. It was dreams of electric strudel for the next three hours.

I came out of my happy daze to the sounds of key cards clicking. The door burst open and in poured Tim, Bert and, to my surprise and delight, Chuck—the man with a verb, a noun, an adjective, and a whole fuckin' nomadic tribe named after him. I jumped up outta bed and ran to him.

"Nerfy Nerds," I yelled, jiggling his belly. He curled his ugly pink lips at me and slapped my hands away.

"God, get off me," he yelled.

I laughed and looked him over. He was wearing beige jeans that were threadbare at the knees, an A's jacket that was neon green, and a hat of the same team with a mustard stain on the bill that resembled a baby octopus. His dirty blond hair was shooting down at all angles like wild hay. His pudgy cheeks and ears were beet red from walking up the stairs and his fig-shaped nose was flecked with peeling skin. I gave him a few more pokes to the gut just for yucks. His big pupils went from baby blue to "screw you." I told him I was nei nornin and shook his hand. Then I turned my attention to the other Chucks. I thought there might still be tension from the snowball fight and subsequent breakup. Instead, what resonated between us was an all-encompassing sense of camaraderie and testosterone-infused adventure that charged our minds, hearts, and souls like so many watermelons hooked up to trillion-watt electrodes and then slammed headlong with wild blue snakes of fire till they exploded in jagged green and red chunks all the way up to the heavens. We got so ecstatic with grab-ass and recaps that the floor shook and the ceiling hummed. Mona was purring at the nodes of our congealed auras, and I hadn't even uttered a peep.

When the exhilaration had smoothed, a new character came into our midst. He had been taking a dump during our little reunion and had missed the memo.

"Hey, gahts, this is my buddy Kartik," Chuck said.

Kartik was a goofy-looking fucker with big lips, loud eyes, and messy black hair. He wore a wrinkled blue flannel buttoned to the tippy top and khakis I was certain his mother had picked out for him. The second Bert and Tim laid eyes on him, they sighed. They had traveled with him (and Chuck) in Amsterdam, where I assumed he'd been a major pain in their asses. To keep things chill, I offered the guy a handshake. He took my hand, but instead of making a casual inquiry about our trip through India, the first words out of his mouth were, "So guyzz, ven are vee going to blow up thee beecheez?"

His question proved my suspicions correct. Kartik was a monstrous tool.

At the hostel bar, Kartik immediately got to asking us about the beecheez we'd gotten thus far. Everyone responded perfunctorily with short recaps of the little bit of action they'd had. Chuck was the only one of us who'd remained silent.

"Didn't you blow up with any nahs on your little trip before meeting up with us?" I asked him.

He bunched his mouth up and nodded his head. "*Yeaaaah*," he said, sarcastically.

"No, no, no, Chuck my man," Kartik cut in. "Tell them about your little date in Lisbon."

Chuck thinned his lips and rolled up his sleeves. "It's not that big a deal," he said. "I was just on the Lisbon metro, and I noticed this old man sitting across from me. He was hella chuck and leaning over his cane with a big beard n' stuff. He started winking at me and pulling his fist back and forth across his crotch. I gave him a funny look to get him to stop but he just smiled at me and went, "*Punheta, Punheta.*" Then he pointed at my dick."

"What the fuck does punheater mean?" Kip asked.

"It means handjob," Chuck said.

Upon hearing this, Kartik exploded into a cackle that made me want to break a beer bottle over his head. Chuck shrugged it off with a slug of brew and a twist of his ball cap. Like he'd done since we were kids, he only let something irritate him so far. Then he turned on it with lazy-eyed indifference and chilled it out of existence.

After a few more beers, we hit the streets of Berlin. The whole way to the metro, Kartik pranced around us with his fingers in the air, yelling, "Hurry up, my men. The beecheez are vayting. The beecheez are vayting."

We took the train over to Hackescher Markt. Dozens of ladies in calf-lace pumps and glittering miniskirts were strutting up and down the streets. A blonde in a pink two-piece approached us.

"Do you guys have zee time?" she asked.

"Sure, my lady," Kartik panted. "It is eleven thirty exactly."

"Vy, sank you," she said. "Vill you like to come viz me?"

"Affirmative. Vow, I love this country. A girl vill fuck you if you just tell her the time."

The lot of us smirked. Chuck stepped forward and smiled gracefully.

"She's a whore," he said.

"Ha," the hooker spat. "If you sink zat, you can just fuck off."

She trotted away in search of another dumb beau. Kartik was left droopy-eyed and drooling.

We shirked the hoes and slipped into a nearby bar. It was smoky and tacky and filled with dudes. I could see Mason's beard burning.

"This is a major cockfest," he said. "I'm outtie."

Before I had a chance to ask him where he was off to, he vanished in the bar haze. The only thing left to do was drink. We ordered a round and started chatting with the folks around us. One guy—a spiky-haired Lithuanian with a gay face—told us he and some friends were on a pub crawl.

"Can we try to sneak in with you?" I asked.

"Why the hell not?" he said.

His group left shortly thereafter, and we followed them. Outside, there was a burnt-out bar hag in an orange hat whistling and calling everyone to her.

"If you're in my group, come line up and take your shots," she yelled.

We lined up with the others. One by one, she dumped a nasty green concoction down their throats. When it came our turn to drink, she blew her whistle.

"You gentlemen are *not* part of my pub crawl," she said. "I don't give a shit if you follow us, but the free shots'll cost ya five euros a pop."

"Free shots, huh?" Bert said. "We coo."

We decided to follow the group around anyway. Our first stop with them was at a kitschy little dump with cracked leather couches, mouthwash lighting, and a lone disco ball dangling from the ceiling. We walked in with the beers we'd brought from the other bar and sidled up to the counter. Not two seconds in, the weasel-faced bartender snatched my drink up.

"What the fuck?" I said.

He pursed his DSLs at me and scowled. "No outside beers," he said.

I had half a mind to drop my drawers right there and streamline a jet of hot piss across his face. I smirked and paid for another beer, sans tip.

Being near that ass-hat gave me anger pangs. I slid over to a booth and drank by myself. I took a few photos for my own amusement. As I was panning across the bar, Bert came into my viewfinder. He was chatting with some odd couple. They had flabby bodies, scraggly hair and big square glasses. The man leaned in and whispered in Bert's ear. My camera flashed just as Bert was pulling back in disgust. I looked down at my viewfinder and laughed. In the photo, Bert was grimacing like he'd just swallowed a gallon of husky cum.

Bert walked over to me and sat down.

"What was that all about?" I asked him.

"Fuckin' tightness," he said. "I was up at the bar just havin' myself a sneer when that bitchin' Scottish couple started talkin' my ear off. Most of what they were saying was just bullshit. Then for some reason, they started talkin' about how they like to have sex with other fools. I was listening only out of weird curiosity. Then they fuckin' asked me if I wanted to go back to their apartment and have a threesome with them."

I burst out laughing. "Sounds like a night!" I said.

The swingers' bar was now a bust. We cut to look for food. There was a bratwurst stand just across the way. We pimped it for a few cheap weenies and kicked it on the curb. The spot we had chosen was a good little lookout; hookers were walking all up and down the cul-de-sac, fixing their lipstick and bending over into car windows. One hooker approached a Mercedes with her twins out. The driver, who couldn't have been more than nineteen, slipped her a note, ushered her in, and stripped her down. They fogged up his windows quick, fuckin' n' howlin' n' whatnot. At one point, the hooker dragged her hand across the windshield leaving a tiger streak on the glass.

Bert looked over at me. "I wonder what Maytn's up to?" he said. "Eeff," I said.

The hooker screamed in climax. We popped the last of our brats in our mouths and grabbed a tram back. It let us off near our place at 4:30 a.m. All of us were thinking about Mason's disappearance when out of nowhere we spotted the fucker. He was sitting on the fountain outside The Factory, puffing on a smoke with his head between his legs. His beard was mangy and red.

"What the fuck happened to you?" I asked him.

"Ooff," he groaned. "I caved in and got a prosty."

"And?"

"And instead of getting laid, I spent two hundred euros on a cheap room and a handjob that made my dick bleed. Then when I tried to protest, the bitch called the bouncer and he threw me out on the street. And I hadn't even pulled my pants up."

The six of us looked at each other and roared. Mason snubbed his barg out on the fountain and walked away grumbling.


"You gahts know what today is, right?" Tim asked, rustling us up out of a cool slumber.

"Whaaaat ...?"

"It's day 42.5."

Bert reached down into his boxers and scratched his balls. "Does that mean we hafta go out and buy you a pregnancy test or something?" he asked.

"Haha. No," Tim said. "It means we're exactly halfway through the trip."

My face locked into place. "Damn, you're right," I said. A rush of black panic blew through me. It kicked me outta bed feetfirst and planted me on the floor. I put my hands to my hips and let off a monstrous belch. Then I yelled, "You heard the man. Now getcher Chuck asses up and let's blow this city apart."

We split up to cover more ground—Bert, Kip, and I in one group,

Mason and Tim in another, and Chuck and annoying-ass Kartik in a third. My little group hit a bakery first to fuel up. As we slipped out the door, licking our *pfannkuchen*-fingers, a man lumbered up in front of us. He was pudgy and rank. He had lamb chop sideburns, beer-stained pits, and lederhosen hiked so far up his fat ass you could see the bisection of his anus through the leather. He moved in short, drunken steps, stopping every so often to scratch himself or pick his schnoz. I snapped a photo of him just as he was trundling under the eaves of a bridge.

"*Komm*," he grunted. "*Lass mich dich durch meine Stadt führen.*"

He took us down scalpel-cut streets through sheets of wind and fog, past Siemens' steeples and into green fields, where people sat chatting with their backs to Greek museums, fountain lips lapping and addled black chapels—so black, in fact, that their domes grew green, one cross gleaming and the other one beeping—inside these halls run red with money, sad Jesus faces, and chandelier honey, silver bat phantoms stretched up to the ceilings, peelings of gold and death's scepter kneeling, feather to his fingers all tipped n' bleeding, scratching out the masses in so many black ashes, dust, bones, prayers n' pods, slipped up the steps of the dome's façade, up, waaay up till we oohed and aahed, one hundred thousand buildings, it's a bit macabre, how so many good people could become so odd, staring at the skies while they stepped on God. Aw, Lawd. Is that a basement? A dungeon of debasement? A dozen bishops illin' while the villain gets his payment? See, we saw old Christo like a porno prince, seed across his knees made his birdies wince, come to tink of it, I taught I taw a puddy splint, what betta kinna pimp den a foo wit a limp? Shucks, I'm just fuckin' wit ya, so was tha troll, prick took ta skippin' on a Spree line stroll. I asked, "Where we goin'?" "Up ta ol' Humbo. It's a funny kinna place, don't ya three Chucks know?" "Yep, that's the place where the concrete's made, Schiller's on the pillar givin' head for dayz, ta' Goethe, n' Mann, n' maybe ta' Hegel, Steiny shoulda been there but they tossed him a bagel." "Well, Jack. Since ya know, let's hit the road." Two-stepped the *Strasse* to the Dem Deutschen Volke, saw only columns and stairs unfold, sages pointin' straight to a football dome. Next we hit the nexus of the would-be thanks, eighty thousand dead next to Soviet tanks, "pranks" said the Germans, or should I say I, a pond full 'a piss's what caught my eye, dotted at the center with a boy n' his Berliner, "Don't ask 'em, dude, they know what's for dinner." Come to think of it, I felt like I was gettin' thinner, we sauced off a doner then we made for the river, passed angels named Lizzy dipped in gold, Prussian-made mansions next to horrors untold, I mean this place was so bad it made the troll go cold, almost three thousand blocks but over six mil sold. Weeeew! We took ta' runnin' till we hit the wall, East Side G's all they do is scrawl, like we saw trippy shit like we'd sucked on a bong, shucked the manifesto with the white King Kong, I'm talkin' six-pointed stars 'cross a wall of shame, swastikas n' sickles, who the fuck's ta blame? Some rain up in Korea? And don't forget Nikita, Stalin pluggin' leaks to prevent the drain. Brain dead muthafuckas from tha bullets 'a Grepos, Schumann's on the fence, might as well be Aleppo, leaped n' grabbed the West, shoulda grabbed him a vest, tossed it off ta' Geuffory fore they blew out his chest. Buh Bam! N' that was that till we came to the center, chips off the block, you can call me a sinner, a winner, or maybe just a ginner; sippin' a Molotov, "Tear down this wall, Mr. Mikhail Gorbachev. Don't forget to steal a kiss n' click out the light, Brezhy's on the left, but you can sleep on the right. Alright, Erich? Bah! We had enough of that. Let's go troll we feelin' suffer n' suckitback." Skipped across the river till we hit us a bar, Berliner Weisse please, rot or grün or huh? It didn't matter anyway. Our heads were a daze. We shook the troll thanks, then he burst in a haze . . . Poof!

Back at The Factory House, we were dead on our knees. We wanted to catch some Z's, but the others were raring to blow up.

"Lemme just make a phone call first," I said. I went to the payphone and dialed Zefir's number. It rang a few times, and I almost hung up.

"Alo?" she answered, startling me.

"Huh-hey, Zefir. It's Johann, How are you?"

"I am fine. You are still in Berlin?"

"Yeah, I was thinking I'd come out and visit you if you're not too busy with your mom."

"When?"

"This week."

"Oh, I'm sorry. After I see my Mom, I will go on vacation with my husband."

"Husband?"

"Yes, didn't I tell you?

"No."

"Johann?"

"Yeah?"

"Did you find translation for your magic words?"

"No." I laughed. "Not yet."

"Don't worry. This will come. Anyway, if you will like, I am going to Greece alone in six weeks' time. Maybe we can meet then."

"Sure, we might just run into each other. Take care, babe."

When I hung up, I was more confused than ever. There was only one solution to my confusion. I hit the bar like a warrior chief with his dick out. All the Chucks were there pounding drinks amidst a huge crowd of sixteen-year-old girls. I felt guilty when I got chubby.

"So what do we do?" I asked Bert.

He grinned big. "It's not what do *we* do that you have to ask yourself," he said. "It's what would *Mason* do?"

I sprayed beer across the counter. "Haha. What *is* that shameless beardface up to, by the way?"

We looked over and saw him with a brew in his hand, explaining something deep to three wide-eyed preschoolers.

"Hog Man's at it again," I said. "Maybe we should take a hint."

We were up and packed by noon. After a very short goodbye to Kartik, we cut to the station and just made the one o'clock. All of us had a cabin together. We tossed our shit everywhere and laid all over the seats. Twenty minutes into my snooze, Mason started badgering me in slurs.

"Dude, roll to the back with me," he said. "There's some nahs."

Nahs, nahs, nahs. The word was starting to make me sick. I told him to fuck off, but he insisted.

We cruised back to the dining cabin. Chuck and Kip were there playing cards, and Tim and Bert were chatting with two Aussie chicks. I crinkled my nose at them.

"Those pussies arready swooped up," I said.

Mason laughed. "Nahs'r back farther," he said.

I shrugged and continued following him. We entered the next cabin where two girls were sitting alone. The one on the right caught my attention first. She was short, svelte, and tan with a sly smile and big brown eyes. To the left was her friend. She was blond, pale, and dumpy with an upturned nose and mean blue eyes. To my astonishment, Mason picked the snotty-looking blonde. I smiled and sat in front of Big Eyes.

"Hey," I said. "I'm Johann."

"Leddy. Nice to meet ya, man."

"Shit. An American," I said. "Brooklyn?"

"Bronx. Close though. Good job. Where you from?"

"Cali."

"Oh shit. I love L.A."

"Yeah, everybody does. Anyway, what are ya doin' out here?"

"Studying. I was in Barcelona for a year."

"Fuck, no way. I was in Madrid. *¿Hablas Español?*"

"Eh, it's crap. You'd laugh at me."

"I'm already laughin' atcha."

She smiled.

"So the school year's up and yer just travelin' around now?" I asked.

"Yeah, we did Paris, Amsterdam, Berlin. Prague's the last stop."

"Must be fun traveling with ol' Smiley there," I said quietly.

"Haha. Who, Kate?"

"Whatever."

"Aw, she's not so bad, man. I think she just misses the beach."

"From the looks of it, she's never seen one."

"You're mean."

"Yeah, I'm mean. Hey, you drink?"

"C'mon man, I was in Spain for a year."

"Let's get a bottle then."

"Arright."

I got the waiter's attention and he brought a menu. We perused it for a bit. Leddy pointed. "My family emigrated from Hungary in the thirties so I gotta go with the Hungarian red."

"Fuck. Ya read my mind."

The wine went down smooth. In ten minutes, we'd blown through half the bottle. The conversation flowed accordingly.

"So Hungary, huh?" I said. "Is your family Jewish?"

"Yeah. How'd you get that? Am I *that* Jewish?"

"Well, you said they came over in the thirties. I just put two and two together."

"Yeah, they got out before it got real bad."

"Do you speak the language?"

"Nah. My grandparents do, but they never taught it to my folks. They wanted my parents to be *real* Americans and only speak English, which is stupid because we're Jews and we have to learn Hebrew in school. I'm not even sure what the hell a *real* American is anyway. I mean I'm American, but I'm also kind of Hungarian and Jewish. And it's weird cuz I can go anywhere in the world, and when I meet another American, I feel a connection. And when I meet another Jew, even if they're from somewhere else, I feel a connection, but it's a different connection. Does that make me less American? I don't know. You know what I'm talkin' about, right?"

"Kind of. My identity is sorta fragmented like that too. On my father's side, I'm German, but we don't speak German cuz his family came over *dayz* ago, so there goes that connection. And then on my mother's side, we're Mexican, which is already a huge mix, and I speak Spanish, but it's old-ass Spanish that my grandfather from Chihuahua taught me, so when I talk to other Mexicans, they're weirded out by me. Plus, my name is Johann, so that cancels out even the American bit cuz what American—or Mexican for that matter—is named Johann? Shit, even being named Johann in Germany is an anachronism cuz only old farts there carry the name."

"Wow. You must've had no one to connect with when you were a kid."

"Well, almost no one."

I gulped the last of my wine and looked back at the Chucks. All of them were drinking and laughing and rattling off in ROAST. A warm feeling came over me.

"What?" Leddy asked.

"Nah, if I tell you you'll only laugh."

"No, c'mon. I promise I won't."

"Ok, but don't say I didn't warn your ass."

For the next hour, I explained the ways of the traveling Chucks to her in great detail. Some of it furrowed her brow, but most of it she grooved on, especially the part about ROAST.

"I think you've got a baumish little thing goin' with your friends," she said, repeating what I'd taught her. "Damn, if you invented it . . . I mean, what culture out there *isn't* invented? It's all human anyway."

"Yeah, I guess yer right."

"I know I'm right, buddy. Ya gotta keep blowin' up. "

"Haha. Hey, speakin' of . . . check where we are."

# PRAGUE

We got off the train and Leddy and I exchanged emails. I didn't know if I'd see the little squirt again so I threw out a line.

"We're goin' to this place called U Kláštera tonight. It's a brewery that used to be run by Czech monks. Maybe we'll see you there."

"Yeah, maybe. We gotta get to our hostel first so they don't give our rooms away. Anyway, it was nice meetin' ya, Johann. I hope this isn't the last."

"Yeah me too Leddy. Yer aright kid."

She and I skipped the handshake and hugged. It lingered for a bit. Kate cut in. "Let's go already."

Leddy rolled her eyes and threw her giant pack over her shoulder. "I gotta go," she said.

When the two were gone, it was time to find a hostel. We tried calling a few spots from the guidebook, but they were all booked solid. Our only recourse was to use the Tourist Information Center. We found it hidden in a gray corner of the station. There was only one window. Behind it sat a potbellied ogre with stained teeth and zombie eyes. He had a half-chewed cigar wedged into the corner of his mouth. The smoke clouding up from it was so thick I thought it might push the window from its frame.

"Yez?" he croaked.

"Um, we're looking for a hostel. Maybe something like—"

"Yez, yez, I knou dis," he said. "Vat you vant . . . two triple?"

"That's fine," I said.

He picked up the phone and called around. Every time someone answered, he barked at them in razor-bladed Czech. After the sixth call, he looked up and snarled. "Steve's Hostel have opening. You all pay now for four nights or no deal."

"Whadduyoo mean we pay now for four nights?" Mason said.

"I mean, you all pay now, sixteen hundred korun each."

"Fuck that! I'm not paying anything until I see the room."

I said, "Can't we just pay for one night up front and then pay as we go?"

The Ogre considered my offer with a giant frown. Mason piped up again.

"No. I'm not even doing that," he said. "No money till we *see* the room. And I'm sure as shit not paying this guy's commission."

"What?" the Ogre snapped. "I get no commission! I only do favor for you, and you fuck me like little bitch!"

"You haven't seen me fuck you like a lil' bitch yet," Mason said, grinning.

The Ogre withdrew into his cloud of smoke. I prayed he didn't have a gun.

"Dude, quit being a fucking hard ass and let's just pay the guy for one night and go to the damn hostel," I said to Mason.

"Psh, I just don't see why it matters if he gets no commission. Why can't we just go down there and pay ourselves?"

"I think this is cool, dude. Let's just pay and get it over with."

Mason handed me his four hundred korunas and sat on the bench. I gathered up the rest of the cash from the others and paid the Ogre.

"*Děkuji,*" he said. "And tell your friend not to be idiot nex' time."

"I can hear you, prick," Mason yelled. The Ogre snarled and picked up the phone. It sounded like the guy from our hostel on the other line.

We got a cab to Steve's and went inside. It was a clean little joint with low lighting and one silent receptionist. We told him we were the guys from the station and he handed us a key.

"The rum is down the holl to left," he said.

We followed his directions and opened the door. I had been expecting a critter-filled shithole with busted windows, but our room was nice and large. It had a full bath, six beds, and a computer with internet. The only things missing were chicks.

"Well, let's bower, change, and blow up," I said.

We spiffed ourselves up and hit the door. It was cool out, and the air was glowing in rings around the black-iron streetlamps. We strolled down thin cobbled lanes under tall baroque facades. A church bell later, we found our spot. It was tucked away in a corner with only the glow of its one window to announce its presence. Hanging there above its gnarled oak doors was an intricately carved clock with the words "U Kláštera" scrawled in gold around its face. We walked inside. The atmosphere was warm and orange. People were chatting and clanking glasses at black wood tables. Waiters in traditional garb were threading up and down the walkways serving up giant plates of food. A fat-bellied man with snow-white hair was belting out Czech drinking songs and laughing. He conducted the sway of the room with the inhales and exhales of his accordion. A blond waitress with her tits poking out of her frilled outfit came up and showed us to our seats. She asked us what we'd like to drink, and we told her a round of her finest. She came back a minute later with six frosty mugs of home-brewed licorice stout. We grabbed 'em from her and held 'em high.

"Here's to poppin' off Prague!" I said.

For the next hour, we gorged ourselves on *svíčková na smetaně s knedlíkem* (Sirloin roast in cream sauce with dumplings), *klobásy* (grilled sausages), *gulášová polévka* (goulash soup), and *smažený vepřový řízek* (fried pork schnitzel). We washed everything down with four pints to the head of good dark beer. We walked out of the restaurant like walruses on stilts. Out of nowhere, a tiny elbow hit my gut. I almost puked.

"Hey, you!" a voice said.

I looked up and saw Leddy standing there. She was dressed in a cute little skirt and leather jacket and had fresh curls in her hair. Kate was in the background, scowling. I ignored her and focused on Leddy.

"We're just going in to eat," she said. "How was it?"

"Fucking baumish! But filling. We're going back to the place now to chuck."

"Haha. Baumish. Wanna meet up with us and go out when you guys'r done?"

"Sure, we'll see ya back here in an hour and then go blow up."

After a short nap, we wandered back to the restaurant and met the girls. Leddy was all bubbles.

"The food was fuckin' awesome, man!" she said. "I had dumplings and pork knuckle and pickled cabbage and fried cheese and beer and—"

"Jesus! You ate more than I did."

"Prolly. I absolutely adore food."

"And how was your meal?" Mason asked Kate.

"Uh, whatever," she said. "I don't really eat meat."

Mason smiled. "Well let's go grab a couple'a shots. Maybe you'll change yer mind about that."

We walked out into the night. I kept next to Leddy as we made our way to the center.

"This is my third time in Prague," I said to her. "Place is fuckin' magic."

"Yeah? What's so magic about it?"

"Well, for starters, it wasn't badly bombed in World War II like Berlin or Frankfurt, so most of its old buildings are still intact. This makes for layers and layers of history just poppin' out from every corner. I mean, Prague's been the center of Czech culture for over a thousand years, and in that time, it's seen dozens of different architectural styles shape its streets. Not to mention you've got dudes like Rudolf II, a Holy Roman Emperor, ruling here in the sixteenth century. He was a patron of the arts and invited tons of alchemists, magicians, astronomers, painters, poets, writers, and whatnot to come and live and work in the city. This turned it into a veritable Mecca of European culture. Nowadays, you walk down any street, and there's either a black-spired church or onion-domed cathedral or candy-striped synagogue waiting behind any and every corner. And to add to it, the streets are always misty and glowing and filled with promise. And since absinthe is fucking everywhere, and you're either hallucinating on that shit or tanked on one or more of the millions of Czech beers, all this craziness gets jacked up to the umpteenth degree. Throw in gads of hot Czech chicks and tons of lime-eyed expats chasing the Green Fairy around with their arms outstretched and their tongues draggin' behind their heads, and you've got one helluva place. I mean, fuck . . . if the devil threw a party, he'd do it in Prague!"

Just then, we walked out onto an open-air promenade. Its tract ran the length of the Vltava and provided a perfect view of Old Town. The spires of Pražský hrad (Prague Castle) stretched up from the horizon like a network of lit vampire fangs. Dripping from their concrete gums in a thousand drops of light were pieces of a mirror image that slid out onto the water and collectivized across its dark skin like so many glowworms in a maze. This image crept and crawled till it went lapping up the arches of the Karlův most (Charles Bridge). I could almost see the gargoyles up top, with their muscled backs and pointy wings, peeking over their shoulders to catch a glimpse of what was shimmering below.

Leddy's eyes bulged. "Boy, you weren't kiddin' about this place!" she said.

We snapped some photos and kept going. We walked till we came to Charles Bridge then turned right. We threaded through a network of tiny streets. Then we entered an open area.

"What's up here?" Leddy asked me.

"You'll see."

We came up on Staroměstské náměstí (Old Town Square) from the back. Its grandeur was unveiled to us in stages. First, we saw a cluster of yellow umbrellas crowded under by scores of beer-clinking night owls. Their shadows were thrown onto a wall of lit facades that wrapped around the square. We stepped inside and looked up. The sight of Týnský chrám (Tyn Cathedral) cracked us across the eyeballs. With its razor-sharp spires stabbing into the belly of the night, it looked like a time-frozen castle in purgatory guarded at its towers by clans of phantom Slavic knights waging war with the sky. Their eerie chants pulled us deeper into the square, past shop fronts selling garnets, past bums with tin cups and cloaks. Our attention was soon diverted to the left by a black-top tower. At its base was Pražský orloj (Prague Astronomical Clock). Just as we turned toward it, its gears clicked and its bells rang. A beautiful Sagittarius purled across its lower dials. The ring of Apostles above spun out in a haunting whirl of ghost mouths and grieving eyes. All this madness was making me want to drink up and climb the walls and howl at the moon.

We burst into one of the bars and started drinking. First, it was beers, then it was *mojitos*, then it was rum and cokes. Pretty soon, we'd moved on to tequila shots and were rattling off about trips and travel and backpacking mishaps. By the time midnight hit, we were all savagely drunk and ready to get close. I moved in to kiss Leddy.

Kate elbowed her in the side. "I wanna go back," she spat.

Leddy rolled her eyes and looked back at her friend. "You need me to go with you, or are you alright?"

Kate folded her arms and pouted. "I guess I'm alright," she said. "You go ahead and do whatever, but I'm fucking leaving."

She got up and left. Leddy's face sagged.

"I gotta go with her," she said. "I just can't let her walk off alone at night in some strange city."

"I understand," I said. "Maybe we'll catch each other on the flipside."

We hugged tightly then broke apart. She looked back once, then walked out the door.


"What the fuck?" Kip screamed.

My eyes shot open and my heart raced. I thought someone had

just been knifed in the face.

"Dude, what is it?"

"I can't find my money belt. It has my passport, credit cards, travelers' checks, and like four hundred bucks in it. If I don't find it, I'm really fuckin' fucked."

Now everyone was awake and sitting up. "Woll, where'd you last see it?" Mason said.

"I hung it on the bedpost before I went to sleep. That's where I last saw it."

"You hung it on your fuckin' bedpost, Kip?" I said. "Dude, you should always sleep with that shit under your pillow."

"Well, I don't see why it matters," he snapped. "It's not like anyone was in here."

Tim's face broke into a sweat. Then he slapped himself on the forehead with his palm.

"Fuck. I can't believe how fucking stupid I am."

"What is it?"

"Last night I just was chuckin' out, and I woke up cuz I heard a strange noise. Someone walked in the room, and I just thought it was one of you Chucks so I didn't say anything. Then when I saw the guy going through all our shit, I thought it might be a robber. I was going to yell out, but I just closed my eyes and hoped he'd go away. I think I was scared he'd have a gun or something."

"You fuckin' pussy," I mumbled.

"Let's look around and see if anything else is missing," Chuck said. "Then, Kip, you should file a police report."

"Ha," Mason said. "Before we go to the fuckin' popos, I'm havin' words with that bitch-ass receptionist. I betcha fiddy bones he's the one who rigged this shit up."

After checking all our crap, Mason stormed up to the receptionist.

"Did you know our fucking room was robbed last night?" he said.

The receptionist glanced at him lazily. He seemed more concerned with the sandwich he was eating.

"I don knou anyfing abou dis," he said. "You gow to *polis* an figoor it out *your*selv."

"Oh, this is bollshit!" Mason continued. "You rigged this up, didn't you? You and that bald shithead at the train station."

The receptionist blinked. He took another bite of his sandwich and looked away.

"Forget it, Mason," Kip said. "I'll just go to the cops."

We walked down to the police station. We were met at the door by a pudgy cop with a five o'clock shadow. He asked us what we needed in broken English. We told him what was up.

"One momen," he said. He lumbered off down a corridor and brought back a female fiver. She looked like a truant officer at a private school that might bust kids in the feet if they forgot their hall passes.

"Yez, vat is it?" she said.

Kip told her his name and what had happened. Her eyebrows went up.

"Vee actually have your passport and trawelerz check," she said. "Dis man who steal your fings try to cash checks and use credit card at store, and ven shop lady ask to see passport, he shou it and she knou he is liar and keep it and call *poli*s. Your money empty, dou."

Kip thinned his lips. "So what do I do now? Just make a report?"

"Yez. You may come in nou, and I vill take statement an report."

Kip went in, did the report, and got his shit. When he came back out, he was fumbling all over himself and dropping things everywhere. He stuffed his cards, checks, and passport in his money belt and slung it around his neck. A tweak of his specs completed the act.

"Dude, some bum's gonna roll by and grab that shit right off yer neck," Mason said. "You better hide it."

Kip smirked and stuffed the belt under his shirt. It bulged like a middle tit. None of us said anything.

We went back to Steve's and decided to find another hostel. We scooped up our packs and left the room in disarray. On our way out, we shot daggers at the receptionist. He ignored us with his feet up and watched the soccer game. Outside, we thought it only appropriate to document this whole disaster. We put our middle fingers in the air and grinned while a passerby snapped our photo.

"Get it, Steve's," we yelled. "Get it square in the ass!"

We wandered the city for hours searching for another hostel. Most of the cheaper options on the outskirts seemed as shady as Steve's. We booked it to Old Town to see what we could find there. We showed up at a joint called Rick's just as a group of Italians were leaving. The cute receptionist put us in their ten-bed dorm at twelve bucks a pop. She assured us with a smile that our stuff would be safe.

By the time we got set up, it was already 4 p.m. We decided to save the sightseeing for the morrow.

"I can't believe that bullshit with the police took the whole fuckin' day," Mason said. "A robber breaks in here, and I'm gonna cut his nuts off."

To prove his point, he whipped out a pocketknife and snapped the blade up. He held it in the air for all of us to see.

"Oh, you won't need that," Tim said.

"Why?"

"Because I've just been thinkin' and like I bought this in Rome and . . ." He rummaged through his bag and pulled out a giant twelve-color megaphone that looked like a prop from Sesame Street. The whole room burst out laughing. "What?" he said. "I could just use it to scream out and scare a robber if he breaks in, ooff?"

"Tim, that shit wouldn't scare a gnat." Bert said.

"Yeah. Using that makes you look like an extreme faggot!" I said.

Tim shrugged and placed the megaphone by his pillow.

Feeling safe now that Tim had shit on lock, we rolled out and grabbed some alcohol and sandwich fixings to start the night off proper. We brought everything back—beers, salami, cheese, cold cuts, buns, tomatoes—and started drinking and saucing and blowing up. Mason set his ass up on the floor and made a little station. The fucker had a po-boy bursting with meat in one hand and a frosty stout in the other and was sitting there cross-legged like a Buddhist *satyr*, munching and chomping away while he grunted about nahs and just let his red beard glow. The thing looked so big and bright, I just had to grab at it.

The second I started, I couldn't stop.

"I'm warnin' ya, Felm. Ya keep fuckin' with my pigs, and I'm gonna hook it up."

"I'm only nei nornin, Maaaaaaayt'n."

I picked and poked and grabbed some more. He threw down his sandwich and got up.

"I warned you," he shouted.

"Wait, where are you going? I'm Nei nornin!"

I never took Mason seriously when he threatened to shave his beard. The thing was like his extra appendage after his cock and was just as essential to his character. I continued getting trashed and forgot about it. Twenty minutes later, Mason waltzed in the room barefaced as a baby's brand-spankin' new ass.

"Noooooooo," I cried.

"You gottem, Felm," he said.

"No bro, *you* gottem! Good luck gettin' any nahs now without your life's blood!"

After we all had a good laugh at Mason's baby face, we got ready to hit the streets. Everyone but Chuck, who was happily ensconced in his covers, sputtering Z's, guzzled the last of their beers and fixed their collars. As we walked out the door, a character slid into our midst. He had hazel eyes and a scraggly ponytail and looked as if he hadn't shaved in weeks.

"*Hola*. I an *Rr*aul," he said. He was carrying a big jug of clear booze. He lifted it and smiled with coffee teeth. "Dju guyss wanna shar?"

"*¿Qué es?*" I asked.

"*Slivovice.*[10] *Es pura checa.*"

We nodded and he poured us off a couple cups. This shit stung our throats like naked fire going down.

"*¡Oye, esto sabe a mierda!*" I spat.

"*¡No tío, es de puta madre! ¡Tómate más!*" Raul said.

We slammed shot after shot till our ears were ringing and our eyes

---

[10] *Slivovice* is a plum brandy of Slavic origin.

were buzzing. We were fully ready to go out and pop off. I only knew of a few big clubs near Staroměstské náměstí that we could do. Raul told me—strictly in Spanish because beyond pleasantries he refused to converse in English—that he knew of a cool bar just across Karlův most. I explained this to the others, and everyone seemed to be cool with it. We shot off one last *"¡Salud!"*, downed a *chupito*, and cut.[11]

We weaved our way through the square and strode out onto the bridge. Its causeway was brimming at the hips with tourists chattering in different languages and laughing street clowns all flipping bowling pins and handing kiddies red roses with winks. Every so often, we spotted a sad-looking musician pouring his tears out through a violin. We all tossed 'em what we could, as did Raul.

When he wasn't listening to the street music or cursing about the gads of tourists, the old Andalou was rattling my ear off in Spanish about everything from politics to pop culture. He had an opinion about absolutely everything and wasn't afraid to share.

"I just think Americans are such bad tourists," he said. "Wherever they go, they bring their big cameras and their McDonalds and their Coca Cola, and it drives me fucking crazy."

"Well, I'm American, and I don't do that shit," I said.

"Yes but you are not really American. You are Mexican and German."

"Well, what is *really* American then, Raul?"

"I don't know. Fat, lazy, stupid white people with guns and no culture, like George Bush."

"We're not all like George Bush," I cautioned. "And even the white people in our country can be open-minded and have vibrant cultures of their own. Take Louisiana, for example. That state is home to the Cajuns, a culturally rich people, and they're white."

"Yes, but they are French originally."

"Well, the Spaniards are Romans originally, and before that, they were nomadic tribes of proto Indo-Europeans wandering the steppes of Anatolia. Does that make you an Italian or a Turk?"

---

[11] *Chupito* is the Castillian Spanish word for 'shot' (of alcohol).

"I guess not. But what's your point?"

"My point is we're all a mix, bro. And no matter how pure you think a culture is, you go back far enough and you'll find that it had other influences from somewhere else. But that doesn't make it any more or less valid."

"Okay. Well, how does that make America any less full of idiots?"

"It doesn't. America *is* full of idiots. But it's also full of cool people. And some of 'em you can find right in your own hood."

Raul and I agreed to disagree. We did so with a handshake.

"So where's this damn bar?" I asked once the air had cleared.

"Just there." He pointed ahead to a slanted two-story shack on the banks of the Vltava. It had one glowing glass eye and a sign above its door that read "Warp."

Strange name for a bar, I thought. We stopped to wait for the others. Five minutes passed and only Mason walked up.

"The pussies went off to some other bar," he said. "And I'm kinda gettin' chuck from the sneer and slivovice so I think I might just go for a lil' walk n' roll back."

"Suit yourself," I said.

Raul and I walked into the bar and up the stairs. They creaked and cracked like floorboards under a killer's nighttime tiptoes. When we got to the top, an orange glow curled around us and pulled us into its distorted womb. Covering the walls like so many rococo mirrors in a madwoman's vanity den were dozens upon dozens of strange and horrible sketches. They were of almost everything imaginable: goblins chewing the heads off shrieking damsels, leeches sucking the eyeballs from cackling skulls, flowers growing from dead and rotting women's vaginas, babies crying out with butcher knives lodged in their bellies, saints being hung, demons being praised, Satan at a Cub Scout bonfire teaching the kiddies to paint with their parents' blood.

We ordered drinks and sat with a group of Catalanes. They switched from Catalan to Castellano the second we pulled up chairs.

"*¿Qué están jugando?*" Raul asked.

"*Peseta*, you guys wanna play?"

I knew about *peseta*. Peseta means "quarter"—at least according to my grandfather—and in its eponymous counterpart, a quarter, or any coin of roughly equal size, is bounced off the table from a distance and into a plastic cup. If it lands inside after a certain number of tries, usually three, everyone else drinks. If it doesn't, you drink.

After an hour of play, I was shit-chewing drunk. This provoked me to spout off like an idiot.

"So you guys are Catalan, right?" I said. "Do you all want independence from Spain or what?"

The group looked at Raul, then at me. A bald dude with hedgehog features and rolled up sleeves spoke up.

"Some of us do, some of us don't," he said. "Since 1979, when our autonomy was won after Franco's death, we've enjoyed a lot of freedoms. We make our own laws and basically run our own country. We are just not legally recognized as a nation. The Spanish parliament calls us a nationality instead. This is easier for us to accept than, say, the Basques, because our culture is more similar to that of the Spanish. Plus, historically we weren't treated quite as poorly as they were."

I looked at Raul. He pursed his lips and bit his tongue.

"Nowadays," the hedgehog continued, "you still have independence movements, but I guess the solidarity isn't there. This is because some consider our identity fragmented. For example, within Cataluña you have us, the Spanish, and the Araneses. Then you have Las Islas Baleares: Mallorca, Menorca, Ibiza, and Formentera, and also the region of Valencia where the cultures are extremely similar to ours, and they speak a variation of Catalan. Only each place calls it something different. In Valencia, it's Valenciano. In Menorca, it's Menorqui, and so on. And each place swears up and down that its language and culture is totally unrelated to, and different from, Catalan. No solidarity, see? Me personally, I'd like to see our country have a shot at being totally independent. But am I willing to kill innocent people for it? No."

I didn't really know what to say after that. Quite frankly, I was too drunk to respond anyway. Instead, I thanked the Catalan crew and bid them adieu. On my way down the creaky old steps, I tripped and almost slammed my face onto the concrete below. Luckily, I had ol' Raul there to catch me. He straightened me up, and we split through the mist.

I woke in the morning with rattling lungs. All the booze and fog had finally gotten to me, and I was coughing up sinkfuls of blood-marbled phlegm dots. I contemplated staying in and catching some rest, but Mona's whispers egged me on. She spoke of adventures, fairytale castles, nahs, and beer, and blowing up. I fought the chuck and drained my demons in the shower. It was a push, but I made it out with the Chucks on two legs by noon.

It quickly became apparent that today wasn't a day for a sick man to be wandering about. The Prague skyline was being drenched in thick sheets of rain, and I was immediately soaked in its catch-up. The only thing pulling me forward was the promise of seeing Pražský hrad again. It loomed there in the distance like a black ice palace, its spires jutting up into the sky's swollen guts.

Once we crossed Karlův most, I stopped and grabbed some cough medicine. The pharmacist who sold it to me—a Czech milf with red lips, black hair, and graveyard eyes—noticed the jewels glistening across my fingers.

"I like your rings," she said, smiling. Her teeth were smoky and crooked, but somehow sensual. I want to say they made her look *more* attractive but then that's just the devil in me talking.

"Thanks," I said.

Outside, her compliment began filling me with horrible joy. I set my med bag down and went spiraling through the rain with my arms out, singing, "Cumshots'a fallin' on my head. Cumshots'a fallin' on face n' asshole. Dicks, balls, n' hairy cocks shootin' off their . . . cumshots'a fallin' on my head, and there you beeeeee, and ya werryin' meeeeeee." I repeated this perverted little ditty some half a dozen times before coming to a halt in the middle of the street. Everything around me was silent. I looked to my right and saw two blondes cupping their mouths under a single umbrella. I made like I was going to walk toward them. Their eyes flashed with terror, and they ran off tock-tock-tocking down the cobbled lane. The Chucks busted up. I turned around and bowed.

"Thank you, ladies and gentlemen," I said. "I'm here till Saturday."

Feeling better now, I chugged some sizzurp and charged with the others up the marble steps to the castle grounds. Directly ahead of us was the Royal Palace—a four-story baroque behemoth with checkerbox windows and pastel hues. In front of it was a black-iron gate swathed in gold leaves. On either side of the entrance, a blue and white striped box housed an iron-chinned Czech guard with white gloves, bayonet, and periwinkle outfit. The two black spires and the verdigris bell tower of St. Vitus Cathedral crept up from behind everything. We snapped a few photos, then veered off to the balcony on the right to catch a view of the city. The fog and rain had mostly cleared. We could see Prague's sprawling patchwork of red and black rooftops. There was a beer stand just there. We ordered up drinks and got a good buzz going.

"Wanna fuck with the guards?" I asked Kip.

"Ooff. Won't they hook me up?"

"Nah, man, I did it the last time I was here and shit was coo. C'mon, I'll take your pic with them and you can flip 'em the bird or something."

What I didn't tell Kip was that the first, last, and only time I pulled that stunt the pissed-off guard went looking for my ass once his shift had ended. When he found me sitting under the archway, he damn near scared the piss outta me with his bayonet rifle. I knew this might happen to Kip. But since he was a newbie and couldn't do the cobra blood, I thought I'd use this opportunity to fuck with him a little as part of his initiation.

The two of us walked over to one of the guards. I waved Kip on.

"Just stand in front of him and throw up the bird when I tell you," I said.

Kip picked at the underside of his chin and readjusted his specs. I thought he'd crap himself before he even got to the guard box.

"Okay, now just turn around, stand there, and do it when I say go, ait?"

"This is fucking stupid," he spat.

"Just do it!" I raised the camera and opened the shutter.

"Alright, now," I yelled.

He raised his hand and crumpled it into a fist. Instead of his middle finger, he raised his thumb.

"Well that was a fucking retarded picture," I said. "Really do it this time or shove that thumb up yer ass."

"I'm coo on this," he muttered.

"Well, then do the jerk-off motion or something so the guard doesn't know what you're doing."

"How the fuck would he not know what I was doing? I might as well pull down my pants and point to my asshole!"

I could tell by the pulsing of his jaw muscles the guard was losing patience. I called Kip a ginormous pussy, and we walked off to St. Vitus where the others had gone.

The cathedral was more impressive than I remembered it. With its serrated points, flying buttresses, ghost-mouth windows, and shiny black slate it looked like a satanic temple crafted from the exoskeletons of giant hell-dwelling beetles. We passed through its maw and into a grand hall of stained glass and haggard messiah statues all bloody and weeping. I felt like I was walking through the gullet of a mutant whale that had swallowed a whole mess of religious artifacts. There were swarms of tourists. We noticed a group of three girls amongst them that were fairly attractive. One of the girls, a slinky brunette with brown eyes, gave me a smile. I ran my palms over my greased-back hair and prepared to approach her.

"I wouldn't do that," Kip said.

"Why?"

He cocked his head to one side and clicked his fingers. His eyes lit up with calculating sparks.

"Because your odds of obtaining her through direct contact are decidedly low."

"Okay, genius. What should I do to get her then?"

"Well, based on my preliminary assessment, she's a flirt, nothing more. Therefore, she seeks to rope guys in with smiles, so she can flatter herself and then reject them when she's finished."

"How the hell do you know that shit, Kip?"

"Note for a second the friends she hangs out with. They're both cute, but in a frumpy way, and neither of them stands out like she does. She's using them as a comparative setting to frame and enhance her beauty. It's a peacocking technique."

"Aright, I getcha. What should I do then?"

"Hit on the blonde to her left. She's the second most attractive of the three, so it's believable you'd approach her first, plus it'll make the brunette jealous. When it does, hold out just until you sense her getting angry, and then make your move. Then you'll get her."

"Aright faggot, I'm gonna give this shit a shot. Wish me luck."

"Good luck," he said, grinning.

I walked up to the girls all swag. The blonde was right in my sights. Just as I opened my mouth to spit, a bald dude in a muscle shirt strode up and grabbed her by the hand. I quickly turned to the brunette for some rebound game. Bert was already in her face chatting away. The third girl, a decent looking redhead, caught wind of what was happening and walked away. I stormed back toward Kip.

"What the fuck just happened back there?" I screamed.

Kip flashed me his pearls and cackled like a nerd.

"I just told Bert to grooge over there and be your wingman with those nahs. I didn't know he was gonna go for the brunette."

"Bullshit. And you knew the blonde had a boyfriend too."

"No, I didn't." He giggled.

"Kip, you're one calculating lil' basterd," I said. "We're just gonna hafta call ya the Kipriolitic Calculator." Kip grinned.

I woke up the next morning with a tremendous headache. It felt like my eyeballs had just had a marital spat and had stormed outta their sockets in opposite directions, pulling my brains out like luggage with them. I vaguely remembered going to some trashy strip club with the Chucks. There was a pirate-themed sex show, and I'd been prodding this faux-Amazon's cunt with a Scottish longsword. Then came the $20 drinks, the $200 prosties, and the priceless moment where Chuck may or may not have run off and fucked some midget in a thong.

I didn't make it outta bed till noon. The plan was to go to the ossuary at Kutná Hora, but I was having second thoughts.[12] Not only had I seen it before, I needed a break from all the madness. I decided to go out on my own.

"I'm gonna head to Karlštejn instead,"[13] I said. "I've been around enough boning for one day. Especially after Nerfy's little escapade."

"I didn't screw that midget," he yelled. "I told you I choked just before we did it."

"Sure ya did," Bert said. "Sure ya did."


I caught a train to Karlštejn. When it arrived, I stepped off and breathed in. I was immediately struck by the purity of the air. It was so crisp I could almost see it wrinkle. As I glided my way through it, I noticed the surrounding countryside. There was a beautiful expanse of emerald hills and thin-stemmed forests, divided in half by a smooth stretch of the Vltava. I floated over a wooden bridge and into the village center. It was an ascending network of red rooftops, church steeples, and streetlamps all snuggled together on either side of a zigzag lane. At the top was a castle with white walls and blue roofs all sprouted up like a cluster of so many giant mushrooms. I tiptoed my way toward it, past horse-drawn carriages, garden terraces, and Czechs sipping beer. When I arrived at the gates, it started to sprinkle. I was just in time to catch the last English tour of the day.

---

[12] Kutná Hora, a city just east of Prague, is famous for its ossuary, silver mines, and grand cathedrals.
[13] Karlštejn is a fourteenth-century Gothic castle built in Bohemia by Holy Roman Emperor Charles IV. The castle houses many royal treasures and holy relics.

After the tour, I wandered into some of the little shops in town to see what kind of local booze I could dig up. The two spirits the Czech Republic is most famous for are slivovice (plum brandy) and absinthe, an anis-tasting drink made from herbs and wormwood. I had tried the latter only once before and spent the evening wandering around Prague for hours in a euphoric daze. It seemed like the way to go. I went right for the tallest, greenest bottle I could find. I paid twenty bucks for it and thought it was a steal. I walked to the next shop. The guy who owned the place was a long-haired musician type with a neat goatee and intense eyes. He stopped strumming his guitar and looked up when I walked in.

"I have a question," I said to him.

"Oukej."

"Is this shit any good?" I pulled out my bottle and held it forward.

The guy laughed. "Dis is verst shit you can buy."

"Really? How can you tell?"

"Becaus it is green. Good absinthe is never green. It is yellow and it always have little pieces of vormvood floating at bottom."

"I've never seen any like that."

"You vould not because you are tourist. You must go to special shop for dis. Dis because dis absinthe very strong in *thujone*."

"What the hell is that?"

"Is what make absinthe to cause hallucinations. Da absinthe you have is one milliliter per liter thujone. It is shit. Good absinthe starting to ten milliliters per liter. Den der is tirty-five and eefen one hundred, but dis is no legal."

"Where can I find it?"

"In special stores. I gif you name. It called Da King, and it have photo of Van Gough on front because he using it."

The guy scribbled down the address of a store off Wenceslas Square. I thanked him and split.

When I got into the city, I went looking for the little shop. I found it after a half hour of scouring the streets in the rain. I could see through the window that it was packed to the gills with bottles of the

Green Fairy. Unfortunately, it was closed. I schlepped my ass back to Rick's with my crap bottle and chucked. Not twenty minutes into my nap I was kicked awake by a watery boot. I peeled my eyes open and saw Raul standing over my bed.

"You're coming out with me tonight," he said in Spanish.

"Why, what's going on?"

"A gypsy jazz festival. I can get us in cheap."

"Gypsy?"

Raul and I shot through the rainy streets and up to an old opera house. We dropped five bucks a pop and went in to see the show. The thing started off slow, hushing the throngs of people with low lights and rolling drums. A line of dark-skinned men in snazzy pants and shirts, flutes and trumpets in hand, strode out on stage and took their places in front of the mic row. One man among them, with black curls, hairy arms and golden eyes, took center stage and gripped the front mic. He was quiet, then snapped our heads back with a blood-curdling wail. The band broke out behind him in a cacophony of blazing horns and spiraling whistles. The whole writhing orb of music rose up from the stage and blew across the audience, making our bones jiggle. My shoulders were bouncing and my knees were kicking. I began laughing wildly with my teeth out and spinning circles around the concert hall. Raul joined me in his own rough and contained way. We fused with the rest of the crowd, locking legs, and beating our fists in the air to the crazy gypsy rhythm.

When the concert ended, I was all sweat and happy red patches. I wanted to go up and chat with the gypsy musicians, maybe even ask them to translate Mona's little phrase. Raul pulled me off in another direction.

"Some friends of mine want to meet us at a café," he said.

I almost told him to fuck off. I'd have done it, but he gave me a look like, Please don't leave. I am so alone in this life. On the way to the café, he ranted between smoke puffs about how he'd told me so with the concert and how I should trust him and believe shit was going to be cool at the café with his buds. We crossed Karlův most and rolled passed Warp to another nook in the shadows. There was a nameless café turning the raindrops to gold flecks with its fluorescent lights. Raul grinned as we walked up to its entrance. I asked him if there would be girls. He turned to me and chuckled.

"Very beautiful ones," he said.

I stepped inside and looked around. Two people rose from their seats to greet us. One was a skinny hippie with a blond mop barely clinging to her scalp. The other was a fat dude with a goatee and a shaved dome.

"These are my friends, blah and blah," Raul said.

My face froze. I could have done the kosher thing and stuck out a cup of coffee with them, but the Chucks had been talking about a trip to a club I loved called Charlie's Fix earlier, and I was dying to blow that up instead. Without so much as a peep, I shook Raul's friends' hands and tipped my hat. Their eyebrows were still wrinkling as I slipped out the door.

I hailed a cab to Rick's. I got inside and the cabbie was this ancient Czech dude with long fingers and a face so haggard it looked like a huge melting prune. We got to talking about the spirit of the Slavs. Homeboy made a fist and raised it.

"All Slavic people are brothers," he said. "The Poles, Czechs, Croatians, Russians, Ukrainians, Bulgarians, Macedonians. Vee are all related. If you vant proof, you see our languages. All Slavic languages have forty percent same vords. Dis mean vee all have some under-standing between us and vee can preserve our culture ties to each udder."

"Wow, that's—"

"But," he continued, shooting a twelve-inch finger into the air, "young people today are ruin dis Slavic culture wis Vestern shit and rap music. Dey do not care about our culture vee have for tousands of years, and dey vant trade it for hamburger and Snoop Dogg."

I felt a horrible pain in my chest. As we pulled up to the curb, Long-fingers pointed one at me.

"Don't ruin your culture like so many stupid young people," he said. I gave him a little nod.

The cab sped away. I ran up the steps and burst into our room. The Chucks were soaked and lying in bed. I bunched my face into a tiny ball.

"What the fuck is this horseshit?" I yelled. "Let's do Charlie's up!"

"I'll roll," Bert said. "That brunette from St. Vitus gave me her number. I'ma hit her up."

"Faggot. Any other takers?"

Kip and Mason crawled out of bed.

"We'll go," they said together.

I nodded and looked over at Chuck. He was snoring with his pillow over his head. I scowled and looked over at Tim. He was wrapped in his sheets and grinning.

"You gonna roll with us or stay here with that player?" I asked him, pointing my thumb at Chuck.

Tim wiggled his shoulders playfully. "I'm gonna stay here with Chuck and chuck," he said.

"I see. Well, keep that megaphone handy in case a werewolf breaks in."

He hummed at me sarcastically. I flipped him the bird and grabbed my coat.

"Let's bunt, gahts!" I said.

Charlie's was fuckin' bumpin' that night. There was a line out the door twenty yards long, and it was studded with tall Czech chicks in black boots and skirts. I could see from where I stood that the club's six floors were bending at the studs with people. Each one of its windows was being sliced up by the spray of lasers and stretched finger shadows. We paid the burly dudes at the front door ten bones a pop. We stepped inside and our mouths dropped. The whole club, I mean the *whole* club, was throbbing at the jowls with thousands upon thousands of ravers, drug rats, mob types, and hipsters all sweating and dancing and breathing on each another in a great big multilayered tower of flesh and sex. And every level of this skin beast was being galvanized to the point of bursting eyeballs by silhouetted DJs atop dark towers firing lights from their ears and beats from their fingertips. At the center of everything was a man who stood as a counterpoint to, but in some strange way, epitomized all the chaos. He seemed almost twelve feet tall and was dressed top to bottom in an open collar eggshell suit that looked pilf'd from a Cuban kingpin's closet. He moved in slow, calculated steps, gliding across the floor as if he were a pimp phantom on a mission. We watched as he crept up to a Marilyn Monroe-type and dappled her a tiny wink. She melted like putty. Then and there the fucker earned himself the chuck name, "Mr. Charlie."

In the late hours of the hung-over morning, I could feel Mona's gentle hand guiding us Chucks away from Prague. Raul had vanished before we'd gotten up. Leddy had booked it out two days before. And Bert, Kip, and I had gotten zippo from the Charlie chicks.

At the station, we bought our tickets to Český Krumlov. Our train would be arriving in five minutes. Before it came, Mason's eyebrows shot up.

"I'll be right back," he said.

He took off toward the back of the station. I followed behind.

"What the fuck are you doin' dude?" I asked. "We're gonna miss the train!"

"Ooff. Just one more thing I have to take care of before we bunta."

I followed him all the way to the dingy Tourist Information Center where our experience in Prague had begun. I smelled cigar smoke and suddenly realized what my buddy had come to do. He strode right up to the lone window and looked the pudgy bald prick—who'd most likely arranged the break-in at Steve's—right in the eyes. The Ogre snarled and shot his chin up.

"Vat you vant?"

Mason leaned his baby face into the window.

"Fuck you," he said sweetly.

The Ogre burst into a rage and nearly lost his seating. We ran laughing to the train and hopped on just as it was pushing off.

# ČESKÝ KRUMLOV

To get to Český Krumlov, we ended up having to take a train and two buses. We arrived four hours later at the outskirts of the city. There was nothing around but a tree and a bench. We had no prospects for hostels.

"What the fuck do we do now?" Bert asked.

"Get a cab to the city center, I guess," I said.

"Oh yeah," Mason cut in. "I'm fuckin' droppin' hella bones on a cab when I can walk there."

Just then a cab pulled up. An old man with flowing white hair and a beard rolled down the window. He told us he'd take us right to the center for a bone a piece.

"Have fun walkin', Assface," I said. Mason got in the cab with a scowl.

Krumlov crept up on us like a black ghost. One minute we were driving past patches of gray apartment blocks. The next we were hugging a hillside and watching as the green steeple of Krumlov Castle poked up through the reeds. Much as a point of lipstick slowly rises from its sheath, the entire rainbow-painted tower of the castle turned upwards at the sky, pulling the rest of the city below with it. In a flash, a lattice of red, black, gray and brown rooftops, all bent and pointed and popping up on top of one another like so many mushrooms in a cartoon field, came stretching up before our eyes. It was enough to tighten a wizard's nutsack.

"Vee have beautiful city, *že jo?*" Merlin said, grinning through his giant white beard.

"You do indeed," I said.

Merlin dropped us off at a tiny wooden bridge that straddled a slice of the Vltava, weaving through the city. We paid him for the ride and went hostel shopping. Most places were fully or partially booked. We had to split up. Bert and I shacked up at a place across the bridge called The Seeker's Inn. Mason, Chuck, Kip, and Tim picked a joint just before it called Hostel Pes (The Dog Hostel).

We all chucked then met up at 8 p.m. for drinks. The place we picked had a long, flowered terrace and was nestled deep in the heart of Krumlov. To one side of it was a maze of shiny cobbled lanes and old buildings. To the other was a black bend of the Vltava rippling with the image of Krumlov tower. We ordered the works there: roasted quail, blood sausage, chicken and poached peaches, stinky cheese plates, sudsy stouts, everything saucy and all drippy and gooey and baumish. To crack the night off, we even ordered a fresh bottle of absinthe. It was green tourist shit, but the label read ten milliliters per liter of thujone. I figured it couldn't be all bad. The minute the shots were poured I started feeling that monstrous black mass claw its way up my ribcage. I closed my eyes and swallowed hard.

"The Czech Republic," I said, raising my shooter. "The sickest shit this side of the planet!"

I threw back the shot. Absinthe spilled down my throat like melted emeralds. It hit my stomach lining hard. I could feel it peel into my circulatory system. All my capillaries started puffing with hazy green fluid. Just as both my pupils flushed like little toilets, I opened my mouth to scream. Nothing came out.

"You okay, Felm?" Tim asked.

"Ooff," I said.

I got up and shuffled to the back of the restaurant. Tim followed me.

"That cool shit passin' you treats again?" he asked.

"Yeah," I said. "It's hard not to think about it."

Tim smiled and put his hand on my shoulder. I could feel the warmth of his wisdom flowing through me.

"Just ride it," he said. I took a deep breath and walked back to the table. Right when I sat back down, I felt better, better enough even to shoot up a lil' more green morphine drip— nuthin' enough to tempt fate or nuthin', just enough to break me in and get my head spiffy for the night. Chuck, on the other hand, was going large. He cleared himself half the bottle in a quarter of the time and piled on six big beers to boot. When he lifted himself from the table, he looked sea-deck fucked.

The six of us, drunk as imps on baby blood at a black mass, went barreling through the twisted streets of Krumlov after Mona's sweet scent. It led us to a club called Dosed which felt oh so apropos, as we were wild reeling eyeballs and green fairy farts leaking from the cracks in our teeth. We burst inside and started to fuse. Everything was all squiggly colored lights and white pops like you might imagine going off over Tesla's head when truly brilliant ideas dawned on him. The people amidst this psychedelic madness were hippies and beatniks no less, flushing out their sorrows with drink after drink of the funny stuff and two-step-traveling their way through an iridescent kelp forest of rippled time. We could hardly keep our drawers on as we slipped into its gangly rainbow grip. The hours flew.

Only camera shot flashes of the night remain. There's me and a married chick locking knees, Bert at the back of a blonde begging please, Mason in the shadows and Tim grinning big, Kip throwing a finger to the demons in his wig. The only one fucked was good ol' Chuck. He came stumbling out of the bathroom after a puke session and went straight for the streets. We followed him to see what was up. We found him hunched over a trashcan yakking himself silly.

"You okay, Nerfy?" Tim asked.

"*Fiiine*," he groaned.

Right when the ol' boy was in the heat of his biggest wretch, some enormous bald black fellow in a ghetto fab suit came strolling out of the club laughing, with a Bohemian minx on either side of him. He saw Chuck vomiting and backed up with fingers splayed.

"Look at dis fucking dood," he said in a thick Yoruban accent.

The girls giggled under their press-ons.

Chuck snapped. "Hey dickhead," he yelled. "Why don't you …"

Chuck could have gone with any number of insults at this juncture. "Go fuck yourself" might have worked. "Eat shit," maybe. Even "Suck my dick." Nope. These were all too standard. My gaht needed something that would really click in and express how he felt about homeboy and his bitches mocking him.

"… come over here and fuck my ass."

The Nigerian guy was so stunned, I thought he might wet his silvery pants right then and there. He wrinkled his big brow and scowled.

"Fock, dis mon crazy." he said.

All of us fell dead on the cobblestones laughing. He grabbed his hoes up without another word and split for the hills.


The next day was an *extremely* chuck one. We spent most of it eating and wandering around Krumlov aimlessly. When night came, we decided to hit the scene. Our destination was a place we'd stumbled upon while sightseeing, called Ghost Dance Bar. It was located down a dimly lit alley. There were cobweb curtains covering its arched entryway. We stepped inside and soaked it all in.

The interior was an elaborate system of ancient tunnels decorated top to bottom with horrifying nicks and knacks. There were red wax candles with flames slithering up the walls, gothic crosses painted in blood, and bejeweled skulls in foggy glass cases. The ceiling was hanging with crucified skeletons screaming out their unhinged jaws. Their maws hopscotched to the back where they fanned out into a glass bar rack stacked with every color of bubbling spider-covered liquor. We headed straight for it and ordered drinks. The barmaid was a teen dressed in shredded black with triangles of pale skin showing through. Her eyes looked like red-tailed monarchs. Her lips looked like she'd just consumed a charred cadaver.

"Vat vill you have?" she asked me, running her fingers through her witch's mane.

"You got tha hundred mil King?" I asked.

"Dis is illegal. Vee only have tirty-five."

Thirty-five was a step up from what we'd had the night before. We ordered two shots each and went to pick a table. There was one big one at the entrance with four girls at it.

"Mind if we join you guys?" we asked them.

"Not at all," they said.

We kicked the night off by lighting the first of our two King shots. We threw them back in a cheer of twisted blue flames. After that, it was beers and chatting. The ladies with us were actually two sets of friends; one American, one Australian. Each had a hottie and beater amongst them. Mason and Bert both went for the Australian nah. Tim swooped up on the American. And all I was left with were two dodo birds staring morosely into their glasses. I shrugged and took my second shot. I watched as Tim giggled with his new ney ney and drew stupid pictures on napkins with crayons, and as Mason and Bert crowded in on their brunette prey who suddenly got all panicky and belted out her Aussie-accented rejection, "Naaaaaauuuuueeeeee."

I wanted to get in on the action, but something froze my mouth in a circle. It was time for a walk.

The second I got outside, I felt sick. My nerves were sizzling and my eyes were blurry. I could feel my stomach turning inside out like a used rubber glove. I went staggering through streets with my fists clenched and my knees shaking. I made it about a hundred meters. Then the fragile equilibrium in my brain tipped. Thousands of vesicles of long-repressed thoughts and memories extricated themselves from my subconscious and floated upwards. I was helpless, with my eyes crossed, watching as two green Tinkerbelles floated up to each bubble and popped it into awareness with a prick of the wand. My head was instantly flooded with blackness. I felt that wretched cloak start to envelop my body just as I turned the corner. I'd have been completely consumed, but a vision stopped me shit cold. Looming in the candlelit shadows ahead was Krumlov Castle, its rainbow tower transformed into a projection screen for my fears. They came spraying forth from my mind in so many foggy and demonic screams and swirled up the length of the colored brick shaft. When they reached the steeple, the entire thing brightened. Each of its illuminated layers of color represented a specific fear I had to conquer. There were many. Fear of drugs, fear of dying, fear of women, fear of flying, fear of love, fear of loss, fear of failure, fear of trying. Above the rest was the fear that started this whole trip. It was the fear that our Chuck culture would disappear or, worse, that it had never really existed in the first place. I saw myself at the very bottom of this tower of fright and knew that it would take a lifetime to scale. Just finding a single handhold would be a small miracle. I got down on my knees and begged Mona to grant me solace. She whispered to me with the winds and told me to look up. I saw the crescent moon in a perfect Cheshire grin with two stars twinkling overhead. The stars held their glimmer for a moment, then one of them blacked out.

I was in a daze the next morning. I forced myself to do a bit of sightseeing with Bert, then came back for a nap. Afterward, Bert and I met up with everyone for drinks. We ended up at a place called The Bohemian that barely had a pulse. There was an old Czech record crackling in the background and some toothless drunk poring over his beer at the bar. We ordered a slivovice or two then called it quits. Bert and I wandered back to The Seeker to finish the night off. Since things were going nowhere, I decided to see about some absinthe.

"You guys got any one-hundred-mil King?" I asked the cute barmaid.

"No," she said, cleaning out a shot glass. "Vee have tirty-five and dis highest."

It seemed I'd never find that elusive illegal shit. I told her to give us two shots of the thirty-five and she poured 'em up. Bert looked nervous as I handed him his shooter. Just as we were about to say cheers and down it, he stopped.

"Eeff. I don't know," he said.

"Don't know what?"

"I don't know about this shot."

Like me, Bert had had bad experiences with hallucinogens. This seemed out of character for him, though, as all of us had been downing absinthe since we'd arrived in Krumlov.

"Dude, this ain't shit," I said. "We blew it up last night!"

"I didn't."

"Bullshit, we all did!"

"Not me. Have you ever actually seen me blow up absinthe?"

"Well, no."

"Yeah, that's because I fuckin' have been. I've been skinin' Midori shots instead n' you faggots just assumed it was absinthe."

"Jesus, Bert. This is the same cool shit you pulled with the cobra blood."

"I know, ooff. I'm scared."

"Well let's just fuckin' do this together. C'mon. We'll break you in with this lil' shit, n' then if and when we find the biggity shit, the *hunno* shit, you'll be boomish n' ready."

"Ait," he said. "To conquering fears, right?"

"That's the gospel baby!"

After a few more shots, we got all oh-mouthed and loopy-eyed. We sat down at a table, laughing, then Bert looked at me seriously.

"I know I've been kind of a pussy on this trip," he said. "It's just been crazy as shit for me, and it's kinda hard to process it all."

"It coo, gaht," I said. "This trip's been a lot for me too. I mean, I may have blown up more than you, but that doesn't mean it hasn't affected me. There were a few times there in India where I almost felt like leaving cuz I couldn't handle it."

"Really?"

"Yeah, man. Like the time I almost snit my France in Manali. That shit wa' cooooo."

He cracked up. "Yeah, I guess I don't feel so bad then. I mean, India was the fuckin' most barg for me, especially after comin' outta Thailand. It was like having a bomb dropped on my soul. I felt so fuckin' depressed. It's only now that I'm startin' to kinda come back into my own and click into it."

"That's so funny you say that."

"Why?"

"Just cuz remember that guy Mace at The Rama?"

"Yeah?"

"Well he said that exact shit about you."

"Really?"

"Yeah, he said he could sense that you were gettin' 'em kinda in India and that you'd come into your own once you got to Eastern Europe cuz the culture was a lil' more inviting for you, in his opinion."

"Damn, Mace was a wise ol' Chuck."

"Dude, no shit. Fool predicted so much. Like that India would change me forever if I let it, and dude it did. So fucking amazing."

Bert paused a minute. His face softened.

"Dude," he said, "I know you think I'm just Respect Guy and fuckin' Culture Guy n' all that, but I have really loved and grown from this whole trip. Even India."

"Yeah?"

"Yeah, man. I wouldn't trade that experience for anything. I mean, it passed me treats, but in a way, it showed me my fears and put 'em right up in front of my face, and I realized that my life's goal was to just keep traveling and blowing up and conquer all my fears. That's really the only way to be free and just totally Chuuuuck."

"I hear ya, man. Actually, I gotta tell ya something, and you gotta kinda keep an open mind when I do."

Bert grew a goofy smile. "I already know you're a fuckin' homo, Felm," he said.

"No, dude, I'm serious. Pretty much only Mason knows about this shit cuz he was there, and to some degree, Blow Up Dude, but dude, this is really serious."

"Okay."

"I feel like I found God in India."

Bert laughed. "Like you did that one night when we all got D and you ran out into that shit-covered cow field in the back hills of L and fell on your knees and started barking at the full moon?"

"Haha. Actually yes, kinda like that. But I'm really seezly though. I saw her."

"Who?"

"Mona."

"Who the fuck is Mona?"

"Bert, just take this with a grain of salt and remember that I was hella D and that you know I'm hella Felmania-ish n' gettem in the head n' shit, but dude, she told me she was our Chuck goddess."

He looked like he was about to laugh. Then his face went dead.

"I'm not gonna say that isn't crazy because it *is* fuckin' crazy," he said. "But I guess there really is a reason we're all friends and we're all together here."

"There is, gaht. I know it in my heart. I mean, we've gone this far with our weird little pseudo-culture, why not take it one step further? Mona may be a dream, but she's our dream. And with those sparkling blue eyes and curly black hair, how can nah nah go wrong?!"

"Oh, now that's fuckin' weird."

"What?"

"Just her description. I've always said that my perfect woman had curly black hair and bright blue eyes. And she always kinda lived inside my head, and when shit would gettem with other bitches, I would just turn to her and she'd fuckin' give ol' Jack Burton advice. I always assumed she was a figment of my imagination, but when you told me that, it just kinda made me go, 'hmm.'"

"Fuck hmm. Let her in, bro! Who cares if she's in your head? She *helps*. Fuck, speaking of conquering fears, just last night she was the one who showed me all *my* fears. And she's the one who's gonna help me—fuck—us conquer them all and build our little Chuck culture one story and one ritual at a time. Damn, that just made me realize something."

"What's that?"

"That culture's about people ritualizing things together to overcome life's fears and build something outta pure love. And that's kinda what we're doin' here. Every blow-up, every explosion, every trip, we add a little piece to the puzzle. Mona's just one more, a *huge* one more, and wouldn't that be cool if someday we could just spread this shit, especially to our Chuck little town and to our ignorant ass country, and just motivate all those genius fools to just get up and bloooow the fucking world up and just learn about all the other cultures out there, too, and even themselves? I mean, if we did all that and hella fools remembered us for it forever, we'd kinda be immortal, huh?"

Bert smiled. "That'd be boomish," he said.

We woke up hungover, but happy. After we shit, showered, and shaved, Bert and I had to cut from The Seeker. We'd only booked our beds for three nights, and the place was now full up with tourists. The only spot for us was at the Hostel Pes with the other Chucks. When we got there, we found it much more low-key than The Seeker. It was basically just a tiny two-story cottage with three rooms, a kitchenette, and a balcony overlooking the Vltava. The woman who owned it, Vlada, was an old suck-lipped cougar with short blond hair and so much makeup she had to squint just to see us. She answered the door in ass-huggers and a cheap blouse and ushered us in with her pointy red nails. We walked in and looked down.

"Look at this lil' guy," Bert said.

Frowning at his feet was a shaggy maroon dog with lips hittin' the ground. He looked up at us with his cloudy eyes and grumbled.

"What's his name?" I asked.

"He Shmudla," Vlada said. She picked him up and lit a cigarette. Shmudla started lapping at the smoke. "Come, I shou you room."

She put us in a room with the other Chucks. They were all stoked to see us. We immediately started chatting about what to do for our last day in Krumlov. Everyone had different ideas. I wanted to make breakfast and shop for jewelry. Kip and Bert wanted to get their tickets for Munich where they'd be meeting Kip's friend. Chuck and Tim wanted to do a bit more sightseeing in old town. And Mason wanted to surprise his Aussie nah at her hostel and try to coax her into saying "Yesss" instead of "Naauuee."

We fanned out across Krumlov and did our shit. That night, after a big homemade pasta dinner, the six of us decided to go in search of the Hunno Mil King. We asked Vlada where we might find such a thing. She raised her tattooed eyebrows.

"Go to small store after bridge wis green door," she said. "It have."

We scooped up some cash and zipped out the door. As it was closing behind us, Vlada called out, "Come to Zion Bar ven finish. Vee have party!"

Now it was on. We trotted across the bridge, poking our heads this way and that in search of the green door. It was dark and misty out with only the dim streetlights sprouting up from the ground to light our way. We came to a break in the path that snaked off to a dusty corner. The walls on either side of it had strange shadows like demon fingers stretching up to their gutters.

"It's gotta be down here," I said. When we got to the end, we found a door. It was pine green and streaked across with ghost semen gossamer.

"Think this is the place?"

"Only one way to find out," Chuck mumbled.

He pushed the door open and we stepped inside. To creaks and cracks, a curious sight flooded our eyes. On either side of us were shelves of old liquor bottles connected with cobwebs. There were red, white, and brown, but not green or yellow bottles. These spirits—the ascending levels of absinthe, if you will—were on shelves behind the front counter. At the bottom, were the cheap cough-syrup greens. At the top, were the banana yellows cluttered to the nuts with so many hunks of wormwood. Manning this impressive collection of beatnik blood was a hunched-up little dude with an upturned egg head and big red schnoz. He was fiendishly cupping his hands over one another and glaring at us under an M-shaped unibrow.

"Pleeeeez, come in," he said.

We walked up to his counter and had a peek at his products. Five giant bottles of the hunno mil King boasting Van Gough's spooked mug stretched across the top shelf.

"Give us the strongest shit you got," I said, pointing upwards.

Mr. Egg looked at me and smiled. He reached under the counter and pulled out a lumpy red cloth. He held it in front of us and slipped the cloth away. What lay in his hand was a potbellied bottle with a curvy neck like a snake's. It ended in a huge, misshapen cork and was filled with what looked like alien urine mixed with psychedelic mushroom hunks.

"Holy shit." Bert exclaimed. "What the hell is that?"

"It is my own special blend," Mr. Egg said. "One hundred fifty milliliters thujone per liter."

"Jesus," I said. "How much?"

"I fink you vill cry if I tell you . . . two hundred dollar."

Our nuts tightened. We all looked at each other with worried eyebrows.

"That's bank," I said. "Let's just get the King and skut."

"Fuck that," Kip piped up. "This is our last night here. Let's just go for it. I'll throw in fifty and you guys can each do thirty."

"Okay," we said. We gathered the money and gave it to Mr. Egg. He smiled hellishly and handed us the bottle.

"You won't be disappointed," he said.

Zion Bar was a place we had seen before. It was a stone's throw from Hostel Pes, but it was always boarded up and silent. Tonight, blades of red fog were shooting through the cracks in its wooden walls. Endless streams of cackling were sailing out its windows. We pushed open its front door—an ebony monster with a crescent moon for a peephole—and wandered in. We found the source of all the hullaballoo in its main den. Five men were sitting around the bar's main table drinking and smoking and laughing. Four of the men had instruments—flute, violin, bongos, guitar—and one just had a beer. I recognized from their coffee skin, narrow eyes, and lanky Dravidian hands that they were Roma. We were apprehensive to join them at first. After all, we were *gadji* or non-Gypsies. We spotted Vlada. She was sitting at the center in her evening finest, batting her peacock lashes at her would-be suitors and throwing up toasts. When she saw us, she pulled open her busted grill.

"Come," she cried. "Vee vill sit. Vee vill drink!"

The six of us piled in around the huge table. None of us knew a lick of Romany, but we made do with Vlada's help, our own broken Czech, and some English. All the guys we met were characters. There was the bongo player with his wild frizzy hair and heavy brow, the flute player with his giant specs and sunken cheeks, the violinist with his twisted Dali mustache and crazy eyes, and the beer-sipper with his long, scraggly black hair and wood gnome's beard. Undoubtedly, the most striking of the five was the guitar player. He had steely gray-blue eyes that lasered through your skin, and a wavy, head-to-chin mane of ashen hair like whipped cream and mercury. The whole time we were mingling, he just nursed a slivovice quietly. I thought he might be uncomfortable with our presence, so I pulled out the special blend.

"You guys wanna do shots?" I asked.

Vlada's eyes lit up. "You find. Oh, and forest stuff, not King. Dis *nejlepší*. Let's to drink!"

Luckily, we had a full liter of the shit. I poured up twelve big yellow shots and handed them all out.

"To tonight," I yelled, holding up my shot. Before I downed it, I made sure everyone else did first. I did this for Bert's sake to keep the pressure high. He looked at me with the shooter to his lips and laughed. There was a certain strength in his wily gaze, almost like it was he who was daring me and not the other way around.

"Get me," he said, throwing back the shot.

"No, Bert. You fuckin' get *me*."

When the thujone hit my tongue, my head turned to wax and got blown to thousands of side-streaking tears by an imaginary flame thrower. I looked around the room and saw everyone in a similar state. Now that we were all clicked in, it was time to make a little music. At Vlada's request, the Roma picked up their instruments and started to play. Things began with a twittering of the flute and a bomp, bomp, bomp of the bongos. Soon the violin squeaked in, edging out haunting cat cries fit to give the moon jitters. This strange accordion mass breathed in and out. Our hearts started pumping and our hands started beating. Gray Eyes lifted himself from the table and put one foot up on the bench. In a swift, counterclockwise motion, he spun his guitar around and rested it on his knee. His fingertips quickly tickled across the strings like drips of wine from a fountain's lip. This kipped Vlada into action, and she burst out yipping and yodeling and screaming like a Persian housewife at a mullah's funeral. The cacophonous roar of sounds set my chest on fire. It was almost like every note being hit was a small voice begging me to sing. I reached deep into my heart and pulled out everything I had. Esoteric lyrics, even mysterious to me, came exploding out of my mouth in every language I had ever been acquainted with. It was a raw, unmitigated blend of English, Spanish, Patois, French, Portuguese, Czech, Farsi, Arabic, Greek, Albanian, Thai, Hindi, Catalan, and German. I was a huge rapping conduit for the souls of world languages. When the last word slipped from my mouth, the room fell silent. I was buzzing at the nodes with super-flow.

At the crack of dawn, we said goodbye to our new friends. There were no emails or cell numbers exchanged, just hugs and grins and real human things. Before I slipped out the door, ol' Gray Eyes called me over. As I walked back toward him, I remembered Mona's phrase. I didn't really know how to approach the subject, so I just wrote the phrase on a drink napkin and handed it to him. He held it up to his storm-drop eyes and smiled warmly.

"What does it mean?" I asked, hoping he'd understand me.

"It mean make peace," he said, chuckling.

"Make peace? All that time and it was something as simple as make peace?"

"Ava, make peace with beast, make peace with beast inside."

Gray Eyes reached into his coat pocket and handed me a baggy. It was filled with hunks of sparkling green herb and tiny bits of mushroom. My heart seized up and my mouth fell open. I slipped into a state of panicked recollection.


It was February 2004, in San Diego. None of us Chucks had moved in together yet. Mason was still up in L-town going to a dead-end community college. Bert was shacked up on the other side of SD with one very coked-out and broke Ned (the Blow Me guy). Tim was twenty miles south, living in a giant apartment all by himself with only his black cat Mofo to keep him company. And I was residing in a shadowy dump with two weirdos near UCSD campus.

One breezy boring night, Tim hit me up.

"I got 'em," he said.

"Shit. What happened?"

"No, I mean, I got 'em—the shrums you wanted."

A capsule of adrenaline burst against my brainstem.

"You got 'em?" I eeked.

"Yeah, grooge over."

A week earlier, I had asked Tim to put his feelers out for some magic mushrooms. I was curious about trying them and would only do so in his presence; he's kind of like my drug guru.

I hurriedly packed my things and blasted over to his place. He answered the door with Mofo crawling around his neck and sparkles in his eyes.

"Here they are," he said, holding up a plastic baggie. Inside were three crooked-stemmed mushrooms with umbrella tops, all threaded through with electric blue veins. I got goosebumps just looking at them.

"Who's the extra one for?" I asked.

"Raja. He's greegin' over tomorrow afternoon to sauce 'em with us."

Raja was one of my weirdo Indian roommates Tim had clicked with. The two of them were major stoners and were constantly calling one another to smoke out and whatnot.

"He's not gonna act bitchin' is he?" I said.

"Nah, he be coo," Tim said.

That night I could barely sleep. I kept wondering what I might encounter on my little journey through the self. Tim told me whatever happened, the worst thing I could do was panic.

"You just have to be Chuck and let it take you," he said.

I knew this was easier said than done. Not two months prior, Mason had shown up at my parents' place one night while I was home for the holidays. He'd brought a bag full of pot brownies. Like an idiot, I ate more than I should have. I ended up calling 911 because I thought I was having a heart attack. It took a full heart scan, two valiums, ten EMTs and twelve electrodes to the chest to convince me otherwise. I felt like such a fool after the whole ordeal. I had to prove to myself I could do better.

When the morning came, I was anxious. I wanted to chew my baby blue up right then, but we had to wait for our third party. Raja finally arrived two hours later. He came lumbering in the room like a giant sun bear, carrying a fifth of Johnny in one hand and a video camera in the other.

"Let's fuckin' blowwww up!" he said in his deep, breathy voice. He had blood-spattered eyes and a jack-o-lantern smile. Once the camera was set up and the starter flick, *Bruce Almighty* was in, Tim went to the kitchen. He brought back three knives, a jar of chunky peanut butter, and a loaf of Wonder Bread.

"What's all that for?" I asked.

"Shrums taste fuckin' *yummy* so you're gonna want sumthin' to sauce 'em with," he said.

"Ait." I lathered up a slice of bread with peanut butter and crumpled my mushroom on top. As it shredded against my fingertips,

I saw tiny puffs of topaz dust spray up from its edges. "This fucker's gonna be poty," I said to Tim. He just looked at me and grinned.

The peanut butter and bread almost completely masked the taste of the mushroom. I detected the faintest hint of cork as I chewed, but nothing that might make me puke or panic. This almost made me think I'd ingested nothing of any importance. I got half an hour in denial's cozy little waiting room till madness performed a grand defenestration on me. It started as a pinch on my stomach or rather, what felt like a pinch, but soon blossomed up into my ribcage like a rose of fire. My eyeballs were sizzling in their sockets. When the flames of anxiety began lapping at the underside of my brain wrinkles, I saw red sirens.

I'm gonna die. I'm gonna die. I'm gonna die, I thought. I looked over at the phone and contemplated calling 911. Suddenly, Tim's words blanketed my mind.

"Be Chuck. Let it take you."

With a lazy grin, I sank down into the couch cushions and tilted my head to the side. I was ready for my ride.

Things began slowly. The three of us floated up out of our seats with the camera and wandered into Tim's room. We plopped down on his messy bed and let ourselves fly. Tim aided the cause by firing up his stereo. He put on the Peppers' "Chasing the Girl" and turned it up full blast. The music tickled my throbbing cortex and pulled me melting away into the realms of psychedelic bliss. I soon began having visuals of an extremely odd nature. First, it was the leopard spots on Tim's comforter dancing up and across the walls, followed by my brain turning purple and swelling up from the bottom of a water cup. Then it was ants on the ceiling and bugs on the rug. I could hardly hold my eyes still when Tim made things madder. Like a deranged chemist, he went rifling through his cluttered shelves. He grabbed up a brush, some paint, and a dusty beret.

"I gotta fuckin' paint it," he cried.

He popped the beret on his scalp, dipped the brush in blue paint, and streaked a leech across either side of his upper lip. He looked like a faux French artist in a Fraggle Rock special.

"You're just gonna paint yer damn face?" Raja asked.

"Not at all," he shouted arrogantly. He fumbled through his closet. He came back out with a splotchy canvas and a corky little warm grin on his face. "I'm gonna just express all my inner explosions on here."

In a flurry, he dipped his brush in every which color and smeared it all across the canvas. Within minutes, he had created what looked like a mass suicide by shotgun. I could almost see wolves howling over the mangled carcasses everywhere. Just to peek at it made me sick.

"I'm gonna roll out n' Chuck on my own," I said, pinching the bridge of my nose.

Tim and Raja were so transfixed in their own little worlds, they didn't even hear me. I left the room with zero resistance and wandered back out to the living room. As I was becoming increasingly introverted, a solo chill-sesh seemed just perfect. I grabbed myself a seat on the sofa and snuggled in.

At first, I was content just sitting there. But soon my thoughts began to stew and bleed down to my fingertips.

I gotta write something, I said to myself. I went over and grabbed the pen and journal I'd packed and sat back down. What flowed out of me was this:

*As I delve into my mind's eye, I can see the sea crumple into a thousand tiny fragments till the fire inside my mind tears at my soul and a chasm of tears flood from the spiritual embodiment of a thousand miles from my heart's only wish to have its head combustible with a heaving thrust of soul fizzle. What ponderous thoughts were sailing through the recesses of my endangered soul! How insane it is to be enveloped in such a pleasant state of madness. As these words dance magical fire before my eyes, I shout with my spirit's only voice. Oh, such vibrant caress. Such vibrant caress! I AM GOD!*

With that, I dropped my pen and closed my eyes. I saw a flash of white light behind my eyelids, then a scene unfolded. I was standing at the nexus of my mind and self, watching as the thousands of doorways between the two opened and closed like the wings of halved butterflies, while screaming and voices and laughter sailed out from their mysterious chambers beyond. Above all this, dangled a pair of women's feet. I tried to reach for them and my toes kissed off. I floated higher and higher till I thought I would break. I wanted to cry out in fear when I heard Tim's words again.

*Be Chuck. Let it take you.*

Just then, I felt an overwhelming urge to be free of everything. With eyes still closed, I shot up from my seat and removed the items encumbering me. I pulled off my watch, my rings, my chains, my shirt, my shoes, my socks, my pants. I went leaping through a crack in my forehead in a thousand splinters of light and flew spiraling toward the living, breathing Van Gough paintings on Tim's wall. As a hovering and separate entity, I could now see myself for who I really was. Everything was visible, all my billions of conflicting parts. The Mexican, the white, the black, the Chuck, the wack, the beaner, the spic, the killer, the lover, the saint, the sinner, the writer, the trekker, the yuppie, the beggar, the liar, the fire, the god, the devil all stitched together in lumpy, iridescent pieces to make a strange and gyrating creature seemed dreamed up by Arjuna after his epoch chat with Lord Krishna. When the vision ended, I slipped back into my closing dome and moved my lips. The words came out effortlessly.

"I'm beautiful," I said. "Jesus Christ. I'm fucking beautiful!"

In only my boxers, I went running back to Tim's room. I threw open the door and looked on. Tim was laughing silently and painting his walls with shoe polish. Raja was drinking whiskey and staring at his fingers. My grand entrance spooked them both. They stopped what they were doing and looked up at me with wide eyes.

"I just saw myself on another plane of reality," I exclaimed. "I'm fuckin' beautiful!"

Raja crossed his eyes and snickered. Tim smiled at me tenderly.

A few weeks after my experience, I began to feel uneasy. No longer was I the liberated soul reeling on psilocybin, but a man of quivering fragments, tiptoeing through life in fear that one swift step might send me crumbling to the ground. One night, in a moment of desperation, I approached Raja.

"I'm afraid of losing my mind," I said to him. "Everything has changed, and I don't feel like I have control anymore."

He looked at me with his lazy red eyes and grinned maniacally.

"Dude, that's funny that you think that," he said.

"Why?"

"Well, because my old roommate did shrums and six months later he went schizophrenic—."

The second the words left his lips, I heard an awful shriek rising from my bowels. It summoned dozens of giant tentacles that went ripping through my body and coiling around my arms, legs, and neck. Soon all that inner beauty I had seen before was blacked out by the shadow of this hideous beast. I was now a madman, reaching up for the sun's rays as the devil cupped my mouth and dragged me down to hell.

For the next four months, I distracted myself with plans to go to Central America. When all the Chucks ended up coming, I found just enough strength to force the beast deeper into my subconscious. This wasn't a defeat or a deletion by any means, but rather a small triumph. I knew in my heart I'd still have to deal with the fucker at inopportune moments, but at least I had a handle on things. Such was the case till the present moment.

# BLED

After a long trek through the Czech Republic, Austria, and Slovenia, we finally pulled into Bled's Lesce station. The tracks were grown over with grass, and the benches were bare. Everything was silent and calm. It almost seemed like we'd shown up just after the last gasp of a plague. The only thing that reminded us of the living were a few bovines chewing their cud in a back field. We stepped off the train and were hit square in the nose.

"Jesus," Chuck said. "Slovenia smells like cow shit."

At a parking lot behind the station, we caught a bus into Bled proper. It dropped us off at a pension named Bled and Breakfast. We booked a dorm room for two nights. It was cramped but cozy with a bath and three bunk beds.

We washed our nuts and hit the town. All the houses in our area were made of gingerbread wood with deeply slanted roofs and crosshatched windows. We wandered by, soaking in the fresh air, and chatting. We stopped for photos when we reached Lake Bled. Its waters were dark green in the center and got lighter toward shore. A bright limestone cliff on the north shore cradled a red-coned castle called Blejski grad. A swath of forest ran below. It grew up in soft patches like a young girl's fuzz. On an islet at the center of the lake was The Assumption of Mary Pilgrimage Church. Its most notable feature was the black spire of its bell tower. It stood like a slanted phantom, the chapel below it cramping its style.

We walked till we entered "new town." It looked like a trendy sliver of Aspen. Amidst its casinos and banks and neatly shaved concrete, we found a tiny enclave of history. It was an old restaurant built in 1805 and aptly named *Stara Gostilna* (the Old Restaurant). The place was warm and glowing, with outdoor seating and walls crawling with ivy. We slipped through the heavy oak doors and were greeted inside by the smiling owner. He was a portly man in a chef's suit, with bottle cap specs and a five o'clock shadow around his bulbous chin.

*"Dobrodošla,"* he said, ushering us in. He seated us at a black wood table cut by hatchets and bought us beers. While we sipped 'em and looked at the menu, I stole glances at our surroundings. The walls were covered in old photos of Slovenian mountaineers at peak tops, elk horns, and stuffed boars' heads. I felt like I was at some sort of hunter's lodge where the best thing to eat would be the freshest kill. I ordered a heaping bowl of venison goulash followed by a thick peppered bear steak. Everything was hot, bloody, and delicious and got washed down with four good pints of Laško—Slovenia's most popular beer.

When dinner ended, we were good and tipsy. We were looking to blow up, but as it was a Wednesday, not much was going on in New Bled. We booked it back to the suburbs and found a little Irish bar there named Mickey's. We went inside and grabbed ourselves a grip of Laškos. Most of the main den was cluttered with drunk and smoking dudes watching football. We moved to the back where there was a foosball table and a ring of couches. Chilling on the couch closest to us were a pair of Slovenian cuties. One was a brunette and the other a redhead. They both had button noses, peacoats, and high heels. We slid in around them and struck up a conversation. They said their names were Lavra and Liza and that, yes, they did come here often.

"Dis is not good night, dough," Lavra said. "You must come tomorrow ven Stanko vill be here. He make all party happen."

"Who the fuck is Stanko?" I asked, chuckling.

"You vill meet if you vill come tomorrow night," Liza said, licking her lips. "He is coolest man in Bled. Dis is why he only come out

Thursday, Friday, Saturday."

"Sounds like a fuckin' winner," I said.

After twenty minutes of banal chitchat, it became very apparent that none of us was going to get any action. All the girls could talk about was Stanko, Stanko, Stanko. It bored us all to fucking tears.

"Let's go chuck back to the room," Tim said to me between Stankos. "You can watch me roll up the gypsy joint."

We bunted back, and I busted out the shit. Tim rolled it up lickety-split and held it up in front of my face with a grin. The damn thing was sparkling white and perfectly symmetrical. It looked like a tiny icicle plucked from the beard of a hibernating wizard.

"You just tell me when ya wanna beef this, Felm," Tim said. I nodded.

It was beautiful out the next day. Since we could only stay two nights at the Bled and Breakfast, we decided to use the good weather to find a new place. We split into two's and combed the town. Tim and I got squat, but Mason and Chuck got lucky. The place they found was five minutes' walk from New Bled. It had spacious rooms and even a little balcony we could chuck out on and skink. Tim and I decided to share a room, as did Chuck and Mason. After a tiny nap back at BnB, we got up and hit the castle.

We did the treacherous hike to the top and took photos. We bought super local, and super rare, *malvazija* red from a little cellar manned by a bald monk with a ghoulish frown and pointy silver eyebrows, then cut back to the room to drop our crap off. After that, we went to Stara Gostilna. I inhaled a plate of venison goulash and four beers, but instead of being happy and buzzed, I was pissed. I couldn't quite put my finger on why. I knew it had something to do with something that was supposed to happen somewhere in Bled that night. I shrugged it off while we looked for a spot to party. All the crummy clubs in town were empty, so we cut to Mickey's. As it was early, and the place was packed, I figured this was where all the locals started. It wasn't until I got inside that I realized a little extra special sumthin' was going on there.

The guy certainly didn't look like much on his own. He was about five seven with a frayed ponytail, a weasel's goatee, and a beer gut bulging from behind a blue sweater that read "Brooklyn." Had I seen him on the streets, I'd have taken him for a chickless bitch with zero moxie. But somehow, through sheer fault of either Slovenian female idiocy or blind fuckin' luck, this dumpy bastard was crawling with beautiful women. Among them were Lavra and Liza. But the one he seemed most preoccupied with was a mastodon blonde named Bojanca. She wore long, tight jeans and a black leather jacket. A serpentine braid slithered down her back. She had an angular face that was somehow soft and beautiful. How this asswipe—who was scratching himself at the bar and making smug kissy faces at all the ladies—ever landed himself such a woman, was beyond me.

When Lavra and Liza spotted us, they called us over. They introduced us to their friend, but we already knew his fuckin' name.

"Guys, dis is called *Staaanko*." Lavra beamed. She said his name like she was introducing a traveling magician. I shook his hand briefly then ordered myself a triple shot of Jack. I sucked it down and stumbled into the lounge with the Chucks. The Pride of Bled and his entourage of sycophantic and starry-eyed females followed. Not one of them paid any attention to us. I just sat there and scowled. After twenty minutes, I was ready to leave. Then Stanko looked our way and said, "You know, America is such ridiculous country. I really hate how dey try to be *po*lis of whole verld."

I was stunned. Not just by the thoughtlessness of his words, but at how much they infuriated me. I mean, I'd mirrored almost that exact sentiment a hundred times before. But to hear it come from someone who wasn't American, wasn't one of *us*, lit me up like a thumbtack to the testicle.

"Yeah, well, I really don't appreciate that fuckin' remark," I snapped.

Stanko chuckled. He snapped his finger for Bojanca to come sit on his lap, then went off again.

"I don't really care," he said. "Every president of yours is starting wars wif so many countries. You act like dis is your verld and you do it right now in Iraq and Afghanistan."

"And you're judging *me* for this?"

"No, I'm just saying dis is bullshit government."

"Oh, so what? Slovenia's suddenly perfect now? I mean, weren't you guys just accused of committing war crimes against Yugoslav troops during the war for independence?"

"This is not a point."

"No, it's very much the fucking point. I'm so sick of people from other countries, especially Europeans with sordid histories, bad-mouthing my country, however fucked up it may be, and then just expecting me to take it in the rear end. I neither made, nor voted for any of the political decisions that facilitated those wars, so I'm tired of fucking hearing about them."

There was a pause in the room. Then Stanko raised his eyebrows. "If you not support these things, then vie you so angry at my statement?" he asked.

I thought for a long moment. The answer finally came. "I guess because no matter how much I hate what my country does, I'm still an American."

Stanko and his Brooklyn sweater had nothing to say to that.

When it became apparent that my presence was no longer welcome in the lounge, I split and went sniffing around the bar for other company. Like before, most of its clientele were local dudes, but there was one pretty girl at the back having a beer and looking lonely. She had deep black hair and a pale face. I realized from her almost glowing complexion that she was a waitress I had seen serving drinks earlier. I ordered a shot of Jack and slammed it. A half minute later, I was at her table with my arms fanned, firing questions.

"So where you from?" I asked.

"Here." She giggled. "I born myself in Bled."

"Oh yeah? Me too. My mother was too lazy to go to the hospital and push me out, haha."

She looked at me cockeyed. I ran my palms across both temples and changed the subject.

"So, uh, what's yer name?"

"Well, my name is—" Before she could squeak it out, a presence broke her flow. I felt a hand on my shoulder, then the conversation went cold. The hand belonged to a stout, bald man with a leathery face and calculating eyes. He had on blue Diesels and a black turtleneck so tight I could see the lobster-back outline of his well-sculpted torso underneath.

"How is it?" he asked, in a soft Irish accent.

"Good," I said. "Who are you?"

"I'm Mickey. And you are . . .?"

"Johann. Wait, Mickey. Do you own this place?"

"I do. And she works for me, the dear."

"Oh, I get it. I'll back off. I've just been having zero luck with the ladies lately, and I'm feeling shitty and . . ."

Mickey's eyes lit up. "Anything you wanna talk about?" he asked.

"Ummm"

Under normal circumstances, I'd have shared nothing deep with him about my love life. But since I was drunk and now chickless, and Mickey looked like a guy that might know his shit, I decided to open up to him. I told him of all my recent trouble with the ladies. I even mentioned Leddy from Prague and how I wanted to go see her after the trip. I was hoping Mickey would have some sage words on how to approach the matter. His advice was, "Fuck her."

"Fuck her?" I asked.

"Yes, fuck her. Now would you like a beer?"

"Sure," I said.

He signaled to the waitress sitting with us. When she left, Mickey started acting very strange. Since I was fiercely drunk, I can't remember everything he did. I just remember that he kept making odd little comments about my appearance and mannerisms, and then when I would react, he'd attempt to calm me with pouty lips, almost like he was calming his uppity poodle.

When the waitress arrived with our beers, I'd had enough of his bullshit. I looked at Mickey like, What the fuck? and he froze.

"You know I'm gay, right?" he said frankly.

"What?" I yelled.

"You know you're my type, right?"

"Uhhhh . . ." I didn't know what to say. I decided to play it off as a joke. "Yeah, sure. Quit screwin' around, man."

An injured expression melted down Mickey's face. I turned to the waitress and laughed.

"He's joking, right?"

She shook her head at me. When I looked back, Mickey was gone.

After that, the night fell flat. I rounded up the Chucks and we all cut. On our way back to the hostel, I told them what had just happened. When I finished my story, I laughed.

"Can you believe that faggot?" I said, referring to Mickey.

I elicited some chuckles from Tim, Mason, and Kip. Chuck just thinned his lips. "You know you really need to get rid of your homophobia," he said. "It's kind of annoying."

I was going to snap back, but my mouth wouldn't let me. I shoved my hands in my pockets and walked ahead with a hot face.

"I'll work on it," I mumbled.


Next day was a day for change. We changed bases, changed attitudes, and changed sights to a new destination. Our goal was to travel on foot all the way out to Pokljuška Luknja—a gorge cut through by a river deep in the Julian Alps.

After we were all settled in our new place, we hit the road. It was long and windy and fed through a bunch of little villages. Each village comprised a few red-roofed houses, a couple restaurants, and a small church. It seemed like every twenty steps there was a wooden nativity scene or a crucifix with a bloody and sleepy-eyed Jesus. While musing at this strange mix of elements, I got to chatting with Chuck. I felt (as did my bruised ego) that I should give him a little insight into one of his fears, as he had done for me.

"You know, you don't have to be so afraid to talk to nahs," I said to him. "Even if they say Hayes D to you, it's still good practice."

He ignored me and hastened his pace. He got five steps ahead then fell back.

"Chuck?" I said. "You coo?"

"Yeah," he mumbled. "I know I have a problem with that. Sometimes I just feel tight about myself and just can't get up the balls to go talk with nahs, eeff."

"Well, lemme tell you sumthin', bro. You've got a lot of game to work with, more than you might know."

"Oh yeah? Like what?"

Now, I'm not one to bullshit a guy when he's down. I knew I had to spit Chuck the truth, and that didn't include telling him he was the hottest thing to hit the ladies since fake dicks. I decided to go the personality route.

"You're a prick," I said.

"Jesus. That helps," he said.

"No man, think about it. There are so many guys out there being walked all over by women because they're too nice. Shit, remember the saying? Nice guys finish last? That shit is true, bro. But you, you've got something special. Besides just being smart and well-traveled and open-minded and even the chilliest, chuckest guy a chick could ever want, you're a natural, wholehearted prick. You've just gotta use that to your advantage man, so when nahs start finding out, 'Hey, this guy blows up, he doesn't take my shit,' they're gonna wanna see how far they can push it. And that's when ya got 'em. That's when ya rope 'em in!"

He looked at me and smiled. "I guess I could give it a shot," he said. "What the fuck?"

Just then, we arrived at a crossroads. Straight ahead was more paved road, and to the left was a dusty path toward God knew what.

"Do we know which way the gorge is?" I asked, looking at Mason.

"No," he replied. "The map dead ends here."

We could have kept going straight but change was in our blood. We turned left.

The little dirt road led us down through shrubland. There was a wall of trees in front of us obstructing our view. We pushed past it and found a river. Its water was crystal blue and flowing gently like the skin of a cosmic portal.

"I bet this takes us into the gorge," Mason said.

Heeding his words, we walked along the river path and followed it toward the source. It had us looping and winding past tiny forest homes, wildflowers, and hills and hills of sea green. At the culmination of everything there was a break; a small gravel lot just before the entrance into the unknown.

"Zalt," we yelled.

We stepped inside. The gorge opened up all around us. Its rocky edges were dripping with peridot tree leaves. Its lifeline was pouring down the edges of boulders in shades of blended ice. I really didn't have any words, so I continued walking. The path under my feet turned to wood and lifted and extended itself all the way up and around to meet the contours of Pokljuška Luknja. The belly of the gorge was enormous, a hundred feet high in some places, with divots and cracks and caves all carving out its dozens of faces. Accenting this rash of crookedness, were streaks of jade plant life dangling down in uneven tendrils. Their longest points tickled the skin of the river.

We followed the curves of the wooden path. They had us weaving in and out under the sky till we came to an outcropping too chuck to skut from. It was damp, dark, and cool inside. There were spots to drop our crap and a bench just big enough for four. As we sat there, looking out at all the beauty, a strange feeling overcame us. It was almost like a dung beetle that had been lodged in our hearts was crawling its way to the surface of our chests.

"Ooff," Tim said. "Wanna blow up?" He looked at me with those warm wise eyes.

"Chea hea," I said. "This is the place, gaht. This is the time."

He smiled and pulled out the perfectly rolled joint. He handed it to me and clicked his lighter.

"You first, Felmania," he said.

The flame hit the tip and I inhaled. I was fucking with fate.

At first, I was nervous, tense. My hands stiffened and my jaws clenched. Everything was rubbery now. No more beauty, no more silence. The voices at the pit of my stomach were screaming to be released. I took two steps down and cut into a run. Where I was going, I did not know. It was a knee-jerk response to *Who*. He was right beside me at all times, whispering in smoke through the trees and flashing his giant, red eyes. I ran and I ran. I ran so fucking hard I could hear my lungs pop. Poof! My knees gave out.

I was standing at the nexus again, panting for dear life, praying I had the will to fight. I made fists like a boxer and took my little stance. The fucker came rushing up and nearly fainted me, all eyes turning white and collapsing to the ground like a pale worm. He was huge, black like squid ink, and torn with muscle and veins. His demonic face was stretched and curved at both ends like a sleeping crescent moon's. Only this fucker wasn't sleeping. He was grinning! Grinning a grin of thin butcher knives and heated eyes and pointy eyebrows and melted-cheese-string cheeks like some hideous creature about to skin a newborn fresh out tha womb. He reached out for me with his wicked fingers and tucked a razor-sharp nail under my chin. I swung and I swung, but he lifted me with ease. I went sailing into the air like an angry bug. I was fighting everything inside me to send him back to his cave. I got a dozen punches in, then I fell limp, impaled through the chin by the nail wicker killer.

I was just about to slip into the blackness when Mona's face lit it up.

"Make peace," she said, in her wild gypsy tongue. "Make peace with the beast."

Her words were like clear water sent straight to hell. My eyes popped open and my body began to swell. Soon I was just as big as him, with a grin to match. I took one step back and let the spirits unlatch. They floated between us in so many different colors; red, green, yellow, blue, black tar rubber. I slipped my hand between the gap, and I offered some love. I said, "Fuck this silly beef. We're the same, my blood." Then homey said the same and we pulled it together, Mona floating overhead now once and forever.

The walk back to our place was peaceful. Everything—all the quivering trees and yellow popcorn fields and hidden churches, even a dead and bloated hedgehog that we came across—was bathed in soft green light. I was so wrapped up in everything, I felt compelled to write one. I entitled it "Peast Out" and set it to the steps of my groove.

When we got back into town, we were saucy as fuck. We stopped at a little grocery store and bought garlic bread, gnocchi, and meat sauce fixin's. Everything cooked up real nice in our kitchen. An hour later, we had a huge, steaming meal on our table.

"Wanna crack yer bottle of malvazija?" I asked Chuck. "I'm gonna open mine."

"Sure," he said. "Maybe that *real* Slovene stuff'll be my liquid courage for the nahs tonight."

I felt like telling him about Mona then and there. I got dangerously close but thought better of it.

"How 'bout I be yer wingman tonight?" I said instead. "Hook you up."

Chuck just chuckled.

With full bellies and plenty of the monk's special brew up in us, we took to the streets in search of a spot to explode. Since we were sick of Mickey's and closer to New Town, we opted to hit the latter. We got to the front steps of a little place called Bled Bar. It looked rowdy but warm. Everyone inside was laughing and howling and clinking beer mugs at big wooden tables under orange lights. There wasn't a single expat in sight. As we walked up to the bar, our little thread of Chuck life stuck out like a tampon string from a bikini fold.

"Let's skink some sneers n' mingle n' blend a lil'," I said. "Foolz'r lookin' at us like we're fuckin' straight *yokels!*"

The looks seemed to die down a bit once we all had Laškos in our hands. It was enough to give us the confidence to go scouting for nahs. Mason went sniffing in earnest. Tim chose the cork route, and Chuck chose the, "I'm going to lean against the bar like a sack of shit and feel sorry for myself because I don't have the balls to talk to that cute chick next to me" route. I knew that even *real* Slovenian wine wasn't gonna get his nuts to pump testosterone. I'd have to do it myself.

"Let's talk to these nahs next to us," I said. The nahs I was referring to were two cute brunettes with big glossy lips and hoodrat loops. They were close enough for a chat and seemed to be eyeing us.

"Ait. We'll talk to 'em," Chuck groaned.

The conversation started well. "Hi, what's your name? Yada, yada, yada." Once the pleasantries were over, I started getting in deep. I expected Chuck to be doing the same. I looked over my shoulder at him. He was standing there lock-jawed with his cock in his hands while ney ney rolled her eyes uncomfortably.

"Chuck's a great cook," I said.

"Really?" his girl said. "Vat you cook?"

"Ah, well, it's pretty good."

The girl's face tweaked.

"He means the *pasta,*" I interjected. "The pasta he cooks is pretty good. Bomb, in fact!"

Chuck hadn't cooked the pasta that night, I had. Shit, he couldn't cook a can of Spaghetti O's to save his first-born son, but that wasn't the point.

"Bomb?" the girl asked.

"You know? Bomb, like good?"

"No, no, no, bomb no good. Vee gonna go."

"What? What the hell are you talking about?"

Before I got an answer, she grabbed her friend and took off. I opened my mouth and yelled, "Come back here and I'll drop a *jizz* bomb on your face, bitch!"

Chuck gave me the look. "Really great, Johann," he said, chuckling. "Ah, well, at least ya got me talkin' to 'em."

As much as it killed me, I'd had enough of skirt chasin' with

Chuck. I needed a front man more adept at flappin' his gums. There was only one dude for me to turn to—the man, the beard, Mason Scot McKinney. As I'd hoped, homeboy's game was on that night. When I found him, he was already chatting up two blond chicks and laying the slimy foundations for what I was certain he hoped would devolve into a threesome.

"Mind if I join?" I asked, sliding in next to him.

"Ooff, chea hea," he replied.

The girls he was talking to were named Nina and Lex. They seemed to take to us till Tim came wandering out of the bar all drunk and squirrely eyed. He took one look at me inching toward Nina and scowled.

"How would you like me to blow you up right now like you blew me up in Thailand?" he said to me.

I looked at him dumbfounded. Thailand? I thought. What had I done? Then it hit me. On our first night in Bangkok, I had fucked him over, and big time. I remember, we were all outside the Tandu House meeting chicks, and just as he was about to take off with his cute lil' prospect, I asked him point blank in an attempt to salt his game if he was gonna fuck her. It had almost killed his chances. It had almost killed his story.

Had I not been tipsy, I might have responded rationally. Instead, I told him to go fuck himself. He walked off glowering. I felt bad that I'd been so harsh, but his ability to hold a silent grudge and then spring it on fools when they least expected was especially irritating that night. I knew I'd have a fight waiting for me when I got back. To avoid this, I tried to push the issue with Nina and see if we could take off somewhere. She only smiled and gave me the number to her and Lex's apartment.

"Call us tomorrow," she said. "Vee go have fun."

With this shred of promise in my head, I went back to our room and confronted Tim. I asked him, "What the fuck?" to break the ice, but he just froze up.

"I'm just sick of you fucking with me," he said.

"How was I fucking with you tonight? Jesus man, weren't we getting along today?"

"That's just it, Johann. It's not tonight, it's other times. Tonight just reminded me of them."

"What, like what happened in Bangkok? Didn't you already bash my face in with a snowball for that?"

"It's not just that. It's how you teased me about not yelling at the robber in Prague, about buying the megaphone, calling me stupid nicknames that you know I hate, talking about dicks and balls all the time, and embarrassing me in public."

"So when did I do that?"

"Oh, your 'Cumshots a' Fallin' On My Face' song on the way to Prague Castle?"

"Oh, that. Well, shit, I'm sorry, man. It's not like you're fucking perfect either. Anyway, I don't wanna fight with you about this. Let's just chuck and forget about it."

I got up at noon and went downtown with Mason to call Nina and Lex. We called their place three times from a pay phone. Nina finally answered on the third try. She sounded exhausted.

"Wanna get together?" I asked her.

"No sorry," she said. "Vee are too hang over and vee have to stady today."

"On a Saturday?" I asked.

"Yes." I'd have pushed the issue but there was no point. Bled was starting to bleed out of me, and I could feel the winds pulling me away.

"Whatever," I said. "Peace out."

Back at the place, things were more chill with Tim. He had taken a shower and jerked off and was ready to cork out and do something with the day.

"Should we check out that lil' island?" he suggested.

"Actually, yeah," Mason said. "I heard it was kinda ait."

On the tour boat out there, I felt lost. What magic was left in this trip now that'd I'd just made peace with the beast? Was it stories? More fucking stories? Hadn't we made enough goddamn stories to fill five books and more? And what good were any of them even if they did come our way? Would they just be more vacuous tales of prosties and blowing up and bullshitting? What good is a fucking story if it doesn't have a point? If it doesn't have a moral? If it doesn't have a message for future Chuck generations to learn from?

These were the thoughts floating through my head as we teetered toward the island. It was an overcast day so everything—the lake water, the hills, the castle, the casinos, the clubs, even the snowy mountains—was glazed with addled brain matter.

When we pulled up to the little port, I was drained. Nothing, not the misty little coves, nor the deep forest greens, nor the red chapel rooftops, nor the fucking crappy cobbled streets, nor the goddamn horseshit little asswipe steeples, could pull me out of my funk. All I could do was drag my sorry ass up the steps to the church and groan.

"This place blows," I said.

Tim softened his eyes. He came up to me all perky and smiled.

"Sorry I was garnk last night, Felm," he said. "I was just drunk and in one of my lifeish Tim moods."

I felt his tenderness again. It put a little juice in my shoulders.

"It's cool," I said. "Let's just check out this stupid island."

The only thing to see there was the little church next to the clock tower. Its interior was simple; biblical paintings, mahogany pews, a silver organ in the back. At the front, there was a nativity scene wrapped in gold leaf. It was bisected by a long white rope.

"What the fuck is that for?" I asked Tim.

"Eeff. Guidebook says it's connected to a big bell up top. If you ring it three times, you get a wish."

"Goody."

I walked up to the rope and wrapped my hands around it. My face read, Who gives a fuck? When I yanked down, there was a delay. I took the damn thing for broken.

"Clang! Clang! Clang!" The fucker finally rang. It was the sound of dullness against a gray sky. I let my wish fly.

"Fuck all the hoopla, Mona," I said. "Just give me some better weather. Blah fuckin' whatever."

# LJUBLJANA

C hucks were in a funk as we pulled into the train station. Not
only had Stanko all but destroyed our game at Bled Bar the night
before, but Chuck, in his infinite chuckness, had cock-blocked Mason
by not getting up and letting him in their room with the one measly
chick any of us had been able to peel away with since Thailand. As we
grabbed our packs, we hardly spoke. We stepped off the train, and I
shifted my thoughts to Ljubljana. In my dreary mind, I couldn't help
but wonder what incredible sights this charming and sophisticated
European capital might hold for us. Will it be hilltop castles and grand
promenades, easy flowing rivers and baroque facades? Indeed. All this
and more from the windows of our first delightful stop ... McDonald's.

I was ass-chapped through my entire Big Mac. Nothing would
satisfy me, not even a blowjob from a pink-skin virgin with honeyed
lips. Mason, on the other hand, was howling to go. The minute we
stepped outside, he spotted a brunette through the McDonald's
window. She couldn't have been more than sixteen, and she was eating
all by herself.

"I'm gonna grooge back in there n' see what's what with this lil'
ney ney," he said, throwing on his black shades.

I sniffed hard and kicked the dirt. "Classic," I said. "Another six
hours of waitin' on Mayt'n."

He came out twenty minutes later with a clean grin and a number
in his hand.

"Nah's name is Franca," he said. "She's bunt'n to her hometown Velenje today, but she told me to call her. I might roll out there tomorrow."

"Spiffy," I said. "Now can we find the damn hostel?"

It took us a good hour to find the Most Def, the hostel Kip and Bert were at. Under normal circumstances, I might have enjoyed the walk as Ljubljana was actually quite nice. It had a little white bridge, Zmajski most, dotted at its corners with green dragons, the jade Ljubljanica river snaking through, and tons of steeples and church domes poking up above the canopy of its Art Nouveau buildings. There was even a red-roofed castle, Ljubljanski grad, perched atop a forested hill overlooking everything. But to my faithless eyes, it all looked like a city of wax waiting for the sun to reduce it to a scattering of grotesque limbs and hard puddles. When we finally found the hostel, all I wanted to do was take a dump.

After my visit to the john, I went into our dorm room. Bert and Kip had just gotten back from lunch. All they could talk about was how sick Munich was.

"You should have met Kip's friend, man," Bert said. "Dude was a fucking Nazi."

"A real Nazi?"

"Yeah. We got fuckin' D one night off hella liters with him, and the fool just started throwing up the Heil Hitler! Right there in the Hofbrau!"

"Wow, how funny."

"Yeah, n' then he invited us to a National Socialist rally. We almost went."

"I'm sure you'd have been right at home," I said. "And how 'bout you, Kip? Does your fuckface Nazi friend know that you're half-Jewish?"

Kip didn't respond. He just adjusted his glasses and went poking through his bag.

I flipped him off and took a nap. I woke up an hour later still pissed but with a prospect in my midst. She was a five-foot-four brunette with a sleazy smile and swamp eyes. She had acne like she'd taken too many loads to the face, but I didn't care, I needed a good romp in the sack. I got up to go say what's up to her. Tim cut me off at the pass. He busted out his iPod and sat her on his bunk.

"Hi, I'm Tim," he eked. "What's your name?"

"Mary," the girl said in a thick Australian accent.

"Mary, that's a pretty name. Hey, Mary, wanna hear some of my music?"

"Uh, sure."

Tim makes every new girl he meets listen to the twangy, strange music he writes. I knew once the earphones went in, it'd be hours before he let her go. I cut in and sat down next to them.

"What's up? I'm Johann," I said to Mary.

"Oh, hello. I'm Mary."

"Yeah, I heard. Listen, you wanna check the city out with me?"

"Well, I've just met your friend Tim here. Maybe the three of us could go together."

"Whatever," I said.

Our little stroll through the city was one giant cock measuring contest. Every time I mentioned my prowess with languages, history, or geography, Tim would drop the fact that he'd written, sung, cut and produced a grip of songs, and that he was nifty with computers. Mary seemed equally impressed with both of us. I had to do Tim in.

"Hey man, tell her about your amazing pet squirrel," I said.

Tim clenched his jaw and turned stiff. I grinned wickedly.

"You have a pet squirrel?" Mary asked.

"Yeah, I do."

"Well . . . that's awesome! Back in Aus, I have a pet chipmunk."

"Oh, that's . . . that's really cool," Tim said. "I've really always thought about wanting to get a chipmunk."

"You've really always thought about wanting to get a chipmunk?" I asked. "That's some stunning use of language there."

"Hey," Mary said, "don't get mean."

"No, it's just . . . whatever. You guys have a fantastic time. I'm gonna go … I don't know … fall on a knife or something."

I left the two lovebirds to their discussion on the joys of feral rodent ownership and went to find food. I needed something rich, hearty, and preferably Slovenian. I found a locals' joint downtown that promised just that. Oh, the food they served me was Slovenian alright: sausages, boiled cabbage, pork loin, spareribs, bread pudding. And after sampling each item, I gave the meal the review it deserved.

"This tastes like cat shit." I told the waitress.

She looked at me like, Who the fuck are you? I threw my knife and fork down and walked out.

At eight o'clock, we all met up at the hostel and went for drinks. I didn't really want to be around anyone, but going to a bar with Mary and the Chucks was better than the alternative—beating off in the shower with cream conditioner, followed by twelve stiff drinks in our dark dorm room, alone.

It was raining out, so it took us a while to find a bar. When we finally did, I ordered up two liters of their hardest brew and commenced getting shitfaced the instant my cheeks hit the seat. I got about five swigs in when Tim came running back from the bathroom, laughing.

"Felm, you gotta see this," he yelled.

I scowled into my beer. "If it's rodent porn, I'm gonna be real pissed."

I got up and went back to the john with him. He stood at the door with his hand to it.

"Check this fuckin' cool scene out," he said.

He pushed the door open and grinned.

My mouth dropped. "Holy shit," I screamed. It looked like some poor fuck who'd just consumed a whole load of red wine and clam chowder, had gotten up mid-dump, spun around, pitched forward, puked, and completely missed the toilet. The entire bathroom floor was carpet-bombed with chunky purple vomit, and a pathetic little turd was still floating in the bowl.

"I bet that guy feels better now," Tim said.

"Oh yeah? Well, that makes one of us."


Tim was all smiles in the morning. I could hear him and Mary above me giggling and smooching and reveling in their stickiness. After about twenty minutes of this, Mary went to take a shower. Tim got up and started fucking with his bag.

"Hey, Felm, man," he said, once he'd made brief eye contact with me. "I, uh, didn't wake you up, did I?"

"Slept like a corpse," I said.

His shoulders dropped. "Oh, well, because . . . you know . . . last night I was trying not to be loud n' stuff."

"Why, did you have gas or something?"

"No, no. I was just . . . well, me n' Mary, we had some really good, good sex and I was just trying not to be loud."

The Chucks cracked up. I cracked my knuckles.

"Nah, it's cool dawg," I said. "Actually, I did hear you both fucking and I heard that bitch snoring her ass off afterward, even poked her in the fuckin' flesh with my two fingers to shut her up. Next time take her to the damn toilet. None of us wanna hear you bangin'."

"Well, you won't have to hear us again."

"Oh yeah. Why's that?"

"Because I'm going with her back up to Bled to go paragliding. We're leaving today."

The second Mason heard this, he grabbed some money from his backpack and split. Five minutes later, he came back smiling.

"Niope, niope, niope," he gloated.

"What?" I asked.

"Just talked to my lil' Velenje ney ney n' she said I could grooge out and visit her."

"Wow. Bravo for you!"

"Hey, whatever man. At least it's something."

"Yeah, something for *you*. I ain't gettin' shit."

Mason chuckled. "I know I'm not one to talk," he said, "but you really need to stop with the hating, Felm."

"Thanks for the tip. I'll keep that in mind for my next beer shit."

After Mason and Tim left, my heart felt like an empty can of soup. I took off in my hater mood and wandered into Prešeren Square. I spotted a chic little time shop and went inside. Most of the bigger-name watches—Rolex, Cartier, Movado, Rado—were out of my reach. I had to settle for something in the three-hundred-dollar range. I went with a Swiss two-tone that cost me almost four. It glimmered on my wrist like a slice of sunshine. My heart was still a can of soup.

# PLITVICE

Our bus from Ljubljana arrived at the national park in the late afternoon. The asshole driver dumped us off on the side of the road. We wandered into the forest, looking for somewhere to sleep. It was still overcast, and the whole area, down to the beads of moisture collecting on the tips of pine needles, was saturated in gloom.

We finally stumbled across a hotel. It was filled with bucktoothed octogenarian tourists, but it was a place to crash. We went up to the front desk dripping and panting. The receptionist gave us a foul look.

"Vat you vant?" he snapped.

"Uh, a room?"

"No room. Unless you vill pay one hundred dollars each."

"Jesus, man. That's murder! You got anything cheaper?"

"No."

"Well do you know someone who does?"

He huffed and puffed. Then he picked up the phone and talked to someone.

"My fren Boris khav room on other side of park for one hundred kunas (fifteen US) each. He vill caming to pick you up."

"Fine," I said.

Boris rolled up twenty minutes later in a tiny red clunker. It barely had room for five people, let alone all our bags. We were squished together like trout in a sardine can. To make matters worse, the place we were headed to was buried deep in the Croatian countryside, some thirty kilometers down a squiggly dirt road the width of pixie stick. When we finally got there, we were pissed, starving, and filthy. Luckily for us, the place was decent. It had all the amenities we needed to at least clean up. Plus, it was only a kilometer's walk from the nearest restaurant. After showers, Boris gave us directions.

"Vak thru valley past orange church to right," he said. "Restaurant is there to left. Harry, it vill close soon."

On the way there, I began feeling antsy with my surroundings. No longer were the hills green and misty, but black with snow-leopard streaks of gray from the fading moon above. I'd have walked easier if some of that moonlight had dribbled down across our path. But as it was, we were tiptoeing down a dark stream, being encroached upon tighter and tighter by the wicked stick-finger trees at our sides. I tried whistling to comfort myself, but it only stirred up the critters. One went shooting into the bushes, and I looked over my shoulder at it.

"What . . . the . . . fuck?" There they were in the trees, those two hideous lumps of hot blood staring deep into my guts. I looked up for Mona, but she slipped behind a cloud. I felt *him* creeping up on me, haunches bent and giant claws extending in my direction. I looked to the left, and there was the restaurant shining like a little bastion.

"Let's go up there," I said, whoofin' it. When I got to the hilltop, I turned to see if *he* was still behind me. All I saw was darkness.

The morning fog rolled in like a boulder, crushing my chest and popping out my eyeballs like a bullfrog's after a hard stomp to the back. I felt like hell from lack of sleep. The entire night, I'd sat up wondering what the fuck was going on. I'd begged and begged for some answers, but Mona had only given me the silent treatment. She may be a goddess, but she's still a woman, I thought.

After a tug in the lukewarm shower, I was ready to hit the park. It was rainy and I was miserable, but at least I'd get to see some nature. Boris drove us out there with all our crap. We thanked him and slipped through the entry gates. Plitvice was almost indescribably beautiful; a cavernous gem of water, sixteen terraced lakes etched in at the sides with tall pine trees. Its falls were like silver manes of angel hair pouring over the boulders. Each time one hit a rocky nub, it was subdivided, becoming brighter, thinner, and silkier, until it finally dissolved into the deep blueness of the pools below.

We wandered through this freshwater labyrinth, snapping photos and soaking it all in. I'd have almost enjoyed myself, but there were two things nipping at my brain. One was the increasingly inclement weather; it was raining harder and harder and it looked like it would cut into our beach time. The other was Bert saying shit like, "Yeah man, this aiiit. I mean, it coo, but I've seen more baumisher shit in Yosemite." After his twelfth statement of this nature, I snapped.

"Can't we just enjoy this for what it is without *always* having to compare it to shit in America?" I said. "We're here to see Plitvice, not talk about fucking Yosemite."

In all my pissiness, I forgot to watch where I was stepping. My foot got caught in the tangles of an unearthed root, and I went crashing into Chuck.

"Oh, fuckin' Observatory Man," he growled.

"Don't call me that name."

"Oh, so what? You can call everybody any insulting nickname you want, but we can't do the same to you? That's fair?"

I walked off on my own. After two hours of wandering around, I went out the gates to look for the others. I found them passed out on the bus stop bench. Kip and Chuck were propped back-to-back, and Bert was lying supine, with his hat over his fro and both hands stuffed into his pants. I looked down at the sloppy mess of Chucks and chuckled. A freckle of warmth softened my mood.

An hour later, the sun peeked out from behind the clouds. Our bus to Split arrived and I took a seat by my lonely. I plugged the Peppers into my brain and looked out my window. The Croatian countryside rolled by. It had jagged cliffs pouring into the blue Adriatic, lone fishing boats rocking to the sea-wave melody, little church-top villages with red-speck roofs, old crooked fisherman perched on porous wooden docks reeling in the day's catch with bending poles, wide green vineyards, small brown huts, and ancient long-nosed women in flowered shawls tilling the fields and stopping to take swigs of water from jugs and wipe the sweat from their faces. It was a silent and hard land, but the slivers of sun and sea made it happy enough.

# SPLIT

We arrived in the city at 8 p.m. The sun was throwing up its big pink sheets across the clouds, and we took to the streets in search of a place to sleep. We started at some rusty train tracks and moved inward. The road led us through a thicket of whitewashed apartments cluttered with flowers, cats, and satellite dishes. Above one of the doors, a sign read "Apartment to have." We walked up the stairs and knocked.

"Yes?" a man said, opening the door. He was lanky and tan with sunken cheeks and a giant crooked mustache. He had a crazy toothless smile.

"We wanna see the apartment. Is it still for rent?"

"Yes. Plis, come," he said.

As it turned out, the "apartment to have" was really just two rooms of a larger flat occupied by Nietzsche, his dumpy but polite brother, and his ancient babushka mother who looked like a cave-dwelling oracle from a Slavic fairytale. Nietzsche let us choose our rooms. Bert and I took the big one near the front door, and Kip and Chuck took the smaller one in back. After a crappy dinner of "Adriatic squids" at some turdhole recommended to us by Nietzsche's brother, Kip, Bert, and I bought two bottles of sweet Croatian rum. We cranked up the music and commenced getting shitfaced back at our place. Chuck nursed an incipient cold in his tiny room, alone.

At night, Bert, Kip, and I went out to blow up. The Split strip looked decent, at least from afar. It was on the water and lined with palm trees. There were balconied bars and little pubs all stacked up on one another in a bleached façade. Had it been a Thursday or Friday, things might have been poppin'. But since it was the middle of the week, most places—as we found out when we got up close—were pretty dead. We continued walking till we ran out of strip. We were going to turn back when we ran into some English guy trying to woo two Canadian chicks.

"Hey, man, you know where any good bars are?" I asked him.

He sneered at me with full red lips and ran a finger through his blond curls.

"It's a Tuesday night, mate," he said. "The only party goin' is the one out on my yacht."

"Wow."

"Wow is right. Forty feet of exclusive party real estate. I'm just tryin' to get these lovely ladies here to join me."

The Canadian girls giggled. One of them burped up her cocktail and almost pitched into the water.

"Well, we'll leave ya to it there, Mr. Adriatic," Bert said.


The next morning, we were hung-over and bored. The only cure was more drink. We bought two more bottles of Croatian rum. We pounded shot after shot and cranked the trance to ear-bleed. Chuck came lumbering in five minutes later. His lips were tight like he'd just sniffed an anus.

"Dude, don't start," I said. "We're just partying a lil'."

"Fuck yourself," he said. "And turn the damn music down. I'm trying to chuck."

"Do you ever do anything else?"

He grumbled and walked off. I turned the music up louder.

At 5 p.m., we hit the streets. There was a huge celebration going on as the Croats had just tied the Aussies 2:2 in the World Cup playoffs. All along the waterfront, locals and expats, clad in red-and-white-checkered top hats and jerseys, were chugging beers and pumping their fists in the air. There were drink stands everywhere, and some crappy rock band was playing. When they started to play "It's My Life" my patience cracked.

"I'm goin' out to the beach," I said. "Who's comin' with?"

"I'll grooge," Kip said.

I looked over at Bert. He was leaning into some grimacing chick and explaining the finer points of his intellect with emphatic thrusts of his drink.

"Go get 'em, tiger," I said.

Kip and I wandered down the waterfront. We came to a sandy little beach with an ice cream stand and bought cones. We sat down to watch the sky color up. A few licks into my chocolate swirl, I noticed the moon peek its face out from behind a cloud. A tinge of guilt tightened my chest.

"I'm gonna hit the water," I told Kip.

"To do what?" he asked.

"Don't worry about it."

I walked out into the frothy tongues of seawater and got down on my knees. I raised my hands to the sky and threw back my head.

"I know you don't wanna talk to me but at least give me some fucking better weather," I shouted.

I knelt there for a moment, heaving under the faded moon. When nothing happened, I crawled back to my seat all sand-caked and finished my cone.

"Who the hell were you talking to?" Kip asked.

I hesitated. Kip's kippy little aura loosened my will.

"Mona," I said.

"Who the hell is Mona?"

"Our goddess. She guides us when we're in trouble, but right now she's doing a damn crappy job of it."

Kip squinted at me through his specs. I expected him to tell me I was mad. Then I noticed something in his eyes soften. I can't imagine what rigorous gauntlet of precisely ordered gears, wires, and chips the spirit of Mona had just instantaneously passed through, but by some miracle, all systems in Kip's enormous robotic brain spelled "Go!" and she just clicked into him.

"I guess that makes sense," he said.

I threw my arm around his shoulder and smiled. The two of us wandered back to the strip and found Bert drooling into his cup in front of a dumpster.

The next morning was beastly. Our heads were swollen like hot melons, and our bloodshot eyes were barely clinging to their sockets. It was hard to move without aching. We packed our crap slowly and stumbled over to the docks. We bought tickets to Hvar Island and crawled onto the ferry. The thing rumbled to life, and we pulled away from Split. The purring of the motors lolled me into a daze. I stared out the window and watched as dozens of islets, scattered across the blue water like the shells of migrating sea turtles, moved by. When the horn signaled we'd be arriving soon, I went outside to check the weather. The sky was nothing but clouds.

# HVAR

We stepped off the ferry and were swarmed by gold-toothed touts. All of them waved their hairy arms at us and swore their rooms were the best. The louder they insisted, the more they pissed us off. We went with some portly bald guy who'd approached us casually. He told us his place was "wery nice" and five minutes from Hvar Town. We followed him up a steep hill, then down into a dry valley where his house was. Not only was it a good *fifteen* minutes' walk, but our room was cramped and ratty with a bathroom out of a Russian prison movie. There were three tiny beds, with a couch acting as the fourth.

"This is a shithole," I told the guy.

He threw his big hands in the air. "Vat shuttle?" he cried. "Is wery nice!"

"Yeah. Look, you better give us a good price or we're walkin'."

"Okay, okay, eighty kunas each, and I even give you towels."

"What a pal," I said.

After taking the room out of sheer exhaustion, the four of us collapsed and took naps. We woke up three hours later, charged and ready to explore.

Hvar Town was as charming as I had heard. Its buildings were thirteenth-century Venetian with red-tiled roofs, vein-streaked marble walls, and bubbled windows dripping at the lips with flowery tendrils.

We entered an Italian-style *pjaca* (piazza) ringed with yellow umbrellas. At the back was a tall white cathedral with a slit-window bell tower. We sat at one of the piazza's restaurants and ordered a huge meal— chicken piccata, linguini vongole, sausage pizza, garlic bread, beers, and garden salad. When we finished, we took a stroll across the docks. The sailboats bobbing in the harbor and the bleached promenades and the Spanish fort on high like a silent sentinel firmly ensconced me in Hvar's little world. I gripped my arms and smiled.

Bert cut into a swag. "Wow," he said. "If this is *this* baumish, I bet Greece is gonna be fuckin' shiiitty."

I pinched my face in disgust. A snake of moonlight slithered across the black waters in front of me. I swallowed hard and suggested we get drinks. Bert and Kip nodded. Chuck just grumbled.

"I'm gonna go back n' chuck," he said.

We hit a place along the waterfront called The Red Carpet. It had outdoor seating, fire pits, heat lamps, a balcony, and a neon interior with plenty of good-looking girls. The second we stepped inside, our mouths dropped open. Tim and Mason were at a table right in front of us.

"Uuhhh, look at these ballahs," Mason said, waving us over.

We walked up and gave them daps. Tim wore a long white smile, and Mason was glowing with pure redness.

"Your beard's growing back in," I said.

"Chea hea. But don't go molesting it too much or I'll shave it off again."

"Ait, ait. So tell me, how was your guys' little trips?"

"Coo," Mason said. "Saw some baumish slices of Slovenia."

"You fuck?"

"Well . . ."

Mason explained how he'd traveled three hours by bus to the village of Velenje, then another two hours to an even tinier village called Šoštanj.

"I met my girl Franca there," he said. "And she took me all around to the little coot churches and parks and stuff. Then we went to her folks' place and they served me a big baumish Slovenian dinner. After that, I went off and chucked with Franca in her room. She busted out her laptop and showed me pics of her and her friends in bikinis. I took this as a signal and gave her a little massage. It was awkward at first, but she ended up loving it so much that she fell asleep in my arms. When she woke up, she looked so pretty with her sleepy eyes that I just had to try and kiss her. I leaned in, but at the last second, she pulled away. I told her I understood, and she smiled and thanked me."

"That's cool," I said. "But it sucks that you didn't end up hittin' it."

Mason shrugged. "Yeah, but in a way snittin' it woulda ruined everything. I really respected Franca and thought she was a hella classy chick, and if she had just let a shameless Scot like me snit it right away, deep down, I woulda thought that was *cool*. It was weird cuz I've gone to great lengths to fuck hella nahs, but ended up learning shit about where they were from. In those few hours with her, Franca showed me a whole different world."

I was stunned. There Mona was, workin' behind my back and helpin' Mason become a better man, and she couldn't even throw me a damn bone and fix the weather. I was on the verge of getting pissed. I glanced over at Tim, and he looked so happy and tan, sitting there with his spiked hair and his breezy collared shirt. I just had to ask.

"Okay faggot," I said. "Tell me your little story too."

Tim expatiated on paragliding, passionate sex, and umbrella picnics on the rainy beach.

"When it was over, I felt so complete," he said. "And that's when I realized, what I love about traveling with you gahts is that we're all on this explosion together, but whenever we want, we can just get lost and split off and have little baumish experiences on our own. It's like little explosions inside of an even bigger more baumisher Chuck explosion!"

"True dat," I said.

"But that's not the crazy shit," he continued. "The crazy shit is when I left and went back to Ljubljana, I was at the station waiting for my train to Split, and I fuckin' walked right past Mason. It was just like what happened here when you Chucks grooged in and saw us. And now here we Chucks all are in fuckin' Hvar thanks to Mona's baumish little ass!"

I crinkled my eyebrows. "How the fuck do you know about Mona? Did I mention her to you?"

"Nah, Felm, Mason did."

"Really?"

"Yeah. We both were so weirded out by just running into each other that we got to talking about weird coincidences, and he told me about how you n' him both kinda saw Mona at the same time at that Manali rave. That got me thinking about if I had ever seen Mona before, and I realized that hella times, chea hea, I had. Even all the way back when we shrummed out, Felm. While you were off trippin' in the other room, I was still painting, and for some weird reason, I just started painting this girl with black hair and blue eyes. I painted her in a bikini on this beach, kinda like the one I was on with Mary, and painted her over all that other crazy, bloody, fucked-up bullshit I had painted before. I didn't have a name for her, so I just thought of her as my guardian angel. Now I know her name though. It's Mona."

There was a noticeable change in the weather the next morning. It wasn't an all-out one-eighty; there were still a few spaceship-sized clouds streaking up the blue with ghost trails. But on the whole, it was a nice day. After we crawled out of bed and brushed away the dingleberries, we wandered down to the docks to see what type of boat we could rent. There was an old Croat lady with buzzard lips and curly hair working the rental office. She told us in her thickly accented but kind speech that it'd be ten bucks a pop for a four-seater. We paid her and went to the liquor store next door. We grabbed an eighteen pack of Karlovačkos and two bottles of sweet Croatian rum for the ride. The bottles sparkled in our hands as we stepped on the boat.

With Chuck at the motor, we cut out from the pier and into the bay. The water was smooth and glittering like melted glass. We moved through it effortlessly, pouring shots and toasting the million-dollar schooners around us. The people lounging on deck mostly ignored us. We putted past them and weaved around the dozens of rocky green islets spotting up the bay. When I saw one with a decent beach, I pointed.

"Let's hit that one up," I said.

Before Chuck could even change direction, I pounded a double shot of rum and went splashing into the sea. The water was chillier than I had anticipated. It shrunk my nuts up to the size of snow peas and made my skin ripple. I nearly lost my junk paddling in.

The beach turned out to be just alright. It had a nice view of Hvar Town and a few cute chicks, but it was all pebbles with little surf to speak of. We tired of it quickly and went looking for something better. Our search took us to five different islets, but they were all too rocky to chill on. We were going to give up when Chuck noticed something in the distance; a chic sailboat rounding the corner of an islet we had yet to explore.

"Let's check that shit out," he said, kicking our boat into high gear.

We jetted out to the tip of the promontory and rounded the corner. We found that the rock wall had been hiding a sanctuary. The beach there was soft, yellow, and sandy. In front of it was a palate of turquoise water, and behind, the walls of an old fortress, studded with palm trees and housing a classy beer garden. The area was sprinkled with well-to-dos floating off their sailboats and bathing in the sand with beers. It was a perfect place to dock our shit-skipper and cause some trouble.

The first thing we did was hit the beer garden. We ordered two liters each and tipped 'em back *tout de suite*, cackling and making asses of ourselves. All our bullshitting evoked snarls from the Croatian upper crust. They scattered from us with an almost antiziganistic fervor and either got back on their boats or picked different spots on the beach to chill at. The only ones, besides the bartenders, that appreciated our presence were three wild dogs roaming the area for scraps. They came up to us right away, despite our lack of food, and licked our hands and loved us. They say animals can sense things. Funny they ignored the rich.

When the sun started to melt behind the clouds, Chuck got uppity and wanted to split. Costa Rica was playing Germany in a few hours and he just had to see it, never mind the sunset and all. Quite frankly, it was a good thing we cut when we did. The bar was closing up, and we were down to our last few beers and shots of rum. On the ride back, Bert and I killed the rest of the booze quick. After that, it was full-on trance time. I plugged in my headphones and hit the deck. With both fists to the sky, I screamed from the nose of the ship as it sliced an ever-widening chevron through the shiny orange waters of Hvar bay.

We dropped the boat off and started up the hill. On our way, we bought two more bottles of rum. As we rounded the corner to our place, someone yelled out, "Hey!"

We looked up and saw Tim on an apartment balcony. We ran up there to see what he and the bearded Scot were up to.

"We're hittin' The Red Carpet at nine," Mason said. "Wanna meet us?"

"Fuck yeah." I said.

We walked back to our place and collapsed on our beds. We were out before our eyes closed.

Waking up after an entire day of drinking on a boat is fucking torture. I'd rather tie my nuts to a zip line and go sailing across the canopies of the Guatemalan jungle with my ass in the air than have to endure a single hour of a post-boat-ride hangover. Tonight, I had to rally though. After naps, I took a long hot shower, snapped one off, drank some water, and hit the booze. It went down rough at first. I could feel my guts burp and recoil, but after a string of swigs, things leveled out. The four of us headed out to The Red Carpet, queasy but stable. Mason and Tim were already on the terrace, drinking.

A pretty brunette with shiny black curls and a smile like a watermelon slice was sitting there with them. I stole a seat next to her and we chatted. She said her name was Jewels and that she had a hubby back in New York.

"Why isn't he here with you?" I asked.

"Eh," she said, "he doesn't like to travel all that much. He's kind of a wimp. I tried to get him to come on this trip with me, but he chickened out at the last minute, so I just said screw it and did it solo."

"You like traveling alone?"

"Yeah, it's cool. I get to make all my own decisions, but it kinda sucks not being able to share the experience with anyone. I've gotta say, your friend Mason here was explaining to me how you guys get together every summer and travel to all these different places. That's so cool. And to think you guys have been friends since you were practically babies. Shit, I can barely remember the names of my childhood friends. They're all married with kids or whatever, living the standard life, but you guys just said screw all that and stuck together and traveled. That's pretty damn special."

Wifey's words hit me like a cricket bat. I looked around the table, at all my closest buds—buds I'd had since I was crunching around the preschool sandbox in my Huggies—and I just fuckin' smiled.

"We do have sumthin' special," I said.


I woke up the next morning in a fantastic mood. My chest felt light, my arms, my legs, my head. It was like a thousand tiny butterflies were clinging to my body and lifting it up to the ceiling. I got up, ready to greet the new day. The sun was beaming in through the windows in dozens of golden blades.

"Fuck, this is baumish," I yelled. "Wait. Did I just say baumish? I did!"

"Shut the fuck up," Chuck shouted. "We're all still trying to sleep."

I looked at my pretty watch. It was seven in the morning.

"Sorry, gahts," I said. I glanced over and saw that Chuck and Kip were in their spots, chillin'. Bert was MIA.

"Where the fuck's Culture Guy?" I asked.

Nobody answered. Three seconds later he came stumbling through the door, still tipsy.

"God, I blew up," he said.

"Really? What happened?"

"Well, while you guys were off chopping it up with Wifey, I cut out on my own for a little D Brute walk.[14] I wandered all up those little streets behind the main square area, then I saw these two bitches. They were both blondes and pretty fuckin' nah, n' I heard 'em speakin' English with Aussie accents, so since I fuckin' love Aussies, I went n' chatted 'em up. One of the chicks didn't really wanna talk, but her even naher friend seemed interested, so I focused my attention on her. I followed 'em for a good five, ten, till that chick's bitch friend said, 'We're leavin'. Then I reached my arm out, wrapped it around ney ney's shoulder n' went, 'You're comin' with me.' Haha! And it fucking worked! Her friend just rolled her eyes n' cut, and I went off with that nah to the beach. When we got out there, I propped her little ass up on this upturned boat n' went to it. It was hella funny cuz as I was takin' off my pants, I realized I had my money belt on, and I didn't want to take it off cuz I was scared it might get jacked, so I whipped it around my waist, slipped a condom on my prick, spread that bitch's legs, and started nailin' it, big time! And fuck, right in the middle of snittin' it, some group of guys walked by and whistled at my big white ass. I was just about to bust, too, n' so was she, n' that shit made us both just crack the fuck up!"

I smiled and patted Bert on the back. "That's fuckin' baumish, gaht," I said.

We met up with Mason and Tim and wandered down to the beach. It was rocky as hell, but I was a mirror for the sun with big ol' smilin' eyes. We set up camp on a sandy outpost and started drinking. The liquor instantly fired the mood up. Tim grabbed his camera and held it in front of me.

"Check this out," he said.

---

[14] The various Chuck nicknames are in the glossary.

He clicked it on and showed me a picture. It was of a crude drawing someone had done in their notebook of a guy hitting on some chick. At first, it didn't mean shit. Then I saw the rings on the dude's fingers.

"That's me hitting on Zefir at the Stansted airport," I shouted.

Whoever had drawn the picture had captured the moment to a T. There I was in my beanie and all my gypsy bling, trying to spell Szczecin and spouting off the origins of each of my rings like an ass. For this last part, they had drawn a bubble above my head that read, "This ring is from Nepal, and this ring is from Kashmir, and this ring is from la la blah blah blah."

And there was Zefir in her snazzy clothes, hiding her ring from me and thoughtfully ignoring my advances.

I soaked in everything with a grin. Then I turned to Tim. "Where the fuck did you see this shit?"

"Two Aussie nahs that were here the day before you gahts came showed it to me. They were sitting right next to you guys at the airport when that shit happened."

"Holy shit. I remember now.

While I was hitting on Zefir, I kept hearing these fuckin' giggles. It must have been those Aussie chicks."

After reveling in it a bit more, we decided to grab some sauce. We were feeling spendthrift, so we went with the priciest joint we could find. It was all flowered up with Greek columns and a terrace. Everyone eating there was a wrinkly geriatric wrapped in a thousand-dollar bathing suit. We waltzed up in our Tivas and board shorts and took seats. We ordered wine all around and lavish plates of seafood and steak. When the bill came, I hardly flinched. I was more concerned with the aluminum foil the waitress had wrapped our leftovers with.

"I'ma fuck wit these rich bitches," I said.

"Tmph," Tim said. "What'r u gonna poo?"

"You'll see."

I ripped off a square of aluminum and ran to the bathroom. I stood in front of the mirror and folded the aluminum into a long strip.

I pressed it, shiny side out, against my front row of teeth. Once I'd worked out all the kinks, I stood back to admire my work. My smile was glistening like a silver space blanket.

"Who?," I yelled out. Unfortunately, the dude taking a dump in the stall next to me had never heard of Mike Jones.

When I stepped out the bathroom, I was grinning like a pinstriped mobster. The sun leaking through the vines on the terrace overhang hit my teeth and splayed bright light everywhere like someone had just tossed up a handful of diamonds. All the rich bitches looked up from their meals to see what had just exploded in front of them. When they got a load of my grill, they almost choked on their Adriatic squid rings. I walked up to the Chucks and clapped my hands together.

"Whaddaya say we go hit the town?" I said.

I strode along the waterfront with the Chucks at my back. My mouthpiece was out in full force like a platinum bazooka. People at cafés broke their necks to check me out. Some of them laughed, but others just looked puzzled. A local fat cat out for a sunny stroll stopped dead in his tracks. When he spotted my grill, he glared at it all bug-eyed and threw his hairy arms up in bewilderment, as if I'd just sprayed piss across his Gucci loafers.

"You like that shit?" I asked.

Muthafucka just scoffed and walked off.

"Damn, it feels good to be a gangsta," I said.

Back at the room, while Chuck was sacked out on the couch, Bert, Kip and I were pre-drinking before we met up with Mason and Tim downtown. Lord knows how the topic came up. I think I had said something about how shameless Mason would get if he still hadn't gotten any pussy by Greece. That kicked Kip's little calculating brain into action.

"Mason should have an evolving, or rather devolving, string of nicknames that corresponds to his levels of shamelessness," he said.

"That's a fuckin' baumish idea," I said. "How do you propose it goes?"

"Well here's what I was thinkin'. We already call him Mayt'n cuz that's all he thinks about. But what if we took it one step further? Like, since he's Shameless Mayt'n we could combine the two and make him Shayt'n. But he also gropes chicks, so we could call him Mowt'n. Then we could do it by increasing levels of transmutation, each one signifying a higher degree of shamelessness. For example, we'd start with just Mason, then Mason becomes Mayt'n, then Mowt'n, then Shayt'n, then Showt'n, then Shrayt'n, if he ever starts raping chicks, then Shrowt'n, and then, when he can't get any worse . . . he becomes Satan!"

"Jesus, Kip. You're becoming quite the lil' Chuck basterd."

"Mason could even have a camp for the bitches he goes after," Bert said. "Call it Camp Shayt'n!"

"Perfect!" I said. "And you know he'd have that shit in Chang Mai or . . . no, Patong Beach."

"How would it be organized?" Kip asked me.

"Well, let's see. First, you'd need a brief description of the whole thing. Sumthin' like, A summer camp started by Shayt'n, run by Shayt'n, for thirteen to nineteen-year-old mentally and emotionally unstable girls seeking relaxation and rehabilitation via alternative treatments in a sunny and soothing outdoor environment. Howzat sound?"

"Baumish."

"And you know he'd make these bitches pay *him* n' not the other way around," Bert said.

"Oh, of course. And that would include room, meals, camp activities—"

"What would those be?" Kip asked me.

"Let's see. Well, there'd prolly be a bunch of shit like 'How to put a condom on a cucumber with your mouth. Uh, sumthin' like 'The Kama Shayt'n Show,' where Shayt'n performs various sexual positions on stage with volunteers from the audience."

"Pin yer mouth on Shaytn's cock?" Bert said.

Kip and I collapsed laughing.

"Yeah, yeah." I gasped. "For that one, the girls would get

blindfolded, open their mouths, and search for Shaytn's cock while he stood naked with his boner poking through a hole in a naked poster of himself!. Hahaha! Oh my God!. And for a follow-up game when the girls were all in bed, Shayt'n could randomly select a cabin, sneak in, pick a girl and play Guess What's in Your Mouth in the pitch black. If the bitch gets it right, she gets a prize!"

This went on for a good hour. Before we knew it, it was eight o'clock and we were steaming drunk. While the others got ready, I chilled at the gate and waited. It was balmy out; seventy-three degrees with no wind. The castle on the hill opposite me was lit up like an oil slick. Everything, even the descending night, felt light. I looked down at my hands and wrists and rubbed my neck. I was dripping with jewelry: two necklaces, two bracelets, a labret, a watch, six rings. All this metal made me feel heavy. I remembered my shrum trip.

"You said fuck it all," I mumbled. "Why not ditch the jewels tonight and see what happens?"

The thought of going out like this made me feel naked. Yet as I slipped each piece off, I didn't feel bare, just myself but lighter. It was like climbing into bathwater the same temperature as your skin; when you close your eyes, it's hard to tell where you end and the water begins.

There were no plans in my head when we wandered into the pjaca. Like my bling, I'd left all my reservations in a neat little pile in the top drawer of the nightstand at our place. I was up for anything, be it a long night of drinking, a roll in the hay with a prepubescent goat, or both. I bounced my eyes around looking for food. They landed on the restaurant we'd eaten at on our first night in town.

"Let's sauce here," I said.

We ordered up a feast; pasta carbonara, pizza, steaks, drinks. In the middle of our chomping, Bert raised his eyebrows.

"Check that faggot out," he said, jabbing his thumb.

I looked over my left shoulder. The guy must have been in his mid-fifties, but his complexion was so even from tanning and Botox he could have passed for thirty. He had wavy gray hair, a Roman nose, and hazel eyes. He wore a thin gold ring on his left pinky and a cashmere sweater wrapped around his neck. In front of him were all the dining essentials a wealthy, middle-aged European man must have at his table; a half glass of wine, a bottle of Perrier, a plate of *escargots*, a crystal ashtray. While he sat, legs folded at the knee, flicking his twenty-euro cigarette onto the cobblestones beneath him, his date, an olive-skin woman with a waterfall of curls and a flowered summer dress, soaked in his every word with flutters of her peacock eyelashes. Neither of them, especially the dude, paid a lick of attention to anything in front of them.

"That guy needs a title," Bert said. "Whaddaya think?"

Judging from the state of things there was only one we could give him. No city or country would do . . . Motherfucker was Mr. Europe.

With a new character on the list, we left our little cathedral-side restaurant and walked to The Red Carpet. The terrace was packed with locals watching the Argentina vs. Ivory Coast game. Mason and Tim had already scored us a table. We sat down with them and ordered drinks. Ten minutes later, the game ended. A waitress came and set up speakers and a mic on stage.

"What the hell's all that for?" I asked.

"Ooff," Mason replied.

I turned my head to spit over the railing. While my eyes were away, I heard everyone at our table crack up.

"What the fuck's so funny?" I asked.

"Felm, you gotta check this dude out," Bert yelled.

I turned back around and looked. The guy had a nose the size of a tangerine and a receding hairline greased back into a ponytail. His skin was saggy and orange and his mustache was streaked with gray. He wore a tight Armani sweater, stonewashed jeans, and shiny black shoes. I crinkled my eyebrows. Bert looked at me, then at the guy, then back at me.

"That guy's you in twenty years," he cried.

I scoffed at the comparison and sipped my drink. Then Mr. Me picked up a guitar and started playing.

"Damn, he's bomb," I said.

We watched for an hour as he tickled off song after song in all sorts of languages without breaking a sweat. When he finished singing "Guantanamera," I was plum proud to have the old fart as my twin. I even went up and got my photo taken with him.

When the show ended, the six of us split to the inner bar. It was Saturday night, so the place was loaded with hordes of foreign chicks fresh off their cruise ships and lookin' to party.

"How does that saying go again?" I asked Bert, as we walked inside.

"What saying?"

"You know, three times a charm?"

"What does that have to do with a monkey's ass in China?"

"Well, we got two misters and it's a Saturday tonight."

"Okay?"

"So . . ." I pointed both thumbs toward my chest. "Feast your eyes on *Mister* Saturday Night!"

I stepped up to the bar and ordered a drink. Nothing fancy, just a Jack and coke. It went down like crushed velvet. As soon as it reached my fingertips, I was snappin' 'em.

You're a swingin' dick tonight, I told myself. Make it shine.

I let a limp creep up on my stride and put a slant to my eyes. My mind was an empty plate, and my mouth was an endless smile. With limbs like jelly, I swaggered out the door to the midnight lounge. I was cooler than an Eskimo in loccs till I caught me an eye. Its owner was a cute little thing with dimples and brown hair. She had on a tight dress that made her milky tits and thighs bulge. As she looked me up and down, I could feel the spaces on my body where the jewelry used to be burn and glow. My receding hairline became a Pompidou hat of embarrassment and my swinging package shriveled up to a cigarette butt and two cheerios.

"What's happening to me?" I mumbled. Soon all my fears came spiraling up outta my soul in a screaming hellfire. I tried to force them back down, but they only shot out my neck and spun around it. I felt a sting and then a tightening. I looked down and saw the Beast's black hand wrapped around my Adam's apple. He leaned his gruesome face into mine and opened his mouth. His fangs were like icicles spackled with rotted flesh. His breath reeked of entrails and bad blood. I thought he'd chew my whole head off when I remembered the drill. I shrugged one shoulder and puckered my lips.

"Kiss kiss, big boy," I said.

A twinkle hit the fucker's eye, then he vanished in a puff of smoke. When it cleared, my lady came back into view.

I strode up and took a seat next to her on the couch. She flipped her hair to one side and crossed her legs. I looked back at the Chucks and saw that they were egging me on. I figured, What the hey?

"Hey, I'm Johann. How ya doin' tonight?"

"Hey, I'm Cheri and I'm doing quite well."

The girl had the kinkiest little English accent. That alone sharpened my teeth.

"How do you like Hvar?" I asked.

"It fuckin' rocks! We just got off the boat today, yeah? But not five hours into our stay, we're partying like celebrities. I guess this is good practice though, tee-hee."

"Whaddaya mean?"

"Oh, well, I'm studying to be an actress at the moment. Do you think I'd make a good one, Johann?"

"Sure you would!" I said.

She crinkled her nose and giggled. "You mean it?"

"Abso-fuckin-lutely. In fact, since I'm so certain you're destined to be a big-time celebrity, I'm gonna make sure you drink like one. What'll it be?"

"You're gonna buy me a drink?"

"Fuckin' A."

She ordered some tutti-frutti crap that ran me fifteen large. I swallowed it with a grin and asked her what was next.

"Let's go for a little walk," she said.

We pounded our drinks and walked out onto the waterfront.

Once we were away from the crowds, she stared at me with drunken eyes.

"Have you ever been skinny dipping?" she asked.

"No," I said, looking away. "But I've been wanting to try it."

She smiled and took my hand. She led me down to an empty dock and kicked off her pumps.

"This is good here," she said.

Once the two of us were in our underwear, we started making out. I kissed her on her lips and neck and ran swirls around her nipples with my tongue. When everything was good n' hard, we shuffled off the dock. I was fit to hang a suit till my tiptoes hit the water.

"Wow, that's cold," I said.

In all the lust, I had forgotten how freezing the Adriatic was. It made my *pito* shrink up like a spooked turtle and turned my libido to mush. I was going to protest, but Cheri was already in the water, curling a finger at me. I clenched my teeth and slipped in.

"*¡Hijo de puta!*" I spat.

The cold stung my body stiff. Cheri had the foresight to swim up and wrap her warm legs around my waist.

"I want you," she said, rubbing her naked pussy against my belly button.

I was having trouble balancing myself, so I shifted forward. The second my feet hit new ground, I went pie-eyed.

"Cheesy dick-fucking Christ," I shouted.

It felt like I was trampling through a bed of ice picks. The weight of Cheri's body made it horribly worse. I threw her off me and climbed up onto the dock. I sat down and looked at my soles. They were swollen to the size of small melons and riddled with black pockmarks. I pinched one and the bloody tip of a spine popped out.

"I think I just walked through a nest of sea urchins," I said.

I tried to stand up and walk. It only drove the spines deeper into my flesh. I winced and redressed myself, putting my shoes on last.

"Are you okay?" Cheri asked.

"Yeah, let's just go back to The Red Carpet and drink."

We walked—I hobbled—back to the club. The second the Chucks spotted me, they went clown balloons out the ass.

"Did you blow up? Did you blow up?" they kept asking.

I took a look at myself and frowned. I was a sopping mess of swollen agony; the fact that I hadn't even gotten laid made everything so much worse. I was ashamed to admit what had happened, but I did.

"Dude, fuck all that," Mason said. "You'd better grab yer nah up quick and blow her up somewhere. Looks like some douche bag's arredy movin' in."

I glanced at Cheri, who was now sitting and drinking on the couch with the friends she'd come in with. Some guy with a bowl cut and a polo shirt was already creepin' on her.

"Hey, my name's Roman," he said. "Ya know, like the empire?"

When I saw Cheri's eyes glaze over, I knew she was so drunk she'd fuck anything. I grabbed her by the hand and pulled her toward the exit.

"Hey, you have her back here in one hour or I'll cut yer fuckin' bollocks off," one of her friends yelled out.

I told her I would.

With nah in hand, I plodded up toward the pjaca, wincing in pain with every step. I was certain my feet were candy apple red with infection by now. The only thing that would make this all worth it would be a good roll in the sheets. I searched in my pocket for the key. I got to the bottom and my heart stopped.

"We can't go back to my place," I said. "I don't have the fucking key!"

"Well, we surely can't go to mine," Cheri said. "Some of my friends are asleep there."

"Should we get a room?"

"Everything's closed, Johann. It's four in the bloody morning!"

The gravity of our predicament set in. I scanned the pjaca hard for a place to bone. All the shops were locked and the tables folded. I was contemplating a back alley when my eyes fell upon a spot. It was dark, concealed, and protected. Nobody would have the faintest clue we were fucking there except the Almighty himself.

"Whaddaya think?" I said, jutting my chin up at it.

Cheri looked over. Her eyes fell open like canyons. "You want to have sex . . . in the bloody cathedral?"

"Why not? We're both going to hell anyway."

We crept behind the cathedral ruins to an alcove bathed in moonlight. It had a smooth floor and three smooth walls. We threw off our clothes and got up against one. The feel of the moon across my back sent an animalistic rage through me. I whipped a jimmy hat out and slipped it on my pecker. My teeth sunk into Cheri's neck just as I thrust myself up between her thighs. The flesh of her back slapped against the marble as she moaned. I lifted her legs up around my waist and heaved harder. The odor of her blood and pussy juice completed my transmutation. I threw my head back and howled.

When the fury ended, I still hadn't come. The alcohol had desensitized me something fierce.

"What *will* make you come?" Cheri asked, her face sinking.

"Well, when I'm drunk, I usually only come from oral sex."

Her mouth cut into a ghostly O and her eyes widened.

"You want me to blow you while God bloody watches?!" she said.

A verbal response wasn't necessary. I simply kicked my jeans in front of her and smiled.

She started slow, wrapping her hand around my dick one finger at a time. When she had a good grip, she started to tug. She developed a nice rhythm. She cracked her little mouth and looked up at me with her big brown eyes.

"You want me to?" she asked.

"Uh huh," I whimpered. Instead of taking me all in, she touched her tongue to the tip and started making hot, moist swirls that grew in circumference. My breath shortened and my eyes rolled back. A second later, I was engulfed in carnal warmth that made my knees tingle. I felt that violence coming up in me again. It was telling me to do things. I'd call these things "bad," but bad is such a relative term. I knew most girls weren't into them. But there were a few I'd come across who were. My college girlfriend Tanya was definitely one of them. When she was barely a teen, she was already knockin' out bisexual threesomes with strap-ons and candle wax. Anal sex, even fisting, were trifles to her. I had thought myself quite the Lothario till she and I had jumped in the sack. She made me feel like a total prude. Almost nothing to her was taboo. In the year and change we were together, she'd encouraged me to do the most heinous things to her. I would only go so far with it. But what I did do, most people would surely label as "bad."

Acting on old impulses, I reached behind Cheri's head and gripped her scalp. Her eyes bulged when my fingers dug in. I ignored this and went ahead. In an accordion motion, I brought her upper lip up against the end of my love trail and back away some three dozen times. I took the gagging and the intense blinking as good signs. She clued me in by chomping slightly on the base of my penis.

"What the fuck?" I said, pulling out in pain.

"I am not a . . . ugh . . . a fucking toy to be abused like that! she said. "Never in my life has someone done something so arrogant and crude to me."

I recoiled into myself, feeling smaller and smaller. Soon I was no bigger than a mouse taint.

"I'm really sorry," I said. "I just thought speeding things up like that was normal."

"Normal? Who have you been having sex with?!"

"Let's just put it this way. If God had a son, the devil had a daughter."

"Well, I don't know what *she* taught you, but just because a girl gives you a blowjob doesn't give you the right to gag her to death with your wanker. Oral sex should be a sensual thing, even a loving thing, not a violent one. And quite frankly, you shag like a beast too. You need to learn to put a bit of love in your sex and not be so afraid of women. We don't bite unless you make us."

Without saying another word, she got dressed and ran off to look for her friends. I was still feeling guilty, so I followed her. By the time we got to The Red Carpet, her friends had left. Cheri looked panicked.

"Do you want some help looking for them?" I asked.

"If you want," she said. For the next hour, we scoured every bar and club in the area. We even went back to her place, but it was locked, and no one answered when we knocked.

"What the fuck do I do?" she said.

"I don't know."

"Oh, you wouldn't." She started weeping as we reentered the pjaca. I was just about to put my arm around her when she spotted one of her friends running off to a jazz bar near the cathedral.

"Oh my God, there's my girl," she cried. "I'm coming, love!"

"Wait," I said. "I wanna tell you something."

She looked at me with spiked eyebrows. I swallowed.

"You really taught me something tonight," I said. "And I'm gonna remember it."

"You learned something from me?" she asked, her eyes now glazing.

"Yeah. I want to thank you for it."

I leaned in and planted a kiss square on her lips. I made it soft so she got the message.


I woke up in the morning to Kip shuffling around. He was searching desperately for his glasses. When he found them under a pillow, he faced the far window and slipped them on. As soon as the couch came into focus, his mouth dropped.

"What the fuck are you doing, Chuck?" he cried. "You've mummified yourself!"

My heart leaped. The first thing that came to mind was Chuck had finally gotten laid and was wrapped in his sheets with another chick. I got up and hobbled my swollen feet into the next room. There was Chuck alright, wrapped head to foot in sweaty bed sheets. Instead of having a chick on his nuts, all I saw was the lump where his hands were neatly folded. He was wheezing pathetically through the indentation in the fabric where his open mouth was. I was going to make a smartass remark but felt too bad about it. I decided to let the poor fuck rest in peace.

On the boat ride back to Split, Chuck was comatose. We begged him to say "fuck it" and come with us to Dubrovnik. He snarled and pitched us a bundle of silly excuses. Besides his cold and the seventy-five dollars it would cost to change his flight, his most pressing reason for leaving was his cousin's sixth birthday. He also said he wanted to make it back to Cali in time to see Kartik before the idiot left for India.

"You're gonna ditch us to hang out with that faggot?" Bert said.

Chuck just grunted and fixed his hat.

We arrived in Split a few minutes later. We walked—I staggered—to the station and found our bus. Chuck stood there and stared at us vacantly as we boarded. When we took our seats, he hobbled off. As I watched him leave, all I could do was think, Chuck's just too damn chuck sometimes.

# DUBROVNIK

We arrived at Gruzh Station in the evening. My soles and toes were raging with pain. The instant we stepped off the bus, we were blindsided by screaming touts. We lowered our brows and shoved our way through. When we were in the clear, Mason pulled out a slip of paper and went over to a pay phone.

"I'm gonna call this guy Slavco," he said. "The owner of our place in Hvar told us he had boomish rooms."

Twenty minutes later, an old red van putted to a stop in front of us. Its tires were balding and its paint was chipped. There was an enormous dent on its left sliding door.

"Looks like a van Mason'd take bitches to Camp Shayt'n with," Bert said to me.

The side door opened and Slavco stepped out. He was a two-hundred-eighty-pounds warthog of a man with pockmarked jowls, rum-hazed eyes, and severe acromegaly.

"I khav two wery clin room yus waiting for you guys," he said. "Only ten euro each, and any time of night and day you call me and I pick you up wis no charge."

"Jesus, that's a helluva deal," I said.

Slavco forgot to mention that his place was twenty km outside the city center. We'd have been pissed, but everything he'd promised us turned out to be true, and he was very accommodating even after we'd handed him the cash for our stay.

"Is anyfing else I can do for guys?" he asked, pocketing the money.

"Yeah," I said, shifting my weight from foot to foot. "Can you grab me a bucket of salt water, some towels, and a steak knife?"

He gave me a puzzled look but brought me what I'd requested. I took everything to the room I was sharing with Kip and Bert and set up a little station on my bed. I had the towel and the knife on one side of me, and a first aid kit on the other. I put the bucket of salt water on the floor. When I peeled off my shoes and socks, I winced. My feet were ringed with dried blood, and the wounds on their undersides were leaking puss and stinky fluids. I contemplated going to a hospital but figured I'd give it a shot myself first. If I fucked something up, I could always have Slavco race my bleeding ass to the emergency room gratis "any time of night and day."

I dipped my feet into the steaming water. The salinity coupled with the intense heat made me choke. It took me a few attempts to get ankle-deep, but I managed. I was just starting to relax and get comfortable with the idea of self-surgery when Tim came waltzing in the room.

"Want me to cut those babies out for you?" he asked. "I'm a fuckin' Ginsu ninja when it comes to this kinda bodacious shit!"

"Fuck yeah," I yelled. "The only thing your corky ass gets to do is sit there and watch."

I pulled my wrinkled and swollen feet up out the water. Tim donned a strange little grin and pulled up a chair. Kip and Bert headed for the door.

"Why you gahts bunt'n?" I asked.

"I hate blood and so does Kip Kop," Bert replied. "We'll see plenty of red hangin' out with the bearded pig."

Bert's little joke softened my nerves. I put my right foot over my left knee and brought the knife's tip against the largest pustule.

"You ready to see some shit?" I asked Tim.

"Chea hea," he said.

I applied just enough pressure to pop a balloon. The knife went sailing through my skin, sending a spray of puss across my board shorts.

"Jesus, fuck," I yelled. When I pulled the knife back out, dark wine came oozing from the wound. I watched it dribble down the sides of my feet, then I went fishing for the spine. Every time my fingernails hit flesh, my nerves lit up like match tips. It took me three or four swishes in the skin, but I eventually hit home. I pulled the half-inch beast outta my foot with an even draw. It came out all in one piece. I repeated this process another two dozen times. Two hours and twenty-four incisions later, my feet were free of spines. I covered them in Neosporin and wrapped them in ace bandages. A couple of shots of old Czech slivovice, and I was good as new.

By morning I was back from the dead. My feet were healing well and I could walk okay. Visions of Dubrovnik's promise were tangoing through my brain. As I got ready, I couldn't stop thinking about the story my cousin Dom had told me. He'd made it here with two smokin' Italian girls on bein' from Cali alone. Who the fuck said I couldn't do the same?

At around noon, Bert, Kip, and I split on a bus to old town. On the way there, a dot of possibility batted its eyelashes at me. She was five-foot-six with black hair and olive skin. Her nose was paper-thin, and she had hazel eyes that could shock the spots off a leopard. I went up to her to see what she was about. When I got close, I saw that she had a violin in her lap.

"You play?" I asked her.

"*Da*," she replied. "I go to lesson now."

"Aw, that's too bad. I was gonna ask you if you wanted to see the city with me. Maybe I can see you later."

"Maybe," she said, smiling. "I probably will go to Club Caliente tonight with friends."

Before I could get her info, the bus stopped and she got off. It wud'n no thang. I was just along for the ride anyway.

Our bus let us off right in front of Dubrovačke gradske zidine—the brick walls surrounding Old Town. I could tell by their height and aged look that they housed a treasure trove of old architecture. My first instinct was to head straight for the entrance and do some sightseeing. My two allies hesitated.

"I think I'ma grab some Karlovačkos," Bert said. "This place looks fuckin' just like Venice, so I'm whatever on it."

"Seezly?" I asked.

"Chea hea."

I looked over at Kip, who was ripping crap from his pockets and spilling it all over the sidewalk in an effort to find God knows what. I was gonna ask him what his plans were after he finished fumbling, but I figured, fuck it, I'll just go this bitch alone.

I slipped through the entrance and got sucked in by a glimmering wormhole. Stradun, Old Dubrovnik's main drag, was a stretch of white sunlight cradling all sorts of Mediterranean creatures. There were onion-domed clock towers stretching up from the bricks, green shutters on white buildings with sagging red roofs, tourists in ice cream-stained trousers gumming humps of gelato and laughing, rings of pecking pigeons with gnarled feet being scattered by silent nuns, coffee-sippers in shades leering at toffee-skinned women in short skirts, dingy side streets feeding off into piazzas with spring water fountains. There were Italians, Dalmatians, Venetians, Croatians. Everyone was all smashed together in one big happy mass looking up at the sun through polarized lenses. I took my pics n' let my thoughts buzz. Then it was time to see it like the steeples do. I dropped my ten euros and shuffled up the steps. Inside the coiled python of battlements I saw much; old Serbian church domes being blasted through with sunlight to reveal their green insect structures, patches of new red, patches of old red, patches of bombed-out columns and bricks, shit to attest to Milosevic's limp dick, plenty of palms with exploding firework fronds frozen in time to make shade for so many mangy cats, rose-dangling gardens, crosses and cannons, crosshatching laundry lines between close-knit buildings with curly-haired Croatian ladies screaming out their windows.

By the end of it, I needed a fucking drink. I went into a little shop outside the walls and bought myself three big Laškos. As I was walking out, I ran into Mason and Tim.

"Hey there, gahts!" I said. "Where ya groogin'?"

"Woll, we just picked up hella sneers n' were thinkin' a rollin' out to Ploče Beach just east'a here," Mason said. "Wanna grooge with?"

"Chea hea," I said.

We walked through Old Town and out to a beautiful yellow beach lined by a curtain of turquoise water. There was a small island with a few sailboats floating around it in the distance. Kip and Bert were already on the beach sunbathing and drinking.

"Did you have a fuckin' ball seeing Venice again, Felm?" Bert asked.

"Choo hoo. Did you have a fuckin' ball sitting here scratching yours?"

"Woo hoo!"

An hour later, we were completely fucked. We left to get pizza when Mason spotted some chick he had tried to pick up on the boat from Hvar to Split. He walked up to her, and the rest of us snickered.

"Hey Mason," I yelled out. "Take ney ney ta Camp Shayt'n n' see if she can guess what you put in her mouth!"

The girl crinkled her eyebrows. Mason sneered.

"Maybe you faggots should both change your name to Respect Guy," he shouted.

"Hey, whatever, ya damn Scot!" Bert fired back.

Mason ignored us and continued chatting. We walked off laughing and got pizza.

In the evening, Bert and I continued our drunken rampage. We headed for Club Caliente to see if Ms. Violin was there with her friends. There was a fat-ass line out the front. It took us twenty minutes and ten bucks, but we pushed through it. The interior of the club was a dump; fake palm trees covered in flickering Christmas lights, gum-stained photos of people pounding long drinks, and a janky dancefloor with a checkered disco ball wobbling overhead. About the only thing *caliente* inside was the smoky air that seemed to increase in temperature every time a new hoard of drunks tumbled through the door. Bert and I decided to make the best of it anyway. We grabbed a couple of drinks and circled the dancefloor. We weaved our way through dozens of sausage-links surrounding single drunk females. When we got to the end of the club, we came up zip.

"What time is it?" Bert yelled.

I looked at my watch. "Almost one."

"Aw fuck. That bitch ain't comin'. Let's just get D n' try to blow up some other nahs."

The hours and the drinks rolled by. By four, the two of us were plum-fucked with nothing to take home but growing headaches. We went up to the bar to ask for a couple of waters. The bartender just scoffed.

"Vee close," he said, throwing a towel over his shoulder. We turned and saw everyone filing out the front door. We hung our heads and joined them.

Outside, people were chattering on their cell phones and trying to find rides. We'd have hit up Slavco, but neither one of us had the means.

"Maybe one of these fools'll let us use their cell," I said. I asked a few people, but they brushed me off. I was going to suggest we take the 6 a.m. bus, when I spotted two dudes walking up. "Let's ask them if they've got a cell we can use," I said.

"Ait," said Bert.

The two dudes looked like pimps from the polar ice caps. Both had on snow-white zoots and big buckle shoes, rakishly cocked hats, and roses in their jackets. They walked in stride and joked in Croat. One was tall with blond hair and blue eyes and the other was short with brown hair and black eyes. Bert and I walked up to them and asked if we could use one of their cell phones.

"Who you need call, man?" the big one asked.

"The guy who owns our hostel. He's gonna pick us up."

Biggie and Too Short looked at one another. There was an instant transmission between them.

"Vee can give you ride," Too Short said.

"Seriously?"

"Da, no problem. Our vip is just close."

"Your vip?"

"Da, vip, you know, car?"

"Oh, your *whiiiip*. Jesus!" I was so stunned to hear hip-hop slang coming from his mouth, I about shit my drawers. Sure the guy was dressed like a pimp, but I didn't think he could talk like one.

"So, ah, what kinda whip ya got?" I asked.

"No werry, is sick vip. You vill see."

We rounded the corner and went up the street. Every time we passed a beater, I thought for sure it'd be theirs. We walked till we came to a *stani* sign. Biggie whipped out his keys.

"Der our car," he said, clicking the alarm. I looked at the row of cars. The one that beeped took the stiff outta my prick. It was a spankin' new Vanquish in flip-flop pearl with peanut butter interior and twenty-inch spinners. I had to pull the drawstring on my chin to flap my jaw back in place.

"That's a fuckin' bomb-ass whip!"

"Chea," Bert said. "Makes my cherry Mustang back home look like Slavco's rape wagon."

We slipped inside the Vanquish and purred down the road. Biggie introduced himself as Nikola and Too Short as Pavel.

"I'm Johann and that's Bert," I said.

Now that we were all acquainted, I thought I'd go deeper. I asked them what was up with their suits and they laughed.

"Vee come from costume party," Nikola said.

"Well, that explains the Fred Astaire look, haha. How was it?"

"Shiiit," Pavel said. "All vee see is same hoes everywhere. Vee go to crib now to call new bitches."

A silence pervaded the car. The pimp duo looked at one another.

"Hey," Nikola said. "You guys is cool. Vant to come to crib wis us and party wis bitches?"

"Abso-fuckin-lutely," Bert said.

Upon hearing this, Pavel spun his head around and unbuttoned his mouth like a bag of diamonds. "You guys ever ghost ride vip?" he asked.

I recoiled and glanced over at Bert. He seemed even less keen on the idea.

"Nah, we never have," I said. "Don't know if we really want to."

"You are from America. Of course, you vant to." Before we had a chance to reply, Pavel switched on E40's "Tell Me When to Go." The song had barely come out stateside, so I was shocked to hear it.

"Let's really not do this, you guys!" I said.

"Oh fuck, vee do it," Nikola said. "Just you vait . . . aaand now!" As E40 spastically shouted out "Ghost ride, ya whip, ghost ride, ya whip," the two morons climbed out of their windows and onto the roof, singing their throats out. We were going seventy kph till we hit a decline and started speeding out of control. Bert and I looked at each other with our nuts stuffed up into our throats. We banged on the ceiling and screamed, "We're gonna fuckin' crash!" When the car reached seventy, we were almost out of hill. Just as we were about to slam into the embankment, the duo climbed back in, snapped on their belts, and laughed. Nikola hit the brakes and we spun a corner and jerked to a halt.

"Vee here," Pavel said.

Bert and I got out of the car stirred and shaken. Our nerves thinned when we got a load Nikola and Pavel's house. It was a cliffside mansion with a Venetian fountain and twelve shiny cars out front.

"You like da crib?" Pavel asked.

All we could do was nod. The gentlemen took us inside their humble abode. Right away, we were hit with a dual staircase that wrapped around the upper floor. There was a grand piano in back, a fountain in front, and an entertainment room on either side.

"Which way do we go?" I asked.

Nikola smiled and ushered us off to the left. We wandered down a couple steps and into a veritable male playground. The room had two stripper poles, a big-screen TV, a leather sofa, a pool table, a fully stocked bar, three arcade games, and a giant glass coffee table in the shape of Serbia.

"You guys are Serbian?" I asked, pointing to the table.

"Da," Pavel said. "From Belgrade."

"What are you doing in Dubrovnik?"

The two looked at each other again.

"Import, export."

"Ah."

Bert and I got comfy on the sofa while the duo changed. They came back a few minutes later in low-cut white robes that exposed their hairy chests and gold chains. Pavel reached into his robe and tossed an eight ball of snow on the coffee table.

"You like da yey?" he asked.

"Fuck yeah," Bert said. "We're from the Yey area."

"Good, vee do before Nikola call bitches."

Pavel broke out a razor blade and started chopping. I was feeling good, but then Vegas came crashing into view. A couple years back I had thrown my buddy a bachelor party at the Rio. One of the groomsmen had brought coke. I was nervous to try it because of my bad shrum trip. Everyone assured me it was not a hallucinogen and that "I had to, it was Vegas." Against my better judgment, I did it. For my efforts, I spent the entire night running up and down the halls in my boxers with a head full of blackness and tentacles exploding out my ass. I didn't want a repeat with the Serbs. But I also didn't want to bitch out and taint Mona's grand design.

Within a minute, Pavel had four nice neat night crawlers of powder ready. Like a gentleman, he handed a rolled five kuna note to us first. Bert took it, stuck the end to the line, and snorted everything up lickety-split.

"That shit's fuckin' baaaaauuuuuumish," he yelled, flicking his nostril. I knew the man did coke, but I didn't know he could take down a line like that. The pressure was on me now. "Don't worry, Felm," Bert said, handing me the rolled bill. "This is some good-ass *shiiiiit*." I swallowed the bathtub in my throat and leaned forward, nostril to bill. "Here goes nuthin'," I said.

Shhhhrrrrrrrip! The coke hit my dome like a .45 slug. I was a ball of jitters till the cool kicked in. I had a drip, drip, drip at the back of my nose, a two-ton ego, and tongue made of gold.

"Woooooooweee," I yelled. "You wudn't kiddin' baby dat sum guuuud azz shit!"

My jive talkin' made the room crack up. The Serbians each did theyself a phat line then Nikola got on the cell. What he said in Serbo-Croat, I couldn't tell. What I do know is that on the other end'a that line was sum hot soundin' ass.

Not ten minutes passed before four fine-lookin' ladies in miniskirts and fuck-me boots walked through the front door. There were two blondes and two brunettes.

"You can choose vateva you like," Nikola said.

I walked up to the brunette I liked and shook her hand.

"I'm Johann," I said. "And you?"

"Merata," she replied.

"Merata, you're beautiful." And fuck if I wasn't kidding. She had caramel skin and wavy black hair, teardrop eyes, and a full pair of lips that puckered when she blushed. Nikola came over and showed us to a room. It had a mirrored ceiling and a tiger-skin bed, a full bath, and an all-glass shower. After giving us the tour, he patted me on the back. I thanked him for his kindness, and he gave me a little wink.

"Jus' don't kill dis bitch," he said. "Vee just gif fresh sheets to bed."

I smirked and closed the door behind his big ass. When I turned back around, Merata was in nothing but a black lace thong and stiletto boots.

"You like?" she asked, stepping closer. The term 'coke dick' was out the window. Before her hand slipped around my prick, the little guy was up and saluting my bellybutton.

"Um yeah, I like," I said.

She closed her feline eyes and pressed her lips to mine. A shockwave blew through me, and my muscles screamed.

"Let's take a shower," I said.

"Okay," she replied.

She grabbed me by the throat and dragged me into the bathroom. Off the bat, I was on my knees with my tongue up her cunt and her nails digging into my scalp.

"Eat me, you pig," she yelled. She thrust her hips into my jaw over and over and over. I felt abused and lucky at the same time. The harder I ate, the harder I got. Soon it was too stiff to bear. I got up off my knees and took Merata by the throat.

"My turn," I said.

Our sex raged all over the place. We hit the sheets, the floor, the closet, the counter, the sofa. By the time we finished, there wasn't a square inch of that beautiful room that wasn't streaked in some kind of bodily fluid. At one point, I damn near skinned my knee off so blood was up in the mix as well, making it look like someone actually *had* been murdered in there. After a quick clean up, we walked out to the playroom hand-in-hand. The scene we saw there made us both grin. Directly ahead of us were Nikola and Pavel with their arms stretched out and the backs of their heads poking up over the sofa. They were grunting, but from their laps, we heard giggles. These sounds were coupled with moans trailing in from the balcony. We looked outside and saw Bert railing his brunette doggy-style over the rim of the spa. We laughed and wandered into the kitchen. Then I leaned into Merata and raised my eyebrows.

"You from around here?" I asked.

She snickered and lit up a cigarette. She took a deep drag from the corner of her mouth and blew the smoke out her nose.

"I'm from Tirana," she said. "You know this city?"

"Yeah, it's the capital of Albania."

"Bravo, you smart guy."

"Thanks. Dubrovnik's kind of a long way from home though.

What are you doing out here?"

Her face softened. For a split second, I saw an immense sadness well up in her eyes.

"You okay?" I asked, putting my hand on her shoulder.

"Fine," she said, slapping it off. "I come here to study."

We sat in silence for a moment. Then I said, "You wanna go out with me tonight?"

Her big eyes sharpened as she scanned me up and down. It felt like a wave of cobra bites against my skin.

"Is that a yes?" I asked.

"Is maybe," she said. "You call me later."

She scribbled out her number on a napkin and handed it to me. Just as she did, I heard Bert wail in climax.

"Sound like your friend just finish," she said. "Maybe we go."

The girls took off with some skuzzy dude in a Mercedes wagon. Nikola and Pavel then gave us a ride to our place. When we got there, we thanked them for completely making our night.

"No problem, dawg," said Pavel, laughing. "Tonight vee go out even bigger!"

"What's goin' on tonight?" I asked.

"Vee take yacht to Brač Island for party," Pavel said. "You vill come?"

"Oh fuck yeah. Can I bring Merata?"

"Sure. She's sexy girl, no?"

"Yeah, I kinda like her."

"I know. But don't fall in love. She crazy!"

"I won't, haha."

Nikola wrote down his number and handed it to me. He started the car and both guys smiled.

"And remember—" Pavel said.

"Remember what?"

Pavel reached over and clicked on the stereo. Bert and I were on the pavement before the song even started.

It was eight o'clock in the morning, but we were determined to tell someone our story. Since Kip was shacked up with us, we figured he'd be easiest. We burst in the door still half-coked and yelling. Not two seconds in, he was up with his specs on, blinking at us curiously.

"Where the fuck were you guys? I thought something happened to you."

"Oh, something did," Bert said. "Big time!"

"Well?"

We looked at each other and grinned. The whole story came pouring out. By the time we finished, the smile on Kip's face was big enough to crack a mirror.

"The guys even gave me their number," I said. "Wanna see it?"

He gave a puzzled look but said "Sure" just the same. I reached into my pocket and handed him the slip of paper. He looked it over with thinning eyes.

"This is Slavco's number."

Bert and I gave it a second to sink in. It took him the same ten seconds it should have taken you to realize that the Ghostly Mafiosi and their coked-out concubines were nothing more than figments of our imaginations.


After a short nap, we told Kip what had really happened. He was tickled pink and cackling. Seeing him in such good spirits inspired me.

"Hey, did you see Mason and Tim after we bunt'd?" I asked.

"No, why?"

"They didn't know you were here?"

"No."

"Oh my God, I have the perfect idea then."

"What?"

"Dude, let's keep this joke rollin' n' say you blew up with us too."

Kip smiled. "What should I tell them?"

"Well, just stick to the story and say that you did a line of coke, too, and that when the nahs came, there were five and you blew up with one named, um . . . Sonia, who had a black ponytail and a green skirt. We'll say you snit it in the room next to me, and the rest can just be the same."

"Arright. Well, should it be me who tells 'em?"

"Yeah. It sounds better coming from you cuz you wear glasses."

"Okay, well, when should I tell them?"

"Soon as you see them."

Later on, Kip ran into Mason and Tim in the communal bathroom. He told them the story and Tim went monkey dildos.

"Baaaauuumish," I heard him yell. Two seconds later, he pushed our door open all wide-eyed and grinning. He sat down on my bed and started cracking his knuckles furiously. "Kip told me about your guys's blow-up with those Mafia dudes, Nikolo n' Powel. Can you maybe call them and see if they can get nahs for me and Mayt'n?"

"Well, I was gonna tell you that," I said. "They're having a yacht party with hella nahs tonight and going to Brač Island to blow up even more. They told me to call them, and I'm sure they'd *care* if you n' Mayt'n came along. These Chucks are hella hoo hoo."

"Did you actually see their yacht?" Mason asked, walking in.

"No, but they had a phat Aston Martin and a huge mansion, I'm *sure* they're fuckin' lying."

"I don't know, it just sounds funny to me. And what if they start asking for favors?"

"Oh, I'm sure they care," Tim said. "These guys are *un*-rich. I'm sure they want mad from wealthy fools like us."

"Anyway," I said, "I care if you believe us, Mayt'n. You'll see tonight."

We relaxed on the beach, then went to dinner. The restaurant was packed with people watching the Croatia vs. Brazil game. Mason was mildly interested. Tim was solely focused on annoying me.

"You gonna call them?" he asked for the thousandth time.

"After I finish my penne, bro."

He gave it his jolly best for a few minutes. I finally got sick of watching him alternate between smiles and frowns while he picked at his food.

"Arright, I'll call them," I said. I went over to one of the waiters and asked to use his cell. He let me for a few kunas, and I fake called our Serbian mob connection. I let the call last for a good five minutes, laughing and yelling and repeating parts of the previous night's imaginary debacle. When I finished, I went back over to the table and explained the situation.

"So it's nine o'clock now," I said. "The guys said they'd meet us at Caliente at around eleven. They'll take us to the docks from there. We'll get on their yacht and roll out to Brač for the party. They said tons'a nahs'll be on the boat with us. We're prolly gonna be blowing up all night, so be ready."

Tim was nearly panic-stricken with excitement. I could barely hold my tongue.

To kill time, we went to a pub downtown. The place was packed with drunks sporting red-and-white-checkered jerseys in support of Croatia. We got beers and sat at a table outside. I rehashed the entire bogus story in vivid detail. I even went so far as describing the taste of Merata's pussy.

"Shit was like a strawberry Jolly Rancher," I said.

"Oh, I can't fuckin' wait to taste whatever baumish lil' nah nah's snuss those guys are gonna hook me up with," Tim said. "Felm, I swear, me n' Mason have been talkin' about this all day n' it's made me smile so hard my cheeks hurt!"

There it was. Tim's famous phrase he used to describe when he was at his absolute happiest. I knew I wasn't gonna find a better time to break it to the poor sap. I cracked my knuckles and opened my grill.

"Hey, my cheeks have been hurtin' from smilin' too," I said. "In fact, I can't even stop smilin' right now. Know why?"

"Woll, yeah, cuz it's almost eleven and—"

"Nah, man. That ain't it. There's an even better reason."

"You mean the party?"

"Nah."

"The yacht ride?"

"Nope."

"The nahs?"

"Guess again."

"The blow-up on Brač?"

"Still not there."

He furrowed his brow like a ten-year-old who'd just had his Blowpop stolen from him. Deep down somewhere in his optimistic little heart, I think he knew what was coming.

"Arright. What's so baumish that you're smilin' so much from then, Felm?"

I leaned forward with my eyebrows pointed and a smile like an upturned boomerang. Reality clicked into Tim's eyes the second I let the words fly.

"I'm smiling, gaht, because everything we've told you is a complete fucking lie."

Mason had been listening. "I fucking knew it," he said.

I ignored him and concentrated on Tim. His face was dissolving like a tablet of salt in hot water. His eyeballs plopped into his beer glass. I started feeling bad for the guy.

"Lemme buy you another, pussy," I said.

I walked to the bar and stood in line. Twenty minutes later, I was back with the beers. There were two new faces at our table. Both were blondes with bronze skin and blue eyes.

"Who are you ladies?" I asked.

"I'm Lacey," the straight-haired one said.

"And I'm Kat."

"Nice to meet you. I'm Johann."

"Oh, we know." They giggled.

"You know? How the hell is that?"

They only responded with more giggling. Suddenly, it hit me.

"Wait, you aren't—?"

"Did your mates already tell you?" Lacey asked.

"Haha. Yeah. Oh my God, lemme see it!"

She went into her bag and pulled out a sketchbook. She opened it to the page and handed it to me.

"I don't fuckin' believe it." There it was, the sketch they had drawn of me hitting on Zefir in Stansted airport.

Now that my pimpin' was immortalized—and Tim's heart was smashed—I was ready to hit the club. I asked if there were any takers, but I got mostly no's, especially from Tim. The only one who sacked up was Kip. I threw an arm around his little shoulders and clicked him the pointed finger.

"Let's go getchoo a bitch," I said.

We strolled to Caliente like Salsa and Don Chipotle. We walked downstairs and ordered beers. The entire place was packed with checkered idiots. We weaved through the mass, looking for chicks. Eventually, Kip spotted one he liked. She was a cute little thing with an apple bottom and a freckle-dusted nose. Her friend was a skinny-legged fatty in a silver dress. She looked like a baked potato on toothpicks. I contemplated an exit strategy. I looked down at Kip and frowned. The little guy hadn't gotten a single piece of ass the entire trip. He looked up at me and smiled.

"You're gonna be my wingman, right?" he asked.

A memory popped into my head. It was of Mason's and my first night in Rio back in '03. The two of us were there with our college buddies, Steve and Brendon. After we'd all hit a skuzzy club, Mason and Steve had gone off with whores, and Brendon and I were left to wander the streets alone. Brendon didn't really have any problem with going to bed sans chick that night. He was a spiky-haired pretty boy with blue eyes and surfer pecs; he could get laid any time he felt like it. I, on the other hand, was at a crucial juncture in my life. It had been four years since I'd been laid, and now that I was in the pussy capital of the world, I wanted to fuck and fast. My opportunity came when we stopped at a diner for snacks. Two Brazilian girls walked up to our table and immediately started showing interest. The one that sat next to me wasn't half bad. She had big juicy lips and tits, curly hair, and enough ass pokin' out her white jeans to roast on a spit. Brendon's chick, however, was quite hideous. She looked like a Papuan mud wrestler wearing a Jheri curl wig. Under normal circumstances, I'm sure he would've had nothing to do with her. But he saw it in my face that I was hurtin' n' needed this bad. So, like the goddamn champ that he is, he went back with us to my chick's apartment, got stoned out of his gourd, slipped a fronny on his prick and fucked that nasty ass all over the place. Motherfucker straight took a bullet so I could get laid. Shit, he even told me he liked it.

Kip was still staring at me when I came outta my head. I spun my frown around one-eighty.

"You bet," I said.

"Anks gaht," he replied.

With me behind him, he walked toward his chick. His gait was stiff and his eyes full of fear. I could almost hear his self-deprecating thoughts. He got just within talking distance of Freckles, then shut down.

"Kip man, say something," I said.

All he could manage was, "Hey."

Unfortunately, "hey" wasn't enough to blow her panties off. Before I could intervene and get us all dancing, the girls went one way and Kip went another. I caught up and tried to convince him to give it another shot, but it was no use. The little guy was defeated. All he could do was drink.

# MOSTAR

S lavco had us in Mostar by noon. He set us up at his nephew
Vladislav's place. It was a dark wooden cottage with pitched roofs
and a flower trough under each window. Vladislav answered the door
with a smile.

"Velcome to my khom," he said, in a raspy voice. He was wearing
board shorts, flip flops, and a shirt that said, "Show Me Your Tits."
With delicate toughness, he ushered us into his home. All its floors
were lined with handmade Bosnian rugs. On its walls, wherever there
wasn't a black and white photo of some grimacing family member or
a war scene from Slavic lore, there was a pair of bagpipes, or a colorful
flute, or a long-necked *šargija* collecting layers of dust.[15] Mason
immediately got a stiffy. While he waxed himself in ethnomusicological
conversation with Vladislav, Slavco showed us to our rooms. There
were only two, a triple and a double. Kip and I took the latter, with the
queen-sized bed. After showers, we all piled in the rape wagon with
Slavco and Vladi. Like real gents, they'd offered to take us to Old Town
for free. On the way there, I began to get nervous. Before I explain
why, let me regale you with a tale.

In the summer of '94, we took a family trip to the Washington
coast to visit one of my dad's old college buddies. I'd been expecting

---

[15] A *šargija* is a long-necked stringed instrument found throughout the Balkans. It is
primarily used in folk music.

to have to entertain myself—and my little sister—with shitty Disney flicks while the adults got drunk and ate ribs; I didn't know my dad's buddy had a daughter. Her name was Lana, and she was a lunatic if she was an inch tall. By the age of thirteen, she was smokin' dope, poppin' pills, fuckin' quarterbacks, and jackin' hood ornaments. She was a slender redhead with purple lips, blue eyes, and black nails. When I first smacked eyes on her, I nearly shit gold.

One sunny Sunday, Lana got an idea. She called over all her shady friends, and they threw me in their truck and took off. They ignored me the whole ride. An hour later, we arrived at a big green lake. We got out of the truck and hiked into the forest. I asked Lana where we were going, and she laughed.

"You'll see, French fry," she said. We walked up a rocky hill and out into a clearing, where I realized we were on a cliff over the lake.

Lana smiled. "You know you're a pussy if you don't jump off," she said, nudging me.

"Huh?" I said.

I inched my way toward the edge with my scrawny legs. It was a fifty-foot drop straight into the icy dark water.

"I'm not doin' that," I said. "I'll die."

"You won't die, ya big vagina. Watch."

She took a rip of Olde E and slipped her sweats off. In a string bikini that could pass for dental floss, she stepped up to the breakaway.

"See if I die," she said, looking over her pretty shoulder. In one fluid movement, she pushed off, tucked into a ball and spun toward the water. Three seconds later, I heard a tiny splash. "You gonna fuckin' jump?" she yelled up.

I looked back at her friends, who were passing joints and stripping down. All of them were snickering at me.

"Yeah, I'm gonna jump," I yelled. "Just gimme a second."

I bowed my head and prayed to Big Daddy. I stepped up to the edge, all Jell-O, with a toad in my throat. The sight of Lana's pea-head bobbing in all that black water made me freeze.

"Here I go," I yelled.

But I didn't go anywhere. I just stood there with a crooked face while people weaved around me and leaped into the water like suicidal lemmings. After that, I was alone. Everyone below kept screaming, "Jump pussy, jump! Jump pussy, jump! Jump pussy, jump!" Every time they yelled, I shrank back into myself. It took enormous mental blocking and a full hour to gather the courage to finally throw myself off that cliff. My jump was far from graceful. I went squealin' like a hot kettle the whole way down, even managed to hit the lake headfirst so that when I came up for breath, I was starin' at my shorts.

For years after that, I went jumpin' off high cliffs to redeem myself. Nothing felt big enough though, not even the seventy-five-footer I'd done in Belize. It wasn't until I found out about Mostar and its ninety-eight-foot bridge that I felt I could put right my embarrassment. Today was the day I planned to make that happen.

I spotted Stari Most (the Old Bridge) as we were rolling up on old town. It was tall, bleached and arched like the upper jawbone of some giant prehistoric shark. To its sides were two clusters of white rock buildings skewered through with minarets. Below everything ran the dark waters of the Neretva. The bridge seemed frozen in mid-chomp, and I found it odd that it had no visible teeth. My reason assured me that whatever teeth were missing on top would surely be waiting for me when I hit the river.

Chilled by this prospect, I engaged Vladislav in conversation, hoping he'd have some soothing bit of perspective.

"I'm planning to jump off the bridge today," I said. "Whaddaya think?"

He scoffed gently and turned around in his seat. "You vill not khav balls," he said. "And if you do khav balls, you vill lose dem ven you hit vater."

The whole van erupted with laughter. I thought Slavco would lose his grip on the steering wheel from all the tears he was pouring onto it.

"How the hell do you know?" I said. "I've done some big jumps in my life."

"No like dis," Vladislav said.

I shrugged and turned to the Chucks. "Wanna blow this shit up, gahts?" I asked them.

"Fuck yeah," Bert said. "I don't care how much I've bitched out on this trip. I ain't gonna feel any better about it dead at the bottom of a river in Bosnia."

"I'm with Bert," Kip said. "Ninety-eight feet is a considerable distance to fall. Any obstruction in the water, be it a rock, log or whatever, would certainly mean broken bones, if not death."

"What about you Vincenzo Mastrianni?" I asked Tim.

"Nah," he replied. "I'm coo. I'll film it though, and if you break your sack, I'll do a little doodle of it in my journal, too, haha. Nei nornin!"

"Get me. Man Hog Beast, you down?"

Mason lifted his two hairy hands in the air and frowned.

"Eeefff. We'll see," he said.

We pulled into an abandoned lot behind an old building. Above our parking spot was a handicapped sign. The stick figure in it was carrying a cartoon assault rifle. I furrowed my brow and pointed.

"What's with that?" I asked Vladislav.

"Get out of van, and you vill see."

I got out and looked around. Every building for a half-mile radius was bombed to a skeleton. The streets were riddled with pockmarks. Every concrete wall was plastered in gruesome and fantastical images of war. In '93 Mostar had been host to an intense conflict between the Yugoslav People's Army (JNA), The Croatian Defense Council (HVO), and The Army of the Republic of Bosnia and Herzegovina. It began after Bosnia's declaration of independence when the latter two parties combined forces against the largely Serbian JNA to prevent the city from falling into the hands of the melting Yugoslav empire. The battle that ensued left half the city in shambles. The other half joined it just after the JNA were driven out and the HVO, backed by Franjo Tudjman (Croatia's former president), turned against the Bosnians in an effort to claim Mostar for the motherland. It was during this battle that the old Mostar Bridge got taken out. It was rebuilt a decade later.

Besides rubble and halved buildings, I noticed other things that spoke of the conflict. The most striking was that at the end of every street there was a Catholic church spire, a Serbian Orthodox cathedral dome, or a Bosnian mosque minaret. The people that walked around these structures were silent reflections of them. They all wore prayer caps, headscarves, or gold crosses with one or two slashes. None appeared to be showing animosity toward the other. This seemed a bit strange to me. Just before we entered Old Town, we came upon a little café. Its face was sprayed out by bullet holes, and its roof was missing. The three people sitting on the terrace looked of various origins. Just above them, there was a tag in English that read, "I choose peace because I've seen war."

The peaceful tag didn't help my nerves any. All that was on my mind now was that damn bridge.

"Let's just get there and do this," I said.

Vladislav and Slavco laughed and wandered off. The Chucks and I walked down a cobbled path to the riverbank. The jump looked manageable till I was staring up at it.

"Jesus, that's fuckin' high," I said. I cupped my eyes and sized the bridge up. The people milling across it looked like mice on a tightrope. "I don't know about this shit," I said. "I wanna be sure there's no rocks."

"I've got an idea," Kip said. He ran over to a cluster of bushes and grabbed a long stick. He lobbed it into the Neretva like he was trying to spear a whole school of fish at once. "This water's pretty fuckin' deep," he said. "I don't feel any rocks, but that doesn't mean you're not gonna hit any."

"You're such a comfort Kip," I said.

At this point, everybody was staring at me. Kip and Bert both had their cameras in hand, and Tim had already set up his camcorder on a high rock to get a full shot of everything. The pressure closed in on me like poisonous gas. All I could hear was that miserable phrase repeating over and over again in my head, "Jump, pussy, jump! Jump, pussy, jump! Jump, pussy, jump!" I wanted to get up there and do it, but my knees wouldn't let me. They locked in place like metal hooks and froze me to the ground. I turned to Mason hoping he was on the same page. He was blank-faced at first. Then a flame lit against his eyes. It leaked from his sockets and around his cheeks till it hit his fresh beard. The thing burst into fire and a giant devil's grin peeled across his lips.

"What'r you thinkin', gaht?" I asked him.

"Eeff," he said. "I'm thinkin' I'm gonna go fuckin' blow it up."

"*Seeeeezly?!*" I said.

Mason dropped his things and cracked his neck. A spike of fear shot up in my chest, and I looked away. My eyes fell upon a boulder across the river. And wouldn't ya know, that charcoal friend of mind was perched on it, one knee up, picking his big white teeth with a splinter of my will. He smiled and shot me a little wink. I bit my lip, flashed him the bird, and turned to face Mason. He was already gone. I looked up and saw him on top of the bridge, stretching his arms and breathing deeply. I dropped my daypack and ran up there. When I got to the top, a crowd had already formed and was cheering him on. He leaned forward to jump. Then a voice yelled, "Stani!"

In a flurry of baked skin and muscle, five blond Bosnians in red Speedos came charging up. One of them, a ripped pretty boy with his ass cheeks hanging out of his shorts, grabbed Mason by the shoulder and pulled him back from the ledge.

"You no able jump kheer until you pay," he barked.

"Pay for what, asshole?" Mason said. "You don't own this damn bridge."

"Vee operate. Vee are Mostar diving team. If you vant jump, you must pay fifty euros first to vatch vee jump, and den you must pay fifty more to khav yourself jump."

"Look, Mr. Mostar, I ain't payin' no hundred fuckin' euros to jump off this bridge. If I wanna jump, I'm gonna do it free."

The two were at the brink of fighting. Before anyone threw a blow, I broke it up.

"Let's just get the fuck outta here, gaht," I said. "It ain't worth it."

Mason flipped Mr. Mostar the bird and came up next to me. As we walked down the bridge, I felt calm.

The next morning, Slavco and Vladi were nice enough to show us to our bus. It was a tin can piece of shit, but at least it would get us to Kotor. We thanked our hosts and got on board. An hour later, we pulled away from the curb with a rumbling fart. Had I not downed two liters of water, I might have been able to enjoy the ride through the Montenegrin fjords. As it was, I sat there dying to piss like an alcoholic trucker with his dick tied off. I could feel my bladder getting fatter and fatter. It soon grew to the size of a medicine ball.

"Gimme your empty Fanta bottle," I told Kip.

He chuckled and handed it over. I made sure no one was looking then pressed dickhole to bottle tip. I was only able to squeeze out a few drops. As I put my dick back, piss sprayed all over my shorts.

"Fuck this!" I said. "I'm telling the driver I gotta take a leak."

I waddled up to the front of the bus and told the oily faced bastard to pull over so I could pee. He grimaced like he'd just bitten into a centipede.

"Sit in seat," he yelled. "Vee arrive in two hours."

"Two hours? I'll die!"

He turned the bus sharply to make his point. I went crashing against the corner of someone's seat and nearly burst in half.

"You're a fuckin' prick," I yelled.

The anus just ignored me.

# KOTOR

T he instant our bus stopped, I jumped off. I hobbled toward the bathroom, holding my giant piss belly. Just before I entered, I passed a group of old Balkan ladies in shawls. One of them—a nice fat one—stood right in front of me and started babbling in broken German.

"*Kann Ich helfen du?*" she asked.

"Yeah," I yelled. "You can start by getting the hell outta my way."

She scowled at me. I pushed past her and stumbled into the dingy bathroom. I went up to the nearest stall and whipped my pecker out. With shoulders hunched and head back, I let out an agonizing groan. I gave it a hard push to break the seal. Soon piss was rushing out of me like Hanson fans at a Slayer concert. As flecks of it struck my face, I rolled my eyes back and let my tongue dangle. There was nothing to be said except, "Ahhhhhhhhhhhh."

When the blast finally ended, I felt thinner. I walked outside with a smile and gave it to the old bitch I'd yelled at.

"*Es tut mir leid,*" I said.

"*Nicht problem,*" she replied. "*Du willst hotel?*"

"*Ja, Ich will.*"

My German was garbage, but hers wasn't any better. We were at least able to communicate. I listened carefully as she explained where to find a hotel. She told me to see a lady at a blue kiosk on the waterfront.

After burgers that tasted like Windex and fried armpit hair, we wandered downhill. We turned a corner and came into a sunny courtyard of cannons, brick walls, and wavy green water. The area was flooded with chatting locals. We spotted the blue kiosk and walked up to it. The nice lady at the counter gave us a five-bedder for ten euros a piece. We took it and followed her directions. Our place turned out to be pretty nice. It had a bathroom, TV, kitchenette, and AC. We napped, changed, and went for dinner. As we searched for a restaurant, we were lulled by Kotor's interior; a neatly woven maze of mossy buildings, glowing streetlamps, and crumbling battlements. We came to a dimly lit piazza with beer gardens and a church. We sat at the busiest restaurant, ready to sauce. Before we even had a chance to open our menus, our skinny, unshaven waiter was at our table, asking us what we'd have. We all ordered pepper steaks, fries, and beers. We got shots of *šljivovica* to kick everything off. Our waiter, whom we later dubbed Mr. Kotor, came out with them in a pubic snap and set them in front of our faces. We held our shot glasses to the sky and toasted to a new destination. The end of the trip was growing near.

The shot went down like a plug of molten lead. I coughed and gagged till my eyes turned red.

"Get that sneer in ya," Bert said. I nodded and took a slug. The beer helped my gut, but it made my head pound violently. I rubbed my temples to squeeze it out. When I opened my eyes, I saw my steak and fries. I forgot my headache and dove into my meal. In three minutes, I finished it with a gigantic burp. I needed something to compact the food. I ordered beer after beer and shot after shot. The Chucks did the same. By nightfall, we were shitty enough to intoxicate a vampire after a single bite to our necks.

The hours flitted past my eyes like playing cards shooting from the disembodied white-gloved hand of a magician in a dark room. When I came to, I was in a crowded Irish pub, drunkenly elbowing my way to the bar. I arrived after considerable effort and raised my hand to order. The guy next to me—a beefy Serb with a unibrow—got served first. He turned to me and smiled.

"I buy you tequila shot, yeah?" he yelled.

"Yeah." I said.

The shots came. They were brimming with smoky gold and had wedges of fresh lime clinging to their lips. We took our limes in one hand and our shots in the other. We raised 'em up high.

"Živeli," the Serb yelled.

I grinned and poured the tequila down my throat. The second it hit my stomach, I jackknifed. It felt like I'd just swallowed an ounce of finely crushed glass. I pitched forward with my hands around my belly and stumbled out the door. When my feet hit stone, I had only one thought: Get back to the room before I puke my fucking innards out. I staggered and weaved my way there. To the people outside partying, I must have looked like a hunchback with a dump to his buns, running away from a botched bank robbery.

When I got to the room, I kicked open the door. I ran to the bathroom and hung my head over the toilet. In three giant roars, I shot my guts at the devil. When the chunks stopped flying, it was the bile. It came down from my mouth in long strings that coiled around the pukey water. I watched the strings dissolve, then pinched my eyes shut. The dry heaves came in violent bursts. It was like a machinegun filled with blanks going off in my throat over and over and over again. When it finally ended, I crawled to my bed. I lay there by my lonely, with a celery-green face. There was so much poison in my veins that my fingertips ached. My eyes were dry as 76 balls, and my throat was in flames. I sank deeper and deeper into delirium. On the ankles of Death, I passed out.


I woke up heavy. My gut was rumbling, and my eyes were glazed shut. I rolled outta bed and crawled my ass to the bathroom. I put my head over the toilet and jammed my finger down my throat. A shower of neon yellow bile came out. I gagged myself empty then crawled back to bed. I went in and out and in and out. I heard the Chucks ask me how I was a few times, but I was too weak to respond. At one point, I woke up to Tim standing over me. He had a loaf of bread in his right hand and a bottle of water in his left.

"I brought this stuff for you, gaht," he said, smiling.

"Jesus, thanks," I said. I choked down some bread whites and a swig of aqua. I had to sleep for three hours just to process it all.

When I finally came to, the Chucks were just arriving from a hike. I asked them how it was, and they laughed.

"Sucks you couldn't'a grooged with," Bert said. "We hiked to the top of this huge rocky hill and the view was hella baumish. Plus, we saw like fidy Mayt'ns wandering around."

"Swine?"

"Nah, Billy goats."

"They're Mayt'n, too, true enough. Only they've got longer beards."

"That's gonna change," Mason said. "We're gettin' to Greece soon, and I wanna have all my shameless powers intact."

"Grow that fuckin' beard out big then," Bert shouted.

"Jesus, that's right. Greece is comin' up," I said.

"So?" Bert said.

"Well, I'm hurtin' from all the boozin'. Fuck, I felt like I was gonna die last night. Shit just made me realize I gotta cool it on the skinkin'."

"Oh I'm skinkin' *mad* too till we get to Corfu," Tim said. "Oh, I am *too*," Kip seconded.

"I don't plan on it either," Bert said. "I think Albania's gonna be the party capital of the world anyway. We'll just keep it coo there and save the blow-ups for Corfu."

"I'm down for a little cleansing sesh," Mason said. "I'll just loll what I can this week while we're in Albania, and when we hit the islands, I'll let all that shameless energy in me radiate from my full-on beard."

"Arright, coo. Now I won't feel like such a pussy for not getting' D with you gahts. But don't worry, after Albania, I'm gonna go tiny. We're all gonna go fuckin' tiny!"

# THE ROAD TO SHQIPERIA

B y noon, we were at the station. Our bus to the Albanian border looked like a huge aluminum can that an ogre had crushed against his forehead then tried to pull back into shape. I schlepped on it and sat down. There was a group of young dudes next to me. They were all wearing the same green T-shirt, so I got curious.

"Where are you guys going?" I asked.

A thick-jawed pretty boy looked over at me.

"Vee debate team," he said. "Vee go now to debate about politics of Balkan region."

"Jesus. That must get pretty intense."

"Haha. Yes. There is lot of khatred. Slovenian khate Croatian, Croatian khate Bosnian, Bosnian khate Montenegrin, Montenegrin khate Serb, and Serb, vee fucking crazy, vee khate everyone."

"That's so strange to me. I mean, your bloodlines are mostly the same. Plus, most of you speak pretty much the same language, if I'm not mistaken."

"No, is true. Is religion that divide us mostly. And vee do speak same language. Except fucking Albania." When the word "Albania" left his lips, I smiled. Its sweet letters soaked into my skin. I sat back and looked out the window. I could feel her coming.

Before I go on, lemme tell ya a lil' bit about me and places like Albania. Back when I was a little squirt—years before I ever imagined

I'd travel the world—I was fascinated by unique and obscure places in the US. While other kids my age might have dreamed of going to states like Hawaii or Florida so they could make sandcastles or piss their parents' money away on overstuffed anthropomorphized cartoon mice, I was obsessed with the weirdo states, and none more so than Nebraska. To most people, it might not sound like much, but to me, Nebraska was the categorical shit. And not because there are so many awesome things to see. There aren't. Basically, you've got Chimney Rock and a couple of beat-up, crime-ridden cities nobody gives a fuck about. But what Nebraska lacks in interesting sights, it makes up for in uniqueness; it occupies one of the least populated areas in the country, it scarcely receives any tourism, it's triple-landlocked, it has one of the largest Czech populations outside of Europe, and it's the only state that looks like a giant feeding leech with its tail severed. All these things combined equaled solid gold tits to me. Mind you, I was rather pressed for shit to do when I ended up going there with my folks at the age of six. But just being in such an off-the-map place was enough to stiffen my little pecker and bring a smile to my cheeks.

When I got out of high school and started traveling the world, I went searching for more Nebraskas. I found many: Ethiopia, Georgia, Burma, Tajikistan, Equatorial Guinea, Djibouti, Suriname, Liechtenstein, Eretria, Moldova, Kabardino-Balkaria, Nenetsia, Kyrgyzstan, etc., etc., etc. These are the places nobody dreamed of, places nobody in their right fucking mind aspired to visit—except me. I had 'em all on a big list and I was checkin' 'em off as I went. When I started planning the World Explosion 2006, all the Chucks were in favor of doing the Italian or the Iberian route and looping back up. But since I was the one doing all the damn work, I decided to take us on an inexorable journey straight to the Nebraska at the top of my list.

There are a hundred reasons why Albania is so unique and special. It's the only predominantly Muslim country in Europe; its people are the only surviving descendants of the Illyrians;[16] its national language

---

[16] The Illyrians were a group of Indo-European tribes who inhabited the western Balkans in antiquity.

has its own branch on the Indo-European family tree; it has the coolest fucking flag on the planet; and so on and so forth. But I'm sure you wouldn't give a rat's filthy ass. Instead, I'll just go on with my story, content that maybe I've inspired you to consider visiting, or at least learning about, other international vacay spots besides London, Paris, and Rome.

We got off the bus at Ulcinj, one of the oldest settlements in Montenegro, and found a private cab to Shkodër in Albania. Creeping up on the border was surreal. The countryside was green and rocky, and the mountains, blue-gray. There was only one cloud in the sky. It looked like a jizz streak across the sun. Its shadow covered a lone cow chewing cud in a vacant field. I got out to take a photo. As I did, I noticed the border crossing; a tin-roofed post manned by two slovenly guards picking their noses and toying with their rusted rifles. I snapped a photo of the cow. Bert got out and photographed the Tweddle Twins.

"Why you take fucking photo?" one of them screamed. "You want I come in your country and take photo of government building like spy?"

"Eeefff, I'd care," Bert said.

"Good. Then put away camera, get back in car, and get the fuck from here."

We got back in the car. Nobody said a word as we crossed.

Driving into Shqiperia[17] was like driving into some haunted patch of Indiana Jones' imagination. There were scary, tilted houses on empty lots, loud gypsy weddings filled with gold-toothed characters in top hats and colorful rags, cracked and ancient mosques humming at the minarets with calls to prayer, old Soviet cars, new-age women in bug shades and tight jeans, fat guys in prayer caps drunk and drooling on the side of the road, villages with dinosaur skin roofs, dino-back mountains, decommissioned building guts, tortoiseshell bunkers with spider-webbed rifles pointing at our car, and lots and lots of windswept roads leading absolutely nowhere.

---

[17] Albania.

When we arrived in Shkodër, I was eager to take a breather. I got out of the cab, paid my two cents, and went for a little circle around the bus lot. Every third person craned their neck at me. I quickly grew tired of being stared at like I had testicles growing out of my forehead. I went back to where the Chucks were and asked the cabby how we could get to Tirana. "You take dis minibus," he said, slapping his hand against the big red clunker next to him. We thanked him and climbed inside.

As we sat down, Bert looked at me and grinned. "Notice anything in particular about this place?" he asked.

I shrugged and looked out the window. I saw people urinating against car skeletons, heaps of fly-covered trash, half-finished apartment buildings, mangy dogs with one eye missing, and even the odd cow wandering around. At first, I couldn't put my finger on it. Then it dawned on me.

"Holy shit," I said. "I don't know why I didn't see it before."

"I know," Bert said. "I mean it ain't India exactly, but it sure has all the familiar symptoms, haha."

# TIRANA

The three-hour ride to Tirana was punctuated by stops to pick up locals on the side of the road. By the time we arrived, we'd taken on half a dozen farmers—some with animals— two portly cops, three old ladies, and a businessman with a snazzy suit and a cell phone. We squeezed outta that hot meat locker the second we stopped. I asked our driver in my meager Albanian what the nearest hotel was.

"Hotel Delhi," he said. "Up there." He pointed to a thicket of dilapidated buildings across the way. I thanked him verbally for the info and mentally for confirming my suspicions about his country.

After homeboy putted off, we just stood there and looked on. The maze of the city was endless, and we had zero idea of how to get to our hotel. Without having to be asked, Mason put two fingers to his temple and narrowed his eyes against the sun. Rippling frequencies started emanating from his scalp, and I could hear Morse code beeping in the background. Once he locked on, he kicked into a hard stride. The rest of us picked up our crap and followed his lead. He threaded us through a labyrinth of barred windows dripping with vines and garbage. Six twists and six turns later, we were at the front steps of a ghetto-ass hotel.

"I studied a map of this area before we got here," he said. "This has gotta be Hotel Delhi."

"Sure as fuck looks like a hotel in Delhi," Bert said, snubbing his barg against a dumpster.

Mason and I rolled up the steps to check it out. We went up three flights till we came to a knotted door. We knocked and waited. A small-headed woman with big eyes and parted hair opened it and asked us what we wanted.

"Hotel Delhi?" I asked.

She nodded.

"Room for five?"

She clicked her tongue.

"Is that a yes or a no?" Mason asked.

"Is no, very sorry."

"Well, do you know of any other hotels nearby?" he asked. She thought for a moment. Her eyes widened a bit.

"Palms Hotel," she said. She pointed off into another thicket of buildings. Mason nodded.

It took us an hour of slugging it out in the hot sun to get to The Palms. It was just outside downtown Tirana. Judging by its name and location, I was expecting something at least halfway fancy. What I got instead were filthy rooms, no AC, and one Jurassic computer down-stairs that ran like it had molasses crawling through its wires.

Fuck, at least it has vacancies, I thought. Kip and Tim took a double. Bert, Mason and I took the "suite" because it had a balcony and a side room for Mason in case he decided to shame it up.

After a hearty meal of "lamb yogurt" at some Albanian dive, we wandered back to the hotel. None of us had any desire to blow up, so we just chatted and street-watched from our balcony. We saw ratty old bums with mangled legs stumble by, people on rusty bikes, and smog-spitting cars. There were even some wild dogs. Every minute, one or two walked by. Most of them were in pretty bad shape; chewed off tails and ears, dirty coats, missing eyes, limbs, whatnot. There was one in particular that caught our attention. He must have been an old fucker cuz his coat was barely clinging to his skin. Both his eyes were bloodshot and swollen, and his legs were thin as toothpicks. Despite his decrepitude, he seemed rather chipper. He came bumbling by our balcony with his tongue out, smiling like a million bones.

"That dog looks like crap!" Bert said.

The whole balcony busted up. The dog looked at us and scowled.


Since there wasn't a lick of booze in our veins, we were able to get up early the next morning and explore Tirana. I had high hopes for my Nebraska as we walked out the door and into the sun. The first thing we saw was a massive drainage ditch. It was filled with smelly black water and ran through the belly of a pastel apartment jungle. The area around it was speckled with bums and burnouts. We cut outta there quick and bunt'd toward the center.

After a long walk down a shady and cracked lane, we hit Skanderbeg Square. It was an odd confluence of buildings, people, plants, and historical relics. There were old men in sheepskin hats sitting on park benches and staring at little gardens—trees potted in concrete blocks running left and right. There was an ancient mosque with a ribbed dome and a minaret like a missile, an opera house like a concrete cafeteria, and a national history museum with a mural of proud countrymen wearing traditional Shqiptar clothing and throwing rifles and swords and shields to the sky. At the head of everything was a giant Albanian flag. As its bloody back and black double-headed eagle flapped in the wind, a bronze statue of the man who helped put it up there—Gjergj Kastrioti or "Skanderbeg,"[18] bad-ass rebel against the Ottomans, sat proudly astride marching stead with a long sword to his hip, chainmail to his chest, and a pointy conquistador's beard to his chin. Gripping his reins and pinching his bushy eyebrows together, he gazed at Albania's distant and glorious future. I wonder if he imagined that five and a half centuries later he'd be staring at a Western Union.

We puttered around the square for a bit. A single picture at a kiosk caught our eye.

---

[18] Skanderbeg was an Albanian military commander who proclaimed himself "Lord of Albania" and went on to lead a 25-year rebellion against the Ottomans in the fifteenth century.

"Isn't that Jim Belushi?" Tim asked, giggling.

"Yeah," I said. "He and his dead brother John are of Albanian ancestry."

"Kmph!"

"Don't laugh, dude. There's a lotta famous people out there that you might not have known were Albanian."

"Like who?" Kip asked.

"Well for starters, there's Mother Theresa. She was an Albanian born in Macedonia. Then there's Eliza Dushku, fuckin' hella nah Albanian-American actress. Then you got Pope Clement XI."

"There's a big name," Bert said.

"Ismail Kadare, the writer," I continued. "The Belushi brothers, of course. Skanderbeg. Enver Hoxha, the communist dictator. I mean the list goes on and on."

"Damn, Albanians are just invading the planet!" Bert said.

We continued our discussion all the way back uptown. We ended up at the canal where we'd started. We looked in the guidebook for more spots. It said the Blue Tower was just nearby. We walked a few blocks and found the big bitch. There was an observation deck on it that looked pretty decent.

"Might as well hit it up," I said.

We strolled through the doors and took the elevator. It let us off at a revolving restaurant circled entirely by plate glass windows. From above, Tirana looked like a wasteland of pastel concrete blocks. All its cracks were visible, all its looming clouds of smog. Despite these flaws, there was a certain charm to it. I actually took pleasure in viewing a city that was so unabashedly shitty.

When dinnertime rolled around, we hit a dumpy little Turkish place right near our hotel. It wasn't much to look at—trashy floors, yellow walls, a terrace with a few plastic tables and chairs. What it lacked in aesthetics, we hoped it would make up for in food quality.

We grabbed a few stained menus and checked them out. Since none of us could really read Albanian or Turkish, we were kinda fucked. We were gonna give up and go somewhere else when a guy on the terrace hooted at us.

"Come to sit wis me," he said. "I can order you food."

We shrugged our shoulders and went out there. I tried not to laugh when I got a load of him. He couldn't have been more than five-five. He had an egg-shaped head with a Friar Tuck cut, big bottle-cap glasses, and ears that looked ripped off a chimp. His attire was modest T-shirt and jeans. But his T-shirt had knots of dried sweat clinging to each armpit fold, and his jeans were tighter than a nun's cunt against his gangly legs. He smoked like a prisoner and leaned like an alley cat. He reminded me of that little Nazi prick with the top hat and bottle caps from *Raiders of the Lost Ark*.

"So where from?" he asked, as we scooted in.

"The States," I said. "California."

"Ahhh, California. Very nice bitches there, yes?"

"Sumthin' like that. Where are you from?"

"I'm from Istanbul. Also very nice bitches." He slid his sharp tongue across his little brown teeth. "You guys fuck any Albanian chicks yet?"

"Nah," Bert said.

"Eh, you American guys would be too nice to them anyway. You need to just grab them and tell them 'Hey bitch! I want to fuck you.'"

"I think your methods are a little off man," Mason said.

"*Hayir*, you are the wrong one. I can promise you this works. Every night I use same method, and I fuck three Albanian bitches, no problem."

"Three a night, huh?" Bert said. "You must be loaded or they're damn cheap."

"I'm not talking about prostitutes. Normal girls at club. Three per night, no problem."

We were slowly growing weary of Mr. Istanbul's bullshit. Mason got up and put a friendly hand on his shoulder. He leaned in with tender eyes.

"I'll always be there," he said.

All us Chucks cracked the fuck up. Mr. Istanbul scowled.

"What is his meaning?" he demanded.

Bert wiped the tears from his cheeks and faced the prick. In his sincerest voice possible he told him.

"Our friend means . . . he'll always be there, rain or shine, to fucking believe you."

# KRUJA

The next morning we went to the town of Kruja. I was stoked on seeing it because it was the site where Skanderbeg had successfully held off advancing Ottoman forces for almost 35 years. We arrived by minibus and walked into town. At the head of its highest hill was a bronze equestrian statue of Skanderbeg. Around its back was a swathe of rocky hills that fettered off into a cradle around old town. From up top, all we could see was a white minaret poking up through a cluster of wooden roofs.

"Shall we bunt in there and just see?" I said.

"Why the fuck not?" Bert said.

We cut down into old town hoping to be surprised. Unfortunately, the only thing that surprised us about it was how unsurprising it was. Sure it was quaint; twisted lanes made of giant gray slabs, old wooden houses, and shops with big, long overhangs packed tight, the smell of ancient history wafting through the hot air. But it was really nothing we hadn't seen before. I felt an interest in Kruja—and Albania as a whole—amongst our group start to fade. Something welled up in me, and I began to panic.

I broke into a sprint and went all through old town, up back alleys, into forgotten shops. Every place was loaded with crap like hand-woven rugs, tiny sculptures of Venus de Milo, dusty plates, tea sets, handbags, dated paintings. I thumbed through all of it, hoping something would jump out at me. I found a few cool postcards, but nothing special. A lady at one of the shops seemed to notice the dismay spread across my face. In choppy English, she asked me what the problem was.

"I'm trying to find something special from Albania," I said. "Like a symbol or some cool emblem."

"Best symbol from Albania is our flag," she said proudly. "Everybody know this."

"No, I know. I love your guys's flag, but I can only put that on my wall. I want something I can wear too."

The woman raised a single eyebrow. With a click of her tongue, she reached under the counter and brought up a huge stack of red T-shirts.

"What size?" she asked.

"Jesus! You guys have Albanian flag T-shirts?"

"Of course we have. They don't make flag T-shirt in America?"

"Well yeah, but I didn't figure they would here."

"Haha. You wrong. We put flag on everything."

"Everything? Even jewelry?"

"Yes. I have Albanian ring right here for you. I make good price."

She made a fantastic price. For thirty bucks, I walked outta there with a T-shirt, a silver ring, a giant flag, a wool cap, and a grip of postcards, all embossed with that big beautiful black eagle. I smiled at everything in my hands. I donned my T-shirt and cap, wrapped the flag around my neck, and slipped the silver ring on my right index finger. I took two deep breaths and was buzzin' to the gills. I threw my fist in the air and went blasting down the road, screaming at the top of my lungs, "Have no fear, faggots, Felbania is here!"

I whipped around the corner and into the main square. Just as I did, I heard ROAST wafting in from every angle. I stood there at the center, panting and grinning fiendishly. When the Chucks came around their respective bends, my eyes leaped from their sockets.

"Albanian flag T-shirts?" I yelled.

"Well, they're everywhere." Kip snickered.

"Yeah, I know but it's like we all had telepathy, and in some baumish way just *knew* that this would have to be the symbol for the Chucks!"

"Haha. I guess," Bert said. "You really blew up though. You got the hat, the ring, the shirt, the cape. I mean, who the fuck are you supposed to be, Super-Shqip?"

"Chea hea. Super-Shqip the dick dippin' pimp. Albanian nahs, line up!"

"Brrrrrrrrrrrrrrrr," Mason spouted.

After the hoopla died down, we found a little restaurant overlooking the mountains. Our waiter smiled when he saw our T-shirts. He gave us a table with a view and complimentary fruit juices. Within seconds, he was back to take our orders. We all got pizza but skipped the beer. Our food came out in a snap and was served with a grin ear to ear.

"Damn. Albanians are nice people," Bert said.

"*Ju falem nderit.*"

We looked around to see who'd spoken. There was a man, whom we hadn't noticed before, sitting two tables behind us, smoking a barg.

"What's that mean?" Bert asked him.

"It mean 'thank you,'" he replied.

"Oh, hey, no prob. You guys are hella nice."

The man bit the end of his cigarette with stained teeth and ran a hand through his greasy curls. As smoke slithered up from his hooked nose, I saw his green eyes brighten.

"I see you like our flag," he said.

"Yeah," I replied. "It's fuckin' awesome."

"Do you know its significance?"

"Woll, I think it has something to do with the Byzantine Empire. Didn't Skanderbeg adopt it from them?"

"Yes, this is where history book tell you it come from, but do you know the meaning?"

"Albanian unity?"

"Not exactly. More like Albanian split personality."

"Whaddaya mean?"

291

"Foreigners come here. They see one of our heads, the polite and kind one. We show this to all our guests. But there is other head. One you only see if you live here. Have you heard of *Kanun*?"

"Yeah, it's an old book of Albanian laws. I forget the guy who wrote it."

"Lekë Dukagjini. He was Albanian prince who live during time of Skanderbeg. See, Skanderbeg was known as 'Dragon Prince' because he fight for our country. But Dukagjini was 'Angel Prince' because he try to preserve our way of life by writing the Kanun. This have all our laws which govern marriage, work, family, religion, tax, even murder. And this is where you find our other side. You know *gjakmarrja*?"

"No, what is it?"

"It mean in Albanian, 'blood-taking.' Part of Kanun state that you may do blood-taking, which mean murder another person, if he kill someone close to you or put great shame on your family. This was old, old practice in the north near Shkodër, but when the communists come, they stop it. Then, not long ago, when communism fall, the police structure, especially in the north, become shit. So people use Kanun again to rule their life, and one thing they keep to stronger than ever because Albania can be very dangerous country is gjakmarrja. So since early nineties, you have thousands of death from this here. Some people even scared to leave their home because maybe someone in their family do bad things, and other people make gjakmarrja on whole family, even children, which really is against Kanun, but nobody give a shit. I think in this way it make Albania even more dangerous country than in Dukagjini's time."

"Jesus Christ, that's nuts," I said.

"Yes, and now you see why we have two-headed eagle on our flag."

# BACK IN TIRANA

The two-headed eagle convo must've put Mason in the mood. The second we got back to the hotel, he started hitting on the cute freckle-faced receptionist.

"When do you get off work?" he asked her.

"An hour," she replied.

"Do you mind if I see you after that? I can walk you back to your place, or we can go get a drink or something."

She bit her lip and twirled her hair uncomfortably. The snorting man-hog wouldn't budge.

"Okay, come back in one hour and we go," she said.

Mason smiled and parked his ass on the lobby sofa.

"I can wait here," he said.

"God, that fucker's shameless," Bert said when we got upstairs. "I mean, does he honestly think that nah's gonna let him snit it?"

"Obviously, or he wouldn't have tried," I said.

"Oh, I know he's gonna get any snuss," Bert said. "We gotta do something to let that faggot know he's an extreme player when he grooges back after not blowing up at all."

"I got an idea," I said. "You still got that raunchy-ass Czech porno mag you bought in Prague with all the cumshot scenes?"

"Woo hoo."

"Okay, well, let's turn it to the nastiest two pages in there, set it up on the sink with all kinds 'a lotion and Kleenex n' shit, and write a little note for Mason to read when he goes in the bathroom that says, 'Just in case you gottem tonight, gaht.'"

"Well shit, I couldn't'a thought of a better idea myself," Bert said.


Bert and I woke up the next morning to our door squeaking open. Mason stepped inside.

"Are you pussies hella geniuses?" he asked.

"Woo?" I said. "Hella geniuses for what?"

"Oh, you don't know at all, iuuul!"

"Haha. Don't get all butt-hurt," Bert said. "We were just nei nornin with ya. By the way, did you end up using the lil' beat off sink we set up for ya, or did ya snit it?"

"I fuckin' used the sink and I fuckin' snit it!"

"Ha! What happened with that nah then?" I asked.

"Oh, it was tight. We went to get drinks at this one bitchin' bar with a hella mosquito-filled balcony and mad fools there. I was gonna try to get lil' ney ney D, but just decided to keep it simple and have a club boda with her. Then she basically just said for me to skunt her home cuz she was chuck. I had a lil' hope in my shamin' heart, so I kept the convo goin' with her and was hella polite about everything. I walked her almost three miles down hella switchbacks, and shit got really tight cuz eventually even my GPS beard knew where the fuck we were. When we finally got to her door, I told her I had a baumish night and leaned in for a lil' kiss, and she just put her hand up and said sick to me. Then she thanked me for walkin' her home and skunted upstairs. I ended up havin' to take a taxi back. It was tight."

"Well, hey, don't worry about Tirana bein' garnk in the nah department," I said. "Our next stop's gonna be boomish for beaches and bitches!"

"Oh baaaad," Bert said. "I think you just gotta accept, Felm, that this country gets 'em big time except for the people are hella hoo hoo and the flag's baumish."

"Nah, you'll see," I said. "Saranda's gonna be *un*-shitty!"

# SARANDA

When we arrived, I was in a foul mood. Some dickhead on the bus had vomited all over my backpack, and my stomach was in knots from eating lamb guts, then enduring thirty some switchbacks. I had formed a mental image of Saranda from the photos in my guidebook: blue waters, sunny promenades, bent palm trees, bitches in bikinis squishing white sand between their toes.

I stepped off the bus with this reeling through my head. My face dropped like a fat pair'a testicles when I got a load of the real deal. Saranda was nothing but a bleached wasteland of unfinished projects, electronics stores, and dusty internet cafés. My stomach grew another knot.

"So much for Albania gettin' saved," Bert said.

"Now wait a minute," I said, taking a deep breath. "We're only in the city. Maybe the coast'll be more baumisher."

"Fat chance'a that."

"Hey, you fuckin' *know*. Let's just find a place and then roll down to the beach. I'm givin' up yet."

We crossed the city till we came to a palm-lined avenue along the water. It had a few simple restaurants and a single hotel with a sign that read "Vacancy."

"You think the Hotel Pito is gonna be ait?" I asked.

"Couldn't hurt to check," Tim said.

The rooms there ended up being okay. They had working showers, decent beds, balconies, and ceiling fans. It was fifteen bucks a head a night. We booked a double and a triple.

Once we settled in, we lathered up and slipped our suits on. On advice of the receptionist, we cut left outside and walked down to where the "best beach in Saranda" supposedly was. On the way there, I prayed to Skanderbeg's big bearded ass that it would at least be decent. When we got there, I smiled big and round.

"Hot damn, this is baumish," I yelled.

The beach was wide and clean and peppered with nahs. Its lip of sea was crystal blue and stretched out as far as the eye could see, and—

I rubbed my peepers and dropped my fists. Like a pretty postcard being ripped in half, the gorgeous scene split away leaving one of horror in its place. Everywhere I looked I saw bloated sea hags in bathing suits. The water was sloppy green and studded with tankers and concrete stumps. Where one might have expected palm trees stood decommissioned oil rigs. Even the sand was crunchy, hot, and full of sticks.

"I think this makes it official," Bert said, kicking a soiled diaper into the water.

"I think yer right," I said.

We all went for a little swim just to cool off. When we tired of swallowing rainbow water-spirals, we cut back up to the room. After an hour of chucking, I began to get anxious. I had almost completely recovered from my near-lethal bout of alcohol poisoning and was ready to cut loose. Those randy juices were flowing through my veins again. They surged up to my brain and made it crackle.

"Let's fuckin' explode!"

I didn't have beer or spirit to do it with, so I grabbed my camera. I ran back and forth between the rooms picking, poking, and snapping photos. All the Chucks thought this was a gas and started doing poses. I got Tim with his shorts down, Mason with his eyes rolled back, Bert shouting at the heavens, and Kip going swirl-eyed. When the tornado of cheesy pics and bullshit died down, we all started chuckling. Corfu was coming and we weren't gonna let this trip go out without a fucking bang.

# CORFU

T wo hours of drool and we were in Corfu. We grabbed our crap
and stepped off the ferry. The only person we were greeted by
was a pudgy Greek guard scratching his underbelly. He ushered us into
a sweaty immigration hall manned by two dead-faced clerks with
crooked cop hats. One bumped the other awake as we walked up.

"Where from?" they muttered.

"America."

"You come through Brindisi?"

"No."

"Bari?"

"Nah."

"Patras?"

"Nope."

"Well, where you khav come from?"

We pointed to the emblems on our shirts and smiled. The guards
looked at us like we'd just pointed to our assholes.

"We came through Saranda," I said. "You know? *Albania?*"

"You come through Albania?"

"Yeah, what of it?"

"Are you military?"

"No, we were there on vacation, for God sakes!"

They shot us suspicious eyeballs but stamped our passports. We thanked them for nothing and went outside.

"You got the number for that place you booked for us?" Mason asked me.

"Chea hea," I said. I gave him the number for the pickup service and waved him on.

While he barked orders on the phone, the others looked at me with curious expressions.

"So what is this place?" Bert asked.

"Ooff," I replied. "You'll see."

Half an hour later, a van pulled up alongside us. There was a giant decal of a woman's ass in a thong bikini covering its sliding door. Next to it was a bearded Greek guy with a lecherous smile, giving the thumbs up and winking hard. Underneath everything in bright pink letters were the words "Dr. Spank's Ass Castle."

Bert sniffed and looked over at Mason. "I take back what I said about Slavco's van being like the one you should use for your camp," he said.

We heard a door slam. The driver came around to the slider and put his hand on the handle.

"Welcome aboard the Ass Express!" He shot off a toothy grin and raised a thumb. His face matched the one on the van.

"So you're Dr. Spank, huh?" Mason asked.

"You got it, my fren," he said.

Dr. Spank threw open the sliding door with a flick of his wrist. Like a curtain being pulled back from a pyramid of gold, the receding door line revealed a cache of olive-skinned backpacker chicks with big tits and short shorts. They all smiled and waved us aboard. We slung our packs over our shoulders and stepped in.

Despite it being over ninety degrees in our meekly air-conditioned van, the ride down to Agios Gordios, home of the Ass Castle, was very pleasant. This was due in large part to sitting next to a group of hot Spanish chicks that couldn't have been more than eighteen.

"You ladies wanna party with us tonight?" I asked them in Spanish.

"Oh *si*, we'll party with you guys big tonight!" a brunette with long bronze legs said. Just as my tongue started to slide out from between my teeth, Dr. Spank let off a holler. We looked in the direction he was pointing, and our jaws unhinged.

"Welcome to pure heaven," he yelled.

The first thing we saw was a whitewashed village. Above it was a resort of royal size and style. It had peach-painted battlements and murals of asses, dorm den upon dorm den, and clubs for the masses. At the forefront of everything, was a parking lot full of ATVs. We pulled up there and hopped out.

"First, we check you in," Dr. Spank said.

We followed him into the reception room out front. It was packed with beer fridges and liquor stands, porno mags, and plenty of sunburnt women. A slender girl with pigtails rushed up to us with shots. They were filled with a smelly pink liquid that made our nostrils sting.

"You guys want some free pink ouzo?" she asked.

"Fuck yeah!" we said.

She fanned the shots out in front of us and took one for herself. With a resounding "Opa!" we held them in the air and dumped them down our throats. The ouzo packed a wallop. None of us had drunk anything in almost a full week, so our collective tolerance was low. Once Dr. Spank saw that the booze was kicking in, he had us come up and check in. I told the receptionist with the pigtails that we'd booked two rooms, and she gave me a baby-faced frown.

"I'm sorry, sir, but we only have you down for a five-bed dorm," she said.

"Jesus. All five of us in one room? That's gonna be fuckin' nuts!"

"Ahh, it won't be so bad. You'll be so busy doin' stuff, you won't even be in the room, tee-hee."

I begrudgingly went for my money, but the Chucks held me back. I asked them what the fuck, and Tim smiled.

"We had a lil' chat on the ferry over here," he said. "Since you've done small amounts in planning this blow-up, we're gonna fuckin' letcha pay for this one, gaht."

"You guys are gonna cover my stay?"

"Well, we'll cover you for one night," Mason said.

I thanked the Chucks, and they paid. We ran outside and down a flight of pink steps to where our dorm building was. It was a two-story hovel with a busted fountain and a grimy terrace. But the view of the beach was nice enough, so we figured our room might be too. We keyed the door and pushed it open. Inside was a row of matchbox beds, a rickety desk, and a small bathroom.

"Maybe the shitter'll at least be baumish," I said. I walked over and opened the door. The place was no bigger than a large outhouse with a single gurgling toilet and a rusty shower in the corner.

Bert was looking over my shoulder.

"Wow! It's gonna be fun bringin' bitches back to this lovely bathroom after we're all done stinkin' it up with our massive dumps."

We lubed up and headed down to the beach. The flight of pink steps that took us there zigzagged through the entire lower complex of the Ass Castle. We passed sagging volleyball nets and cracked basketball courts, drained-out swimming pools, and empty gyms. We walked by "The Ball Room"—the Ass Castle's very own nightclub. Its outer walls were covered in peeling graffiti, and its grounds were strewn with garbage and dead leaves. I spotted a used tampon baking in the sun.

"Good thing we don't have to pay to get in this fuckhole," I said.

We arrived at the cafeteria. Its air was spotted with flies, and there were no tablecloths covering its janky tables. There were two sweaty cooks working the kitchen, and fifty sun-fried backpackers waiting around for their orders. The meal prices were outrageous, and everything offered looked like it would be better served on a baby diaper than a plate. We looked through the big windows and saw the beach sparkling in the sun.

"Let's just grooge down there and go swimming," I said. "The water'll make it all baumisher."

I cut into a run and busted out onto the hot white sand. As it crunched under my feet, I assumed the crucifix spread. Head to sky, I screamed out a giant, "Fuck yeah!" My body hit the water like a fat sack'a dicks. I was enveloped in liquid blue warmth. It carried me in spins till my eyes shot above it. I saw Tim running toward me. He kipped up into a jump kick with his skinny legs and went sailing at my head. At the last second, I ducked. Tim crashed into a swirl of seafoam next to me.

"You gay ass man," I yelled.

He laughed and splashed me in the face. I returned the favor then came at him for a headlock. Just as I did, I heard three bombs go off behind me. I spun around and saw the other Chucks coming up from the water.

"Oh, you gottem," they yelled.

Our whole little area erupted into a massive splash war. You'd think it was a shark fight, but it was just us Chucks, playing in the sea, teeth out, and free.

After judo chopping the surf, we rolled up to a stilted lounge area. We stretched out across the chairs then heard giggling. In a swarm of pastel bikinis, the Spanish chicks from the ride over came trotting down from the upper deck. Their little olive bodies were glistening with suntan lotion, and their tits and asses were held firm by their suits. They waved as they passed us and flitted down to the beach. We watched with saucer eyes and shoelace drools as they cat-walked up to a spot to plop their buns. We all wanted to go down there and hit on them. It was just a question of balls.

"I'm gonna wait till tonight when we're all good n' D," Bert said. "Then it'll be easier."

"I agree," Kip said. "Odds are they'll be more willing to have sex once they get some alcohol in their systems."

"What are you thinkin', Conchelli?" I asked Tim.

"Eeff," he said. "I'm thinkin' we wait till tonight too."

I looked over at Mason. He was already bearing fangs behind his big red monster. "What'll you faggots give me if I grooge down there and get those nahs to let me give 'em back massages?" he said.

"Haha. You do that," Bert said. "And we'll each buy you a sneer tonight."

"Is that a deal?" Mason asked, looking at the rest of us.

"Chea hea," I said.

He slipped on his black loccs and cracked his knuckles.

"You gahts just watch," he said. "I'm gonna have these lil' hussies beggin' for more Shayt'n by the time I'm done with 'em."

He strode down the steps to the beach. When he hit the sand, he sucked in his gut and held up his chin. He metered his steps so as not to scare the girls. When he got within two feet of them, he broke into a disarming half-smile and began gesticulating calmly. None of us could hear what people were saying. Bert and I created our version of what their dialogue might have been.

"So, uh, how'r you ladies doing today?" Bert used his deepest and grumbliest voice.

"Oh, *muy bien*," I cooed. "You have mucho beard. Very scary."

"Oh, don't be scared, the beard likes you. Hey, you mind if I just get in there and give you guys a lil' back massage? I promise not to tickle your pussies from behind . . . unless you want me to."

"Oh, no, *señor* beard. We okay. We don' wan' back massage from hairy sasquatch man. It is too—"

Before I could finish my sentence, Kip gave me a little elbow. I looked back up at the beach and gagged. There was Mason, hunched over two of the Spanish girls. He had both his arms out and was massaging their necks and whispering things in their ears. We all stared at him in awe for a moment. He must have felt our eyes on him because he looked up at us and grinned.

"Haha!" Bert choked. "That goddamned Scot pulled it off!"

That night, we donned our finest wrinkles and strode down to The Ball Room for dinner. We stepped inside and saw a tasteless feast for the eyes. In the center of everything was a scratched-up dance floor. A lopsided disco ball dangled from the ceiling as did a mess of twisted pink ribbons arranged in the shape of a big fat ass. A pink-lit bar was in the back. There were cracked Greek nudes wearing dildo-nose masks on either side of it. Off to the right was a small DJ booth. The fucker up there must have been drunk because he was spinning Ace of Base's "The Sign" at super high volume. Nobody in the place seemed to mind. They were all seated at their plastic dinner tables laughing and drinking and carrying on as if something tasteful were resonating from the spider-webbed speakers above them.

We resigned ourselves to the bullshit and chose an empty table among the dozens. The night's only salvation at that point short of a group orgy could be good food and drink. We waited patiently for our servers to come out with it all. It took twenty long minutes, but finally they came.

"Jesus Christ, I hope we don't have to party with these douchebags tonight," Bert said.

Our servers were greased-up, muscle-bound bro-tards with tribal tats, puka shell necklaces, and spiked hair. Each wore a Greek flag around their waist as a skirt.

"Maybe they'll all grooge back to Dickhead Island once they've served us," I said, chuckling.

Two of the morons came to our table. They practically tossed the plates at our faces, then walked off. When they were beyond earshot we looked down at our 'meals.' Each consisted of three items: pruned peas that looked like gorilla boogers, a smear of old mash the likes of which I'd once seen hanging from a yeast-infected vagina, and as a centerpiece, a hunk of freeze-dried meat that could have doubled as a reconstituted buffalo chip. To wash it all down, we were given already open bottles with peeling labels that read "Zorba the Greek."

"This beer tastes like rat piss!" Bert said, after his first sip.

I was hoping our hideous-looking meals might at least be palatable enough to take the taste of the beer from our mouths. We loaded up our forks with a dripping stack of everything. We stuck it on our tongues, bit down, and chewed.

"I'd rather guzzle this damn pimp beer," Tim said, with a sack of half-chewed food bulging from the side of his mouth.

"I've got a cure for that," someone said in a thick English accent.

We looked up to see who had spoken. The guy had an oblong head, droopy nose, and pathetic eyes. His skin was the color of curdled milk, and his build was that of a malnourished ten-year-old. His shoulders had a slight hunch, and his neck a slight crook. I was just about to say it, but Bert beat me to it.

"This player looks exactly like Ned," he mumbled.

Ned was the one we always used to bag on when he was still with us.

All of us were humorously intrigued by what this surrogate Ned—his name turned out to be Pip—meant by "cure for the bad beer taste." We invited him to pull up a chair and speak his piece.

"This beer's crap, yeah?" he started in.

"Yeah," we agreed.

"Well, you've got to add something to it to make it taste better."

"Whaddaya suggest?" Mason asked. "I mean I could shoot a load in this beer, and it would prolly taste better. Doesn't mean I wanna drink it afterward."

"Haha. I'm not talking about your spunk. Have yous ever heard of a shandy?"

"Is that like when you crap on somebody's chest?" Bert asked.

Pip furrowed his brow. The joke hung in the air for a minute.

"Oh, wait. That's a Hot Carl," Bert said.

"Okay so a shandy, mates," Pip continued, "is beer mixed with either ginger beer or lemonade. Now, I know it doesn't sound appetizing, but I promise, adding either of these ingredients to this rotten beer will improve its taste significantly."

"Where are we gonna get ginger beer or lemonade?" Mason asked.

"Well, certainly not here. You're going to have to settle for Sprite. In fact, I have a Sprite shandy in my glass right now. Would any of yous like to try it?"

None of us volunteered. After a few seconds, I shrugged my shoulders.

"I'll try it," I said.

Pip smiled and handed me his glass. I put it to my lips and took a modest sip. "Hey, that's pretty fuckin' good," I said.

I passed the shandy around for the rest of the Chucks to try. They liked it, too, and each wanted one of their own. We were just about to get up for Sprites when the music cut off. A microphone came down from the ceiling and everyone hushed. A few seconds passed, then up came one of the bro-tards. He was gleaming trap to calf, with an ass-crack chin, Mickey Rourke chops, and a wavy black doo.

"Look at this fuckin' tool," Bert said.

"Tool" hardly did him justice. The man was more like a whole shed.

"We're gonna need to give this fool a Chuck name," I said.

"We could call him Maynard," Tim suggested. It took us a moment to get it. Everyone cracked up but Pip.

"Well, who's Maynard?" he asked.

"The lead singer of the band in question," Bert shouted.

We laughed again. Maynard cleared his throat and put the microphone to his lips.

"Tonight's a big night." he began. "We're all here from everywhere. Got some big stuff planned for you ladies and gents. In fact, speaking of ladies and gents, we're gonna switch those roles up tonight. Yup. That's right guys. It's Tranny Night."

Everyone cheered. Maynard chuckled to himself.

"And you all know what that means," he continued. "Ladies, you dress up like guys, and guys, well, you know the deal. Now, everyone finish eating and get yer tranny on."

We all looked at each other. Bert was the first to break the silence.

"Well, I'm fuckin' dressin' up like some ladyboy faggot tonight," he spouted.

"Oh, I am too," Kip seconded.

The rest of us nodded our heads. I cracked off a couple'a queer jokes just to ensure my loyalty to the cause, then downed my drink in cheers with the others. All that froth and sweet stuff ripped into my bladder. I excused myself from the table. I left The Ball Room to relieve myself. On my way to our room, I ran into Julia, a twiggy

Spanish blonde from the bus, with whom I'd flirted earlier.

"*Hola*, Juan," she said, walking up to me with a sly little grin on her face.

"Hola," I replied, gripping my pito. "What's up?"

"Oh, nothing. We girls are just wondering what we should do tonight. Do you have any ideas?"

I wanted to tell her I had a lot of ideas. I had enough sense not to voice them.

"Not really," I said. "We're probably just gonna drink and hang out at The Ball Room."

"Oh, us, too. Hey, but I was talking with my friends, and we were thinking we should all get together and . . ."

The instant the words left Julia's mouth, my chubby shrank and my piss evaporated. My blood crystalized, and my eyes crumpled in their sockets.

"Is something wrong, Juan?" she asked.

"Ah . . . ah . . ." But I couldn't respond. I was wrestling with a bad, bad memory.

When I was just a hair over fifteen, I had my first real crush. Her name was Anita, and I met her in some online chat room late one night while buzzin' off too much caffeine. Our conversation had started simple. I'd seen she was from Livermore, so I shot her a "Hey." Before I knew it, we had plans to meet and study. Two days later, she showed up at my front door with all her books. She was dressed like a *chola*; baggy overalls with one strap undone, tube top hugging her breasts, long red nails, geisha-white face, sleekly painted lips and eyes, black curls draped over one shoulder. I was immediately attracted to her. I'm certain my jeans reflected that.

"Hey,' I said, trying not to blush. "I'm Johann."

"Yeah, I figured that," she said, smiling. "I'm Anita. It's nice to meet ya."

"You too."

I showed her back to my room. My heart was beating so hard and fast I thought it might crack my ribcage.

"Well, here it is," I said, opening the door. She stepped in and dropped her pack. With one slow turn, she soaked everything in.

"You sure have a taste for the morbid," she said.

At that time, I was going through my pseudo-goth phase. To proclaim it, I'd plastered my walls with pictures of everything from werewolves biting screaming maidens in half, to maniacally grinning skeleton alchemists mixing up deadly concoctions. I shrugged my shoulders and cocked my head to one side.

"Whaddaya think?" I asked.

Anita grinned. "I kinda like it."

Over the next two weeks, Anita and I met up almost every day. Each time we 'studied,' we grew increasingly flirtatious. At the end of the second week, we had our first kiss. When her lips locked with mine, my heart bled a tender little pool. In the throes of that special moment, I remember thinking I'd do anything for this girl. Somehow, she must have sensed this the second our kiss ended.

"You wanna do something awesome for me?" she asked.

I pulled back and crinkled my brow. "Sure," I said.

She smiled like the skeleton on my wall and reached into her backpack. With a graceful flick of the wrist, she pulled out a sparkling makeup kit complete with hair curler, lipstick, eyeliner, mascara, and every kind of cover-up.

"What the hell is that for?" I asked. "You want me to do your makeup?"

"No, I don't want you to do *my* makeup," she said.

"Then what are you suggesting?"

"Well, I'm not really suggesting. In fact, I'm telling you. Today, I'm gonna make you up like a girl."

Had it been anyone else, I'd have told 'em to go fuck themselves running with a big fat stick. I mean yeah, I was kind of a goth, but I wasn't *that* kind of goth. The furthest I was willing to take it was the morbid posters and, occasionally, a little black nail polish. I protested, but it was all in vain. Eventually, my heart overran my stubbornness, and I puckered my lips in defeat. It didn't take long for Anita to get me done up. Fifteen minutes and she was laughing hysterically and telling me to go look in the mirror. I walked to the bathroom with my head down and my shoulders hunched. When I got to the sink, I took a deep breath and looked up at my reflection. My hair was curled and coming down on all sides in thick spirals. My face was polished to an angular shine. My lips and eyelids were dressed with sharp black points. Had I not been wearing my flannel and baggy jeans, I might have passed for a fairly attractive, though kinda masculine-looking, Mexican prostitute.

Anita brought out her camera. I pleaded with her not to photograph me. We went back and forth for an hour. Then she grabbed my dick.

"I promise to make out with you *and* show you my tits if you do this," she said.

"Okay."

I stood up with a boner and cracked a half-smile. Anita raised her camera and stuck it to her eye.

"You have to fucking promise me something now, Anita," I said.

"What's that?"

"That you'll show it to no one."

She pressed the button and the flash filled my face.

"I promise," she said.

The second that photo was developed, Anita took it to school and showed everyone. When the Chucks saw it, they didn't really care, but some of the assholes Bert hung out with, whom I mentioned previously, made it their mission to ridicule me about it. At the forefront of this effort was the bane of my high school existence, Buddy Stubbs—hick dickface extraordinaire. Like any self-respecting motherfucker, Buddy took great delight in torturing me. If he wasn't ragging on my name or my mixed heritage, he was calling me Tecumseh 'cause of my long black hair or bagging on my style of dress. In the months before I'd met Anita, the prick's little act had pretty much run dry. That photo was just the shit-storm he needed to start opening his mouth again.

Every day for weeks he waited for me near my car, smoking with his cronies and thinking of new ways to call me a faggot. It didn't even matter that I was dating a girl at the time; I was considered gay by him and his moronic cadre of rednecks because I'd let someone put a little bit of makeup on my face and take a picture.

So when Julia asked me and the Chucks to do Tranny Night with her and her girlfriends, the sublimated effects of all that torment came bubbling to the surface. I'm fully aware of how irrational this sounds, but I thought if I dressed up in drag that somehow, in some way, all those nasty things Buddy had said about me would ring true and I would become, in a word, gay.

With the word ringing in my ears, I came to. Julia was standing there scratching her head.

"Juan, are you okay?" she asked.

"Yeah, I'm just tired," I said, pinching my eyes. "Maybe I'll just wash my face in the sink and—"

A noise broke my speech. It sounded like bees being crushed in a meat grinder. It got louder and harder and tighter. I plugged my ears with my fingers and squinted. Through the haze, I saw a figure materialize. He had his legs crossed, with an elbow on Julia's shoulder and a big fat grin on his ugly face. The fist of madness closed around my heart.

"You sneaky motherfucker," I muttered. The Beast took his elbow off Julia's shoulder and dropped the grin. With red eyes fixed on mine, he started walking toward me.

"Keep comin'," I said. "I've seen all this crap before."

As he moved closer, his gait hastened. He got within inches of my face then came to a halt.

"Ease up," I gulped.

He sneered and flashed his eyes. As his black flesh started to peel up in smoke, I unclenched my jaw. "Fuckin' A," I whispered. The smoke around him formed a dark gray cloud. It coiled up like a viper, then started to dissolve. I coughed and brushed it from my face. I was just about to strike the conversation back up with Julia when I heard,

"Hey, you fuckin' faggot." I leered into the vanishing smoke. A man stepped into a streetlight shaft. The unctuous yellow glow crawled up his face. Once the last morsel of darkness had been eaten away, I frowned.

"Buddy Stubbs," I said. "What the hell is your funky ass doing here?"

He pulled a bent cigarette from the pocket of his wranglers. He put it to his lips and lit it with a silver Zippo. He took a long, self-satisfied drag. When his lungs were completely saturated, he emptied them through his nose and knocked me in the face with a dead-eyed gaze.

"I knew I was right about you," he said. "Shit, here ya are in fuckin' France or whatever, gettin' ready to dress up like a bitch again."

"Who gives a fuck?" I said. "It doesn't make me a fag!"

"Oh, yes it does. First yer dressin' like one. Pretty soon ya got a big black guy behind ya goin' balls deep while he eats some fried chicken off yer back."

"You're such a fucking redneck piece of shit," I yelled. I threw my dukes up and charged at him. Just as I pulled my fist back, a light clicked on in my head. "Son of a bitch," I said.

I stepped back, knelt, and looked up. As my ears filled with fellatio references, I closed my eyes and started to pray. I went deeper and deeper into a humming trance. After what felt like a month-long disembodied fling through space, I came crashing down ass first in the middle of a humungous crater. I dusted the soot from my hair and stood up. All around me were thousands of ashen grooves, sliding upwards and fusing with the infinite starry blackness. In an effort to absorb it all, I broke into a spin. I spun and I spun till I was dizzy, knee-buckled, and hunched. I burped up a bit of barf but held it back, fingers to lips. I looked up to gulp and saw a shack. It was a cozy little one-room with a rakishly tilted roof. Smoke was puffing up from its red brick chimney and a single lit candle was glowing behind its window. I walked up and peered through the warped squares of glass. I saw nothing but a rocking chair and a desk, a neatly made bed, and a suspicious-looking chest. I was going to go inside and investigate but something broke my will. It was gentle and melodic but sliced the air in half like a sheet of thin steel.

I walked around back from where the strange sound was emanating. I saw a horse-drawn wagon and a great big garden. The garden was filled with wine vines of every kind. Only these ones weren't yellow, green, and brown, they were crazy-fool blue, hoppin' with madness like the eyes of a bum who'd crawled his way to enlightenment with a bagged-up bottle to his bearded lips. There was a rustling amongst these bad boys and then a delicate snap. Two vine-curtains parted and out stepped my woman.

"Wow," I said, taking her in. She was dressed in a blue Flamenco dress with asymmetric *volantes* and a beaded *mantón*. Her wrists, ears, and fingers were looped with silver, and every inch of her soft skin was positively glowing. Her topaz eyes lit up like firecrackers when she saw me. A delicate smile slipped across her crimson lips.

"Hello, Johann," she said, hooking a finger through her curls.

The sheen from her hair seemed to rub off on her fingertips. I felt that warmth inside me grow, then I spoke.

"I can't make peace with him this time," I said. "He's got me tricked."

"He hasn't got anyone tricked," she replied. "You have."

"I have? What do you mean, I have? I know what's what. I know I'm not a goddamn faggot!"

She let the words hang in the air. While I stared at them, she tended to her garden.

"What I mean to say is, I'm not a homo just cuz I dress up like a chick."

"Is that what you think the problem is?" she asked.

"Of course, that's what the problem is. That, and the fact you brought me all the way out here to the fucking moon to play with my head!"

"You should watch your words."

"You've heard me cuss before. What's the big deal?"

She closed her lips again. I probed my brain till I hit a nerve.

"Oh, you mean my words to describe gay people? They're part of ROAST. That's how we talk."

"How you talk is part of how you'll be remembered. Do you want the Chucks to be remembered as a world culture that puts down one of the world's cultures?"

"I guess not."

"Okay then, you have your answer."

With that, she vanished between a tangle of vines. I was ripped up by my feet and shot back into space. Time bled by in trillions of liquid seconds. I felt a stretch and a pop, then bang! I was back on the street staring at Buddy's wretched mug. He was still coming up with new ways to tell me what a faggot I was. Between the "shit-stuffin' man pleasers" and the "big, fat ball jugglers," I struggled for a modicum of mental clarity. I thought about what it meant to stop using pejoratives for gays. I applied this understanding to myself, and my answer slapped me dead across the face.

"It's not that I'm *not* gay," I shouted. "It's that if I were, it wouldn't fucking matter because being gay isn't a bad thing."

Buddy's eyes lit up red. He threw his head skyward and let out an agonizing roar. As the sound of it fanned outwards, I heard the crackle of sizzling flesh. It rose to meet his bellow, then the two clapped together in a thunderous blast. At that very second, his body cracked apart. The fragments were suspended for a moment, then in a grand poof, they broke into a drifting smoke. I watched with a smile as he floated away. I blew him a kiss and wished him farewell.

I blinked and looked back at Julia. She was staring at me like I'd just severed my nuts with a blade of glass and handed them to her for safekeeping.

"Where did you go off to?" she asked.

"Don't worry about it," I replied. "Point is, I'm back. And fuck yeah. I'd love to do Tranny Night with you and your girlfriends. I'm sure my bros would too."

I woke up to something choking my crotch. I looked down and saw my hairy legs bursting out of a mini skirt. I raised my hands to my face and saw my nails. They were long and red like Thai chilies.

"Good Christ," I muttered. I looked over and saw the Chucks flopped out on their beds. Tim was in a black cocktail dress with a rose on his ear, and Mason was in a frock and pumps. Kip had on daisy dukes and a tight blouse. A wad of Kleenex was running from his left tit.

"What the fuck happened last night?" Bert said, sitting up. He was wearing an extremely tight red leather slip. His ugly balls were hanging out over his leg. "We seriously shoulda gotten laid."

"You mean you and Kip didn't blow up with those Canadian nahs?" I asked. "Christ. I saw you guys fucking skinny dipping with them down at the beach."

"I know. I fuckin' know what happened. One minute we were in the water naked with those two bichin' Canucks, and the next they were walkin' off laughin'."

"Maybe they caught a glimpse of your balls."

"Fuckin' baaaad! I think they were just so damn D they forgot to fuck us. It coo. Next time I'll just bring a club, knock 'em over the head, and drag 'em to a cave!"

"That's fuckin' nice," I said.

"Haha. I'm only nei nornin."

"Hey, speakin'a clubbin' bitchin' chicks," Mason cut in. "How 'bout those really sick Spanish chicks we switched clothes with last night?"

"Yeah, what was up with that?" Tim said. "I thought for sure I had a lil' romance going with one of those ney neys."

"Oh you did," Mason said. "When all of 'em had fuckin' boyfriends."

"What?" I said. "How the hell did you find that shit out?"

"Your friend, Julia the Alien Twig, told me after she got hella D. Basically, she said her and her friends were just fuckin' with us the whole time to see if they could get us to dress up like chicks."

"Brrrrrrr! That's the first time I've had that shit happen. Whatever. Let's just get our clothes back and blow up."

We spent the entire day on the beach, frying our skin red. When evening came, we headed down to The Ball Room for another stunning meal squeezed from the crack of the aptly named castle we were staying at. This time we were served cold fish sticks, apple sauce, and green beans. I'd rather have eaten my toenails.

"This kinda shit makes me skin crawl," the guy across from us said. "And that's saying something considering what me and me friend Jakey here went through to go on this trip."

"Really?" I said. "What was that? Wait, lemme guess . . ."

Judging by their appearances, it couldn't have been much. They were a couple'a spiky-haired Emo boys with wrists as thin as paperclips and pretty little faces that looked like they'd scarcely felt the strike of a raindrop.

"You guys had to work a couple'a dead-end jobs at some boring-ass department stores, right?" I said.

"Haha. Naw, mate. You're way off," Jake said. "I'll let Sammy here tell ya the story though. He tells it better than me anyway."

"So here's how it started," Sammy began. "We both left Sydney and were out in London livin' the dream, yeah? We had jobs at a great boozer, girls every night, getting fucking pissed. Champions, right? Wrong. A few months into it, we lost our bloody jobs. The old bloke who ran the place said we came in off our faces too often. He fired us, the dopey bastard, and told all the other boozers in the area not to give us work. We were left with two options—go back to Aus and have another go at graduating from uni, or stay in London and finish the two-year trip we'd set out to do."

"Two years? Jesus Christ! Where the fuck were you gonna find the money for that?" I asked.

"You're not gonna believe where we *did* find it, mate."

"Where?"

"At the hospital, as medical guinea pigs."

"Bullshit!"

"Honest. You can do it, too, if you're ever short of money. It's easy. We were checking the want ads for ways to earn easy cash and we came across it. They needed two test dummies at a hospital near where we were living, so we went in and they gave us the job. It was actually rather fun at first. We got dressed up in hospital pajamas and all that. They gave us each our own beds. Then they gave us the test products. I got some funny asthma inhaler and Jakey had to take these pills to exfoliate his skin. At first, everything was ace. Free meals and whatnot, even if they were sort of bodgy. But a few days into it, we started feeling the effects of our products. Mine gave me a chronic cough that got worse and worse. I thought I was gonna cough me bloody lungs out by the end of it. Jakey had it worse than I did though. For the first part of it, he was fine and all, but I remember I woke up one morning as he was coming from the dunny cuz he was groaning and making all sorts of noise. There he was with his arms around his stomach, his pajama top off, and his whole bloody body was bright pink."

"I took me top off to check me whole self after having a shit cuz I saw me face in the mirror," Jake said. "Bloody scary. I thought I was gonna die before the nine days were up."

"You guys had to do this shit for nine days?"

"Yeah," Sammy said. "But it was worth it, believe me."

"Why, how much did you guys get paid?" Mason asked.

"You won't rob us if we tell you?"

"Um, no."

"We each got nine thousand pounds."

"Oh, I'll always be there," Mason said.

"Be where, mate?" Sammy asked.

"Nowhere," I said. "It's an inside joke. Anyway, now that you have all this dough, where the hell are you gonna go?"

"Everywhere. The rest of Europe, Africa, Asia, the Americas. Jakey's got family in Macedonia, so we're off to visit them next. After that, who knows? We've got plenty of money, so it could be anywhere."

"Well, if you blow all of it before you leave you might wanna hit Dr. Spank up," Bert said. "I'm sure he'd love to run some 'medical tests' on you guys."

"Christ, I'd hate to see what those were. See how much bodgy pink ouzo you can drink before you die or something. I'd rather face the inhaler again, haha."

As dinner came to a close, Maynard's oily, muscled ass got on the mic to announce the night's activity. I prayed it wouldn't be another lame dress-up party.

"Tonight is Culture Night," he said. "And since we're in Greece, it's gonna be Greek Culture Night. Are you guys fuckin' ready?"

A few people coughed. Bert farted.

"Ok, then," Maynard continued. "Let's get in a circle and get this party started!"

Everyone got up from their respective tables and formed a huge circle around the dance floor. Once we were all sitting cross-legged, Maynard and his league of extraordinary dingleberries started the show.

"Okay," Maynard said. "Let's have two people get up here and Greek dance."

Most people seemed baffled as to what exactly Greek dancing was. Without explaining it, Maynard and his cronies selected a dude in a ball cap and a fat girl in a black top to perform. They grabbed each other's hands and started swinging their arms together. It looked like a hammock tied between two palms trees, blowing in the wind.

"No, no, no," Maynard yelled. "That isn't Greek dancing. This is."

He ushered the couple offstage and started clapping. To the tune of a crackling *bouzouki*,[19] two hairy dudes in black shirts with open collars came out. They stood side by side and gripped each other's elbows. They did a few quick shuffles, broke the line, bowed then took off.

"Wasn't that incredible?" Maynard shouted. I wanted to run up there and shit across the guy's flip-flops. He stopped me by screaming,

---

[19] Greek guitar.

"Now it's plate-breaking time!"

The Dingleberries put stacks and stacks of plates in a circle. In the middle of it, they placed a big silver bucket with a ladle poking off to the side.

"I bet this'll be rich," I said.

A plate whizzed toward me and broke at my feet. Plates started flying in every direction and shattering all over the crowd. We covered our heads and ducked down low. When the one-sided war was over, Maynard got on the mic again.

"That's Greek Culture, people," he said. "And now that you've been initiated, we're gonna reward you guys by serving all of you a big giant ladle of our very own pink ouzo."

For the next ten minutes, the crew went around imploring everyone to drink from the ouzo-filled ladle they dangled in front of their faces. Most did it, if reluctantly. I was going to skip it, but I figured getting a little tossed would be the only way to handle the rest of this travesty. When the guy came over, I grabbed the ladle from his hands, poured its nasty contents down my throat and burped.

"My, that's tasty," I said.

The guy grimaced and served a few more people. Maynard got on the mic again.

"All of you drank like brave Greek warriors," he exclaimed. "I'm very proud of you. Now, I'm going to give you a special surprise performance. Hit it, man!"

There was a loud fumbling in the back. The lopsided disco ball spun to life and house music came blaring from the speakers. There was a click, then a heavy hiss. The floor was filled with fog and lasers, and the oiled bozos went dancing around in circles. Each of them grabbed a female partner and made her straddle his waist.

"Shake that ass, ladies," Maynard yelled. The girls started grinding their hips and fake-moaning. The men humped them harder and grunted like warthogs. I sat there scowling at the freak show. As I did, I thought, my God, I hope people don't see us like these douchebags.

I woke up with a head full of molasses. I crawled into the shitter and jerked off. I felt the tiles closing in around me. After I came, I got an idea. I wrapped a towel around my boner and walked out. Everyone was still asleep.

"Gahts, we're in Corfu," I yelled. "And Corfu ain't just the Ass Castle. There's a whole island out there. And we should fuckin' explode it."

"How do you propose we do that?" Mason asked, shielding his eyes.

I threw my hands up and let the towel fall from my naked cock.

"ATVs," I yelled. "I saw them in the parking lot when we came in."

"Ait," Tim said. "Now put your dick away."

We packed our provisions for the day and headed out to the parking lot. Dr. Spank was already out there flicking his boogers and checking the oil on one of the ATVs.

"Hey you guys," he said. "You wanna rent some of these fuckers? They each seat two people so you can pick up some pretty girl."

"How much for a day?" I asked.

"For you, special price. Twenty-five euros each and I throw in nice helmet."

"Twenty and you got yerself a deal."

He took the hundred euros from us with a wolf-toothed grin. He tossed us our helmets, then gave us our pick of the ATVs. I took a blue, Tim took a yellow, Bert took a brown, and Kip took a green. The only one having trouble selecting was Mason. He puttered around the lot stroking his beard.

"You think I should go with the black one?" he asked.

"You know goddamn well which one you should go with," Bert said.

Mason grinned and mounted a pig-blood red one. The rest of us mounted ours and donned our shades. With smiles to the sun, we turned our keys. Our engines roared to life, and we blasted off.

We zipped through the countryside feasting our eyeballs. We saw sun-soaked olive groves and big-horned goats, hot forgotten villages, and elders in wool coats. All this ancient stood beside the recent. There were smart cars and snazzy cafés, chicks in pink tank tops licking their *crème brulées*. We wound through the wrinkles of this anachronistic handshake for what seemed like days. Suddenly the road ended and we were left with a sign.

"Pelekas?"

"Yeah," Mason said. "I was looking at the map earlier and there should be some pretty baumish beaches around here."

We rode down a tiny dirt path till we came to a clearing. The beach there was small but decent. Around it was a ring of porous cliffs grown over with scrambled green. There were sand dunes and tide pools and gnarled trees growing up from the rocks. The water in between was see-through teal. It was studded with half-surfaced boulders and kelp like eels. We slipped off our sandals and went splashing in, laughing. It was all sun and diamonds till we looked on ahead.

It was there in the distance . . . large, black, and crooked like a foot soldier of the damned, frozen in mid-march as it made its way up through the earth's crust, only to hit water instead of land. Its jagged eaves were filled with razor-sharp points and pockets. It had barely a discernable top to spring from, and what it did have looked like it would skin the meat clean off the feet of anyone who even attempted to stand thereover. I tried to suppress the thought I was having. It wiggled itself to the surface and forced me to blurt it into existence.

"Should we make up for Mostar and jump off that big bitch up there?" I asked.

As soon as the question left my lips, an eerie silence spread across us like a rash of crabs. I could almost hear our cumulative heartbeat purr out of control. We looked at one another, sweat pouring off our brows. We knew it was time to separate the bulls from the cows.

"I'll fuckin' do that shit," Mason said. "I got robbed by that speedo boy pussy back at the bridge."

"That's one," I said. "Anyone else groogin' with?"

Kip and Bert both let off a big fat "Yeah!" The only one left was Tim. I glared at him. He scratched his neck and puffed through his nose. The seconds drizzled by. Finally, he spoke.

"Chea hea, fuck it," he said. "Let's go bodacious on this big bitchin' cock."

We shot into the crystal water and went arm-lapping toward the rock. Every time we scooped our mouths up to take in air, we caught glimpses of it in the distance. It grew bigger and bigger like a super bad guy from an eighties videogame after consuming a power-giving piece of fungus. Each of its growth spurts sent our heart rates that much higher.

When the water thinned, we reached forward till we grabbed land. A couple twists and pulls and we were up on a ledge.

"Dude, I can even stand on this tight shit," Tim said, shifting his weight from foot to foot.

Mason and I were in similar states. Underneath our feet was a network of volcanic glass with surgically sharp curves and points.

"We're gonna even be able to climb this rock," Mason said. "I mean look, Felm, it'd basically be a death sentence just getting up there."

I lifted my eyes to where he was pointing. The draw of the motion wore my neck out.

"Ooooofffffff," I said. Over sixty feet of skin-ripping agony awaited us. I swallowed my teeth.

"You think we should say Hayes D to this shit?" Mason asked. "I mean, it's not like we haven't done hella bargaretty jumps before."

"I can't believe this is coming from you of all people, Beardo," I said. "You were the one who almost conquered the fuckin' Mostar Bridge."

"Yeah, but that was just a barg jump. This is a barg jump and an even more barg-ass climb."

"His beard is right," Tim said. "You're *un*-shitty when it comes to climbing. The rest of us gettem."

Tim had a valid point. Of the three of us, I have the most climbing skills. Since I was barely a toddler, something inside has always compelled me to scale things. This was first made manifest when, as a two-year-old, I climbed to the very top of a fifty-foot pine tree in our backyard. I can still remember my mother and father pinching their faces up in horror as I waved to them with my tiny hand from up high. Ever since then, I was hooked.

"I know I'm the better climber," I said. "So I'll go first, gahts."

I tiptoed up to the rock face. The handholds were like greasy scalpels. I bit my lip and gripped one. The points dug into my skin. I took it and pressed on. I wedged both feet into sharp notches. The pain spiked and spread inwards. I had to move fast.

"I'm just gonna blow this bitch up all in one go," I yelled. I took a big breath and focused my eyes skyward. All my muscles tightened. I went farther and farther, slamming my palms and soles up against the rock. I could feel them start to split and bleed. I relied on the leverage of my stomach and elbows. This introduced an awkwardness of motion that opened me up to wider bodily injury. I was able to keep it to a minimum till I reached an overhang. I threw my right arm over the top and clubbed my elbow.

"Harvey Christ!"

I fanned my arm out to see what had happened. There was a chunk of flesh taken from the tip, which was pooling with blood. I shook it off and intensified my gaze. In four swift, stomach-grazing motions, I was up and over the outcrop. I stood up and looked down. I was covered in bleeding scrapes and bruises. I cracked a tiny smile. I panned my head to take it all in then threw my fists in the air.

"Fuckin' get me," I screamed.

Over the next twenty minutes, Mason and Tim struggled their way up the rock. I tried to guide their movements as best I could. In the end, they avoided serious injury; a few deep scrapes but that was it. After a high five, we stepped up to the edge and looked down. The way seemed clear except for a few ambient boulders. I told the Chucks, "Let's blow it up." Then I heard someone shout. I looked over at the shore to see if it'd been Bert or Kip. They were both watching us intently but neither signaled liked they'd said something. I called out to them just to make sure. They shrugged and said sick.

"Down here," a voice said. I looked toward the water again and rubbed my eyes. There was a girl there treading. She had soft blond hair, big hazel eyes, and a crooked little mouth that told sweet lies. I asked her, "What tha dilly?" and she told me to jump. I smiled with surprise and said, "I'm no chump."

"Oh, no? Then what's taking you so long, bud?"

"Haha. I'm just sizing up my surroundings."

"You're sizing up your surroundings, huh? I've seen plenty of people do that jump right off, and I've only been here a few days."

"Is that so? Well, have you ever done it?"

"Oh, shit yeah. Where I come from, we do jumps like that all the time."

"And where exactly is that?"

"The Cayman Islands."

"I've been there. Which city, George Town?"

"Nope, you've probably never heard of it. It's near a bunch of volcanic glass formations way out in the country."

"You mean Hell?"

"Hey, yeah. Damn, you know your stuff."

"Well, I'm pretty good at geography. Hey, after this we should grab some lunch or something."

"Arright. But if you wanna have lunch with me, you gotta do something for me first."

"What's that?"

"Jump, you big pussy."

I pulled my head back. "Excuse me?" I said.

"You heard me," the girl said. "Jump, you big pussy!"

Her words hit me like a pickaxe to the neck. I went shrinking into myself till I vanished in a cocoon of lifeless flesh.

"I don't like the way you're talking to me."

"Huh? I'm just messin' with you. Plus, I'm kinda hungry, so if we're gonna get lunch, quit being such a big pussy and jump."

Crack! Memories of that fateful day at the lake came surging up through my cortex and spilled out into every area of my brain. I could hear Lana and all her horrible friends chanting, "Jump pussy! Jump!

Jump pussy! Jump! Jump pussy, jump!" I was on the brink of blipping out like a TV screen. At the very last second, I exerted my will. I stuck one toe over the ledge and filled my lungs. Once they were ballooning with air, I looked down at the girl and winced.

"I'll do this," I said. "You just watch."

I rocked back on my heel to gain momentum. When I came forward, I was stopped mid-rock by what I saw. There was the girl still floating and smiling. Only difference was she had smoke snakes trailing up from her nostrils.

"I can't fucking believe it," I said.

"Whaddaya mean? I just told you to jump. Why don't you go ahead? It's nice and warm in here."

Her words warped and expanded till they were hollow and black like endless hell-bound chasms. They gave way to her eyes that lit in flames till the hazel in them was burnt to a glowing red crisp. Her skin turned black, and her teeth turned long. She went lurching up outta the water as if propelled by a machine.

"That bitch showed you hers and filled you with wine. Jump, you big pussy, and drink some'a mine!" With that, she tossed up her claws in vainglorious flare. Things started sizzling, including my hair. All around the cove popped pillars of fire, blood streaked the sky and the water turned mire. I looked to the sun for a shred of dear hope. It crumbled to soot and went up in smoke. There in its place stood a big black hole, and from it flew monsters and horrors untold. There were demons and goblins and devils galore, ghouls with axes, and witch-fingered whores. They spiraled and swooped to a symphony of madness, all paying tribute to the paragon of badness. With ounces of strength left to will my poor limbs, I lifted my fists for I'd forgotten those hymns. And then in a flash of star-speckled light, they popped in my brain and told me, "Don't fight! Make peace with that beast, lest hell be your home. Give him a kiss on his big black dome." Now, much to the suffer of that fucker from Hades, I puckered my sucker and told him, "Oh, baby!" He squirmed in his hatred and let off a shriek, as I embraced my fate with one fearless leap.

Splash! Everything that was black went golden and blue again. I swished around in the water smiling as the smoke trail vanished. When I poked my head up to check the status of my two gahts, I saw Mason in the front and Tim in the back. The latter gaht was assessing while the former was bracing.

"You gonna blow up?" I asked Mason, as he neared the edge.

"Chea hea," he said.

He put toe to point and shut his eyes. He clenched his fists, and I could almost hear his brain sizzle. I can't be sure of the details of his struggle. It didn't matter. Mason's got the balls of a Billy goat and a beard to match.

"Yuuup," he cried. He went sluicing through the wind in a flash of ginger. When he hit the water, I thought he'd broken something from the slap.

"That was fucking *un*-baumish!" he said, surfacing with a gritty giggle.

We turned our attention to Tim now. All we could see of him were two big eyeballs and a line of spiky hair.

"Dude, I know it looks bigaretty, but it's baumish," I said. "Just close your cheatie eyes and say sick to it."

"No, Felm. I can't do this shit. I'm coming down," he said, peaking over the rock ledge.

"Don't be garnk, gaht," I yelled. "Just say sick to whatever bitchin' shit's holding you back and do it."

"I can't. It's too barg."

"Want me to roll up there and blow it up with you?"

"Eeff."

"I'll take that as a yes."

I was quicker up the rock this time. I incurred a few more scrapes but nothing major.

"You ready to say phat ice to this shit?" I asked Tim, as I walked up to the edge. He was standing there, knee-buckled and shivering like a lamb in an abattoir. I put my hand on his shoulder and told him, "Choo oot. The trick is, you've gotta just care. Trust that Mona's got yer back and just leap into that shit."

"You don't think I'm acting like a savage fucking child?"

"Did you think I was acting like a savage fucking child all those times you helped me through my drug trips? I mean, I was gettin' 'em with shit you said sick to all the time, and you cared mad. But you still helped yer gaht. Through the shrums, the absinthe, the loll, all that shit. You're a cheatie space cadet but I fuckin' am. And you still blew me up. Now we're on Felm territory, so I gotta do the same for you!"

Tim smiled and faced the water. I did the same. There was a long pause. Then I blinked.

"Banzaaaaaaaaaaaaaaai," Tim yelled.

The rest of the day was a breezer. We zipped around the countryside on our ATVs, snapping photos and cackling like conquistadors. When we got saucy, we ate at a little Greek place with a grapevine terrace. The owner—a local dude with a mane of shiny curls and a big gold chain glistening from behind his open collar—served us up big plates of moussaka and *dolmades* [20] and *pasticcio*.[21] We sauced it all off while chatting about the jump. I felt like giving Bert and Kip a bit of shit for not having done it, but in the end, I decided not to.

Six o'clock rolled around. We dropped our ATVs off and thought about dinner. We all agreed we couldn't stomach another meal of freeze-dried cardboard. We hit the town and found a Chinese joint that had decent Szechuan beef and pretty alright sweet and sour pork. We wolfed our food down in a hot minute. When we finished, we thought about where to drink. There were few bars around, and they all looked like crap. The Ball Room was our only real option.

We arrived there around ten. Much to our surprise, everyone was wearing normal clothes.

"That's weird," I said. "I thought when we got here, reception told us there'd be a theme for every night."

---

[20] *Dolmades*: stuffed grape leaves.
[21] *Pasticcio*: a Greek baked pasta dish made with tomato, ground meat, spices, and a *béchamel* sauce.

The DJ got on the mic. "Tonight's Hip Hop Flow Night," he shouted. "Come up to booth n' spit yer werst!"

Tim looked over at me and grinned. "You should go up there and pull Brotha Felms," he said.

I've had an affinity for hip-hop and gangsta rap since I was a kid. I'm not sure what initially triggered it. Maybe it was my perennial desire to shock my parents into paying attention to me. Maybe I thought it would transform me from something dorky, weak, and awkward to something pimp, powerful, and smooth. Whatever the case, I took to it like stink on shit. I can still recall the day it happened. I was about twelve years old. I had gone out that fateful afternoon on my bike to see what I could dig up downtown. All the old haunts—the bridge, the creek, the flagpole—were dead. I decided to hit up an old music store across the railroad tracks to check if any new releases had come in. The kids at my middle school had been raving about this rap album cut by some medical professional and his nosey canine. I wanted to see what all the buzz was about.

I walked up in that bitch all dork. I had on my McHammer-style Gecko Hawaiian pants, my black T-shirt, my oversized Nikes, even my bean-dip-stained Yokahama Giants cap that my dad had bought me in Japan, pokin' way up at an angle so the front wave of my flattop was in full view. I walked over to the hip-hop/gangsta rap section straight up lookin' like a dick in a finger forest. People's eyes were crawlin' all over me. I ignored 'em as best I could and started my search. I sifted through a bunch of garbage I didn't recognize. Then I found it: Dr. Dre's *The Chronic*. The guy on the cover looked hard as a brick. He had the lazy-eyed gaze of an assassin, and a clean black cap to match his clean black skin. I was jealous of him immediately. I knew that whatever this doctor had to say would cure me of being a raging dweeb.

It didn't take long for Mr. Dre's music to influence my style of dress. Within a month of purchasing his album, I was wearin' a black cap real low with sagged baggy jeans, fresh Adidas, and an oh so sweet T. I let my hair grow long so I could slick it back under my ball cap. I walked wit a limp just so fools knew. All this was only part of my transformation. I didn't just wanna look like Dre. I wanted to rap like him too.

The path to Gangsta's Paradise was a rocky one. Other phases in my teenage development—the goth, the rocker, the puritan—got in the way. Around the age of seventeen, I was able to reconnect with my thug. This time it was through a different rap artist. I remember first hearing his shit through Bert. We took his old candy apple 'Stang out to 'Donalds one day during lunch and he whipped out the man's album.

"Check this baumishness," he said. He stuck it in his CD player and put it on full blast. What emanated from the speakers was pure bliss. It was gangsta rap, no doubt, but it was different. Instead of just rappin' about blunts, forties, n' bitches, this dude was takin' it to a completely different level, talkin' 'bout shredding baby guts n' fryin' nigga nuts n' cappin' bitches in the pussy n' all that crazy shit. I couldn't believe what I was hearing. I mean, here was a man who had even sicker thoughts than I did, and he had the fuckin' balls to lay 'em on the track.

"That shit's fuckin' siiiiick!" I said.

"Oh, it is sick," Bert agreed. "In more ways than you know."

"Whaddaya mean?"

He grinned big. "Well, first off, this dude's from Sac Town, so he's NorCal instead of SoCal, unlike all the other bitchin' rappers. And the name of his album is *Season of da Siccness*. And the name of the song we just listened to is 'Siccmade,' haha!"

"That's some sick shit."

"Oh, but that's not the sickest part. Sickest part's his name."

"What's that?"

"Brotha Lynch Hung."

Boom! With Dre on one side and Lynch on the other, I resurrected my thug. I took to learning all the lyrics to all my favorite rap artists' songs. Not just Dre n' Lynch's shit, but Pac's, Bone Thugs', Biggie's, Snoop's, Cypress Hill's, the list goes on and on. By the time I hit twenty, I had the lyrics to more than a hundred rap songs memorized. Absorbing a song was a snap. That is till Busta Rhymes came out with "Break Ya Neck." That song was pussy-greased lightning fast. Wow! The way he rolled over all those lyrics with his tongue? You'd think it was "Flight of the Bumblebee" played across clit tips instead of piano keys. I didn't just want to learn this song, I wanted to commit it to motor memory so that the instant I started spittin' it, it would flow out of me as effortlessly as silk piss. I practiced that shit for a good week till I had it down perfect. I knew the ins and outs of every stanza, all the changes in pitch, tempo, and intonation. Christ, I could rap it as well as Busta. Only thing was, I didn't have the balls to do it in front of anyone.

One night in the spring of '03, I went to a kegger that one of my college buddies was throwing. It was in his crummy apartment in south San Diego. Everybody was smashed or passed out when I got there. I grabbed a beer and got busy doing my own thing. I sat down at the community computer and started sifting through the songs on the playlist. Sure enough, there was "Break Ya Neck."

"You don't know nuthin' 'bout dat shit," some dude said.

I swiveled around in my chair. He was a black guy, thin as Q-tips, with a shaved head and big white teeth. He came creepin' over to me. I just glared at him.

"Not only can I rap this shit," I said. "I can do it perfect."

"Bull-fuckin'-shit!" he said. "I got five says you choke, bitch."

"You're on," I said.

I clicked on the song and dipped my beanie real low. I was a cocoon of concentrated darkness. As soon as Busta spit his first lyric, I broke outta the zone and started rapping. My mouth ran off like a Gatling Gun firing oiled bullets. I didn't miss a single beat. The song ended, and I recoiled back into my little black self. The dude looked impressed, but still had a smirk.

"You can copy otha rappers, n' das tight, but you wanna be bad in a room full'a MC's n' you gotta know how'da flow, baby."

"Oh, I can flow."

"Serious? Spit somethin' right now, off tha top'a ya dome."

"I will later," I said, turning away. "Right now, I just want another beer."

The truth was I couldn't flow to save my life. Sure, I'd done it a couple times in private with mixed results, but I was by no means an expert. I wanted to get better at it, ascend in the ranks of the thug, as it were, but I was too scared. It was easier just to bury my fear and inability and pretend like the desire to improve didn't exist. My little plan was going fine for a while. I even tricked myself into thinking that my flow sesh in Krumlov, despite it being in front of a bunch of drunken Gypsies who didn't understand what the hell I was saying, was a big step outta the dark. I didn't realize how wrong I was till that DJ got on the mic and called people up to his booth. The prospect of standing in front of a crowd of mostly English speakers whom I didn't know and flowing twisted my guts up. I looked over at Tim with my nuts on my tonsils. I questioned myself till I thought of our trip. The answer was simple; I had to do it.

I pounded a few Zorbas and walked up to the booth. The DJ looked surprised.

"Hey, you brave," he said, pointing inward with both index fingers. "No one usually come up to flow on Flow Night, so I just do in Greek or khav Nikos from bar come up."

"I guess I'm stupid like that," I said. "Hand me the mic and let's do this shit."

He handed it to me and clicked off the music. I thought he was gonna go right to an instrumental, but he got on the other mic and made an announcement.

"Tonight we khav first victim for flow," he shouted. "Please to welcome . . ." Everyone in the club stopped what they were doing and turned toward the booth. Their gazes felt like a million tiny lasers zapping apart my flesh. "Excuse me, but what is name?" he asked me, covering his mic.

"Name?"

"Yes, yes, your rapper name. What is?"

"Jesus Christ, I don't know, just—"

"Jesus Christ, ladies and gentlemen!"

The whole room burst into laughter. DJ Dickhead fumbled with the mic. "Okay, my man will rap now," he said.

He clicked on the disc player, then cranked it till the speakers hummed. The song started shaky then pulsed into full gear. I put the mic to my lips, then froze. Everything went black.

"Damn that was sick flow, man!" the DJ said, shaking my eyes back open.

I looked at him, then at the crowd. People were smiling and cheering and holding up their drinks to me.

"Did I really do that great?" I asked.

"Yeah man, it was tight. You khad crowd going crazy!"

"That's funny because I don't remember a damn thing I said."

I got down outta the booth to go wash my face. Though people were congratulating me, I still thought I'd bombed.

When the fanfare died, and The Ball Room emptied, I went up to the reception bar for a few more beers. The bartender was bobbin' his head as I walked up. I asked him what he was listening to and he shrugged his shoulders.

"Some rap the DJ from downstairs gave me," he said. "It's good."

I didn't think much of it till he turned it up. It took a few lines then the artist's identity slapped me in the face.

"Hey, that's me," I yelled.

The bartender looked at me like I was nuts. He asked me to recite a few verses to prove it. I gave him a blank stare.

"Haha. You didn't rap this, man," he said.

I furrowed my brow and thought hard for a moment. Suddenly one of my lines came to me: "MC's tryda figa my flow, they think they on to it, but these is God's words B, I'm just a conduit."

Once the last word left my mouth, the voice on the track repeated what I'd just said. The bartender stopped spinning the lip of his glass and smiled.

"Hey, not bad man," he said. "You should keep rappin'."

"Thanks, dawg. I will."

I woke up still glowing from my win. As I lay in bed smiling, my thoughts were cast astray by the rip of wind through squeezed butt cheeks.

"Fuck yeah," Bert yelled, from the bathroom.

"Dude that's fuckin' hot," I said, sitting up.

Bert's nasty fart prompted me to take notice of the equally nasty state of our room. I glared at the piling filth and suddenly felt the urge to move.

"Let's explode the island again ATV-styly," I said. "Only this time let's grooge into town and fuckin' even give this tight place our business."

None of the Chucks put up a fight on that one. After bowers, we were out the door.

We headed to a place in town that rented scooters and ATVs. The woman who ran the joint had bright red hair and luscious breasts hanging from her blue top. The first thing I thought of when I saw her was putting the ATV idea on hold so I could bang her on her desktop and cum on her tits. It took great restraint to approach her politely and sublimate this image.

"We'd like to rent some ATVs," I said, smiling. "How much for a whole day?"

"Fifteen euro," she said. "Best deal in Agios Gordios."

"Damn. You ain't kiddin'. Dr. Spank is charging us twenty. And his kinda blow."

"This because Dr. Spank is asshole. Remember my name for next time. I'm Athena."

"Okay, Athena. We'll take five ATVs for two whole days then."

"Are you sure you want ATV?"

"What do you mean?"

"Well, you look like tough, strong men. Why to get something with four wheel like little child when you can khav something with two wheel like real man?"

"You mean a scooter?"

"*Ne*, I mean a scooter."

"But none of us has ever ridden one before."

"Is easy, I show you if you want."

We looked at each other like "ooff." I could tell the consensus was muscle over hustle.

"We'll just go with the ATVs," I said.

Kip stepped forward. "Speak for yourself," he said.

We all turned around and looked at him like he was bat-balls bonkers. Even Athena raised a thick eyebrow.

"You sure you wanna do this?" I asked him.

"Ch," he said.

"Just sit on it straight." Athena said for the third time.

Kip fixed his glasses and readjusted his little legs. With an awkward flick of his wrist, he started his bike up again.

"Arright, now please to go slowly," she reiterated.

Kip licked his lips and turned his bike handle. It purred along for a bit then jerked into inaction, nearly sending him over the handlebars.

"How can you travel to other side of planet and still not know how to drive scooter?" Athena asked. "*Oi!* Let me show one more time."

After the sixth try, Kip had garnered enough balance and coordination to at least drive his scooter on flat ground. We decided that was good enough and started our engines.

"Please don't to die," Athena yelled as we rode off.

"Don't worry, we won't," I yelled back.

Things went relatively smoothly at first. Kip was at least able to go up small hills and make a few sharp turns without losing too much control. After half an hour of looking over our shoulders to make sure he hadn't spun off a cliff, we began gaining confidence in him. It was precisely at that moment that we heard him cry out, "Ja-Jesus!"

We turned around to see what had happened. Poor Kip had hit a road bump and was wobbling off into a ditch. He regained control briefly by jerking his wheel to the left. He over-twisted the throttle control and went firing off toward the cliff next to us.

"Put on your brakes," I screamed.

His eyes flashed with terror. He squeezed the brake, and his bike came to a smoking stop just before the asphalt ended.

"Who wants to trade with me?" he asked. "I'm done."

None of us wanted to. We were all perfectly comfortable on our ATVs and had no intention of getting on that fucking scooter only to be thrown off a cliff. Problem was, we knew any one of us had a better chance on it than Kip did. It was just a matter of who was going to sack up first.

"I'll blow that shit up," Bert said. "Hand it over."

Bert learned to maneuver the scooter much quicker than Kip did. He was fine with taking it around corners and up hills. His only problem was he was afraid to increase his speed on account of his weight. Once he tired of being the last man in line, he stopped and hopped off. He looked disappointed with himself but still asked if anyone wanted to trade with him.

"Man, I'll do it," Tim said. "I weigh *mad* so this should be buff."

Tim proved to be the best scooter rider of the three. So good in fact that we were able to blast through the countryside and make it to the main coastal highway right on schedule. Our plan that day was to ride as far south as we could. As none of us really knew what that meant in terms of destinations, we decided to stop at a little beachside restaurant in the middle of oooff to figure it out. The place was breezy, with plastic chairs and stilted tents. We took a seat nearest the beach and busted out a map.

"Way I see it, we basically have two choices," Mason said. "We can either roll up to Molos on the upper side of the lower tip of the island or roll south to this place called Kavos. They're really the only places that are actually on the beach in the south, according to this map."

"What's the difference between the two?" I asked.

"Eeff. Either could be bitchin' or baumish. The book says Kavos is more lively, but that don't mean shit. The Ass Palace was recommended in the book, and it was *coooo*. I guess we're just gonna hafta guess."

"Kavos," Tim blurted.

"Why do you say that?" I asked.

"I don't know, I just got this feeling in my Tim gut that maybe it'd be boomish. Plus Mona whispers and chea hea. It's also the most southernest. I just think Kavos. I have a corky feeling."

"Ait, fuck it. Kavos gahts?"

"Ch," Mason and Kip said.

"Bert?"

"Ooff, whatever. Anything to say sick to The Ass Palace. You guys order me a gyro. I'm gonna jump in the water."

Bert slipped off his shirt, revealing a brilliantly white torso of dough. As he walked off toward the beach, the rest of us raised our eyebrows.

"Is he gettin' 'em?" I asked.

"Ooff," Tim said. "I think he just feels garnk cuz he gottem on the bike."

"Well, I gottem on the bike, too, and I kinda care now," Kip said.

"Yeah, but you know Bert, if he gets 'em he shits on himself. So now he's just gonna dough out in the water for a while."

"Haha. Dough out." I laughed. "He *is* a fucking Dough Boy. I mean, look at his pale ass out there sloshing around like a dead seal. I think we should just call him Dough Boy from now on."

"Yeah," Tim said. "He may need that from time to time."

"Need it, or knead it?"

"Both. He needs his dough and sometimes he just kneads it, haha."

We ate and hit the road. As we barreled along the highway, the promise of Kavos whispered in our ears. We had visions of pristine beaches, blue waters, and tiki-bars oozing through our minds. Amidst all the dreaming, we missed our exit.

"Fuck balls. What do we do?" I said.

"Well, we can turn back," Mason suggested. "It's about a half hour ride to the exit. But since we're here, I say we check out what's around for a bit."

"And what would that be?" I asked.

"Supposedly down that way, there's a cool lil' lake called Limni Korisia. We could blow that up."

I looked in the direction he was pointing. All I saw was flatland.

"Ooff. Let's make it quick."

"Yeah. I do really wanna get to Kavos," Tim said.

The trip to Limni was blind. We rode till the wavy heat lines in the distance disappeared against the sky. We thought we'd hit beachfront but instead hit sand dunes. Past them was a thin slick of water the color of baby shit. It was teeming with mosquitoes and egret corpses.

"I don't really think we can swim out there," I said.

"Woll, we can at least ride around in the sand dunes," Kip said. "I mean we're here."

He had a point. We revved our engines and shot into the shrubland. We made it over a few bumps then got half swallowed by the sand. It took a few tries, but eventually, we were able to pull our wheels from the sparkly sucker-mouths beneath them. The only one who stayed stuck was Kip. He was planted directly in front of me with two large bushes on either side of him.

"Dude, you gotta grooge outta the way, gaht," I said. "This is gettin' kinda tight."

While he fumbled with his specs and tried to kick-start his engine, I watched the other Chucks go sailing over the sand dunes just past him. I was able to tolerate his klutziness for a bit. Then I snapped.

"Skunt the fuck out," I yelled.

"I'm trying," he said. "Why don't you just go around me the long way?"

I did what he suggested begrudgingly. On my way out around the bushes, I dropped one last turd.

"Geeky little bitch," I muttered.

By the time we finished fucking around, it was almost evening. We contemplated going to Kavos but figured it was too late. Tim was furious with the decision but choked it down. We rolled into Agios after sundown. We rode up to The Ass Palace parking lot where we parked our bikes. We spotted a poster there that read, "Toga Party Tonight." I asked if anyone wanted to dress up. Everyone said maybe, except Kip. He still wasn't speaking to me.

We walked down to our dorm. As Chucks were going in the room, I spotted something on our balcony table. It was a pair of cheap aviators with gold rims that someone had left behind. I picked them up and smiled.

"Check these babies out." I said, busting up in the room.

Mason, Tim, and Bert looked at the aviators with mild interest. Kip shot 'em a quick glance then peered back through his glasses.

"Think I should roll out tonight in my toga with these sick bitches on ma' face?" I asked, slipping them on.

"Chea hea," Mason said.

I looked in the mirror and grinned big. Then I switched it up.

"Ya know, actually these look kinda bitchin' on me," I said. "Why don't you have 'em, Kip."

"Me?" he said.

"Yeah, man. Take 'em. I think you'll look better in 'em."

Kip whipped his specs off and grabbed the aviators from me. He put them on with both hands. After a few adjustments, he pulled away and let the room have a look.

"Damn playa you ballin' in those," Mason said.

"Yeah," Bert agreed. "You look like fuckin' Diego, the Colombian drug lord."

Kip flashed a giant white smile and ran his fingers through his hair. He arched his head up toward the mirror and got a load of himself.

"I think I'm gonna blow up with you tonight, Felm," he said.

Kip and I stripped our bedsheets and wrapped them around our torsos. Bert skipped this part but rolled with us anyway. The Ball Room was packed with toga-clad morons. Everyone was piss-drunk and falling all over themselves in a wave of hiccups and pink. We slammed three Jack n' Cokes each then hit the dance floor. We tried to get our hands on some ass, but all the chicks were either too drunk or too involved with one of Maynard's shithead minions. We resigned ourselves to the bar and continued drinking. We tossed it back till 3 a.m., then went stumbling up to the reception bar to see if we could find some stragglers. We ordered Zorbas and mingled. None of the chicks in front wanted anything to do with us. We moved to the back hoping to find at least one girl that was willing to talk to us.

"Hey mates," Pip exclaimed, holding up his beer.

"Shit. Hey man."

We sat down at the table across from him. He introduced us to the plain Jane he was chatting with, and we gave her a nod.

"So what are yous up to tonight?" he asked us.

"Same thing as you are, man," I said. "Just dressing up in a toga and getting shitfaced."

"Haha. Right on, right on. One question though, how come he doesn't have his gear on?" Pip pointed to Bert with a playful smile.

Bert crossed his eyebrows. "I'm not afraid to get dressed up in a toga," he said. "Shit, I dressed like a bitch just the other night."

"Didn't mean it that way," Pip said. "It was just an observation."

"Oh, sure ya meant it that way, Eeeeeeeeags."

Eags, short for Eagles, was a nickname we used to call Ned. He earned it because his pale skin, shaved head, and pointy nose made him look a lot like a baby bald eagle. I assume, since Pip was the spitting image of Ned, Bert thought it would be appropriate to call him Eags. Pip, though, had no fucking clue what he was talking about.

"Eags?" he asked. "What on earth does that mean?"

"It means you're a fuckin' faggot n' I gotta grab a picture'a ya."

Bert reached into his pocket and pulled out his camera. Pip tried to ignore him and resume his previous conversation. The flashing and the clicks made it tough. Kip and I cupped our mouths politely. Bert's hilarious idiocy broke us down. When our laughter reached a roar, Pip finally spoke up.

"Can you please not take pictures of me?" he said. "I'm not this damn Eags person."

There was a moment of silence where Bert's inebriated brain

CHUCK LIFE'S A TRIP

considered the request. Suddenly his eyes went bleary again, and he threw up his hand.

"Yeah, ya fuckin' are," he yelled. "Now, turn yer head the other way n' lemme get another shot'a ya, Eags."



"Dyaaaaaard," I said, opening my eyes. I stretched my hands up till my biceps were wrung of their blood. When that familiar sleeve of relaxation hit my wrists, I dropped my arms and let my head dangle off to the right. I saw Bert there lying face down on his bed in nothing but his boxers. He had an empty Zorba in his hand, and there was a glob of drool glistening at the corner of his mouth. This brought back memories of the previous night. I picked up a pillow and threw it at his head.

"That was kinda fuckin' nice what you did to Pip last night, Brute," I said.

Bert peeled back his eyelids and shot me a red-eyed glare.

"Fuckin' care mad 'bout what I did to Eags last night. That faggot had it coming."

"Yeah, but you didn't hafta keep taking pictures of him after he told you to stop. Once or twice was more than enough."

"Don't get all high and mighty on me. You were right there laughin' it up while I did it. *Iuuul.*"

"Granted," I said. "And so was Kip. But none'a that shit woulda happened if you hadn't started it. I mean it's just fucking stupid. It makes us look like dumb-ass Americans. And I know you care *maaaaad* about that cuz you're a fuckin'—"

"Gahts! Gahts!" Tim cut in. "Choo oot. It's a fuckin' really cool thing to be fightin' like this on our last few days of the blow-up. Now Felm, I know you wanna be the ambassador n' shit. And Bert, I know you just get Brutish when you get D, but sick. This is our last few days, and today is extra skloomish cuz we're greegin' to Kavos. So let's *be* bitchin' and just get along for coot Mona."

"Ait," I said.

We got ready and went down to Athena's. The ATVs were looking nice and shiny out there in the sun. I whipped my leg around old bluey. Bert walked up to his yellow ATV and scowled.

"I'm tradin' this bitchin' shit in for a scooter," he said.

My mouth fell open. Kip dismounted his ATV and walked up behind Bert.

"What are you pooing?" I asked him.

He bit his lip and looked at me with his Diego shades on. "I'm getting a scooter too," he said.

Athena gave both Chucks a few stern pointers, then sent them off to ride with us. They had a tough time of it at first, but eventually Kip found his coordination and Bert found his speed. Seeing them master the harder vehicle made Mason and me a bit jealous. We compensated by pushing our ATVs to the limit and speeding unnecessarily. This provoked the others to jack their speeds up as well. Within seconds, we were a writhing mass of metal and Chuck buzzing through the twisted trees whilst narrowly missing old goats and Citroens.

We curved and we jumped and we spun. After a big long drag up a rocky path, we found ourselves at the peak of the island. All below us, we could see olive groves and shiny blue water. Splicing this madness in half was the straight paved highway leading directly to Kavos. The instant Tim got a load of it, he broke into jitters. His eyes started smiling and he turned up his hands.

"Gahts, this is really amazing," he said. "I mean, I just fucking thought of this!"

"Oh, here we go—another *Tim* idea," Bert said.

"No seezly, gahts. This is so baumish. I mean, this is so fucking baumish. We're here in Corfu on this world explosion together, and I just saw what happened back there and realized we're like a team cuz we all push one another to just say sick and blow up. And I just think that, why should this ever end? I mean, I know we hafta say goodbye to Mona for a while once we grooge back to L, but that doesn't mean we can't still explode in some team-type fashion. Like, think about this. We could start a band."

"A band?" I asked.

"Chea hea. It's pretty much perfect if you look at it. I mean, we've got all the elements. Beard Fleas with his rough Scottish beard can be our bassist. Bert with his loud, obnoxious, fast-talking brutishness can be our drummer. Brotha Felm with his sick but hella baumish smart raps can be our lead singer. Sebastian, God bless his Chuck, can be our front man announcer-type dude that just blows up cuz he's hella loud and just wild. Chuck can be our band manager cuz he's hella just chuck n'll get us good deals cuz he's kinda a dick. Me, I'll play guitar and just cork the fuck out. And Kip . . . well, ooff . . . Kip won't really play any instruments, but yeah, Kip's going to law school so he can be our lawyer in case you, Felm, or Bert or Sebastian or Mayt'n do some crazy shit. I mean, I think this is a baumish idea. We could get on it right when we get back and start writing lyrics and making music and then videotape all our performances and put them on YouTube. I mean, you know people watch the garnkest shit on there. I'm sure they wouldn't wanna watch us at all. Then maybe if someone in the music industry takes notice, we can send them our album and start doing gigs. We could be famous and just blow up forever!"

Tim's little idea invoked that special warmness in all of us. It sprouted up from our hearts and out through our ribs. It curled together gently to form one solid orb. Everything around us disappeared. In the comfort of this space, the minutes were all ours. We'd always be together.

# ROAST
## (Result of a Small Town)

The creation of language is not a new thing. It's been going on since our monkey ancestors realized it was communicatively more effective to use grunt combinations to refer to objects, actions, and aspirations than it was to simply point and growl. While nobody knows what those first attempts at complex communication might have sounded like, we do know that they gave birth to a vast number of languages over the ensuing millennia, roughly 7,000 of which survive till this day. The reasons for such linguistic diversity in this world are many; they include isolation, miscegenation, colonization, revolution, globalization, and social experimentation, to name a few. Though arguably all these factors played a role in the creation of ROAST at some point or another, the foremost driver behind the dialect's birth was the Chucks' collective desire to codify our conversations about the naughty things we did so that those around us, especially our parents, would be none the wiser.

To achieve this goal, we initially employed the two tools that were most readily available to us: our wits and our senses of humor. We found that by simply referring to certain things sarcastically whilst using a comic tone of voice only we could detect, we could have whole conversations about taboo topics that were at the very least confusing to outsiders.

As we got older and our communal activities went to another level of taboo, it was in our best interests to encrypt our shared dialogue even further. To facilitate this, we utilized the following tricks and techniques.

- **Word shortening:** The shortening of a word to disguise its nature from the listener. An example is *ait* for "alright" and *prolly*/*akshlly* for "probably/actually."

- **Rhyme scheming:** Using a word or phrase that rhymes with another word or phrase to conceal the meaning of that which is being referenced. A body of rhyming schemes is often referred to as "rhyming slang."
  Examples: *Snit one's France* for "shit one's pants" and *Welcome Back Kotter* for "water."
  The Cockneys, a group largely comprising blue-collar workers from London's East End, are famous for having an especially rich rhyming slang-based dialect of English.
- **Phonemic alteration:** Changing the phonemes or 'sound units' of a word to disguise its nature. Examples: *Friss* for "piss" and *frit* for "shit."
  The Boonters, a group of Scots-Irish farmers from Anderson Valley, California, whose main town is Boontville, are noted for having frequently used phonemic alteration to help create their English dialect, 'Boontling.'
- **Tangential sarcasm:** A form of sarcasm we often employ, whose related vocabulary, phrases, and references evolve in a tangential fashion in the areas of phonemics, orthography, and concept. For an example, see *bitchin'*.
- **Verbs, etc., from proper nouns:** Using people's names and nicknames to create related verbs, adjectives, and nouns. See, for example, the adjective *alb*, the noun *albert,* and the verb *alb out* from the name Albert Einstein.
- **Double and triple sarcasm:** See, for example, *Uh uh!* and *un-*
- **Meaningful sounds from common words and phrases:** See, for example, *Ah 'ah!*, *Wah 'ah!* and *pussy squeal.*
- **Grunting to denote sarcasm:** See *ROAST grunt.*
- **Scrunching phrases to form single words:** See, for example, *ooff.*
- **Using the first letters of words and names to refer to things:** See, for example, *Get D* for "get drunk" and *M* for "masturbate."

- **Words and phrases adopted from other languages and dialects:** Of this ROAST-enrichment technique, it could be said that the language, or rather the dialect, that has had the single greatest influence on ours is, was, and always has been Ebonics—African-American vernacular English. This is largely because most of us since childhood have been listening to gangsta rap and hip-hop, two genres of music, largely populated by Ebonics-speaking African-Americans that exploded across white suburbia in the early 90s when we were growing up. Though we do steal from Ebonics quite often, we almost invariably use the words in a sarcastic sense and have even employed them to create new words, expressions, and phrases that are unique to ROAST (See *blow up star*).

Since we started traveling, our dialect has seen an influx of words from the languages with which we've been in close proximity the longest. These languages include Mexican Spanish, Brazilian Portuguese, Czech, Thai, Hawaiian, Russian, Greek, Swahili, Amharic, and others. On some occasions, we've taken the words adopted from these languages and adapted them (see *loll*). On others, we've simply plucked them as they were and added them unspoiled to our lexicon (see *mzungu*).

While it may be true that ROAST, with all its borrowings from different languages and its style similarities to other English dialects, is merely a hideously mutated and sarcastically slanted amalgam of Ebonics, Cockney, and Boontling, peppered with Northern California slang and foreign vocab, the match that struck it into existence was very much the result of a unique and priceless formula—all of us together, experiencing the trials of life at the same time, in the same place. It was, in short, the **R**esult **of a S**mall **T**own.

# ABOUT THE GLOSSARY

**Terms**

There are over 550 alphabetically listed entries in the full ROAST glossary. They include words and expressions both homespun and adopted, place names (especially those we've modified), names and nicknames of people either in our group or associated therewith, and a body of vocabulary and phrases from Standard English, NorCal Slang and Ebonics that, although existing unaltered as part of our lexicon, is almost invariably used by us in a sarcastic sense. Some entries have been altered to protect identities. In such cases, I've tried my best to keep them as close to their original forms as possible.

The terms I've chosen to include in this abbreviated glossary are generally representative of what we call ROAST. There are at least 300 other terms which I could have included but elected not to for reasons of brevity, redundancy, or preservation of privacy.

It should also be noted that what you will find on these pages is current. This means that a sizable number of entries are for words, expressions, place names, etc. that were created by us after "The World Explosion 2006"—the trip upon which this book is based. Most of these more recent terms were created in Prague, where four of us have been living on and off since 2012. We continue to invent new terms on a monthly, weekly, and sometimes even a daily basis.

**Entry type**

There are twelve different entry types, one or more of which can be found immediately after the entries themselves. They are: *adj.* (adjective); *adv.* (adverb); *excl.* (exclamation); *inter.* (interrogative); *n.* (noun); *num.* (number); *phr.* (phrase); *prep.* (preposition); *pron.* (pronoun); *pr. n.* (proper noun); *v.* (verb); and *v. phr.* (verb phrase).

## Pronunciation

Standard English spelling is used throughout to approximate the pronunciation of each ROAST word. In most cases, this gives the reader a good idea of how to voice what he/she reads. Where it doesn't, an explanation on the appropriate pronunciation is given.

## Definitions

The definitions are brief, but hopefully not so that they fail to capture shades of meaning. A semicolon separates each entry's alternate meaning. Notes are occasionally given to indicate variant connotations or applications of a word or phrase, or to state frequency of use.

## Etymology

Word origin, often followed by examples and/or specificities of that word or phrase's usage, is included where it may be useful. On occasion, a relevant story is also included.

# GLOSSARY

**Ah 'ah!** *excl.* An expression used when giving someone something, especially when you are trying to get that person's attention. "Ah 'ah!" can be uttered in a high-pitched fashion to express delight in sharing or handing over the object in question, or in a low-pitched fashion to express discontentment or frustration. The origin is the phrase, "Here you go, gay-ass!"—something we all used to say as adolescents when giving things to one another. Over the years the phrase was shortened to "Here gay!", then to "Here gah'!" and eventually to its current form, "Ah 'ah!" The apostrophe before the second "ah" represents a pronounced glottal stop. A failure to enunciate it will result in the speaker sounding like a complete dumbfuck when he/she attempts to hand something to a Chuck in ROAST.

**Ai' la'** *phr.* Alright later; alright bye.

**ait** *adj.* Okay; all right; decent; decently (*adv.*).

**akshlly (prolly)** *adv.* Existing as a fact; really; actually; (probably).

**alb** *adj.* Of inferior intelligence; stupid; dumb.

**alb out** *v.* To make a stupid mistake; to forget, esp. something obvious.

**albert** *adj.* Of inferior intelligence; stupid; dumb; a stupid person or idiot (*n.*).

**always be there** *v. phr.* To entirely disbelieve someone or something; to be very dubious.

**'Anks ga'** *phr.* Thanks, buddy.

**Any** *pron.* None. No (*adv.*).

**Baaad!** *excl.* Fuck that!; Fuck off!; What-fuckin-ever!; That's bullshit!

**ball out** *v.* To have a mishap while partying; to commit one or a series of party fouls.

**baller (ballah)** *n.* A total loser (esp. one who frequents parties); a party-fouler.

**ballfighter** *n.* A cigarette lighter.

**barg** *n.* A cigarette. Physically fit; tough; difficult (*adj.*).

**bargaretty** *adj.* Very physically fit and/or tough; very difficult.

Variant forms: **bigaretty**; **biggity**.

**barged out** *adj.* Extremely muscular; grossly ripped.

**baumish** *adj.* Great; awesome; excellent; delicious (when referring to food). Variant forms: **bamish, beemish, bombish, boomish** and **skloomish.**

**baumishness** *n.* Greatness; awesomeness; excellence; deliciousness (when referring to food).

**bav** *v.* To have (especially a cigarette or joint).

**be in love** *v.* To be really angry at; to really hate; to disdain.

**beardy** *adj.* Any one or any combination of the following adjectives: irritable; shameless; intolerant; creepy; rude.

**beef ('em)** *v.* To smoke (cigarettes).

**beef the faggot** *v.* To smoke the hookah.

**Bell** *pr. n.* The American fast food chain, Taco Bell.

**Big P.** *n.* Prague; Praha (in Czech).

**bitch** *n.* A cowardly man; a wimp; a dumbass.

**bitchin'** *adj.* Of inferior quality; not all that great; silly; ridiculous. "Bitchin'" found its way into ROAST via 60s California surfer slang. In this dialect of sorts, it meant (and still means) "awesome," or "exciting." When we got ahold of the word, however, we used it in a sarcastic sense to describe pretty much anything that we deemed substandard or ridiculous. The phrase we most commonly employed for this in the beginning was, "That's *bitchin'!*" We soon shortened this to *"Bitchin'!"* then *"Yitchin'!," "Kitchin'!," "Chin!,"* and then just *"Ch'!"* When a newbie Home-Chuck named Bob Cock started hanging around our group, he noticed us using the exclamation *"Ch'!"* quite frequently, but mistakenly thought it meant "Yes!" and not "That's silly!" or "That's ridiculous!". His interpretation of the phrase was so hilarious to us that it stuck and is still used to this day. Multiple variations on *"Ch'!"* (meaning "Yes!") have been created recently. See **Chea hea!, Choo hoo!, Feeoow!, Shoo!,** and **Woo hoo!**

**bitchiness** *n.* Silliness; ridiculousness, lameness.

**bling** *n.* Fancy, shiny, and/or gaudy jewelry, esp. when worn by a rapper or gangsta; cheap, dull, and/or poor quality jewelry, esp. when

350

worn by a wannabe rapper or gangsta.

**blow Mona up** *v.* To travel, especially to a far-off destination or around the world.

**Blow Ned!** *excl.* An expression we use to express disdain for pretty much anyone or anything.

**blow up** *v.* To party hard; to travel (the world); to fuck; to have intimate contact with; to do something wild or out of the ordinary to the umpteenth degree; to do or experience anything good or bad in an extreme or exaggerated sense.

**Blow-up Chuck** *n.* A Chuck who blows up. To earn the title "Blow-up Chuck" one must not only have grown up with us but have traveled with us at least once and done a proper job of it to boot. See **blow up** and **Chuck**.

**Blow-up Guy (BUG)** *pr. n.* This Blow-up Chuck—referred to as Sebastian Frazelli in the book—got his nickname for being the natural embodiment of everything that is blowing up in ROAST (see **blow-up**).

**blow-up star** *n.* Somebody who is well-known or even famous for their blowing up (i.e., world traveling, partying, fucking, or doing anything wild or out of the ordinary to the umpteenth degree).

**blowy upy** *adj.* Lively; exciting.

**boda** *n.* A soda; soda.

**bold** *adj.* Cold.

**bone** *n.* A dollar.

**bones** *n.* A lot of money. Very expensive (*adj.*).

**bot** *adj.* Hot.

**bower** *n.* A shower, especially a long and satisfying one. To shower (*v.*).

**Box** *pr. n.* The American fast food chain, Jack In The Box.

**Brrrrrrr!** *excl.* Fuck that!; Fuck off!; What-fuckin-ever!; That's bullshit!

**Brute** *pr. n.* This is the most common nickname of the Blow-up Chuck referred to as Bert Thompson in the book. "Brute" is not only a phonemic alteration of the name "Bert" but a nominal representation of his brutal and obnoxious dark side that comes out when he binge drinks. Bert's other nicknames include "Culture Guy," "Respect Guy" and "Dough Boy."

**buff** *adj.* Lacking in muscle; weak; easy; easily done.

**bunt(a)** *v.* To go; leave.

**care** *v.* To not care; to be indifferent; to not give a shit.

**Carl's** *pr. n.* The American fast food chain, Carl's Junior.

**Ch'!** *excl.* Yes!; Absolutely!.

**chayz** *n.* Crystal meth.

**chayz out** *v.* to smoke a lot of crystal meth.

**Chea hea!** *excl.* Yes!; Absolutely!. Variant forms: **Choo hoo!; Feeoow!; Shoo; Woo hoo!**

**cheatie** *n.* An adorable little guy or girl; a precious little thing. Adorable; precious (*adj.*).

**Conchelli** *pr. n.* This is the most common nickname of the Blow-up Chuck referred to as Tim Frazelli in the book. It is a scrunched, vaguely Italian amalgam of "Corky Tim Frazelli." Other variants include **Conchenni, Chonchennzi, Chennzi, Chenni, Chelli, Yelli, Yenni,** and **Yeet.**

**Choo oot** *v.* To chill out; to relax. Chill out! (*excl.*).

**chuck** *v.* To chill with gusto; to unwind completely and let the stress of the day dribble from your joints; to sleep, especially peacefully. Highly relaxed; comfortable; tired; exhausted (*adj.*). A member of our group (*n.*).

**Chuck life** *n.* Our fiercely nomadic yet sublimely relaxing way of life.

**chuck out** *v.* To chill with gusto; to unwind completely and let the stress of the day dribble from your joints; to sleep, especially peacefully.

**Chuck-name** *n.* A nickname we invent for anyone we consider to be part of our group.

**cluh** *n.* A nightclub; a disco.

**coo** *adj.* Un-cool; lame; stupid.

**cool** *adj.* Un-cool; lame; stupid. "Bullshit!"; "I don't buy that!"; "That's wrong!" (*excl.*).

**coot** *adj.* Precious; adorable.

**corky** *adj.* A misspelled version of the word "quirky." We often use this word to describe Tim as he is the corkiest of all the Chucks

**cork out** *v.* To behave in a corky manner; to do strange but endearing little things.

**cry of** *v.* To do something effortlessly; to defeat someone easily.

**Czuck** *n.* A Chuck living in the Czech Republic.

**D** *adj.* Drunk.

**Damn!** *excl.* Big deal!; Who cares?

**dayz** *n.* A long time.

**Donald's** *pr. n.* The American fast food chain, McDonald's.

**dough out** *adj.* To loaf around in a state of depression or melancholy.

**Dyaard!** *excl.* This sucks!; What am I going to do?

**Eags** *pr. n.* A nickname we gave the Home Chuck known as "Ned" in the book because he resembled a baby bald eagle.

**Eeff?!** *excl.* I don't know!; Who knows?; I'm sorry but . . .

**even** *adv.* Not even; not at all.

**ever** *adv.* Never; not ever; at no time; not at all.

**explode** *v.* To party really hard; to travel (the whole world); to fuck a lot; to have a lot of intimate contact with; to do something really wild or out of the ordinary to the umpteenth degree; to do or experience anything really good or bad in an extreme or exaggerated sense.

**faggot** *n.* A loser; a douche bag; an asshole. Also refers to the hookah.

**feed 'em** *v.* To make a really big mistake; to be doing something really poorly; to be in a really poor state; to have something really bad happen to you; to die.

**Felm** *pr. n.* The most commonly used nickname for yours truly in the book. My other monikers include **"Felmania," "Felbania,"** and **"Felmenistan."**

**fidy** *num.* Fifty. A fifty-dollar bill (*n.*).

**fight the chuck** *v. phr.* To resist the temptation to lounge around on your ass all day.

**fool** *n.* Guy; dude, esp. when referring to our peers in a negative manner.

**freak of** *v.* To do something truly effortlessly; to defeat someone extremely easily.

**friss** *v.* To piss; to take a piss. Piss; urine (*n.*).

**frit** *v.* To shit; to take a shit. Shit; feces; a breast (*n.*).

**fritties** *n.* Titties; breasts.

**Fuck yeah!** *excl.* No way! Absolutely not!


**gaht** *n.* Dear friend; comrade.

**garnk(at)** *adj.* Of inferior quality; not all that great; silly; ridiculous.

**gay** *adj.* Of inferior quality; not all that great; silly; ridiculous; homosexual.

**get it** *v.* To get it (a cock) in the ass; to get butt-fucked; to make a really big mistake; to be doing something really poorly; to be in a really poor state; to have something really bad happen to you; to die.

**Get it!** *excl.* Get a cock in your ass!; Get fucked!.

**Get me!** *excl.* Get my cock in your ass!; Get fucked (by me)!.

**get 'em** *v.* To get them (multiple cocks) in the ass; to get butt-fucked by many dicks; to make a really big mistake; to be doing something really poorly; to be in a really poor state; to have something really bad happen to you; to die. Often abbreviated to **gettem** in the present and **gottem** in the past.

**give treats** *v.* To beat the shit out of; to cause bodily injury to.

**ghost-riding** *n.* When a person starts their car, sets it in motion, then either climbs on top of it or gets out and dances around it while it's still moving.

**go tiny** *v.* To party incredibly hard; to go incredibly big.

**greege** *v.* To go; to leave; to come; to spend (the night).

**grooge** *v.* To go; to leave; to come; to spend (the night).

**grunge** *v.* To go; to leave; to come; to spend (the night).

**gunk(a)** *adj.* Of inferior quality; not all that great; silly; ridiculous.


**hang (out)** *v.* To avoid; to stay away from; to not be present any longer.

**har har** *n.* An adorable little guy or girl; A precious little thing. Adorable; precious (*adj.*).

**Hayes D!** *excl.* Fuck that!; Fuck off!; What-fuckin-ever!; That's bullshit!

**headz** *n.* people.

**health out** *v.* To consume unhealthy food or drink; to exhibit symptoms of unhealthiness or sickness.

**Heavy D!** *excl.* Fuck that!; Fuck off!; What-fuckin-ever!; That's bullshit!

**hee-hey** *n.* A blowjob.

**hella** *adj.* Very; extremely; a lot of. Or: not very; not at all; not much/many.

**Home Chuck** *n.* A Chuck who pretty much chucks in L-Town; a Chuck who rarely, if ever, blows Mona up. (See **Chuck**, **blow Mona up** and **L-Town**.)

**hoo hoo** *n.* A cool guy you can pal around with. Cool; chummy; buddy-buddy (*adj.*).

**hook 'em** *v.* To make a really big mistake; to be doing something really poorly; to be in a really poor state; to have something really bad happen to you; to die.

**hot** *adj.* Very unattractive; disgusting; revolting.

**huge** *adj.* Very small.

**hunno** *num.* One hundred. A hundred-dollar bill (*n.*).

**ice** *v.* Fake diamonds of any sort.

**insane** *adj.* Not all it's cracked up to be; full of hype.

**Iuuul!** *excl.* Fuck that!; Fuck off!; What-fuckin-ever!; That's bullshit!

**kick ass** *v.* To perform poorly; to not function well; to stop functioning entirely.

**kick it** *v.* To avoid; to stay away from.

**kid** *n.* Guy; dude, esp. when referring to our peers in a negative manner.

**killer** *n.* A weak, non-threatening person. Weak; non-threatening (*adj.*).

**King** *pr. n.* The American fast food chain, Burger King.

**Kip Kop** *pr. n.* A common nickname of the character referred to as "Kip" in the book. He also goes by "The Kypriolitic Calculator" for his high-powered intellect and tendency to calculate the odds of such-and-such occurring.

**kiss someone** *v.* To get really angry at someone; to get furious at someone.

**Kotter** *n.* Water; a glass or bottle of water. See **WBK**.

**L-Town (L)** *pr. n.* Our hometown of Livermore, California. We sometimes refer to it by the first letter of its name.

**life out** *v.* To contemplate one's life; to be depressed and thinking about the state of one's life.

**lifeish** *adj.* Depressed; melancholy; down in the dumps (especially about the state of your life or life in general).

**live** *v.* To die; to break down; to stop working; to expire.

**loll** *v.* To smoke marijuana; to get stoned. Marijuana (*n.*).

**loll out** *v.* To smoke a lot of marijuana; to get totally stoned.

**loll'd** *adj.* Smoked up; stoned.

**lots** *adj.* Very little; very few.

**love** *v.* To be angry at; to hate; to disdain. Anger; hatred; disdain (*n.*).

**M** *v.* To masturbate; to jack off.

**mad** *adj.* Very little; very few.

**matter** *v.* To not matter; to be of little or no importance.

**Mayt'n** *pr. n.* A common nickname for the Blow-up Chuck referred to as "Mason" in the book. We call him this because it appears that mating, which sounds like "Mayt'n," is all he thinks about. His other nicknames include "Beardo," "Beard Fleas," "Hog Beast;" the list goes on.

**member** *v.* To remember.

**millions** *adj.* Extremely little; extremely few.

**Mona** *pr. n.* The Chuck goddess of travel, adventure, culture, language, love, and wisdom.

**murderer** *n.* A very weak, non-threatening person.

**mzungu** *n.* "White person" in Swahili, the national language of Kenya and Tanzania.

**nah (nah nah)** *n.* A hot chick; a beautiful woman.

**nah out** *v.* to have sex or intimate contact with a chick, especially a hot one.

**Nei nornin!** *excl.* Just Kidding!

**Nerfy Nerds** *pr. n.* A common nickname for the Blow-up Chuck referred to as "Chuck Sunday" in the book. It evolved from us having called him "Cheatie Chuck" as a way of poking fun at his endearing laziness.

**ney (ney ney)** *n.* A really hot chick; a really beautiful woman.

**Niope!** *excl.* Yes!; Fuck yeah!

**NorCal** *pr. n.* Our home, our pride, Northern California.


**Oh yeah!** *excl.* Fuck no!; Absolutely not!

**Ooff?!** *excl.* I don't know!; Who knows?; I'm sorry but . . . The expression "Ooff?!" comes from a sarcastic phrase we used to say long ago when we didn't know something. That phrase was "Well, I *hella* know?!" which meant "Well, I *really don't* know!" Over time, this phrase was scrunched to "Wlahelakno?!", then to "Wlalf?!," "Ooff?!" and more recently to "Eeff?!" and even "Alf?!". Besides just using "Ooff?!" to profess a lack of knowledge about something, we also use it at the beginning or end of a sentence to express our condolences when delivering someone bad news or to back out of a commitment as politely as possible. See **Eeff?!** and **Uulf?!**.


**pass treats** *v.* To beat the shit out of; to cause bodily injury to.

**pigs** *n.* A full beard.

**player (playah)** *n.* A total failure with the ladies; someone who has absolutely no skill with women.

**poo** *v.* To do.

**poty** *adj.* Potent; strong.

**pull a someone** *v.* To do something someone else would have done in a certain situation. This expression usually carries a negative connotation.

**pussy** *n.* A movie.

**pussy squeal** *n.* A high-pitched, throaty squeal that we use for five purposes: 1. To clear tension. 2. To make each other laugh. 3. To express disdain. 4. To get someone to toughen up. 5. To lock someone in a "pussy squeal battle." The pussy squeal developed from the phrase, "Oh my God, pussy!" which we used to say sarcastically when we thought someone was complaining about something that was no big deal to us. Over time, we shortened the phrase to just one long "Ohhhhh." This gradually morphed into the pussy squeal we know and love today. Besides just using the pussy squeal to get someone to toughen up or to express disdain, we also take advantage of its humorous sound and cathartic effect to clear tension between us and to make one another laugh. One way we often achieve the latter is via a "pussy squeal battle" that can unfold in one of two ways: 1) Two Chucks start squealing at one another off the bat and keep going till one laughs, at which point the other wins. 2) One Chuck makes the pussy squeal face—generally, front teeth over bottom lip, eyes rolled back, head slowly bobbling—at another Chuck while he's not paying attention. He holds the face until his friend notices it. At this point, the Chuck making the face breaks into the squeal, and if the other Chuck laughs, he loses.

**The Peppers** *pr. n.* The band, The Red Hot Chili Peppers.

**The pussy** *n.* The hookah.

**ROAST grunt** *n.* A deep, reverberating grunt with undulating tones that we use with certain words in ROAST to indicate that we intend their meaning to be sarcastic.

**rupe** *n.* A rupee.

**sauce** *v.* To eat (especially a lot of delicious food.) Food, especially a lot of delicious food (*n.*).

**sauce it up** *v.* To spend a long period of time eating (a lot of delicious food.)

**sauce off** *v.* To eat the last bit of a meal (especially a large, delicious one.)

**sauce out** *v.* To go have a meal (especially a large, delicious one.)

**sauciness** *n.* Deliciousness; a lot of delicious food.

**saucy** *adj.* Delicious; hungry. A homosexual (*n.*).

**saucy baumishness** *n.* Extreme deliciousness.

**saustrisizery** *adj.* Beyond delicious.

**savage child** *n.* A pussy; a wimp.

**say damn to** *v. phr.* To reject or refuse completely; to decide not to.

**say Heavy D to** *v. phr.* To reject or refuse completely; to decide not to.

**say Hayes D to** *v. phr.* To reject or refuse completely; to decide not to.

**say house to** *v. phr.* To reject or refuse politely; to decide not to.

**say late to** *v. phr.* To say goodbye to; to say "later" to.

**say phat ice to** *v. phr.* To reject or refuse completely; to decide not to.

**say sick to** *v. phr.* To reject or refuse completely; to decide not to.

**say tight to** *v. phr.* To reject or refuse completely; to decide not to.

**scared** *adj.* Fearless; intrepid; bold.

**scream of** *v.* To do something with consummate effortlessness; to defeat someone with complete and total ease.

**Seezly?** *excl.* Seriously?; You've gotta be kidding me!

**shrum out** *v.* To ingest or smoke magic mushrooms.

**shrums** *n.* Psilocybin or "magic" mushrooms.

**sicc-made** *adj.* Completely sick in the head; deranged.

**sick** *adj.* Ridiculous; lame; stupid.

**skink** *v.* To drink (alcohol).

**skunt(a)** *v.* To go; leave.

**skut** *v.* To go; leave (abruptly).

**small amounts** *n.* A bunch; a shitload.

**snalk** *n.* Alcohol.

**sneer** *n.* A beer; beer.

**snit (it)** *v.* To have sex or intimate contact with.

**snit one's France** *v.* To shit one's pants. Rhyming slang.

**snuss** *n.* Pussy; vagina.

**sobe** *adj.* Not sober; drunk; intoxicated.

**take a bower** *v.* To take a shower.

**take a friss** *v.* To take a piss.

**take a frit** *v.* To take a shit.

**T.C.** *adj.* Too cool.

**tight** *adj.* Ridiculous; lame; stupid.

**tiny amounts** *n.* A whole bunch; a whole shitload.

**Uhhhhhhhh!** *excl.* Something we Chucks yell to express happiness or excitement or to make fun of someone who we feel is a wannabe gangsta.

**Uh uh!** *excl.* You know you love it! (in the sarcastic sense). Back in the day, when one of us was complaining about something bad that had happened, we used to tell that Chuck the doubly sarcastic phrase "Uh uh! You don't *love* it at all!" as a way of both poking fun at them and getting them out of their funk. Over time, that phrase was shortened to just "Uh uh!" Nowadays, it is almost invariably accompanied by a slow, wide-eyed shaking of the head. To the outsider, it may seem illogical to have a doubly sarcastic phrase. But see we used words like "hate" and "love" in the singularly sarcastic sense so often that the only way we could truly be sarcastic with them was to use them "appropriately" whilst at the same time uttering them with our classic sarcastic **ROAST grunt**—something that is sometimes identified in writing via the use of italics. Believe it or not, using the phrase *"Uh uh!"* in the doubly sarcastic sense has become so commonplace these days that we've had to start using it in the triply sarcastic sense—a sizable feat to keep track of—just to make each other laugh.

**un-** *pref.* A prefix we use in combination with the **ROAST grunt** when we want to make a normal word sarcastic and add emphasis to its meaning. Thus, to express tiredness you might say "I'm hella chuck," or you might just say "I'm *un*-chuck!"

**Uulf?** *excl.* I don't know!; Who knows?; I'm sorry but ...

**Wah 'ah!** *excl.* An expression used when asking for something from someone, especially when you are trying to get that person's attention and/or have just given them something of your own. It can be uttered in a high-pitched fashion to express delight in asking for the object in question, or in a low-pitched fashion to express discontentment or frustration. "Wah 'ah" is simply the reverse of **Ah 'ah**, which we use to hand someone something. The added "W" comes from the word "well" which we used to say in its entirety in conjunction with "Ah 'ah" to express that we wanted something from someone, especially after we'd given that same someone something of our own. The apostrophe before the second "ah" represents a pronounced glottal stop. As with **Ah 'ah,** failure to enunciate it will result in the speaker sounding like a dumbfuck when he/she attempts to ask for something from a Chuck in ROAST.

**Way** *pr n.* The American fast food chain, Subway.

**Way!** *excl.* Yeah right!; That's ridiculous!

**WBK** *n.* Water; a glass or bottle of water. "WBK" is an acronym for "Welcome Back Kotter"—a comedy show we used to watch on *Nick-at-Night* back in the day. Since the word "Kotter" sounded like "water," we began calling water—be it a glass, bottle, or the item in general— "Welcome Back Kotter" or simply "WBK." Shortly thereafter we started using just "Kotter." All three forms are used presently. See **Kotter.**

**Woo?** *inter.* A ROAST interrogative that can mean "Who?", "What?", "When?", "Where?", "Why?" and "How?". "Woo?" is our strange combination of all six interrogatives from Standard English. We often use it in a soft tone to question what's going on around us.


**Yeah!** *excl.* No!; No way!

**yey** *n.* Cocaine.

**yey out** *n.* To snort a lot of cocaine.


**Zalt!** *excl.* Oh my god!; Holy crap.

CPSIA information can be obtained
at www.ICGtesting.com
Printed in the USA
FSHW022126181019
63187FS